OLDUVAI COUNTDOWN

A JACK CANN MEDICAL THRILLER

MICHAEL WOODS, MD

PUBLISHED BY INGRAMSPARK

Michael Woods, MD
Lawrence, KS
Admin@MichaelWoodsMD.com
www.MichaelWoodsMD.com

INTRODUCTION

This is an updated version of the original *Olduvai Countdown*, published in 2014. I couldn't know how directly this fictional work would collide with the nonfictional realities of the Coronavirus Pandemic — COVID.

As our world continues to heal from COVID's devastation, this revised, updated version of *Olduvai Countdown* provides an inspirational story of hope through adversity during a personal and world crisis of epic proportions.

As one would hope, my writing has progressed across the arc of the past eight years. I have benefited from feedback readers have provided during this time, both in-person and via online reviews. One review, in particular, rekindled a concern I had as I wrote the book:

"This book is quite good. It is, however, complex. If you have a master's degree or doctorate in medicine, biology, virology, gene sequencing, etc., this is the book for you. However, if you don't, there is just TMI."

This, justifiably, made me wonder, "When I revise the book, should I simplify my writing to make it 'more understandable' to the non-medical or less scientifically inclined reader?"

As a result, I started thinking. And what I thought was *Jurassic Park*. Yes. That one, by Michael Crichton, was published in 1990. We've all seen the movie, but what about reading the book? I'm a doctor, as was Crichton, so, as part of my research, as good doctors do, I picked up a copy to read select parts, especially around DNA isolation, cloning dinosaurs, and other complex, scientific aspects of this fiction novel that sold a bazillion copies and spawned one of the most successful movie series of all time.

Before I tell you what I found, I'll share some additional, important context related to my re-reading, sparked by a conversation with my wife and educator par excellence. Before I started reading, we were talking about the reviewer's comments. Her comments went something like this: and "In 1990, Crichton was likely pushing the limits of what the 'average reader' would understand about DNA and cloning technology. Thirty years have passed since his book. Today, given the advancements in science and education, kids *in grade school* know about DNA. By the time they're in high school, if they have paid attention (not a given, I admit - my comment), the topics in *Olduvai Countdown* are not, in fact, too complex for the 'average reader.' In addition, the ubiquity of the internet and immediate access via mobile devices has made access to information easy — literally, keystrokes away." It's easy for people to look stuff up, and I hope that my writing and the story are compelling enough that folks will do so if and when they want to understand something they do not.

What did I learn from reading *Jurassic Park*? In brief, Crichton wrote with a similar degree of complexity, extrapolated to the year of its publication. He uses plants' genus and species names, such as *Serrena veriformans*, and notes the spores contain "a deadly form of beta-carbolize alkaloid." He speaks of laboratory techniques, like the Loy antibody extraction for DNA isolation; cellular mitosis; colchincinoids; paleo-DNA; restriction enzymes; and the nucleotides — adenine, thymidine, guanine, and cytosine — the building block molecules of DNA. He even used DNA sequence string illustrations in the book — as I did in *Olduvai*. In brief, Crichton used the most up-to-date information of the time to weave a compelling international bestseller.

It gave me comfort to find out Crichton wrote this way. It also validated my approach to writing this book and those to follow.

So did I ignore the reader's feedback? No, and yes. No, because it led me to question and do a bit of research, finding that the original version of the book was likely not out of reach of most readers. But also yes, because in the revision, I paid a great deal of attention to those parts the reviewer likely found challenging and made changes to improve clarity — and in some cases — simplify, without compromising the integrity or scientific underpinnings of the story.

I did ponder including a glossary of terms and resource links. Still, I decided against it, having watched the alacrity with which the current generation whip out their cellphones, looking topics up faster than a gunfighter's pistol draw. I have included several drawings for the reader — one of cell anatomy and one of a mitochondrion to assist them in visualizing critical portions of the book.

In summary, I firmly believe this post-COVID revision is better than the original. The general public will find that understanding even the most complex scientific portions is well within their grasp.

ANATOMY OF A CELL

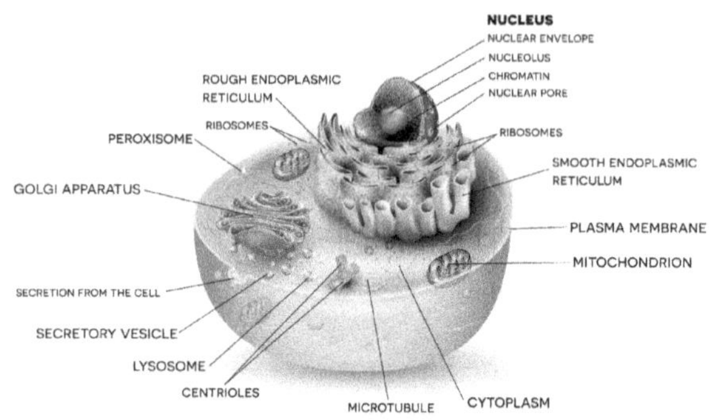

Mitochondrion

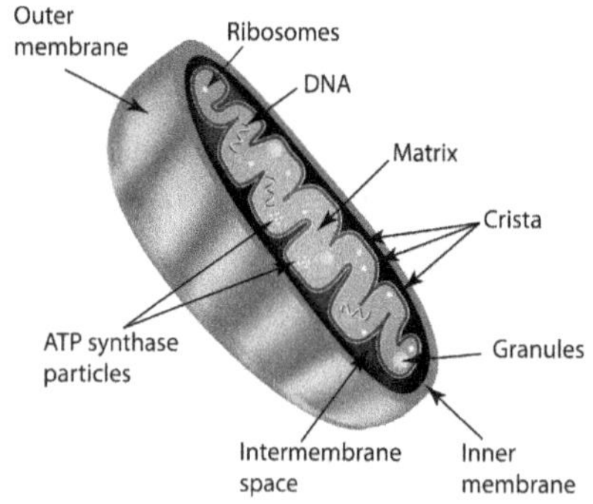

CHAPTER 1

Abasi's eyes popped open as if somehow controlled by the azimuth of the rising sun. He stretched and hopped out of bed quietly to not wake the others in the two-room mud and thatch house. He loved mornings in Mto Wa Mbu.

He stuck his head out of the hut and watched a few villagers trudge by making the daily trip to the well to replenish their drinking water and catch up on local news. He liked to listen to the well talk—never real news like what was happening elsewhere in Tanzania—just little details necessary to the day, the here and now.

Abasi's mother was preparing breakfast when he heard children laughing outside and the scuffling sounds of feet kicking a ball. Some of his friends were already playing soccer in the morning cool to avoid the hot afternoon sun, burning energy from a good night's rest. Without hesitation or asking for permission, he was out the door.

Abasi ran hard just to keep up, the youngest in the scrum. His twine belt, knotted in front, bunched the khaki shorts tightly around his bony hips, preventing them from falling around his ankles. Both of his pencil-thin legs could have easily fit through one leg of the shorts; each deep breath accentuated his bony ribcage, but not in an unhealthy way. His smile seemed permanently fixed, and his eyes were wide, bright, smiling as wide as his mouth.

The other boys were already out of sight, having tumbled out of the alley and rounded the corner of the house at the end of the alleyway, plunging after the ball, their trail evident from the kicked-up dust hovering at eye-level. Running headlong into the cloud, Abasi's eyes filled with dirt, and he began to tear. It slowed him, but he kept moving, eyes closed, toward the noise reverberating in the village center.

Another sweep of his hand and the watering cleared as he rejoined the group, playing more a game of keep-away than soccer. He charged into the middle, kicking furiously, laughing. One of the larger boys struck the ball hard, and it careened off another's head, bouncing high in the air toward a side alley, a spoke off the wheel of the village center.

Abasi watched the ball descend from the sky and land between the dull clay walls of the houses forming the narrow byway. He stared down the alley for a moment as if the ball's temporary disappearance had been an incomprehensible act of magic.

Abasi positioned himself to see down the alley, and when the ball hit the ground, powder-dry dirt poofed up. He watched the small cloud hanging in the air for a few seconds until a gust of wind whipping through the alley spontaneously molded it into a dust devil, rising like a phoenix from nothing. It swept toward him between the short, story-high shacks, bouncing between the houses like a spinning top rebounds off whatever it hits. He watched as the brown, swirling vortex slowly moved closer, becoming denser as it sucked up more dirt every foot it advanced. For a moment, he thought he should run, but his curiosity was more significant than his fear.

He noticed two men at the well talking, oblivious to the boys and the slow-moving brown funnel. The thinner of the two men had a full beard, wore a muted green tropical print shirt, and stood. The other was a shorter, plump, elderly gentleman, shoeless, toothless. They were chatting, their water containers full; neither appeared in a hurry to lug 50 sloshing pounds back home. The pudgy one was sitting cross-legged on the edge of the stone wall surrounding the hole that dropped 30 feet into the earth to water.

Abasi's grin widened even more than usual as it became apparent the men were completely unaware of what was about to happen. Seconds before they were engulfed by the mini-cyclone, one of the men saw the funnel, whites of his eyes gaping. He attempted to warn the other, but he closed his mouth to avoid spitting dirt all day.

It appeared as if the earth had consumed the men when the irregularity of the well disrupted the symmetry of the swirling wind and the dust devil exploded chaotically into a cloud. Abasi watched as some of the brown haze fell back to earth; the rest carried high into the sky, swept away to succumb to gravity beyond the confines of the town. He tilted his head in consideration, wondering where each particle had been before landing in the alleyway.

The other boys had disappeared to retrieve the ball, but Abasi stood watching the men who had resumed their conversation. He thought it remarkable that they could pick up where they were so quickly following the mini-maelstrom.

He wasn't sure, but it seemed as if the man sitting on the well's edge was teetering back and forth ever so slightly—as if he were keeping rhythm to some inaudible musical score. Abasi squinted. *Yes, he's swaying.* His smile faded for the first time that morning as the man slumped over, folding in half at the waist, the weight of his pelvis carrying him back into the gaping crevice. The thin man shouted for help simultaneous to a reverberating splash.

The commotion raised the alarm of those within earshot. A small platoon of villagers arrived, surrounding the well, peering over the edge, and calling to the man bobbing face down, motionless. Abasi fought his way out of the crush, pushing and wriggling through a forest of legs.

Retreating to the edge of the village center, Abasi had a panoramic view of the throng. A would-be rescuer, a man in his mid-30s, well-toned, muscular, and visibly healthy in appearance, became unsteady on his feet and slumped to the ground, apparently fainting. An older man, shirtless and bald, and a middle-aged woman in a flowing red dress, her copious hair loosely confined by a bright yellow kerchief—perhaps relatives of the swooning man—turned him over and dragged him away from the crowd to prevent him from being trampled by other helpers descending in chaos. A man leaned over him and held his cheek next to the still man's nose.

"He's not breathing!" he shouted. A small group of folks close enough to hear the pronouncement rushed to the breathless body, standing over it in confusion and terror.

Abasi watched another man go down next to the well— and a woman. More people congregated in the town center, trying to help but not knowing what to do. Abasi watched as potential rescuers bent over to help a victim, themselves crumpling over, breathless.

Abasi's head was swimming, and he felt dizzy, confused. His legs wouldn't work, even though he wanted to run away. He watched as men and women fell to the ground as if the hand of Hell had reached up out of the well and plucked their souls mid-stride.

The connection between his brain and legs sparked when he thought of his mother, and he turned to run home. Bodies littered the alleyway.

He ran through the curtain hanging in the doorway into his house.

"Momma! Momma!" Abasi shouted.

He couldn't see inside, his eyes not adjusted to the dark from the bright morning sun. He squinted and then closed his eyes, slowly opening them to the dark room. He could make out the outline of a few things—the stove, the small table. He stepped forward into the room and tripped over something on the floor. He knew what it was without looking as he crawled over to the corner of the room, sobbing.

CHAPTER TWO

The lieutenant commander read the incoming message twice, eyes widening and mouth agape. He turned to the ensign and said, "Get the captain on the horn, now, please."

The ensign, looking puzzled, stammered, "Sir, it is 03:12. Are you sure you want me to wake him—*now?*"

"Get... him... *now!*" the senior officer commanded in a low but deliberate voice, glaring at the young seaman.

The commander knew the young man must feel a tremendous amount of intimidation as he picked up the phone and dialed the captain's quarters — there would be an angry voice on the other end. He noticed a bead of sweat glistening on the ensign's forehead.

"Yes?" said the captain in a bleary, barely audible voice.

The commander could see the ensign gulp. "Captain, the commander would like to speak with you, sir."

"This damn well better be important. The seas were calm last time I checked, and we weren't at war, Ensign. What the hell time is it anyhow?" the captain said, now more wakeful.

"Uhh... it's 03:13, Captain, sir."

The ensign handed the phone to the commander. "Captain, sir, I need to see you immediately. There is an—a— serious situation, sir."

"Well, spit it out, Commander!"

"Sir, I think this would best be delivered to you directly. May I come to your quarters?"

The commander could feel the captain's confusion in the silence. "Yes. Come on down."

Moments later, the commander walked into the captain's private quarters.

"Sir, we just received a message from the Department of Defense. A small town in the north of Tanzania named Mto Wa Mbu appears to have been attacked with a chemical or biological agent. It's about 175 miles from the coastal town of Tanga. The Tanzanian president has requested U.S. assistance."

"What's the situation?"

"The details are sparse, sir. Many dead. Some victims may still be alive, but it's too soon to tell how extensive the attack might have been, sir. Whatever happened, aerial reconnaissance by the Tanzanian Air Force indicates no signs of ongoing hostility. The perpetrators seem to have vanished. The Tanzanians are hoping we will help sort this out. Washington has directed us to support their efforts immediately."

"What can we expect from the Tanzanians, Commander?" asked the captain. "I don't know a damn thing about 'em."

"They're friendly to the U.S., sir. Pretty stable country. Democratic. They've been helpful to us in tracking down terrorist splinter groups in Eastern Africa. Generally, we're good to go with them. We have a green light to use their airspace, full stop."

"Well, get on with it then, Commander. And keep me updated," the captain said.

"Yes, sir," the commander replied as he closed the door.

The commander called his junior officers to brief them and outline his plan.

"We'll put two Seahawks in the air in the next 30 minutes. They need a refueling stop at a Tanzanian military base 25 miles inland from Dar es Salaam—the largest Tanzanian city. They'll then head northwest to... to... How the *hell* do you pronounce this? *Mto Wa Mbu*? Make sure an NBC officer is on each bird," he said, referring to military personnel specially trained to investigate nuclear, biological, and chemical attacks. He paused and shuffled through some notes. "And one of 'em needs to be Marks." There were moans from a few juniors, which stopped immediately as the Commander peered over the top of his horn-rimmed glasses.

He continued, "The military dress for this little jaunt is *MOPP gear* for everyone." More moans. "In case anyone missed it, " the Commander continued, "I said MOPP gear—that's right girls—good 'ol *Mission Oriented Protective Posture* gear. We need to expect the worst."

A lieutenant in the back said, "Commander, there must be some shit goin' down if we need to wear MOPP."

"Yes, Lieutenant, there is. And I recognize that MOPP is the bane of NBC duty, but my job is to complete the mission and keep you alive in the process," the commander said.

"But, sir..." The commander raised his hand, cutting him off.

"I understand that a rubber suit isn't exactly the type of thing any of you would willingly wear in the desert. Or anywhere, Lieutenant. But it is the greatest protection you'll have in a situation that smells like nerve gas. So, with that, you're dismissed."

A six-year-old Tanzanian boy walked to the kitchen and paused, confused. He looked around the room. Something was missing. The usual breakfast aromas of chapatti and ugali, as predictable as the sun rising, were absent. The boy, curious as to why he was the first one up, called out for his mother. No answer. His second call, too, was met with silence. A third call, more urgent, loud, scared. Nothing.

He ran to his mother's room to find her lying in bed. "Momma?" he said as he gently touched her shoulder. She didn't stir. "Momma!" he shouted as he tried arousing her, now with as forceful a shake a six-year-old boy could muster. The entire body of the 30-year-old woman moved, stiff with rigor mortis. The little boy, realizing the truth, slumped to the floor, his whimper evolving into a wail.

As the choppers circled above the village, Chief Petty Officer Marks, the NBC officer in charge, could see bodies strewn around a well in concentric rings, like the ripples caused by a stone thrown into a still pond. It was surreal—the well was an epicenter of death. Marks thought it looked like some bizarre, choreographed Broadway play from above. As they descended, he could see Africa's carnivorous animals feasting on the dead.

He thought whatever had killed the villagers acted instantly, bodies having fallen as they were taking their last step. There were a few signs of life, a child here and there as if planted for dramatic effect.

As the choppers swooped down into the village, the meat-eaters scattered, lumbering toward the outskirts of town, bellies full.

Marks instructed the recon crew to put their NBC masks on, transforming them into alien-like beings. They landed in a large garden patch about 50 yards away from the well. Marks instructed the pilot to remain ready to take off quickly if hostiles forced an unanticipated retreat.

A lieutenant junior grade stepped from the deck of the helicopter. Marks thought he saw the junior officer shiver as he hit the ground. He frowned in disgust behind his mask. *Jesus...*

The green lieutenant said, "It looks like a war zone—or at least what I think a war zone might look like." He had never been in combat. There were dead bodies everywhere. He shouldered his M-16, ready to cover his comrades.

Marks didn't hesitate to hop onto the ground. The CPO, unlike the wet-nosed young man, had been to hell and back, as he liked to say. He had been in every U.S. conflict since the '80s. He strode quickly toward the center of the village, the lieutenant trotting along behind like a lost puppy, looking dazed.

"Relax," Marks quipped. "Whoever or whatever did this is long gone."

Marks headed for the epicenter of the dead zone, stepping over bodies bloating in the considerable mid-morning African heat, flies swarming. Confused and scared, a few surviving children cried over bodies, presumably their parents. Reaching the city center just yards away from the well, he knelt and unzipped a bag, pulled out a Geiger counter, and flipped the switch. He knew that he was getting background radiation, which exists naturally in the environment, without looking at the gauge.

"Well, it ain't nuclear," the crusty CPO said. "Only radiation injury these folks could have is sunburn, and I don't think they much give a damn now."

He put the counter away and pulled out a pack of M-9 chemical detection papers. While the paper doesn't identify what kind of chemical agent was used, it tells you if any of various aerosolized compounds have been released, like mustard or nerve gas. Marks had put it to good use—and saved lives—in Iraq in the early '90s and Syria in 2013. He tore open the packet, took out a piece of the paper, and rubbed it on a corpse's skin. He expected it to turn pink, confirming a liquid nerve agent as the culprit. "White. Just plain 'ol goddam vanilla white." He scratched his masked head with a gloved hand. "What the hell is going on here?" he said.

He turned to the group, which in turn looked at him, half expecting a proclamation of discovery and hoping to get back on the chopper. "I would bet dollars-to-donuts this woulda been positive," Marks said, as he held up a white scrap of paper. "What sort of crap did these fuckers use?"

Mark's paused, then said, "The only thing left is a biologic. Boys, our job just got a helluva lot harder." He nodded toward a small collection of survivors standing at the outer edge of the dead zone. "And I feel sorry for those poor little bastards. It's probably just a matter of time for them. Whatever got their parents will get them before the sun sets."

The next thing out of his bag was the kind of thing one would see in a morgue: large, trocar-like needles, scalpels, various tubes, clear plastic vials, scissors. Minutes later, the choppers were lifting off with a Coleman cooler containing vials of blood, skin biopsies, hair, feces, scrapings from oral and nasal cavities—and two body bags.

The choppers lifted off in a cyclone of dust. A little boy of no more than five or six years old, huge khaki shorts held up by a knotted bit of twine, stood staring at the aircraft, tears in giant, bloodshot eyes, and arms stretched skyward in a *take-me-with-you* gesture. As seasoned as he was, Marks felt a lump in his throat and quickly looked away.

"Get us the hell outta here," he barked, looking at his watch. It was 10:34. As the Navy helicopters ascended and turned south, they saw an incoming red-and-white chopper with the letters WNN painted on the side.

"Jesus, word spreads fast... even in this God-forsaken land. How in the *hell* does the World News Network know *already*?" Marks said. He watched the civilian chopper for a moment, long enough to see that they intended to land in the village.

"*Goddammit*! It's hard enough managing this shit without having to worry about a bunch of newshounds gettin' killed. Turn this thing around. We gotta scare 'em off." The Seahawk cut a hard turn and was beside the slower civilian craft within seconds.

Marks peered out the Seahawk's tiny side window. He could see the pilot, someone sitting in the co-pilot's seat, and, through the open side of the chopper, a TV camera pointed down at the village. A woman in a white safari shirt with short, cropped black hair awkwardly leaned over to ensure she was in the shot, talking into a hand-held microphone.

"Tell them to shut their bird's door and get the hell outta here," Marks said. Complying, the Navy co-pilot flipped to all-frequencies mode and commanded them to leave the village immediately.

The woman turned to look at the Navy chopper and shrugged her shoulders as if to say *screw you*. Marks watched as she defiantly turned to her pilot and pointed toward the ground.

"Jesus! She's tellin' him to land! Get nose to nose with them, now!" Marks commanded. The Navy pilot deftly maneuvered the Seahawk and in seconds was face-to-face with the civilian chopper, about 20 yards between the tips of their rotor blades. The civilian pilot was shaken up, but his commander, the obstinate reporter, stuck her head up in the cockpit. As the WNN chopper continued its descent, marks could see her lips moving and knew what she was saying.

"We can't have them exposed to whatever's down there and then go back and prance around the Tanzanian capital, or it'll be like the goddam COVID wildfire shit we just finished cleaning up. If they land, we'll have to take them back with us and throw their ass in quarantine until this mess is over," Marks said.

He thought for a second and then said, "Shoot the ground underneath them—*NOW!*" The co-pilot flipped up the cover on the Gatling gun trigger and fired a burst under the nose of the news chopper, the dry ground exploding from the impact of 30-millimeter rounds.

The panicked WNN pilot careened the WNN vessel up and veered away. Marks saw the reporter, eyes furrowed in anger, her middle finger pointed skyward in a salute intended for him.

Marks grinned behind his MOPP mask. "She's a feisty little thing," he said, with no small amount of admiration.

"Instruct them to go directly to their point of origin in Dar es Salaam — and that we'll be behind them to ensure their safe arrival," Marks said. The Seahawk followed them for the half-hour journey, turning towards the *Shilo* only after the WNN crew had exited the chopper.

"That woman reporter has more balls than lotta Navy men I know," Marks quipped, grinning, as they pulled away from the civilians.

"Take us straight back to the ship," Marks instructed the pilots. "The goddam little WNN incident has eaten up enough fuel to make this exciting."

Twenty minutes before reaching the *Shilo,* Marks radioed the ship. "Is the welcoming party dressed in MOPP?"

"Affirmative," the radio replied.

"And they're ready for decon?" Marks pressed.

"Affirmative. Hypochlorite is ready to decon men and machines," the radio confirmed.

Marks shook his head knowingly. "Well, that'll kill anything we're bringing on board—bugs or drugs."

Lt. Grimes, looking puzzled, said, "Drugs?"

"Jesus, Grimes..." Marks said, shaking his head. "Nerve agent, son. A nerve agent."

"Oh..." the lieutenant replied quietly.

Marks looked out and saw the deck dotted with MOPP-clad Navy personnel as they approached the Shilo. "Well, look at that," he said. "They listened to me for once. Hopefully, the *Eisenhower* is ready to fly the body somewhere they can figure out what the hell is going on. I imagine Bethesda will have their hands all over this crap."

CHAPTER THREE

Jack shoved back from the microscope, wheels on his chair squeaking in a painfully high pitch, removed his wire-rimmed glasses, and rubbed his eyes. He'd seen enough dead cells for a while. He glanced at the clock, squinting. He had worked through the night. Again.

He thought about calling Marla, but mid-reach for the phone decided against it. She wasn't a morning person and had probably already figured out he wasn't coming home. He grinned to himself, knowing he would catch her good-natured hell later in the day. *You love dead cells more than you love me,* she would pout, feigning emotional trauma.

He walked out of his office, smiling when he saw two of his lab rats—Ph.D. candidates—already at the bench working. "Mornin'," Jack said.

The two looked up. "Morning, boss," they said, grinning.

He poured a cup of coffee out of the pot that had been on all night, the steady heat slowly reducing it to an acrid liquid with the consistency of light crude. He winced at the smell as he raised the cup to his lips. Tolerating the unpleasant taste was easier than making a new pot. *More sugar.* He reached for a packet and tore it open over the cup. Better, but only marginally.

Besides the occasional clink of lab glassware, the only sound in the lab was the background of the early morning news on low, barely audible, emanating from a circa 1980s boxy TV set. When one of his lab protégés brought the TV into the lab a semester ago after discovering it in a post-semester dumpster dive of particularly rich finds, Jack had been pissed off. He was not a TV person. However, he had gotten used to having it on early in the mornings to see what was going on in the world, according to the WNN filter anyway. He typically watched for a few minutes and went back to work as it blathered quietly for the rest of the day. It seemed to keep his doctoral candidates happy. To Jack, it was like a telephone call with a distant relative: it never communicated much of importance, and the only way to quiet it short of hanging up was to set the receiver on the desk and keep working.

He walked back to his office, put his feet up on his desk, and cradled his mug, warming his hands. He noticed the Rubik's Cube sitting by the phone. *They're always messing with me.* His lab rats would sneak in and mess up the cube thinking this time he wouldn't be able to solve it—at least, not quickly. He reached over and picked it up as he slurped more coffee. He set his mug down and, with uncanny ease, aligned the six colors as if it were a connect-the-dot puzzle for a six-year-old. Jack's skill with Rubik's Cube was a snapshot into the way his brain worked—he had always been able to glean simplicity from complexity, especially when others were confused by what they saw. The first time he saw one of the complicated puzzles on the checkout counter in Duckwall's Department Store in Smith Center, he awed the small group of stumped adults by twisting it into place in 30 seconds. He bought one the next day, after mowing the neighbor's yard and being paid the king's ransom of $7.50. Since then, he always had a Rubik's Cube close by. Everyone—from his siblings to college roommates, and now his lab rats—needed to prove they were the ones that could mess it up to the point he couldn't solve it—at least not as fast as he had solved the last person's attempt.

After consuming half of the coffee, he rolled back over to the microscope and continued working until a knock on the doorjamb.

"Uh, Jack?" said Ian, one of his assistants, peering around the corner of the doorway.

"Yeah?" Jack said, almost startled.

"You'd better come see this."

"See what, Ian?" Jack asked.

"Something on the news." Jack noticed Ian's face was grave.

Jack followed him out of the office, immediately looking over at the TV. He could see an aerial view of an African village, dead bodies strewn randomly across the ground as he approached. The footage looked staged, like a bizarre Andy Warhol-like fantasy cartoon, bodies surrounding a well as if they had died in a vain attempt at straining with their last breath to obtain a drink of water from some mythical fountain of youth. A woman's face, a reporter, bounced in and out of view, her lips moving, but no sound. The end of the clip was from the perspective of the cockpit, a huge military helicopter filling the screen and firing a massive machine gun toward the civilian craft.

"Turn it up!" Jack urged.

The other assistant, standing by the set, complied. The audio was a voice-over by a woman reporter, the aerial clip being looped—only about 90 seconds in total—as she spoke.

"According to our sources, there are no signs of violence, no sign of natural disaster of any sort. Whatever has happened seems to have killed everyone in the village. From the air, it looks like individuals dropped dead in mid-stride. The U.S. military has already sent in a team of experts in nuclear, biological, and chemical warfare, known in military parlance as their NBC team. The military prevented us from landing in a rather aggressive manner, as you can see from this clip." Jack bristled at the comments regarding the Navy's involvement. Ian noticed.

"What's the whole shivering thing?" he asked Jack.

"I'm not exactly a fan of the armed forces," Jack said with more edge than the underling had ever heard from his mentor.

"Why? What happened?" Ian prodded.

"I'm old enough that I saw our Armed Forces do things—disturbing things—like invade Grenada and Panama. Between that and the 9-11 crackdown on civil liberties, plus the whole Iraq and Afghanistan thing, it really made me despise the government—especially the military," Jack explained. "They seem to think they can do whatever the hell they want. Now, shut up—I want to hear this," Jack said, indicating the conversation was over.

"Although this reporter isn't able to confirm it, our WNN medical experts suspect a contagious, obviously lethal infection—bacterial or viral." The video loop was now in a small corner box, the majority of the screen now filled with the face of the reporter. Although her face bounced in and out of the screen, Jack noticed she was an attractive young woman in her 30s—attractive enough that he wondered how she ended up in rural Africa, as opposed to some major U.S. city as an up-and-coming TV beat reporter.

"A second, although a less likely possibility, is some highly toxic gas, like sarin, a nerve agent used in chemical warfare," the reporter continued. "As to the group responsible for perpetrating this cowardly act against an innocent African village, well, there are no leads at this time. With war and inter-tribal conflict in some neighboring countries, it could be virtually anybody, although Somalian warlords are highly suspect."

The reporter paused, dramatically tilting her head down and to the left. "This is Riley Mills for WNN, reporting from Dar es Salaam, Tanzania."

Jack knew what was going to happen next. While he was debating whether to call them, the phone rang. It was 5:36 a.m. Central Standard Time. He sighed and shook his head.

CHAPTER FOUR

With absolute certainty that he knew who was on the other end, Jack picked up the phone and said, "Hi, Catherine. What took you so long?"

"Oh, shut up," Catherine said. "I just found out about it five minutes before WNN. Jesus, I don't know how they do it! One day they're going to get there so fast they'll become part of the casualty list!"

"Hey, just because you're the head of the CDC doesn't make you so special," he teased. Jack adored everything about Catherine. At first glance, she was an intimidating individual, both in stature and beauty, but in reality, she was a gentle soul with a Mensa-like intellect. He admired her humble origins; she had grown up in rural New Mexico, in relatively poor circumstances. She had shared with him that it was there at an early age she had witnessed first-hand the ravages of unbridled but treatable disease—and the kind of poverty that forced people to choose between medicine and food. She impressed upon Jack that, for most people, a grumbling, hungry stomach was always more immediately noticeable than the slow, silent killers of diabetes, hypertension, and heart disease. Jack was awed at what she had become—the first Latina CDC director in US history. Her goal was to help the masses. Now she was in the position to do it.

"Whaddya think is going on? Any ideas?" queried Jack.

"Not really. Acts infectious, and that's where I'm playing my cards. The rapidity with which it struck is remarkable. We aren't getting lots of cooperation out of the Department of Defense." Jack knew the DoD irked Catherine as much as the military did him, especially in situations where infection could be the source of a catastrophe. Their mode of operation was always secretive. Jack's perspective was that openness and transparency were good, especially where infectious disease was potentially playing a role.

There was a short silence, and then Jack said, "Sounds a bit like *Ebola*. The last outbreak was 20 years ago in Gabon and The Republic of the Congo, so it's about time it rears its ugly head again."

Catherine, pausing, said, "Could be. But it could also be as simple as *Neisseria meningitis*. God, I hope it is. At least we can treat it. Pop everyone in the butt with four million units of penicillin, and we're done."

"Wishful thinking, Catherine. I seriously doubt it." Jack paused, unsure whether to say what he figured Catherine was thinking, too. "Any chance it could be a new COVID variant? I mean, we've hardly had enough time to take a breath since delta."

"Jesus. What a joy you are!" Catherine responded. "You've become a buzz kill since you left the Ivy League spotlight, Jack. Life must be pretty damn boring since you figured out — oh, let's see? HIV, Ebola, and SARS."

"Hey, I love my quiet life and would prefer to have it stay that way," Jack responded.

Catherine said, "Anyway, let's stop speculating and get some data. Whatever it is, it's lethal, and we need to get a handle on it before it spreads. God knows if it gets out of Africa — as COVID got out of China — it will be an even bigger disaster than it already is. Frankly, I don't think the world is ready for another 18 months of quarantine and masks."

"Hey, I'm all about data, but where do we get it? WNN? If you happen to have the CEO's phone number in your back pocket, hand it over," Jack said.

"I need to call my contacts in Washington," Catherine said. "And you, Jack, need to get your ass on a plane to Atlanta. Today."

Jack sighed loudly. "Catherine, can't we just wait and see what the DoD comes up with? I, really, *really* don't want to schlep myself down there only to turn around and come home when this is put to rest by the military."

"Well, I guess we could do that, Jack, but I've already made your flight arrangements. I dispatched one of the CDC jets—it's already headed your way. You leave in four hours. Go home, pack your bag and kiss Marla goodbye. I'll see you for a working dinner tonight. With luck, you'll be home by the weekend."

"It ain't that easy, Catherine. Marla may have a few things to say about my sudden departure," Jack said.

"Ahh…but we both know you're so convincing when you want to be, Jack. You must be. She moved in with you," Catherine said with glee in her voice.

CHAPTER FIVE

"But why does it have to be you? I mean, it's a big country with lots of smart people. Doesn't Catherine know anyone else?" Marla was less than pleased Jack was whisking off to Atlanta.

"Catherine and I go way back, honey," Jack said. "We met in San Francisco in the early 2000s when I presented some work on rapid vaccine generation. Catherine cornered me after the presentation—she asked me tons of questions, popping them off at machine-gun speed. I was taken so aback by her questions that we went to dinner and continued to talk—it wasn't a romantic thing. We've remained close friends. She trusts me, and from the sound of things, this is a pretty big deal," Jack said. "Besides, it's probably only going to be a couple of days. I'm guessing between the CDC and military; this thing is almost sewn up."

"I dunno, Jack. I don't have a warm, fuzzy feeling about this. There's something creepy about the fact this started where it did," Marla said.

Jack stopped cramming wadded-up underwear into his duffle and looked at her, puzzled. "Africa? What's so creepy about Africa?"

"It isn't just Africa, but *where* in Africa. Mto Wa Mbu is part of Olduvai," Marla said in a tone that suggested he should know exactly what she was talking about.

Jack straightened up and put his hands on his hips. "Honey, I don't have a clue as to what you're getting at."

"It's basic physical anthropology stuff, honey. *Olduvai Gorge*—otherwise known as the *cradle of mankind*—is in the lake region of northern Tanzania. It's where Louis and Mary Leakey discovered the remains of the earliest human beings back in the 1930s."

"Well, that's fascinating, and all, sweetie, but I don't know why it's creepy. New stuff crops up all the time—HIV, Ebola, COVID — etcetera, etcetera. It's just another virus that transitioned from animal vectors — monkeys or bats something. No big deal," Jack said.

"Well, it feels creepy to *me*. Anything cropping up where humans first appeared as a species seems just a little freaky."

"Come on, Marla. I mean, how long ago did that happen? One hundred thousand years or something like that?"

"No. At least 200,000 years ago."

Jack grinned at her and shrugged in a gesture of *so what* as he shouldered his bag.

"And aren't you forgetting something?" Marla asked. Jack grinned.

"*No.* We'll celebrate when I get back. Promise," he said, leaning over and kissing her.

ONE YEAR AGO · THE FREE STATE BREWERY · DOWNTOWN LAWRENCE, KS

Just weeks after moving back to Lawrence from Boston, Jack met Marla Qiu, a tall, slender Asian-American woman from Oklahoma. She was finishing up her doctoral degree in physical anthropology. They met at the Free State Brewery on Massachusetts Street, a hometown microbrewery whose name reflected Kansas' aggressive and all-to-bloody position during the Civil War. Jack was sitting on a barstool watching Jayhawk hoops, eating a burger the size of a salad plate and sipping a dark, bitter stout with a thick, creamy head. Marla, looking a bit tousled, sidled up to the bar and sat down on the only empty stool left, which just happened to be next to Jack's. She ordered a pale ale, plunked down the cash, and quaffed it dry like a thirsty pirate on shore leave, much to Jack's dismay and frank admiration.

"Rough day?" Jack queried with wide eyes, leaning back, unsure if this would bring a smile or wrath. He wasn't so sure this petite Asian woman, who had just downed a pint without taking a breath, couldn't kick his butt. He hoped for the smile or at least some other non-lethal response.

Marla looked at Jack, who thought she looked somewhat taken aback, and said, with a slight Southern accent, "You might say that if you consider doing your doctoral thesis defense in the category of a hard day." Jack felt like she was sizing him up and likely came to the same conclusion that he had—she could, in fact, probably kick his ass.

"Why don't you buy me another beer, and I'll tell you about it. You know us Asians can't metabolize alcohol very well, so if you buy me another beer, there's no telling what I'll say," Marla said, grinning. Jack was pretty sure she wouldn't hurt him now but wasn't so sure she couldn't drink him under the table.

"What's your doctorate in?" Jack asked. He tipped his head up toward the barkeep, catching his eye and motioning for him to come over.

"Physical anthropology," Marla responded, scrunching up her nose, pretending the utterance revolted her.

Jack smiled. His mind was running way out in front of his judgment. He marveled at the series of juxtapositions that seemed to be bundled up in this woman. "Let's see," Jack said. "An ale-quaffing Asian-American woman with a Southern accent is studying physical anthropology in the Midwest."

"So? Why the smile? I suppose you're wondering what the hell I'll do with a Ph.D. in physical anthropology," she said, cocking her head, half frowning at her newly delivered pint.

"Actually, no, I wasn't. I wondered why an ale-quaffing Asian-American woman with a Southern accent was studying physical anthropology in the Midwest; Jack paused. Then he said, "Now that I think about it, I can't see why I should question what someone else would do for a living. I don't exactly have a mainstream job," Jack said.

"No?" queried Marla.

"Not unless you consider a guy who watches little genetic packages slowly kill something or cause cancer a popular career choice," Jack said, pausing. "It's fun. You should try it sometime."

Jack noticed her fake surprise as she said, "So you're a defense contractor?"

"Very funny," Jack said, liking her more with each verbal parry. "No, I'm a virologist at KU. I study viruses. Mainly ones that humans worry about. Very boring stuff — except for like the last 18 months and the surreal bullshit COVID put us, virologists, through"

He winced and paused, thinking of the 5 million people that evaporated from the earth from COVID. He took a long pull from his beer, and when he looked back at Marla, he knew the last exchange created some discomfort.

Jack broke the silence. "Now that you mention it, what are you going to do with your degree?"

"Well, since a lot of physical anthropologists don't make much money, I thought I would apply for food stamps," Marla said. "My thesis helped my literacy, so I figure I can complete the application now. Maybe unemployment, too," said Marla, smirking.

"Un-huh. Sure," Jack said, shaking his head, grinning. *She stuck the landing with that comeback. Nice.*

Marla added, "I'm an associate professor on The Hill, too. In the Anthro department. My real interest is migratory patterns of early hominids."

"Fascinating. In my world, humans are just fomites— especially kids— they're just carriers of the viruses I like to study. They always bring home the damn cold!" Jack said, trying to be a bit more lighthearted.

Marla took a pull off her beer. "Now that you know what I do, I could probably teach you a few things."

There were a few moments of considered silence. Jack spoke first. "Why the interest in physical anthropology?"

"It started with a fascination of the Native Americans in Oklahoma. The Cherokee, the Comanche, the Kiowa, the Kansa — the tribe the State of Kansas is named after. I became interested in how North America was populated via the Bering Strait migration. Dreadfully dull, eh?"

"Did you forget whom you are talking to?" They both laughed.

Jack enjoyed the conversation as it meandered and expanded, covering topics from the arcane to the common to the esoteric. He sensed their attraction to each other growing— a genuine attraction beyond a casual meeting in a bar. Jack couldn't tell what was hotter—her intellect or her body. Whichever, the other part came in second by a gnat's eyelash. He hoped she was feeling the same. He knew she was when several more ales and hours later she suddenly leaned over, put her hand behind his neck and pulled him over, and kissed him.

"Wow," Jack managed to stammer out. "Let's do that again!" Marla willingly obliged. Jack, suddenly self-conscious, suggested they leave. Marla enthusiastically agreed and was halfway out of the Brewery before Jack had his wallet out to settle up with the bartender.

Marla met him at the door and put her arm around his waist as naturally as if they had been together for years. "How about you show me your place?"

The connection he felt at Free State was heartily—and mutually—confirmed within the hour. The sex was as enthusiastic, affirming, and mutually gratifying as their intellectual exploration had been and lasted just as long. He collapsed about 4 a.m., exhausted, silently thankful to be in her arms, hoping it was mutual.

Jack was the first up. He smiled at Marla, sleeping soundly, her body tantalizingly outlined by a thin, white sheet, as he slipped to the kitchen and started the coffee.

"So, I hope you realize something that I did—or rather completely failed to do—and would have to say I'm completely embarrassed," Marla said.

Jack jumped, startled by her voice. He turned to find her leaning against the doorway. His shirt hung down just far enough to cover her hips, and she had unconsciously buttoned it such that her cleavage was front and center.

"Sorry! Did I scare you? The coffee brewing wafted into the bedroom. It woke me up... I found one of your shirts and thought I'd join you. Hope it's OK."

"My God... " Jack was stunned by her beauty. He was hoping that she wasn't regretting the night. He sure as hell wasn't. He wanted to burn the visual of the way she looked now —standing there—permanently into his memory and see the real thing every day.

Jack said, "Yeah, you startled me." He paused, then asked, "What are you embarrassed about?"

"I don't know your name," Marla said deadpan. "And you don't know mine."

"Oh my God! You're right! Were we *that* drunk? Or just that into the conversation?" Jack said, shocked.

"Who cares? Probably a little of both," Marla said. She walked over to Jack and stuck out her hand. "Hi. I'm Marla Qui. And you are?"

Jack reached for her hand and said, "Hi, I'm..." He paused, puzzled. "Wait a sec. What did you say your name is?" Marla looked at him quizzically.

"Marla Qui. Spelled Q-U-I, but pronounced, 'chew,' she said.

A broad grin split Jack's face. "Marla! It's me! Jack Cann! From Smith Center! I can't believe it's you!"

Marla looked confused, eyes darting to and fro as if searching for something.

"From Smith Center?" Marla said.

"Yes! Don't you remember?"

Marla broke into a smile, then laughed. "Of course I do, Jack! Oh my God! I can't believe it's you!"

"When did you leave Smith Center? Weren't you about eight?" Jack said.

"Yes, I was eight. I had such a crush on you! I hated leaving," Marla said.

"Where did you go?"

"We went to Oklahoma, down by Bartlesville. My dad's family homesteaded some land down there in the 1860s, and we went back when my grandfather became ill. I graduated from high school there, then went to Oklahoma State. Got my degree in Anthro and moved to KU for my Ph.D."

"I have such amazing memories from our time together... playing on the farm, doing the chores. I remember you would come to help me with the dirtiest damn things— cleaning out the farrowing house, mucking out horse stalls..."

"I told you I had a crush on you. You don't think I hung out with you because I thought shoveling shit was fun, do you? I just wanted to be with you. I kinda hate to admit that after all these years..." Marla said. "I even remember helping set irrigation pipe for the corn. And that crop duster! Remember that insanity?"

"Geez, can you imagine anyone doing that today? I mean to stand in a cornfield and hold red flags up so the spray plane could drop organophosphate pesticide on the field? Seeing that plane level off and running like hell to get out of the way...” Jack was laughing so hard his eyes teared up. “It was lunacy!” Jack spat out, gasping for breath.

They spent the rest of the weekend together, knowing they had found their match. They moved in together a few weeks after reuniting and, as Jack’s parents liked to say, were living in sin.

CHAPTER SIX

She was strumming her fingers on the desktop in an increasingly rapid cadence, her anger approaching the boiling point.

Riley Mills had just become the worldwide TV persona of a mysterious African tragedy, but she was pissed. No one chased her off a story—not even some gun-slinging macho Navy boys. The tipping point reached, she hurled a coffee mug full of pens against the wall, the pens scattering like shrapnel and creating a staccato-like clatter as the mug bounced off the plaster only to shatter on the grey concrete floor. She slumped back in her chair, fuming. She wasn't used to losing, and this felt like a loss. *U.S. Navy: 1; Riley Mills: 0.*

A fellow reporter stuck his head in the office. "Everything OK?" he asked.

"No, goddamn it! It isn't OK! I just got stiffed on a story that's being covered up. I needed to get on the ground and get critical info," Riley said.

Her colleague paused, wondering if it was safe to say anything. "Well, they may have saved your life, Riley," the man countered. Her glare slowly faded to questioning furrowed brows.

She thought for a moment and sighed, "Well, maybe. But I still feel like something isn't right," she said. She tilted her head, thinking, eyes focused on nothing. She looked back up at him and said, "I just can't believe all those dead people lying around the well. Something about the whole scene—other than the dead people—is bothering me."

"I know what you mean," said her colleague. "Pretty surreal."

Riley looked up at the TV screen in her office. It was, of course, tuned to WNN, and her story was being shown again, volume down. She squinted with the intensity of someone seeing it for the first time, despite having seen it about 40 times.

Her eyes widened, suddenly understanding what was bothering her. "There weren't any kids among the dead!" she exclaimed with near glee.

"Jesus..." she said in a whisper, a look of panicked realization washing across her face. She stood, lost in her thoughts. "There were kids there—kids that were still alive. And the Navy left them. *We* left them!" Riley said. "I was so damn annoyed at the military; I totally missed it." She bolted out of the room and headed for production. She walked fast, wanting to run. Reaching the door, she knocked twice, a subconscious formality before bolting in and startling the young man at the editing console.

"I need to see all of the footage from the village story," she said to the man.

"Riley, we aired everything. You've seen it about a hundred times already."

"No, I haven't seen it all. We aired only the footage shot while we were directly over the village. The camera was rolling from about a mile out of the village as we approached it. I need to see that," Riley said.

The technician rolled his chair over to another monitor, typed something, and clicked. A window popped open, and a video clip began rolling.

They were looking out of the front of the WNN helicopter, the desert flying by beneath them. The village was visible on the horizon, tiny hut-like houses growing larger in the screen. The Navy chopper was just starting to lift off the ground as the news crew approached, the WNN aircraft slowing.

"Look, there," she said, pointing to a tiny figure under the Navy chopper hovering about 25 feet above the ground. "What's that?"

The tech zoomed in on the area of interest and sharpened the image with some digital magic. "You mean here?" he asked, freezing the video.

"Yeah," Riley responded. "Look below the Navy chopper." The tech complied. The detail was remarkable. A little boy, arms reaching upward toward the helicopter, clearly pleading for them to take him. Riley felt a pang in her stomach.

"Can you make it bigger and keep the clarity?" she asked.

"You got it," the tech said.

The two WNN employees were now staring at the face of a village boy, eyes pleading for help, arms stretched upward. He was wearing oversized khaki pants held tight to his waist with a twine belt. Riley's eyes began to tear—something that never happened, certainly not at work. The tech just stared.

"Jesus... There was a kid still alive in the village," the tech said.

"And we left him. We left a little boy there to die. Just like..." Riley's voice trailed off as if she were somewhere else. She clumsily groped for a chair to sit down. "What..." she paused and swallowed hard. "What if he wasn't the only one?" she said, looking over at the tech, their eyes meeting.

"You had to leave him—or them," the tech said. "They weren't going to let you land."

Riley thought for a moment. "Yeah. You're right." She stood up and started to walk out, pausing at the door. Without looking back at the tech, she said, "Can you send me a copy of that little boy's picture by email?"

"Sure. Why?" the tech asked.

"Well, we left him, but that doesn't mean I can't go get him. Besides the fact he's just a little boy, there is more to this story than I originally thought," Riley said as she walked out of the room.

She sat down at her computer, opened the email, and clicked on the picture. The little boy's face again stared at her. It was as if he were making a personal plea to her. She felt pain in her chest as she tried to suppress feelings she hadn't experienced in years. She printed the photo, cut it out, and put it in her reporter's notebook. As she leaned back in the chair, she thought maybe she didn't lose to the Navy. Perhaps it was just halftime.

Riley got back to her apartment late. She felt irritable and didn't understand why. The kid's face floated around her consciousness all day. Now he was intruding without permission, and it exhausted her. She went to bed and, after trying to read for a while, gave up, turned off the light, rolled over, and drifted off.

She tossed and turned in the purgatory between sleeping and not sleeping. The boy's face was still there as if to taunt her. But why? For what? And what the hell is that smell?

She jolted awake and sat straight up as if having a seizure. She smelled alcohol and cigarettes in the air, faint but distinct. She reached over and turned on the light, anxiously looking around the room. Water dripped on her forearm. She stared at it, confused. Another drop. She reached up and touched her cheek. She was crying. Confused, she flopped back against the pillows and stared at the ceiling as another tear slowly trickled down the side of her face.

CHAPTER SEVEN

Jack's CDC jet landed at Andrews Air Force Base at 4 p.m. EST. He was pissed because Catherine had re-routed his plane from Atlanta to Bethesda. She wanted him to keep an eye on the DoD.

As he was disembarking, a giant C-17 Globemaster III touched down. He watched as it lumbered up to the same hanger as the CDC jet. Jack watched as a slew of military vehicles descended on the Globemaster, the number of armed military personnel disgorged by the vehicles reminiscent of clowns piling out of a tiny circus car.

He watched as the back end of the military transport plane dropped down, and two body bags were transferred to ambulances.

Jack was unceremoniously escorted to a waiting car that took him directly to the hospital. Two MPs greeted him, who took him down a dizzying array of hallways to a door on which a sheet of white printer paper was taped with the words TOP SECRET hand-scrawled in red ink. *How bush league.*

"In there," one of the MPs pointed.

"Excuse me?" Jack said.

"You need to go in there," he said.

Jack cracked open the door, light from the outer hallway escaping into the room like a Hollywood searchlight. A small group of military personnel turned and looked at his head poking through the doorway. He stepped in and shut the door.

"Hi. I'm Jack Cann from the University of Kansas. Uhhh, I mean from the CDC. Director Montoya sent me up from Atlanta to see if I could offer any insight." The group stared silently for what seemed like an inappropriately long time, at least to Jack.

"Is there an issue?" Jack asked.

"We don't need civilian help, sir," one of the corpsmen said. Jack bristled but held his tongue, the young military man's arrogance justifying his disdain for the military.

"Corpsman, I'll handle this," a man said, stepping forward. "I'm Lieutenant Rick Matthews, and I'm in charge of this operation." He paused, looked back at his colleagues, then said, "So, Mr. Cann, what is it that you do that's supposed to be helpful?"

Jack fought the urge to say what came to mind. "I'm a virologist with a specialization in genetics. The CDC is suspicious that whatever this is, it's viral—perhaps something new. Dr. Montoya thought it would be a good idea if I popped in to watch and offer my input to the DoD."

Jack could tell they weren't impressed. Picking up on their reticence—*or is it just bald-faced conceit?*—he added, "But I'm sure you guys have this well in hand, so why don't I just take a seat where I have a decent view and stay out of your way?" He took a deep breath and exhaled inaudibly. *Dick.* The corpsman and physicians turned and carried on as if Jack weren't in the room. He walked over to a chair and sat down.

He looked around, studying the surroundings. He heard the Corpsmen using the letters LFU in reference to a glass self-contained work area immediately in front of him. Short for laminar flow unit, he figured—a negative pressure system that sucks the air into the room to prevent airborne dissemination of infectious agents. The inner chamber was entered through a double-door system, one leading into an antechamber, the second into the LFU autopsy room. On the ceiling and the two sidewalls of the antechamber were oversized showerheads. Small placards had hypochlorite on them, placed just above a faucet-like handle on a control panel outside of the unit where the corpsmen were standing. There was a small, two-by-two foot square door inside the antechamber and small nozzles, also labeled hypochlorite. Jack assumed that samples could be passed through this opening for bagging and transport to another room for preparation as needed.

The corpsmen addressed Rick as Lieutenant Matthews and another officer, a woman, as Lieutenant Hermans. The officers called each other by their first names, Rick and Lucy. He gathered from the conversation that Matthews was a pathologist and Hermans was an infectious disease specialist.

As Jack observed the two officers suited up in incredibly uncomfortable protective suits—things the corpsman referred to as MOPP gear—he couldn't help but notice that Lieutenant Matthews was quite the physical specimen. He was a tall, fit Navy doctor with a handsome, chiseled face—he could be the poster child for any branch of military service in any country in the Western Hemisphere. Jack imagined he could have convinced anyone that he was an aircraft carrier captain.

His partner, Lieutenant Hermans, was the female opposite of a poster for anything—short, teetering on overweight, brunette hair with stray gray streaks piled in a messy bun — a quintessential middle-aged schoolmarm.

Jack studied the MOPP gear. Each suit had a cooling and air filtration system large, white-ribbed hoses running from battery backpacks along the neck and around the sides of the helmet. He watched as they tested the built-in radio communicators that allowed them to speak to each other and the technicians to monitor the conversation.

The physicians stepped through the first door of the antechamber and closed it behind them. There was a hissing sound as the vacuum of the LFU was activated. Jack thought he saw Lucy shiver with the metallic ker-lunk of the metal bolts on the door locking from the outside behind them. A red light shone above the second door at the opposite end of the short corridor. The showerheads began spewing the decontaminating solution over them, lasting about 15 seconds. One of the corpsmen announced, "When the green light goes on, you can go through the inner door, Lieutenants. It should be about another five seconds."

Jack watched the whole scene through the glass. *This must be the longest five seconds those two have ever lived through.* He hated the military, but he wasn't devoid of compassion for anyone. He knew their hearts must have been beating in their throats. He was authentically concerned for them. If this was a rogue virus or bacteria of some kind, no telling what could happen. He felt slightly nauseated at the thought. *I have to start eating breakfast.*

The green light popped on simultaneously to another hissing sound, and a diaphanous mist enveloped the two doctors as the inner door opened.

"The only thing missing," Rick commented to Lucy, "is a shrill violin note, and this would be a great horror flick." The remote speakers relayed the comment to the group outside of the LFU. Jack smiled.

Everyone in the room knew that one tiny breach of technique could have one or both physicians end up as fresh specimens on the autopsy table themselves. Jack's mind took it a step further: *If one of them tanks and crashes through the window of the LFU, we're all screwed.*

"Which should we start with?" Lucy said.

"I don't think it matters," Rick said, looking slowly from the bagged corpse to Lucy.

Jack watched as they moved to the bag closest to them, paused to look at each other, and each heaved a long sigh as Rick unzipped the bag. Spreading the bag open revealed a black male, less than six feet tall, moderate build, somewhat bloated, in full rigor mortis. The corpse had a blank, eyes-wide-open stare, the corneas clouded in death. He looked about 40 to Jack. They stripped the bag from the body, lifting his head first, Rick rocking him from side to side while Lucy pulled the bag down toward the feet. The dark body contrasted sharply with the gleaming, stainless steel table. The table had a concave surface to funnel stray body fluids to the center and toward the feet, where a hole allowed them to drain into a bucket.

"I'm about to help with something I haven't done since med school," Lucy said.

Rick muttered, "Complete, compulsive, thorough." Jack noticed Lucy was puzzled by this comment. Rick saw, too, so said, "Oh, those are words beaten into my consciousness during training. This is one case that needs to go perfectly. The entire damn world will eventually know what went on in here."

Jack watched as Rick pulled a microphone down from an overhead boom and switched it on. "This is Lieutenant Rick Matthews. The time is 17:22 EST. The specimen is a black male, native of Africa, and measures five feet, ten and one-half inches from the vertex of the cranium to the bottom of the calcaneus on the right. His estimated time of death is between 36 and 60 hours ago, occurring in his native village in Tanzania. There are no signs of external trauma or injury on the anterior or posterior sides of the body. There are no signs of external hemorrhage."

After describing the body's exterior in painful detail, Rick clicked the mic off and scrunched up his face. "Jesus, this is even freaky to a pathologist. I mean, this guy just dropped dead on a continent known for ethnic violence, and there isn't a scratch on him. You'd think in a place where guns and machetes are as common as sand; you wouldn't have to go to the trouble of using biological or chemical agents to off someone." Lucy nodded her head in agreement. Jack was hoping it was biological or chemical weapons. *At least we know how to treat the known biological stuff.* He was more worried about some new, as yet unknown virus—a new strain of Ebola or HIV. *God forbid this is COVID 2.0.* Jack intentionally banished the thought from his mind.

Rick handed Lucy some cotton swabs. They each sampled various orifices of the body—mouth, nose, ears, anus, and genitals—placing each swab separately in culture solutions for bacteria and viruses. Everything was meticulously—and painfully—labeled.

Rick turned to a stainless steel table and picked up an autopsy knife. "It looks like what I carve my Thanksgiving turkey with," grinned Lucy, in another awkward attempt to relieve the tension.

"Yeah, it isn't meant for delicate work, but then I'm not a surgeon either," quipped Rick. He made a V-shaped incision from each shoulder, starting just above the armpit and connecting them in the center of the chest just below the breastbone. Jack noticed the incision went completely down to the bone in one swipe of the knife, a testament to Rick's experience and the knife's sharpness. The V was made into a Y with a third incision, starting from the point of the V on the chest and continuing down the middle of the belly and to the corpse's pubic bone. This wasn't as deep as not to cut into the abdomen or injure the organs, potentially obscuring important information. The second sweep of his hand exposed the fascia of the belly, a long, tough tendon-like structure, beneath which lie the internal organs. A heavy scissor was used to cut the fascia from the pubis to the point of the V, laying open the belly. Next, a bone saw was used to cut the breastbone and upper ribs. A rake-like object was pulled down from above the table, suspended from a trapeze-like pulley, and hooked under the breastbone. Rick cranked the ratcheted pulley, lifting the bony chest wall from the underlying heart and lungs. A quick slice of the knife divided the esophagus and trachea at the base of the neck, and then, using scissors, Rick stripped the organs out of the body cavity. This process would have appeared to be nothing short of gross mutilation to the casual observer. Jack, slightly nauseated, nonetheless admired Rick's dexterity.

Jack watched as the physicians stood back and paused, looking at the organs. "Well, anything jumping out at you?" Lucy asked. Jack was peering into the chamber, craning his neck, squinting to see as if he would spy something the two doctors just 12 inches from the specimen might miss.

"Unfortunately, no. Grossly, everything appears normal. Hopefully, the microscopic exam and cultures will prove more helpful."

Cutting into each of the organs confirmed Rick's initial impression. "I don't see any sign of gross abnormality: no hemorrhage, no necrosis, no discoloration, no nothin'. I didn't expect it to be easy, but I thought we'd at least have a clue after the gross exam. Hell, I don't even know what organ to focus on."

Rick began taking small pieces of tissue from each of the organs and putting them in small jars with formalin to prepare for routine microscopy.

A piece of each organ was placed on a special culture dish and another in a test tube filled with a blood-and-broth solution to coax the growth of the causative agent. Homogenized pieces of each organ were placed in human cell tissue cultures, standard practice to grow viruses. Jack watched this part of the process with particular scrutiny.

Lucy had the painful task of labeling each specimen. Jack smirked, thinking she must feel a little like she was in his Biology 101 class. Each sample was carefully placed in incubators kept at the same temperature as the human body.

"I'm putting my money on a viral etiology," posited Lucy. Jack nodded his head in agreement. No one noticed. He was pretty sure that they didn't care what he thought.

"Could be bacterial, too, I guess," Rick said, trying to keep a broad perspective.

Lucy, arms folded, noted, "Yes, I suppose. We'll know within a week, one way or another. Who knows, if it is something new, it could have an incubation period much longer than we expect."

Again, Jack nodded. *At least they're not idiots.* He had concerns that this would not be as simple as throwing some tissue in a broth and cooking it for a bit. Tracking down HIV took ages. COVID took far less time due to all the advancements, but still... Jack figured the Navy brass would be breathing down their necks the whole time, unable to understand why they were waiting on some unknown bug to grow.

"Great. Thanks for cheering me up," Rick said.

Lucy grinned, "My pleasure. You didn't think I was going to sit around waiting for the results alone, did you?"

"No, but I was hoping we would walk out of here today with results," Rick said, dejected. They put the remaining cultures in the incubators and sat down. They each took a long draw of water through the straw-like mouthpiece in their suit, which was connected to a liter-sized water bladder within the outfit.

Jack observed the two physicians. He could make out their faces behind the clear mask and could see the furtive back and forth glances; each was wondering what the other was thinking.

Jack broke the silence. "Now what?"

"About the only thing left for us to do before calling it a day is to take a look at the brain," Rick said.

CHAPTER EIGHT

06:00 · MARCH 11 · DAR ES SALAAM, TANZANIA
(22:00 EST · MARCH 10 · U.S.)

Riley had convinced the home office to let her go back to Mto Wa Mbu to follow up on the story. WNN had pulled a few strings with the U.S. Embassy to get some MOPP gear for their East African personnel, arguing that if the cause was infectious, their folks should be protected as U.S. citizens. Riley's MO was different. If there was a story — great — but this was about saving a little boy that she didn't even know was still alive.

Dressed in the heinous gear, Riley and her crew piled awkwardly into the SUV. Pulling out of the driveway, the SUV bounced violently, as if they had driven over a tree stump jutting out of the pavement. The driver exited the car, freaking out.

"Jesus Christ! I—I—hit someone!" he stammered, hands on his head and twirling like a ballerina, while repeating *Jesus Christ* mantra-like.

Riley tumbled out of the vehicle. "Whaddya mean you hit someone? I didn't see anyone. Did you?" Looking at the cameraman still sitting in the vehicle.

"No way," he said.

Riley walked around to the driver's side, where the sandaled feet of an African man stuck out from under the truck.

"Shit," Riley said. "That's all we goddam need. The Tanzanian police will be all over us for this." She stood looking down, hands on her hips. She walked out into the street a bit further to see if a policeman was in the vicinity. There was very little street activity. No—there was no activity.

"*What the...*" Riley's stomach lurched, and the back of her throat felt hot, acidy. Lying on the sidewalks were dead Africans—not one or two, but twenty, thirty—she couldn't count. She turned around and was greeted by the same horrific scene down the street behind her.

"Riley? What's wrong? I mean, besides the fact we just ran over someone?" the cameraman asked. "You're not prone to silence." She motioned him to come. He joined her, and Riley knew from his face he saw the cause of her silence.

She stood for what seemed like hours until aroused by the sound of something that sounded like crying. She tilted her head, listening. Yes. It's crying. She moved toward the whimpering sound, mentally cursing the MOPP gear. She rounded the corner, and on the ground was a small girl, not much more than five years old, sitting beside the body of her mother. Across the street was another child, also near an adult body.

Riley realized that whatever had happened in Mto Wa Mbu had also come to Dar es Salaam—in less than a day and a half. She thought of the boy in the village, arms raised, pleading for help. She looked down at the girl. The realization hit her squarely, suddenly. *The kids aren't affected by the infection!*

"Get over here! And bring the camera," she yelled. The videographer came trotting over.

"What?" he asked.

"Look," Riley said, pointing.

"So. A kid. So what?"

"Did you notice the kid is alive?" Riley said, dripping with sarcasm. "And that one over there, too? And that one?" she said, pointing further down the street. "Whatever is killing the adults doesn't seem to affect the kids—at least, not yet."

"Yeah, I see what ya mean," he said, handing Riley the microphone and backing up to get a shot incorporating Riley and the kids. "OK, get it right on the first go. I'm going to send this live to the wire service."

Riley composed herself and took a deep breath. It was all impromptu for this shoot.

"This is Riley Mills for WNN, in Dar es Salaam, Tanzania." Her voice was muffled and a bit mechanical, coming through the MOPP mask. "Yesterday, we reported that some type of presumed infection wiped out a small village in north-central Tanzania. Now the largest Tanzanian city appears to be under siege by the infection. As you can see behind me, dead bodies litter the streets, and there is very little activity. While COVID took days from exposure to death, whatever this is killing much, *much* more quickly. However—and I do believe we are the first to notice this extraordinary fact—children seem to be unaffected by the disease." The videographer swung the camera down toward Riley's feet, showing the little girl, her eyes swollen from sobbing. He paused for dramatic effect, as if the sight of a mourning child required it, before re-focusing on Riley.

"Whatever kind of infection this is, it's moving with incredible speed, covering over 450 miles from Mto Wa Mbu in just over a day. Africa is in crisis, and this WNN team is in the middle of it. We will continue to report until it's... not possible. The world, as we know it, may very well be in jeopardy — again." She paused intentionally to let her last sentence sink into the audience's consciousness. "This is Riley Mills, WNN in Dar es Salaam, Tanzania."

The cameraman left the camera shouldered. Riley could tell he was thinking about what she had just said.

"Ahhh, not to be a wimp or anything, but shouldn't we be getting the hell outta here? I mean, I'm dedicated to my job and all, but not too sure I want to die doing it. It's time to go home—as in the U.S.—as in now," said the cameraman.

Riley considered his comment. She thought of the little boy from the village. She looked down at the little girl. *Who do we save? How do we decide which children to take with us? I mean, COVID didn't affect kids right away either, and it supposedly wasn't as severe as the adults.* She realized the answer to her questions were opposed absolutes: *Take all the children—or none of them.* She wanted to take them all — save them all. But she knew there was only one answer, and it wasn't the one currently tugging at her heart.

"Riley?" the cameraman said. "You OK?"

"You're right," she said.

"Right about what?" he asked.

"We can't take them all back. We can't take the kids," Riley said.

Confused, her companion said, "I didn't say that..."

"But there's a story here, and we've already been exposed to whatever it is, so you can go, but I'm staying," she said. "We know it hasn't spread much further than here because we just watched live reports from Mozambique and Zambia, so I'm going south."

"You'll have to go without me," said the cameraman. "I'm headed home, man."

Riley walked past the driver, still looking down at the body he hit. Riley looked at him and said, "Jesus. You can stop beating yourself up now. He was already goddam dead."

She climbed into the driver's seat of the idling vehicle and rolled down the window. She leaned out and said, "Fine, go home. But call the WNN station in Maputo and tell them I'm coming. I'll need a video guy. Got it?" she said. "And call the airport and have them get the chopper ready. Tell them we're going to Maputo in an hour."

"Yeah, I'll call 'em," he replied, pulling out his cell phone.

Riley put the truck in gear, pulled into the street, and, navigating between dead bodies on the road, headed for the airport.

CHAPTER NINE

Jack was getting tired. It had been a long day, and it wasn't over. He rubbed his eyes and continued watching the morbid scene in the LFU.

Standing at the head of the table, Rick incised the scalp of the corpse beginning above the eyebrow, carrying it along just above the ear, then down and around the back of the head. After connecting the right- and left-sided incisions, he peeled off the scalp, revealing the whitish-pink bone of the cranium. Jack winced as Rick picked up the bone saw and flipped the switch. The irritating sound of the vibrating blade pierced through the inner sanctum of the LFU as Rick began sawing through the skull. Jack nearly hurled. Lucy used a turkey baster-like, giant syringe to drip water slowly onto the saw blade, keeping it cool and preventing bone dust from flying into the air. The process was slow, even with power tools that looked to Jack like something more appropriate at home on a greasy garage workbench.

Once the skullcap had been circumferentially cut, Rick took a thin knife, inserted it into the bone incision, and cut the underlying dura, a tough membrane lining the cranial cavity. Beginning at the front of the skull, he carried it down the left side. A grayish, mucousy fluid oozed out as he approached the ear level. It wasn't cerebrospinal fluid, which is watery and clear, but thick, grayish-yellow snot-like stuff.

"What the…? Grab a specimen bottle and culture this stuff up," Rick said, almost in a panic. Jack grimaced.

"What the hell is that?" Jack said. The two physicians were so focused that they didn't even hear him.

Lucy held a bottle under the back of the skull. Several long strings of goo slowly dripped in.

"Rick… there are…uh… it looks like little tiny pieces of tissue in this stuff."

Jack's queasiness persisted. He couldn't imagine Rick and Lucy wouldn't soon be hurling in their face masks. Jack thought that the smell would have been unimaginable had Rick and Lucy not been breathing filtered air.

"We'll do a smear of it as soon as we get the head open." Slow, steady pressure and jimmying the skullcap with a small crowbar-like tool created an odd, indescribable sucking sound as the skullcap separated from the rest of the head. Rick, eyes focused on the task, said, "You gotta watch this part. If you pull too hard, the suction can rip the top half of the brain off. In my crowd, that would be considered poor form. And besides, it's gross." He lifted the bowl-shaped bone away from the rest of the head, and the look on his face told Jack that something wasn't right. Jack stood on his toes to try and see what was causing Rick's expression.

Rick stood back, skullcap in his hands, head cocked. "Well, I think we're on to something now." The brain did not fill the cranial cavity. Instead, the skull was filled with the same mucous-like material that had oozed out just moments before. Only a few visible gyri—the convoluted surface of the brain that most people would recognize—remained. Still, it was certainly enough to allow Rick to recognize it as brain tissue, even if it had not been sitting in the cranium.

"I've never seen anything like this," Rick said. "You?" Lucy shook her head slowly, staring in disbelief at the grayish puddle, which was the consistency of pudding. "It looks like the brain has undergone autolysis... it has broken down into this goo... like something has partially digested it."

Jack's mind was racing. *What the hell kind of virus or bacteria would cause this?* He struggled to recall even a single case report of anything remotely similar. Nothing. He was blank. He felt fear, but he wasn't sure if it was because he couldn't remember something he thought he should or because he was worried that they had just encountered a new, lethal, infectious agent.

"OK. Fine. I haven't seen an autopsy since medical school. Isn't this what you would expect from a body that has been dead for nearly 48 hours?" Lucy asked.

"Well, to some degree, yes, if it weren't for one small detail. This guy has been refrigerated since he was on the ship. He'd only been dead about 24 hours before that. It's unlikely this would happen in that time."

"But we don't know how long he'd been dead when he was picked up—not exactly, anyway."

"True, but I still doubt it would explain *this*," countered Rick.

"Well, for the sake of argument, let's say this isn't natural autolysis. There's no virus or bacteria for that matter that is known to do this," Lucy said, looking at Jack for confirmation. It was the first time they had acknowledged Jack's presence, let alone give him a furtive glance in hopes of a glimmer of affirmation.

"You mean none known yet," Jack said. The thought that yet another new infectious agent was lurking about the world less than a year after COVID, one that could turn a brain to jelly, was almost more than he could fathom. Jack noticed

Lucy unconsciously backing away from the hollowed-out, brainless corpse.

"Yes, nothing is known yet. I guess we better get the cultures of this stuff cooking," Lucy said, breaking the silence. She went to work putting the goo onto the culture plates, broth-filled test tubes, and human cell cultures and placed them in the incubators. Rick focused on putting some of the more solid brain tissue into specimen jars, hoping the microscopic exams would shed light on what was going on. Jack knew enough about tissue decay that he had a sinking feeling that the specimens were too far gone to provide helpful information.

Jack glanced at his watch. 11 p.m. He was exhausted.

The doors to the room swung open and one of the corpsmen Jack had met earlier entered the room, pushing a TV on a cart. "You all gotta see this. The cat's out of the bag," he said. *Well, that's dramatic.* The corpsman flipped a switch and turned to WNN. They watched Riley Mills reporting from Dar es Salaam. Jack assumed they were all having the stark realization he was: their challenge was rapidly becoming far more extensive than a small Tanzanian village in the middle of nowhere.

CHAPTER TEN

He was beyond tired. Working all night, walking home, and taking a late morning nap in Lawrence was one thing. It was something entirely different to fly to Baltimore, watch an autopsy right out of a horror flick, get back on a jet after midnight, and fly to Atlanta to attend a high-level CDC meeting.

Jack got to his hotel room, chucked his duffle bag into the closet, and slumped down on the bed. He welcomed the softness. His cellphone rang simultaneously as if the bed was programmed to ring it with the slightest pressure on the mattress. He sighed. He knew it was Catherine. She probably told the hotel front desk to call her the minute he checked in.

"Hi, Catherine," Jack said tiredly as he sprawled out on the bed.

"How the hell do you always know it's me?" Catherine said. "Did you get your packet of information and read the agenda?"

"Well, I got a packet, but I just walked in the room, and I thought it would be nice to take a moment to—well — pee. Long flight from Baltimore, you know. Somehow I thought you wouldn't have an issue with me waiting to open my packet until after peeing," Jack said. He looked at his watch. *It feels like I've been to hell and back today.* He quickly quit feeling sorry for himself, remembering the autopsy.

"Do your damn business and get down here, Cann. We have a frigging global disaster on our hands, and we're waiting on your bladder!"

"It'd be easier to get down there if you would hang up so I could go to the bathroom. My bladder's screaming at me," Jack said. The click told him he had made his point.

A few minutes later, bladder silenced, Jack stepped out of the elevator and walked into the lobby. Catherine, her assistant, and four members of her epidemic rapid response team were assembled, each in their own disheveled, post-travel attire.

"Finally, Jack. Lord, you would think you were the head of the CDC the way we're waiting on you." Catherine turned and headed toward the hotel's meeting rooms. She pushed open the door to a small conference room equipped with laptop computers and a giant flat-screen TV on the wall at one end of the table.

Jack set his computer down as Catherine turned to the group. "I'm having breakfast brought in for us in about an hour. Until then, I'd like to start picking brains." Catherine took her seat and motioned to the room attendant to dim the lights. The attendant complied and turned the TV and a tape recorder.

"Each of you is here for a specific reason. I suspect you've at least heard of each other, but let's start with brief introductions anyway. "Jack," she said, smirking, "We waited on you to show up last, so why don't you go first."

"Yes, el Presidente," Jack said. He thought some of the participants looked a bit perplexed, not knowing he and Catherine went way back. He concisely explained who he was.

The introductions were brief and business-like. A pathologist from Stanford, an MD epidemiologist from Emory, a Ph.D. microbiologist from Kansas State University, and a U.S. Army colonel, a logistics specialist.

The Stanford physician was a fifty-ish-year-old female pathologist focused on laboratory medicine. She was attractive and fit with bobbed blonde hair and a personality that exuded friendliness and competence. Jack thought her manner of speech would have allowed anyone to conclude she was from California.

"So, like, I guess I'm here because of my interest in laboratory medicine, but I am turned on by infectious disease. Catherine asked me to participate because of my experience with the Laboratory Response Network that came out of the anthrax scare two decades ago. I helped put that network together and have been involved with the CDC on an as-needed basis, like, ever since." Her introduction resulted in a few puzzled looks.

"The CDC organized a group of labs after the anthrax attack in 2001," Catherine said. "It's a national network of local, state, and federal public health, hospital-based, food, veterinary, and environmental testing labs that provide laboratory diagnostics and gives the CDC the capacity to respond to biological and chemical terrorism. It'd be able to serve in the event of other public health emergencies. The CDC was mandated to create and maintain the network on an ongoing basis. We have over 140 labs in the U.S. and abroad now, primarily in Canada and Australia. It's a collaborative effort with the FBI."

"Has it ever been activated?" the Emory MD queried.

"Yes. A little more than 1,400 mobilizations worldwide since 2015," replied Catherine. "But only a handful of times in the U.S. — for some hurricanes, Zika virus, and COVID. It works in the U.S. because any of the fifty states can call the CDC if there is a suspected biological or chemical event. The Laboratory Response Network and a rapid response team—you guys—would tackle the situation. Canada and Australia have their country-based teams that report to the CDC, but we don't have teams elsewhere in the world. That's why you're here now. We are going to be focusing on the situation in Africa." Catherine paused and nodded toward the pathologist. "Doctor, continue, please."

"So, anyway, my role on the team is to, like, advise on specimen collection and culture methodology, as well as to troubleshoot other laboratory-based questions or glitches," she concluded.

"Thanks, next please," said Catherine. Jack shifted in his chair to look at the gentleman from Emory.

The epidemiologist was the oldest member of the team, pushing the mid-sixties. He was a bookish sort, tall and gaunt with sucked-in cheeks, sickly looking, like a cancer patient after his last chemo treatment. He wore thick-lensed, black horn-rimmed glasses that were constantly sliding down his nose from their weight, requiring subconscious, frequent correction. He did this with his middle finger, which Jack noticed immediately. It seemed like he was subtly flipping the bird for no apparent reason. His voice was much deeper than one would have guessed, and its booming effect could startle an unsuspecting audience. His Adam's apple was so prominent on the front of his needle-thin neck that it was impossible to not stare at it, at least momentarily, as it bounced up and down in cadence to his speech. "Catherine and I go back to her days in New Haven. She was a student of mine doing a residency in public health. It took a lot of talking for me to get her to stay on —she wanted to go back to the big skies of New Mexico. But fate took it from there," he said, pausing.

"Please, that's enough," Catherine said.

"No, no!" the Stanford woman said. "What do you mean, 'Fate took it from there?'"

Her epidemiology colleague persisted. "Within two years of Catherine's academic appointment at Emory, politics, and providence took over. The dean of the School of Public Health was killed in a horrific car accident while driving to the shore for a weekend. The department was in turmoil, not to mention mourning, and was rudderless. Catherine stepped up and provided unbelievable leadership. She completed the unfinished budget and pushed it through the byzantine university approval process. She organized the class schedule, lobbied for her colleagues' approval, and won their support. Her skill matched her efficiency in navigating the typically dangerous political waters in an Ivy League school."

Jack picked it up from there. "Yeah, before she knew what hit her, she was at the helm as the new dean of the School of Public Health in one of the most prominent schools in the country. And the fact that she did so as a double minority—a Latino woman—caught the eye of many people in Washington,

DC. When the Democratic administration took over the following year, she was asked to be the director of the CDC. Kinda hard to tell the president of the United States 'No,' huh Catherine?"

"Enough!" Catherine commanded. The edge in her voice told Jack the biography lesson was over.

"Anyway," the professor continued, "Catherine asked me to be on this team a couple of years ago. My role, at least as I understand it, is to look at the situations we encounter from an epidemiological perspective and to devise strategies to prevent the spread of infectious agents, if possible."

Jack noticed he almost seemed intimidated by Catherine. He was well aware that Catherine's beauty, combined with her ability to command a room, was intimidating.

"Next," said Catherine, nodding to the Kansas State microbiologist.

He introduced himself and explained, "I'm a Ph.D. microbiologist like Dr. Cann, but my interest is bacteria. I'm on the faculty of Kansas State University in Manhattan, KS, and an adjunct professor at the medical school in Kansas City. I also work with the National Bio and Agro-Defense biocontainment facility in Manhattan, part of the federal response infrastructure." He was in his late fifties but looked more like 45. He was an avid outdoorsman and looked it— broad-shouldered and square-jawed, with piercing gray eyes, salt-and-pepper hair, and the reddish complexion of a recent sunburn, obtained during a 60-mile mountain bike race he had competed through the Flint Hills the week before. He explained that his expertise was in bacterial resistance mechanisms. He was well known for having uncovered some key mutations in antibiotic-resistant bacteria that led to several recent breakthroughs in designing novel drugs to treat resistant infections.

"Catherine asked me to join the team about six months ago, so here I am."

"Colonel?" Catherine prompted.

Sitting at the end of the rectangular table facing Catherine was a petite brunette, hair wound in a tight bun, and formal Army attire. A silver eagle was perched on her right collar. She was attractive in a severe sort of way. "Yes, Dr. Montoya. I'm a colonel in the United States Army, as you no doubt now know. I am the military liaison to the team and a logistics specialist here to support the team." Jack thought her voice was quite pleasant, and her face softened visibly after she started speaking. Her manner of speech was disarming yet confident, something that had served her well in navigating upward through the male-dominated military. "I'm here to ensure clear, bi-directional communication between this team and the DoD, as well as make sure you have everything you need, or at least that the military can provide."

"Great. Thanks, everyone. Let's get started," Catherine said.

"Catherine," the Emory physician said, "what is the radius of the area affected so far?"

"Everything, so far, seems to be within a 400-mile radius from the initial village. Why?"

"Well, it gives us a bit of an idea of how rapidly this thing is spreading and where to focus our prevention efforts," he replied. "But if it has spread 400 miles in each direction in, what? Less than two days? I don't think we can react quickly enough to prevent Africa from becoming annihilated if it can't be slowed down. I mean, how long, at a couple of hundred miles per day, would it take to get to South Africa? To Egypt?"

The colonel spoke up. "Africa is about 1500 miles across at that latitude and is about 5000 miles long. Simplistically, at 200 miles per day in all directions, the entire continent will be affected in less than two weeks." Jack was impressed that she pulled this out of her head.

"That seems about right," the Emory doc said. "And it assumes that there has been no travel of individuals from the affected area to currently unaffected areas, and we all know, people are traveling. If for no other reason, they'll be fleeing the advance of the disease. This could make the COVID crisis look like the common cold."

"Any opinions on whether this is viral or bacterial?" probed Catherine.

"Catherine, I don't think we have enough information to say. Could be either," Jack said. "Hopefully, the cultures from the autopsy will point us in the right direction."

"Yes, but the cultures just started cooking late yesterday —what? Only about eight hours ago, so it isn't likely we'll have any information until at least tomorrow—maybe 48 hours. Is that correct?" Catherine said, looking at the colonel.

"Figure two or three days before we hear back on the autopsies," the colonel said. "We picked up and iced four more bodies in Africa this morning in case we need them."

"Well, in that case, I don't think we should speculate as to whether it's viral or bacterial, but should focus on preventing spread, at least until we get useful information out of the Navy," Jack said.

"I agree," the epidemiologist said. Everyone nodded in agreement.

Jack said, "I think we should consider starting anti-retroviral therapy in Africa as soon as possible. It could be a waste of time, but it might make a difference." Catherine was nodded.

"I think we can pull that off pretty quickly," Catherine said. "I can have all of the U.S. manufacturing plants overseas divert their shipments to West Africa. We can have the drugs on the ground tomorrow and use the military to distribute." The proactiveness of the idea injected the group with a sense of hope.

The door to the room opened almost simultaneously with a staccato knock, startling the entire group.

"Is the colonel here?" said a diminutive, wiry man in a squeaky voice.

"Yes?" Catherine said, irritated at being interrupted. She nodded toward the colonel, who was not hard to miss in military dress.

"An urgent message for you," the squeaker replied, handing her a folded piece of paper.

The colonel read the note. "Well, folks, pack your bags. We have a meeting with the DoD later today—in Washington. We'll leave from here in 30 minutes. The aircraft is waiting."

"Well," Catherine said, hands on her hips, "looks like the head of the CDC is no longer calling the shots."

CHAPTER ELEVEN

The CDC team was exhausted — Jack especially so— it was the second time he had been in the DC area in less than 12 hours. They were escorted from Reagan National to the hotel. Jack was surprised to see where they were staying. He leaned over to whisper to Catherine. "I think I want a government job."

They checked into their rooms and were told they had an hour to rest and freshen up before the 8 a.m. meeting. Jack quickly showered, dressed, and passed out on the bed. It seemed the alarm went off before his head hit the pillow.

He walked down the hall to the elevator, got off on the second floor, and walked into the conference room five minutes to eight. The other team members were already there, clustered together and talking about the most recent reports of African death.

"Hey, Jack," Catherine said. "Nice of you to join us."

Jack pointed at his watch. "I'm early." He looked around the room. Seats were pre-determined by name cards around the table. Only the Federal Government would make sure name cards were made during a crisis.

"Jack," the epidemiologist said, "we were just talking about the rapid spread of death in Africa. WNN reports deaths in the Congo, Zambia, and even eastern Angola. Have you heard anything more than what WNN is reporting?"

"No, sir, I didn't hear anything in my sleep," Jack said, grinning. He noticed the TV in the corner of the room. "Hey, turn it up," Jack said. The professor complied, and they listened to the same attractive black-haired reporter Jack heard back in Lawrence.

"I would assume any significant change in information would be routed through the colonel first, considering she's linked to the DoD. Have you been informed of anything different than what's out there on the networks?" Catherine asked, looking from the TV to the officer.

"No, Ma'am," replied the colonel. "You are correct, in theory, that I would be notified, but things don't always work that smoothly at the Pentagon. And Riley Mills seems to know as much as anyone," she quipped sarcastically.

A knock on the doorjamb stopped the conversation, and two individuals dressed in Navy whites stood at the room entrance. Jack looked up to see Lieutenant Matthews standing in the doorway.

"Dr. Montoya?" the Navy man said.

"Yes? I'm Dr. Montoya," Catherine said, standing to greet the military duo. Jack thought Catherine seemed taken aback, almost hesitant. He quickly concluded he had just witnessed Catherine's surprise at being confronted by a military man who was the very picture of handsome. He grinned, never having seen Catherine react in such a manner. She was always in control.

"I'm Lieutenant Rick Matthews, United States Navy, Medical Corps. This is Lieutenant Lucy Hermans," he said, motioning Lucy forward, "Also Navy Medical Corps. Our commander asked us to debrief you on the autopsies of the Tanzanian victims."

"Great. You're right on time. Please have a seat," Catherine said, pointing to empty spots at the table. Jack was watching Catherine, and although it was hard to tell, he thought he detected a faint blush. He could tell she was trying not to look at him directly.

Jack watched the handsome lieutenant walk to his seat. He recognized Jack from the day before and nodded to him as he set his briefcase down on the table and pulled out a folder. "Dr. Montoya, if you're OK with it, I would like to show what we've uncovered to this point," he said, pulling a jump drive out of his pocket and handing it to her. Jack thought he saw their fingers touch in the handoff. Now he was sure Catherine was turning rosy.

"Absolutely," said Catherine, taking the drive from him, smiling, but averting her eyes from the lieutenant's. She popped the drive into the computer's USB port, and the lieutenant walked over to the computer and took over.

The lieutenant began, "As you no doubt know, we were asked to autopsy the bodies of two African males that were sent to us from ground zero in Mto Wa Mbu. They had been down for an estimated eight hours before being picked up and placed in refrigerated body bags and transported to Bethesda. We initiated the studies within roughly 36 hours of death, and the bodies were kept cold during that time. I don't want to be dragging this out with you because, frankly, we have obtained essentially no useful information from the work of the past 18 hours or so." Jack looked around the room. Faces had transformed from eager anticipation to stunned concern. The lieutenant reached over and turned off the overhead lights, and with a few clicks, the large flatscreen TV lit up. "In a word, all gross findings were normal, adjusted for time of death."

"Yes, Lieutenant. Dr. Cann had told us as much," Catherine said.

"While that's not too unusual, we can usually identify clues on microscopic exam. In these cases, however," he said, advancing to a photo taken through the microscope, "the cellular decomposition was so advanced as to be uninterpretable." The TV showed what appeared to be a pinkish-red smear—like strawberry jam on a window. "This is the myocardium—heart tissue." He rapidly advanced the pictures. "This is brain. This is kidney. You get the picture. Each of these is indistinguishable from the other. I can only tell you it's heart, brain, or kidney because I took the samples. If I gave these slides to the best pathologists in the world, they wouldn't be able even to tell you what tissue they came from," the lieutenant said.

"Any other tricks you can use?" Jack asked.

He thought for a moment. "Yeah. But it's a long shot."

"What?" Jack pressed.

The Lieutenant hesitated. "EM."

"What the *hell* is EM?" the Colonel asked. Jack smiled. She looked embarrassed when she realized she had sworn.

"Electron microscopy," the Lieutenant said. "But it may be much work for nothing, given the state of decomposition."

Using EM isn't standard in post-mortem exams. Even when light microscopy was unhelpful in examining tissues, EM was capable of magnifying structures two million times their actual size and could still help pick up subtle clues that would otherwise be missed, even in partially decomposed specimens.

"Sounds like it's worth a try," Catherine said.

"Lt. Hermans, could you please update the group on your findings?" her partner asked.

"What's more disturbing than normal pathological findings is that all microscopic screening for bacteria is negative too, at least so far. The virulence of whatever this is would indicate that it would have at least survived long enough to be seen by microscopy. The first cultures were taken just shy of 24 hours ago, though, so we may see more in the next 12 to 24 hours," Lucy said. "Of course, if this is anaerobic or viral, it could be longer—72 hours, even a week."

The only sound in the room for an uncomfortable period was the whir of the computer's fan.

The lieutenant spoke again. "It's Lieutenant Hermans' and my opinion that we didn't find anything not because there isn't an explanation, but because the bodies were too decomposed to allow us to find the cause. It's been very frustrating work." He closed the laptop and flipped the lights back on.

"Dr. Montoya?" Catherine replaced him at the head of the table.

"Well, not the best news of the week, but then, how much worse can it get when so much of eastern Africa is already dead?" Catherine said. "So, ideas, anyone?"

The Stanford pathologist spoke first. "Lieutenant Matthews, it seems that you need a fresher body, correct?"

"Yes, that would be extremely helpful," the lieutenant said. "I know that the DoD is already working on that, but the logistics are challenging. There are four more bodies, supposedly fresher specimens, headed this way. We're told they were frozen within 30 to 120 minutes after death."

The colonel chimed in, "The logistics of getting a fresher specimen is something I can comment on. I've been working with the DoD on behalf of Dr. Montoya and the rapid response team. One of the challenges is that Africa is so big and much of it is so remote that being in the right place at the right time with the right equipment is nearly impossible. The local research capabilities are minimal. Most places are lucky to have a light microscope in a major hospital. And considering that an infectious agent is still the primary working hypothesis, setting up clean research rooms in a contaminated environment is virtually impossible. The DoD is not willing to compromise the safety of our military personnel by loosening their precautions around handling the bodies. Full MOPP is required, adding a level of difficulty, and in some sense, impracticality to the situation."

"Well, then," replied the Stanford doctor, "What's the plan?"

"In some ways, more of the same. We have military forces stationed in Africa trying to get fresher specimens; in all honesty, I don't know if it will work because things are chaotic," said the Colonel. "And there are potential ethical issues with just picking up someone off the street who just dropped dead—next of kin and all that stuff. We should continue to utilize Lieutenant Matthews and Hermans as they have been involved from the get-go, so it would be useful if you considered including them on your team, Dr. Montoya."

Jack thought he saw the corner of Catherine's mouth indiscernibly flicker upward in a smile. He marveled at the subtle signs of attraction that everyone else in the room seemed to miss, but then, he knew Catherine better than anyone else in the group.

"It makes perfect sense to have them on the team," Jack said, saving Catherine from having to say it.

"Yes, obviously, it's a wise move," Catherine said, affirming the suggestion. "Lieutenants? Will we be able to accomplish that? Do I need to talk to someone to ensure that happens?"

"Well, Ma'am, I already took care of it in the hopes you would approve," the colonel said sheepishly. "I called Bethesda with the DoD's blessing, and they now are under your command, Dr. Montoya."

"Aren't you efficient," grinned Catherine. "So, anything else I don't know about, Colonel?"

"Yes, there is," she said, pursing her lips, a new tone of seriousness in her voice.

"First, you all need to understand that what I am about to tell you is confidential—and I mean so confidential that you don't talk to anyone—no loved ones, no one, about what I am about to tell you. Agreed?" Every voice agreement with intrigue and trepidation.

"The situation in Africa is worse—far worse—than the networks are communicating. The U.S. Air Force and our NATO allies, along with remaining African forces, have managed to create large no-fly zones over the advancing front of death, preventing news helicopters and planes from reporting the actual extent of the disaster. Jack noticeably bristled.

"Dr. Cann, we aren't trying to hide it for subversive reasons. We're hoping to prevent global panic. It's been less than three days since Mto Wa Mbu, and, for the most part, there isn't a living African adult in a million-and-a-half square mile across the mid-section of the continent. COVID killed 5 million in 18 months. We estimate there are — *conservatively* — 300 million dead in Africa today. So what WNN is reporting barely scratches the surface, and we won't be able to keep them out much longer. It's impossible to patrol every road, and we've already seen how persistent this Riley woman is. And more horrific — there's no one to take care of millions of orphaned children, from newborns to teenagers. The humanitarian crisis is beyond comprehension. Children will fall ill soon or begin to die of thirst or water-borne diseases like cholera. Access to clean water is dwindling too fast to address with our limited resources. Adults drop dead unexpectedly in the worst places— into ponds, lakes, streams—contaminating water sources. It was bad enough just to have to deal with dead adults, but our urgency to find a solution to save adults from death will also save millions, maybe billions of children in the long run. I'm a logistics specialist, folks, and I am at a total loss as to how this is going to be managed." Jack thought she was about ready to cry; she was visibly affected by the scope of the situation and the effect on children.

There was silence while Jack and the rest of the team absorbed what they had just heard. Finally, he spoke.

"Well, they call us the rapid response team. Let's get on the ground and see what the hell's going on firsthand. I mean, I've always wanted to go to Africa. Now seems like a good time for a virologist to go."

Catherine said, "Jack, this isn't exactly like visiting Denver. It's Africa. And people are dying right and left from an uncharacterized, highly communicable disease. You'd have to wear MOPP gear—on an equatorial continent."

"Catherine, whatever it is, it's moving fast, and we can't let it come to us. We need to play offense here. And as far as MOPP gear, how much worse can it be than the rubber sweatsuits I used to wear at wrestling practice in a room intentionally heated to 90 degrees? How bad can it be?"

The team members filtered out of the room, Jack lingering with Catherine.

"Jack, are you sure you want to do this?" Catherine asked, putting her hand on his arm, eyes narrowed.

"Want to? *Hell, no!* And Marla will be justifiably fucking pissed. But Catherine, in three days, half of Africa is dead. If we don't stop whatever this is now, it will be knocking on our door tomorrow. And the way this is going so far, it could be the last knock we ever hear."

CHAPTER TWELVE

Riley looked out of the helicopter window as they flew south over Dar es Salaam. It was an open-air morgue. It was like some B-rated horror movie set. The video of the little boy in Mto Wa Mbu had become a recurrent, intrusive vision, each time accompanied by low-grade nausea and an ache in her chest. Each time she thought of him, it was worse—both deeper and more intensely gnawing. She reached into her pocket for another chalky antacid tablet, the kind with some artificial sweetener added in an unsuccessful attempt to improve its nastiness. Her fingers brushed the notebook in her pocket. She remembered the photo, took the out notebook, and pulled the picture out from between the pages. Staring at the boy, she slowly chewed the tablet.

For the first time in her life, she felt powerless—not due to a lack of information — but because of too much of it. Death surrounded her. Personal loss was everywhere, inescapable. And she was playing a leading role in a story that was evolving too rapidly to comprehend, let alone stay on top of.

The flight was long, and the drone of the helicopter's engine and the rhythmic vibration from the whirling blades was pulling Riley into a stupor. She was exhausted from the lack of sleep and emotional strain. She tried to stay awake, but her head lolled to the right and back, her snoring obscured by the rotor's noise.

The girl walked into the kitchen. She was hungry, and it was dinnertime.

"What's for dinner, momma? I'm hungry," she chirped as she set her school backpack down. She should have known better than to utter the words. Her good-natured attempts seemed out-of-place in the depressing, smoke-filled room.

"I'm not making you anything, you piece of shit," her mother snarled, venomously, as she took a drag off a cigarette, ashes fluttering down to the table in a wispy, grey cylinder of powder. The girl watched her exhale the smoke and take a drink of what looked like water, but the smell around her was musty, fetid. Vodka. "But now that you mention it get me something to eat! And get that other bottle of vodka and bring it to me!"

"Yes, momma," the little girl said, trying to maintain the flowery lilt in her voice, hoping it would help. She delivered the vodka first, hoping it might lead to the silent trance she knew was only a glass or two away, sparing her from hours of abuse. How long just depended on how drunk she already was... Her mother immediately filled her glass and drained it halfway in one glug.

The girl put some water on to boil and pulled a box of mac and cheese out of the cabinet. Seven years of fending for herself—ducking blows, stealing money to buy necessities, scrounging for food—she was self-sufficient by age eight. At fifteen, it was all just part of the daily dance.

She dumped the macaroni in the boiling water. "Dinner will be ready in about 10 minutes, mom," she said, turning to look at her mother. She had slumped over the table, unconscious, cigarette burning between her fingers. For a moment, the girl thought about letting it burn down and sear her fingers, knowing that it wouldn't even wake her, but she couldn't do it. She would just write about it in her journal later. She had long ago given up talking about things with her mom, resorting instead to writing down her thoughts, a mental catharsis of sorts. It prevented her from yelling back and suffering the consequences. She pulled the butt from between her mother's fingers and tamped it out in the ashtray. She filled a bowl with the pasta and went outside on the porch to eat it in the fresh air so she wouldn't taste the room in her mac and cheese.

The smell of cigarette smoke in the cockpit awakened Riley.

"Put out that cigarette," she commanded. The pilot stared at her blankly.

"I don't smoke," he said. Riley sniffed. The smell was gone. She looked at the pilot, brows furrowed in confusion.

"The way you were twitching around over there for the last hour, I think you were dreaming," said the pilot.

"I guess. I don't remember," Riley said.

By the time they landed in Maputo, reports of an ever-broadening zone of African death had begun to surface in the media, including Mozambique. Death had traveled the 2,130 miles to Maputo more quickly than the helicopter took them. There wasn't a soul alive at the airport.

She commandeered a car at the airport—there was no one to rent one from, so she took one. Driving to the WNN station was like déjà vu, navigating around dead bodies in the street and passing crying children, distraught over the loss of their father or mother or both.

She tried to take her mind off reality by listening to the radio, but this was folly. In just under three days, death had spread to the north and east and south of Tanzania with the rapidity—and ruthlessness—of an uncontrolled wildfire on the Serengeti. The newsman's voice seemed tinny, distant, cold.

"It seems from this reporter's view, that the apolitical scourge will spare no African country: The entire southern half of this continent—the Congo, Zambia, Mozambique, Zimbabwe —every country to South Africa and north and east to Kenya, Somalia, Sudan, and Egypt are reporting wide-scale death." Riley shook her head in disbelief. "The most distressing aspect of the entire situation is not necessarily the dead, but those who are alive. The pathogen does not seem to affect kids who are not yet sexually mature. Children who have not reached puberty are being spared for obscure reasons."

The reporter paused, the dead air creating tension. He resumed in a sadder, lower tone. "This awful tragedy is only made horrifically worse by the fact that millions of children throughout eastern and southern Africa have become orphans in a period of just days. It appears that the line of death swept across Botswana and into Namibia but may be slowing as it spreads into South Africa. Currently, there are only scattered reports of death in Johannesburg, leading this reporter to hope we may be spared this horrific fate."

Riley had just arrived in Maputo and was already exhausted but knew she had to stay ahead of the wave of death. She had to go to Johannesburg. She stopped in the middle of the road, folded her arms across the steering wheel, put her head down, and sobbed.

She looked up after several minutes, her sense of self-pity replaced by the resoluteness that had served her so well, time and again. She sat back in the car seat and looked around, finding a map. Opening it up, she found Johannesburg and traced a finger from Maputo to the city. About 350 miles, she estimated. I can be there in six hours. That puts me there about midnight tonight. She put the car in gear and slowly let out the clutch.

CHAPTER THIRTEEN

The President of the United States was already feeling washed out and exhausted at the start of the day. He had not rested well and had a rare feeling of surliness. His Cabinet rose as he walked in. He motioned them to sit down with a wave of his hand. He understood protocol; he just didn't like it.

"Coffee, Mr. President?" said an aide behind him.

"Yes, please. Between watching WNN most of the night and taking calls from Africa, I'm a bit out of sorts," he said, his accent more discernable due to his tiredness. He would have liked to have had his coffee in the quiet of the bedroom before entering the fray of the day. He could tell from the background buzz in the room that it wasn't going to be a typical day. The Cabinet members' anxiety was vibrating in the air.

President Lopez was the first Latino president in the history of the United States. He was an oddly attractive man. The sun had branded him at a young age, growing up working beside his father and mother in the commercial produce fields of California. The deep creases in his face, including oversized crow's feet angling off the corner of each eye, highlighted twinkling, grey-green eyes—a result of some odd genetic hiccup in his family. They could communicate deep care and love, or they could cut you in half, as many political opponents had learned.

As an Arizona senator, he had swept to power in a come-from-behind, crushing defeat of the conservatives two years prior, running on a platform of inclusiveness and moderate liberalism that had appealed to a country beaten down by the economic woes brought on by an anemic response to a global pandemic and the cult-like fervor of the prior administration. Benefitting from a Senate majority, he had been able to get down to business quickly, especially around the domestic agenda. The connections he had developed as a young man working in the fields spanned the grassroots working class to the elite politico in the Arizona and California state governments. He leaped to the national stage as a junior U.S. Representative by fighting for—and winning—equal wages and a state-sponsored benefits package for the naturalized working immigrant population. The minority-majority quietly lined up behind his presidential campaign and decimated the conservative party that had arrogantly assumed they'd retain the White House.

The Secretary of State, Elaine Morrow, began speaking before the first mouthful of the black liquid had reached the president's stomach. "Mr. President, no doubt you appreciate we're facing a massive humanitarian crisis in Africa." Ms. Morrow was a moderately attractive, middle-aged woman with icy blue eyes and auburn hair, each feature underscored by the jet-black power pantsuit she was wearing. As the past ambassador to Russia, she had earned a reputation as an incredibly savvy negotiator, with a sixth sense for creating novel solutions in tense situations.

"Ms. Morrow, I don't need the State Department to tell me the obvious. WNN has done that already. It would be nice to hear something that we know that everybody else in the world with a TV set doesn't." He knew he sounded edgy and that his team recognized it. Usually, his demeanor was more gentle, even equanimous—not wishy-washy or indecisive, but balanced in delivery. Recognizing this, he said, "I'm sorry. That was impertinent. Let me try again."

He thought for a moment. "I've seen everything you've all seen on TV, and I was on a video call with the Prime Minister of Mozambique at about 3 a.m. As he described what was happening locally and asked for assistance, he disappeared from the screen, dead, I presume. For me, ladies and gentleman, that was a very unpleasant first, and it highlighted something for me that perhaps you've already understood."

"What's that, Mr. President?" asked Ms. Morrow.

"We are utterly unable to rely on local governments to be of any help because there's no leadership at the local level. While this occurred to me yesterday on some level with the Tanzanian crisis, having one's counterpart die mid-sentence was a particularly graphic," the president said.

"I suggest we do whatever it takes to ensure we're prepared at home for the onslaught of this virus—or whatever it is. We need to pull back all of our resources, Mr. President," said the Secretary of Homeland Security. He was a thin man with crew-cut hair and sharp features, a former marine.

"Well, that's fine," said the Secretary of Health and Human Services, "Except for the fact that it's already here. We have reports of pockets of African emigrants dying all over the U.S. in ethnic enclaves. I've been on the phone with Director Montoya of the CDC, and she's already initiated steps to contain the infection. From my perspective, we should use our local resources at home and use our deployed forces for humanitarian missions. I don't know how we, in good conscience, can simply abandon millions of helpless children on the continent of Africa.”

President Lopez listened attentively, his chin on his hand, entirely focused.

The ex-marine harrumphed. “Well, that’s all well and good, but a touchy-feely approach isn’t going to secure our borders.”

“Mr. President, with all due respect to Homeland Security, I agree with HHS,” said Ms. Morrow. “I think we need to call NATO and get them involved. We have no idea when—or if—this infection will stop. MOPP gear seems to be protecting our troops, and this isn’t an issue of security, at least yet.”

“And what happens, ladies,” the feisty military man said, intentionally highlighting his feeling that they were females rather than colleagues, “when the oil from Africa stops flowing because there isn’t anyone left to run the goddam refineries? That seems to go directly to our security concerns,” he said.

“Yes,” said the president, “And everyone else’s too. I certainly don’t want to be toe-to-toe with Russia and China over oil.”

“Again, Mr. President, activating NATO for humanitarian reasons gives us the ability to put forces on the ground in strategic locations to serve two purposes, one overt, the other covert.”

“Yes, I was thinking the same thing, Ms. Morrow,” said the president. “We send them to assist the orphaned children while they can also secure key production facilities.”

“Exactly,” Ms. Morrow said.

“Do it,” said the president. “We’re done here for now. Ms. Morrow, could you please stay for a moment.”

“Absolutely, Mr. President.”

After the others departed, the president said, “Ms. Morrow, some of Homeland Security’s concerns are justified. With emigrants dying, it’s clear that the infectious agent has somehow been brought into the country. What has Director Montoya done in response to the situation?”

“I was going to debrief you on that, now, sir, as it involves federalizing the National Guard. She wants you to activate the Guard in all states to assist in quarantine and morgue support services,” said Ms. Morrow.

“Morgue support? Are there really that many dead?” asked the president.

“Not yet, Mr. President, but she’s anticipating the worst, given our recent experience with COVID. In Africa, what is happening is magnitudes worse — but our cities will have tens of thousands of dead.”

"Go ahead with the National Guard, and you'd better get FEMA involved too. They're already trained for disaster mortuary management."

Ms. Morrow walked out of the room. The president stayed seated. He imagined FedEx Field, home of the Washington Commanders football team, lined with body bags end-to-end and side-to-%side.

CHAPTER FOURTEEN

The carpet in the jetway told him he was a long way from home, a luxury by his prior standards. But that was Africa. This was America.

Enzi had just arrived from Tanzania after a 36-hour journey. He hadn't seen his family for four years, and he missed them terribly. To say he was excited was an understatement.

The Sibale family had moved to Atlanta to find their piece of the American dream. The 30,000 other East African immigrants in greater Atlanta made it seem like a home away from home. They found jobs easy to come by — Americans shunned manual labor. They were more than happy to work, and, on a relative scale, they felt rich. With time, his family could afford the ticket to bring Enzi over to rejoin them.

Enzi identified his luggage and found his way to the sidewalk along the front of the terminal. He had left a message on his older brother's cell phone, saying that he would meet him curbside at the airport. He waited for over an hour in the insane heat and humidity of Atlanta, continuing to call. Nothing. He tried his father. Another message was left. He decided to take a cab, even if it cost precious dollars.

He hailed a cab and struggled to lift his wheeled, oversized luggage into the trunk. The cabbie offered no help. He gave the driver the address and asked, "How much to go?"

"How'd ya speck me ta know that?" the cabbie said, scowling. "It ain't far; I know that. You want me ta take ya or not?"

"Yes, please," Enzi said. He sat back, thankful for the car's air conditioning. He hadn't traveled in many air-conditioned vehicles. Enzi noticed large military trucks headed into the airport as the cab departed the terminal.

The cab pulled up to a sprawling apartment complex just north of the airport twenty minutes later. It was crawling with ambulances and police cars. Gurneys lined the sidewalks, white sheets covering, Enzi presumed, dead bodies. His family had told him that the area they lived in wasn't the safest place, but he hadn't expected this.

The driver navigated the chaos to the building number Enzi had given him. Enzi paid and collected his trunk. As he headed for unit 384B, jittery with excitement, Army National Guard vehicles began blocking off the roads into the complex.

He wondered if it was related to the Army vehicles he saw going to the airport.

He lugged the trunk up a flight of stairs, plopped it onto its wheels, and rolled it about halfway down the building to his brother's apartment. He opened the door and stepped in, hoping to surprise his family. The first thing he noticed besides the apartment was sweltering was a putrid smell—a cross between rotting meat and sewage. Combined with the heat, the effect was repulsive. "Hello?" Enzi said hopefully. There was no response.

He stepped further into the apartment, pushing the trunk in front of him. He was walking through the living room when he saw his mother's feet poking out around the kitchen corner. He moved quickly to her, kneeling. A swarm of flies exploded out of her mouth in a black whirlwind, her body bloated, eyes open, bulging, fixed.

"Momma!" Enzi cried. He felt shocked at finding his mother dead, but what he was feeling in his body was not that —he felt like gravity was sucking him into the very earth upon which the apartment had been built. He wanted to gasp for air, but his lungs felt frozen, moving no air. He wanted to embrace his dead mother. Gravity helped him because he was now lying on her chest, unable to move, his face just inches from her chin. He felt flies on his tongue, crawling back and down his throat. Then he felt—nothing.

16:00 MARCH 11, ATLANTA CITY MORGUE (22:00 MARCH 11, MOZAMBIQUE)

The scratched, stainless steel swinging doors crashed open, and a gurney carrying an occupied body bag rolled through, pushed by a toothless, burly man, wearing thick, plastic-rimmed glasses dressed in dirty coveralls. He looked more like a backcountry mechanic than a coroner's assistant. "Gotta 'nother, doc!" he shouted.

The morgue manager, feet propped up on a metal, government-issued, gunmetal gray desk, peered over the top of the newspaper, frowning. "Jesus Christ... What the hell's going on around here?" he said.

"Ain't just here," the assistant said, almost nonchalantly. "Black folks are dyin' all over the place."

"What the hell ya talkin' 'bout?" said his boss.

"Radio's saying it's happenin' lots of places—Dallas, New York, Kansas City, Denver. You name it; it's probably happening there, too. Even in London and France and stuff like that." With that, the manager picked up the TV remote, clicked the TV on, and navigated to WNN.

"Jesus, will you look at that!" said the manager, pointing at the screen. Dead black people were lying in the street. A disembodied voice of a reporter was narrating as the screen flashed from city to city, showing the chaos.

"In light of the East African situation and what's happening on the ground in the U.S., the head of the CDC, Dr. Catherine Montoya, has implemented quarantines of major proportions on neighborhoods nationwide, using National Guard units for enforcement. Dr. Montoya says her actions are intended to minimize the panic and limit the potential for the infection to spread. Military personnel, dressed in what we suspect are HazMat suits, have set up barricades and strictly enforce access to and from the affected areas. Medical personnel is helping triage any survivors, who at this time appear primarily to be children."

"Goddamn. Will ya look at that! The Army has all that stuff to protect them, and we're sitting here with a bunch of people who died from that shit," the manager noted, disgusted.

The reporter continued. "Of course, the obvious question is how this all relates, if at all, to what happened two days ago in Tanzania, when our reporter, Riley Mills, first broke the story on the small East African village that was wiped out by what may be germ warfare." A photo of Riley filled the screen.

"While the CDC is intent on preventing the spread of disease to the living, a huge problem has resulted from this wave of death. A hundred dead bodies would be a challenge to any city. Past civilian disasters—the Kansas City Hyatt disaster, the Oklahoma City bombing, Katrina, and 9/11—have taught us much. The lesson was reinforced a thousandfold by COVID. The number of dead bodies that seem to be piling up may be impossible for any city to handle. FEMA has been activated by the president and is setting up open-air morgues—large quarantined spaces—in football stadiums and parking lots." The camera panned back, revealing hundreds of body bags lined up side-to-side at a local high school's football field.

CHAPTER FIFTEEN

The president watched the screen as the Reverend Franklin Jones stepped to the podium to begin the news conference, looking crisp in his black suit. The white shirt and solid red tie created an intimidating aura as if the broad shoulders mounted on his imposing 6'3" frame weren't enough. Although clearly of African descent, his skin was lighter than many, the influence of several forced Caucasian "indiscretions" in the remote past.

The camera panned the crowd. Reporters were in the front, but the rest of the auditorium was filled with the reverend's supporters, all of them black-skinned.

Reverend Jones was a board member of the NAACP and one of the most influential black leaders in the country—religious or otherwise. The President personally knew him and had hosted him in the White House, even asking advice on racial issues. They were both minorities and had much common ground.

Lopez knew the reverend wasn't known for being quiet if he perceived an issue of importance to his followers. There was no question that he loved the limelight, but he was genuinely committed to doing the right thing, even if it meant pushing a few of the buttons that he knew would get him into hot water. The president admired this quality and admired the man. He considered him trustworthy and, frankly, a friend.

As the reverend was collecting his notes, Ms. Morrow said, "Well, Mr. President, you need to be prepared for public criticism around what's happening, even if we don't know what's causing this mess." The press secretary silently shook her head in agreement, slightly behind the president.

"I know what I think, but what are you thinking?" the president asked.

"The only population affected thus far is people of African descent. It could easily —logically — be made into an issue of race."

The president leaned back in his chair, hands behind his neck, and took a deep breath. He was well aware of being discriminated against—to feel singled out because of heritage or skin color.

The conversation was interrupted as Reverend Jones began to speak.

"Good evening, ladies and gentleman, my fellow countrymen. Over the past few days, we have witnessed an unprecedented series of events that can only be described as horrific. Beyond comprehension. People of African descent began dying several days ago, first in eastern Africa, now worldwide." He paused. "Today, the tragedy arrived on our shores and is ravaging neighborhoods across the land. I hesitate to say that it seems likely that hundreds of thousands have died today in this country, if not millions. The pace of death is so rapid as to preclude counting. The cause of this is as yet unknown—or so the media — and our government would have us believe."

"Crap," the president said. "Here we go…"

"The very fact that this… this scourge… is not killing white folks—or people of any other color for that matter—leads me to believe things may not be what they seem, what we're being lead to believe, if only by hearing nothing from the administration." The reverend paused with great effect.

The president felt as though Reverend Jones was staring at him through the camera. The reverend took a deep breath and began again, "I'm known for asking hard questions; questions that make people uncomfortable, shift in their seats, look at their shoes. In this time of crisis, it is no different, so I must ask if this is an intentional act by some person or group— the QAnon, Neo-Nazis, Proud Boys, or some other white supremacy group—to wipe out people of color!" The reverend's supporters angrily erupted at his words. He held his hands up high, beckoning them to quiet down. After several minutes of continuous urging, it was calm enough for him to continue.

"The rate of death in our brothers is so high that I must ask if there will be any survivors, other than the children, who seem to be protected in some way. It's a blessing for our people that the children live, but a curse for them, now fatherless, motherless, as they wail out for help that will not come." Another pause.

"Brothers and sisters of all colors, your black brethren have survived centuries of being pushed down, abused, tortured, enslaved, murdered. As hard as their oppressors tried —those who wrongly thought they would succeed at the Devil's work—segregation failed," the Reverend said. "But now there is no escape. Just outside the doors of this building are armed troops, forcing us to stay in our neighborhoods, where the disease is spreading like a forest fire, sure to burn us all to death. The same troops that protected us in 1957, escorting our children into the halls of Little Rock schools, now enforce our imprisonment."

"This is no time for political correctness, for working through appropriate channels. We demand answers from the administration and people of America now! They must surely hear our pleas for mercy. The Jim Crow segregation days were left in the dust of past decades. Now, some malignancy has been loosed on us, resulting in our exclusion as participants in unified society—a more frightening, permanent exclusion—extermination. It appears, my brothers and sisters, we are on the brink of terminal segregation." The Reverend's voice quivered as the last two words left his throat. "May the great, almighty God bless you, my brothers and sisters—those of *all* colors—and strike down those who would loose this plague on us!"

The live audience was silent for several minutes until there was some commotion in the center of the crowd. The camera panned the crowd. The president sat forward in his chair, straining to see. People were kneeling in the center of the throng around a black man—who had fallen to the floor, dead. Bystanders were initially confused, but a look of horror was soon visible. The president recognized the buzz in the audience as a premonitory sign of crowd panic and wondered how the reverend would handle the situation.

Off-camera a voice started singing. At first, the words were unintelligible, but slowly it became more chorus-like, growing and becoming discernible. The TV camera refocused on the pulpit. The reverend was singing Jesus Loves Me, one hand raised, gently rocking from side-to-side, eyes closed. Those closest to him had joined in, arms locked, moving in unison. The nervous twitter died down, replaced by beautiful voices united in song.

The TV cameraman repositioned himself, so he was slightly behind and to the right of the reverend, able to capture most of the room on the screen. The president continued to watch, lips pursed, brows furrowed in compassion, as black men and women slipped through the interlocked arms of their swaying companions and fell to the floor, dead. Initially unsure of what to do, the remaining individuals calmly rejoined their arms and continued singing until the next person succumbed, each appreciating the hopelessness of struggling against the obvious. In 15 minutes, all but a handful were dead, the remaining chorus now a small group—including the reverend. And it was all on live TV.

The president concluded that the cameraman was likely in MOPP gear as the footage continued to roll. He wondered how the others in the room were still standing, given that all other blacks had fallen dead. He managed a weak smile as he said, "Only the reverend could calm a crowd facing certain death with a song." He wondered if he would ever see the reverend again.

The president stood up and turned to Ms. Morrow and the press secretary. "I need to address the people."

"Yes, you do, Mr. President, but not in public. We'll use our White House-based TV crew," said the press secretary. "The marines have secured the entire perimeter of the grounds and are in full MOPP. No one is being allowed to enter or leave the White House to protect you and the first family."

"It'll be a damn short conference. All I can say is that we have no idea what is going on," the president said. "Not exactly something that will inspire the people's confidence."

"How will you address the reverend's assertions that this is a plot to wipe out the black race?" the press secretary pushed.

The president looked at her in disbelief. "That can't be an honest question, can it? I mean, it's ludicrous to imagine that whatever this infection is will only affect black people! I'm not a scientist, but it would have to be a first in nature for that to happen. And that's exactly how I'll address it. Most people are logical and hopefully will understand that."

"Yes, sir," the press secretary said.

"Well, Mr. President, at this point, it's critical to reassure the nation that we're doing everything we can to find the cause and develop a cure," Ms. Morrow said. "Your message will affect not just the U.S., but the world. Our allies will be looking to you to lead the way."

The president paused, considering her advice. "You're correct, Ms. Morrow. I just hope we are doing something meaningful to get to the bottom of this. Have we heard anything from Bethesda? The CDC?"

"Not yet," she said.

"Well, then, we better hope Reverend Jones survives," said the president.

"Why?" asked the press secretary.

"Because we need all the prayers we can get."

CHAPTER SIXTEEN

In the bowels of the Naval Hospital, in a windowless, dark room, the huge metal tube of the electron microscope, the EM, erupted out of the floor, looming over the two scientists, giving the appearance of a lab one might expect on an alien spacecraft. The low light in the room cast shadows, adding to the eerie effect. EM examination was a long shot, considering the amount of tissue necrosis that had occurred, but optimism often suppresses realism in dire circumstances.

Lucy's work didn't require the use of EM, so the mammoth instrument fascinated her.

"It's been years since I've even seen one of these things," she said. "Can you remind me how it works, Rick?"

"Sure. Prepping the specimens is a pain in the ass. Takes a couple of days, pretty much. The specimen is put in an air-tight chamber, right here," he said, pointing to a small square door centered at the base of a cylindrical tower that rose about six feet above their heads.

"All the air is pumped out of the chamber to create a vacuum. The scope produces charged electrons that bombard the sample. The vacuum enables the electrons to hit the specimen, without them being deflected by air molecules randomly floating around in the chamber."

"An air molecule is big enough to deflect the electrons?" Lucy asked.

"Yeah. The electrons bounce off the specimen and generate a picture that appears on this small screen," Rick said, pointing to a small flat screen on the side of the stainless steel monolith.

As they waited for the unit to power up and the EM's vacuum chamber to do its magic, Lucy could hear the tick-tick of the clock in the room. Rick hummed a song, unrecognizable to Lucy, trying to minimize his anxiousness. Lucy saw right through it.

"Do you always jiggle your leg three times faster than the actual beat of the song you're humming?" she asked, trying to lighten the mood.

Rick was not capable of feeling less stress at the moment. He felt the responsibility for finding answers to the horrible fate of the village in Tanzania was his. He shot an angry look toward Lucy that quickly faded to frustration.

"Damn it, Lucy. I just feel like nothing has been going right for us. Everything is negative. I'm sick of negative this and negative that."

"Just because we aren't finding anything doesn't mean we're failing. It also doesn't mean we're missing anything," Lucy observed.

"How could we not be missing something? These people didn't just die from fucking sun exposure!" Rick countered, almost shouting.

Lucy paused, tilted her head in thought. "Rick, this might sound stupid, but the fact is, we can only look for things we know exist. Your ability to explain things is based on... uhh... it's relative to your prior experience and what is already known. The only reason we're concerned about another COVID variant is that we've dealt with COVID variants."

Rick sat back, put his hand behind his head, fingers interlaced. "Yeah," he said. "Maybe. Something is seriously wrong here, we can't explain it, and the goddam DoD is breathing down our necks looking for answers. I'm not sure Einstein could help us."

Lucy was so focused on their discussion that she was startled by the loud beep indicating the vacuum in the EM was complete. Rick reached over and pushed a white button, switching on the microscope. The screen, the EM's equivalent to the eyepieces on a light microscope, lit up, similar to a high-definition, black-and-white TV. It looked more like a bad picture of the surface of Mars than anything that had come from a living person. They could see irregularities and shadows of necrotic tissue without actual form. Rick turned a dial clockwise, increasing the power of the magnification. He adjusted the specimen to the right, left, then up and down. He took a deep breath, leaned back in his chair, puffed his cheeks up, and slowly exhaled through pursed lips. Lucy, sitting slightly to the right and behind him, not sure what to feel, stared at the EM's screen. Lucy knew Rick had the same sinking feeling: nothing. Nothing at all.

After a long silence, Rick spoke. "Shit!" He picked up a clipboard and hurled it, Frisbee-like, against the wall. The metal clip flew off the board, clattering along the cement floor and bouncing off the opposite wall before coming to a rest. Still in near shock from a worthless EM picture, Lucy was unfazed.

They looked at each other as Rick slowly reached for the phone and dialed the rear admiral's number at the National Naval Medical Center, just a few blocks away. A pleasant, well-trained receptionist answered. "Rear admiral's office. May I help you?"

CHAPTER SEVENTEEN

"Tell me you're fucking kidding. Jack. If this is a joke..." Marla said in a not-so-happy tone of voice. It wasn't the kind of conversation Jack would have elected to have by phone.

"Honey, it's not a joke. Someone from the RRT needs to go and see what's going on in Africa. I have the most experience with viral disease, so it's me."

"So they chose you? Of all the people the DoD could send, they *chose* you?" Marla pushed.

Jack hesitated, then said, "No."

"Goddamit, Jack! You volunteered?"

"Sort of—well, yes. I volunteered. But..."

"What the hell were you thinking?"

"Marla, honey, the Africans need help. Millions of children have lost their parents, and if we can't figure out what's going on and stop it, the continent will be one big orphanage. Children die of starvation or dehydration." There was no response. Jack could hear her sniffling.

"Honey, I just wish you would have asked me first. I understand about the kids over there. I just—"

"I'm sorry, Marla. It's all happening so fast. I just said the first thing that came to mind. Next thing I know, I'm packing for Africa."

"When do you leave?" Marla asked.

"In an hour," Jack said. He wished he were with her but knew it wouldn't make it easier. There was a pause. "Honey?"

"What?" Marla said.

"Honey, I'm doing this as much for you and me and the U.S. as I am for the Africans. You know as well as I do what could happen if it gets here..."

"Yeah, I know. But one slip-up over there—one tiny breach in your gear..."

"I know... I love you. I should go..." he said as he hung up.

Jack awoke with the sharp, descending turn as the plane lined up to land in Johannesburg, South Africa. He flopped his seat back up and peered out the window. Columns of whitish-gray smoke punctuated the sky, billowing up from funeral pyres as far as he could see.

They had taken off from Bethesda four days into the crisis. There had been only sporadic reports of death in South Africa at that time. In the 14 hours of flight time, the situation had dramatically worsened, with no fewer than 50 percent of the country's adults dead now.

A youthful-looking Air Force captain helped Jack into a MOPP suit. The cumbersome attire had Jack rethinking the whole idea of coming to Africa. It wasn't the thin, pliable rubber of a wrestling sweatsuit. It was heavy and thick and smelly. And it was completed with a gas mask that reminded him of the pictures of the old diving bell helmet. His facial expressions betrayed his thoughts.

"You'll get used to it soon enough. The most important thing for you to remember—wait—the two most important things for you to remember is, one, never, ever take any part of the suit off unless you are told to do so, and two, drink at least a quart of water per hour in this heat," the Captain said.

"If I'm gonna be drinkin' that much, and I'm not supposed to take anything off, where do I pee?" Jack said logically.

"Try not to. But if you do, you'll go through a decontamination process in an anteroom before entering the facility. We've one building that's considered a safe environment for de-suiting."

"Got it. Should be fun," Jack said, rolling his eyes.

They walked down the back ramp of the C-17. The sun was glaringly bright after the dark hull of the aircraft. They were met by more MOPP-garbed personnel that Jack assumed were military.

"Dr. Cann, nice to meet you," one of the suits said. "I'm Major Winters, U.S. Army. I'm the commanding officer of this detachment. I hate to say it, but you may have come for nothing. We're estimating that about 80 percent of Johannesburg adults are now dead." Major Winters paused momentarily, head tilting slightly down and to the right as if distracted.

"What? Major? Is there something else?" Jack asked.

"Well, it's the damnedest thing..."

"Yes?" Jack pressed him.

"It's like everyone, but the Africans got vaccinated or something," the Major said.

"Whaddya mean?"

"Dr. Cann, the people still alive are every color but black."

CHAPTER EIGHTEEN

The RRT was sweating, sequestered in a small, hot room in Washington, DC, while Jack was sweating half a globe away.

"Does it bother anybody that the kids are spared, at least so far?" the Kansas State microbiologist said. "I mean, why is that? What would possibly explain that?"

"It's possibly related to their immature immune system," the infectious disease doc suggested.

"What are you thinking?" he said.

"Well, whatever this is may be something that only a mature immune system recognizes, and when it does, it over-reacts and creates SIRS, leading to death," she explained.

"What is SIRS?" the colonel asked.

"Systemic Inflammatory Response Syndrome. The entire body reacts with intense inflammation, most often to an infection. Once it starts, a cascade of events leads to total organ failure and death. It isn't pretty," the doctor explained.

"But kids have an immune system, so why... I mean, I'm not sure I understand," pushed the colonel.

"By the time we reach adulthood, our bodies have been bombarded with infections, both bacterial and viral. Hundreds of viruses cause the common cold, adenoviruses, or the Epstein-Barr virus that causes mononucleosis—you know—the kissing disease. Bacterial infections cause strep throat and staph infections of the skin. Gastrointestinal infections caused by bacteria or viruses cause diarrhea, nausea, vomiting—rotavirus, Shigella, typhoid. Influenza is a viral illness. Each time an individual catches something different, it builds their immune system, making it more competent. It sort of gets cataloged into the immune system's memory. Think of it as adding another reference book to a library — another resource your body calls on when challenged," the doctor explained patiently.

"Yes," interjected the microbiologist. "Remember the H1N1 flu scare? They started vaccinating people backward of how they would for the typical seasonal flu. Usually, the vaccine is first given to the older population, especially those over 65 years. It's because the new strains of seasonal flu are things that younger folks seem to have more resistance to, in theory. After all, their bodies have been exposed to the newer strains of the virus, if you will. But with H1N1, the elderly were more likely to have immunity on some level because it is the re-emergence of an older strain of virus related to the killer strain of 1918. So with the H1N1, young kids were vaccinated first, since it was a virus their bodies had never seen before, and were, therefore, more susceptible to."

"Exactly," the doctor confirmed. "Only in this scenario, it may be that the lack of exposure to a broad range of infections that is preventing serious illness in children. Does that make more sense, Colonel?"

"I understand. Thanks for that," the colonel said, smiling with appreciation.

"I agree it's possible," Catherine said, "but isn't that kind of a long shot?"

"Yes," replied the doctor, "but I think it is worth keeping in the back of our minds. I think the autopsies will tell us if it is a factor. The postmortem findings of SIRS are not subtle."

"Excellent. Thanks. It's the best theory so far. More data should help us," Catherine said.

"It's so hard," the Colonel said. The others looked at her.

"What's hard?" Rick asked.

"Having no real idea what's going on, while millions of children are probably going to die."

CHAPTER NINETEEN

Jack spent very little time in South Africa. He saw everything he needed to see in a short time, and it was depressing. At Charlotte Maxeke Johannesburg Hospital, the basic hurdle was that most of the hospital's staff were African, now dead. Remaining researchers had to go into the field to collect specimens — not a massive challenge until you mixed in the factor: fear. Not all of the remaining staff contributed to the effort, choosing to stay home and hunker down, hoping to avoid the infection, as if any bacteria or virus, measured in microns, couldn't slip through the window sill or under the door or down the chimney.

The research was carried out in a manner that was unlikely to help. Jack noticed they had started some tissue cultures for viruses and the routine bacterial stuff, but beyond that, efforts were minuscule compared to what was staring the world in the face.

Jack had been given carte blanche in Africa by the CDC and DoD. Transport planes loaded with anti-viral medications had been dispatched to Africa from the Americas, Europe, and Asia. There were so few survivors in Johannesburg that he rerouted most medicines to western Africa, where adults were still alive. It all seemed sloppy to him, a crapshoot as to whether anything could staunch the tsunami of death that had swallowed eastern and southern Africa in less than a week.

He was back on the military jet less than twelve hours after landing in Johannesburg, headed for Nigeria with the hope of being of more significant help.

Riley had been in Johannesburg most of the day, although it could have been any city in eastern or southern Africa. Everything was the same: death, wailing children, and unfettered carnivores. The constant macabre paradoxically allowed the low-grade, persistent nausea she had developed over the past few days to abate, and her ability to navigate the environment was, as a result, better.

She walked into the InterContinental at Tambo Airport, exhausted from a non-stop drive from Mozambique and the better part of a day meandering around Johannesburg in a smelly MOPP suit. She popped her hand down on the bell at the front desk to summon the personnel, not even considering that they might be sprawled out behind the counter, dead.

A TV was on in the lobby. She smiled weakly when she noticed the channel was set to WNN. She started to look away when Tambo Airport, Johannesburg, SA, scrolled across the bottom of the screen, the video showing a military transport plane lumbering down the runway and slowly lifting into the air. She quickly walked over and turned up the volume. The reporter, not surprisingly, had a South African accent.

"An expert from the CDC sent on behalf of the U.S. government and the U.S. Department of Defense has just left Johannesburg, bound, our sources tell us, for Nigeria. To date, there have not been reports of death in western Africa, and there is a worldwide effort to initiate antiretroviral therapy for those still alive in Africa. The U.S. government's not-so-subtle message for South Africa is that we are on our own. The South African government is encouraging people to stay off the streets to—if it's even possible—avoid contracting the infection."

Riley stood for a moment, then turned and headed back to the airport. She felt like she was chasing a ghost but figured if the U.S. was sending their expert to Nigeria, it was a good bet that's where she needed to be.

Jack wasn't the only one baffled by the events unfolding in Africa. The RRT's implementation of antiretroviral therapy in western Africa seemed to have stopped the disease's spread. However, in the eight days since the African disaster had started, answers still eluded the global scientific community.

Jack hadn't seen anything like it—the lightning-fast spread of the malady was such that obtaining fresh specimens had been—and remained—a considerable challenge, thwarting every effort to isolate the presumed infectious agent. Jack was relieved that the people were still wearing MOPP suits to prevent the spread of the disease and prevent the workers from contracting the lethal sickness themselves.

He knew Rick and Lucy had done four more autopsies, one on a body that had been picked up and cooled with ice in a village hospital within an hour of death. It wasn't optimal, but it was better than nothing. Gross inspections of the bodies were all the same: normal. Even the brain was intact—not a single abnormality was identified. And still, nothing grew in the cultures.

The microscopic exams on the most recent specimens were not as worthless as the earlier specimens. Some cellular details could be made out, but the changes generally seemed characteristic of the stage of death and not specific to any identifiable cause. Screens for known poisons, both man-made and natural, continued to be negative.

The RRT continued to meet daily, even though Jack was in Africa. When possible, he would teleconference into the meetings. The team desperately sought experts from around the globe, but theories were eliminated almost as fast as they were espoused.

While there was a great relief that implementation of anti-retroviral therapy had halted the disease, there was a sense of unease in concluding they had indeed found a solution since they had not found a cause. The lack of answers and the treatment seemed to have stopped the disease was a catch-22.

"I simply don't understand how a disease could sweep through the better part of an entire continent and leave us with no clues," the Stanford pathologist said.

"Well, I wouldn't say we don't have any clues," Jack said through the crackle of a speakerphone.

The Emory doctor leaned back in his chair and cleared his throat. "What are you thinking, Jack?"

"Well, if the response to the antiviral drugs is real, we can conclude that we're looking for an RNA-based virus, like HIV. If that's the case, our job should be a bit easier. We can just use the same isolation techniques from the HIV process to identify the bug—at least in theory."

"How long would it take to find out if that'll work?" asked the colonel.

"Best case scenario—a couple of days," Jack said, uncertain with his response.

"What's wrong, Jack?" Catherine asked. Jack knew she sensed his discomfort an ocean away.

"Well, what's bothering me is that nothing has grown in the tissues cultures yet, so if this is a retrovirus, why isn't it growing?"

After a pause, Catherine said, "Anything else, Jack?"

"Yeah. I hate MOPP gear."

CHAPTER TWENTY

Jos, Nigeria, smack-dab in the middle of the country, has a half-million residents and was where the U.S. flew their expert to from South Africa. Riley was able to ascertain that much from watching her own channel. She figured they picked Jos because if anything happened in Nigeria, the expert would be centrally located and could quickly get anywhere in the country. While there was not the same kind of large-scale death seen in other parts of Africa, there were small pockets of death around the city and throughout Nigeria. It was enough to make people edgy, and it was still consistent with a person-to-person transmittable agent.

Finding where the U.S. had sequestered the expert was another story, but with the help of the local WNN office, she found the military safe house less than 24 hours after hitting the ground. She set up shop across the street in a third-story rented room.

Riley, sitting in a straight-backed wooden chair directly in front of the window, peered down at the U.S. headquarters for the sixth day running. She was wearing down—the continuous surveillance was beyond tedious, especially given that nothing was happening. Each day since her arrival had seemed like a month, considering how quickly eastern and southern Africa had succumbed.

There were some positives, however. She was now MOPP-less, having scored a month's supply of generic antiviral meds on the street. She figured they were working for the masses, so they'd work for her, too. She had become rather nonchalant about the whole thing, figuring MOPP or not, she had likely been exposed at some point back in Tanzania, and it was just a matter of time before she was infected. She had the occasional fantasy that she was somehow immune. She understood this was folly and that if she had contracted the disease, the drugs were now suppressing it—maybe curing her. But she was done with MOPP, permanently.

Each day, not at any particular time, three MOPP-dressed Army personnel left the building, apparently going out for exercise—it never seemed like a mission. Upon seeing the door open, Riley had just enough time to throw on a hooded tunic and clamor down two flights of stairs to follow the small group. Between her hoodie and the Army folk's MOPP-induced limited peripheral vision, she had remained undetected.

Her cup was empty, and being the pathologic coffee drinker she was, she got up to refill her cup. Nigerian coffee was unexpectedly good—an indescribable hue of brownish-black with an oily sheen on the surface. She walked back to the window and took a gulp. Looking down, she noticed the door to the U.S. occupied facility open, and the MOPP-dressed personnel headed down the alleyway. She nearly choked, putting the cup down so forcefully that liquid exploded six inches into the air before the majority of it miraculously fell back into the vessel. She grabbed her tunic and sprinted out, taking the stairs two at a time. She burst out the door. She couldn't see them, so she headed to the alley.

She arrived at the alleyway entrance, but they had disappeared, and with three other narrow paths branching off, she worried she had lost them. She ran down to the first alleyway. No sign of them. She took a guess, quickly moving down the middle alleyway, looking from side to side, as she moved past yet another branching spoke.

Riley looked left when the three MOPP-suited figures unexpectedly appeared from the right, almost running into her. She instinctively pulled the hood up, blending into the surrounding natives before they saw her face.

She lagged back, following them from about 10 yards behind, peering out from under the hood, never completely revealing her face. Two of the individuals were heavily armed with M-16s. The third, positioned between the other two, had no weapon. They were guarding him, and Riley assumed he was the CDC expert.

The late morning heat was boring into the black asphalt of the pavement, ribbon-like waves of heat cutting the air. It had rained earlier, the thick post-storm humidity intensifying the heat. She could only imagine how hot and miserable the MOPP suits were—the occupants must have needed to stretch their legs and see some different scenery to tolerate such suffering electively. She felt sorry for the government folks.

She followed the small group as they wandered with no urgency through the city streets of Jos. The middle one picked up the pace, flanked on each side by armed companions. Riley could see they were chatting the best they could through the masks, gestures being a necessary part of the exchange.

She followed them around a corner, walking down a narrow alleyway for about a hundred yards, to where it opened into a small square filled with vegetable and fruit-laden stalls. It was the local marketplace, teeming with activity. There were so many people that the crowd slowed her pace considerably, making it harder for her to keep up. The Army guys were taller than the natives, and the MOPP gear was easy to spot—and of course, the automatic weapons of the Army folks, combined with the insect-like outfits, resulted in a parting of the crowd and easy passage. Despite the imposing look, the masses weren't bothered by the foreigners.

In the middle of the market, surrounded by what seemed like a hundred people, Riley heard a commotion behind her. Startled, the soldiers shoved the unarmed man behind them, spinning and shouldering their weapons. The crowd was pushing toward a man lying on the ground amid the feet of market-goers. Riley worked her way against the crush to the edge of the market to avoid the jumble and watched the scene unfold, perched atop a short wooden box. She wished she had a videographer with her.

She was only about ten feet from the soldiers when she heard the unarmed American ask, "What is it? What's going on?" Neither of the soldiers responded, apparently processing what was happening.

After a moment, one of the men lowered his weapon; eyes still fixed on the crowd. "Nothin'. I think some old man just fainted. The sun's so damn hot it's no wonder."

"Oh," the unarmed man said, turning to head out of the market. He took a step, paused, and turned around slowly as Riley watched. Then she noticed another man, just to the right of the MOPP group. She rapidly surveyed the market. Another woman was on the ground next to a cart piled high with melons, her stall mate patting her face with a damp, multi-colored rag, attempting to revive her.

The nausea Riley had successfully eluded days earlier slapped her again. She felt limp, weak, incapable of movement. She watched helplessly as people died, one after another, falling to the ground while the Americans remained upright, in stark contrast, like the few old-growth trees that survive a forest fire. A young man dressed in a brightly colored shirt fell at her feet, lifeless. Having fallen backward, he stared unblinkingly up at Riley. Vibrantly alive moments ago, the market was completely silent—except for bawling, frightened children.

One of the armed soldiers looked in Riley's direction. She stood out now, as any living adult would have among the crumpled bodies. One of the masked figures was staring at her when she realized her hood had fallen back in the commotion, her face exposed. She did not attempt to cover up as the soldier nudged the unarmed, shorter figure and pointed at her.

The three MOPP suits began walking towards her. She turned, and one of the soldiers shouted, "Halt!" She turned to see him pointing his weapon at her. The unarmed man put his hand on the weapon and pushed it down and away from Riley as he walked up. She could see his bespectacled eyes behind the mask, wide as if he recognized her. He did.

"You're that reporter! You... reported from that little village in Tanzania!" She shook her head slowly, still trying to clear the fog of fear—and horror—at having just witnessed the deaths of sixty, eighty, a hundred people.

"Why are you here? You're exposed to the infection, and we have no idea what the hell it is!" the man continued. "Why in God's name would you be here? And why wouldn't you be wearing something to protect yourself?"

Her brain engaged. "Yes, I'm the reporter from Mto Wa Mbu. Who the hell are you?"

"I'm Jack Cann. I'm here with the military to help figure out what's going on."

Riley squinted, trying to see more of his face. "Well, I know who you are too. You're that researcher the CDC sent to South Africa last week."

"Yup. That's me. Come on. We need to get you out of here," Jack said, turning. He ran into one of the soldiers who had stepped up right behind him.

"I'm sorry, Dr. Cann, but we won't be taking her with us," said the armed figure.

"What the hell are you talking about? Of course, we're taking her with us. She's an American citizen," Jack said.

"It doesn't matter, Dr. Cann. She's been exposed, and we have strict orders. She will not be going with us," he said. Riley felt panic in her chest, heart pounding hard and fast as if a boxer were using her chest as a punching bag from the inside out.

Jack looked up at the soldier. "We're taking her with us, goddammit!" Riley notices Jack's gloved fists clenching. He was visibly shaking with anger.

She stepped forward and said, "But I've been on antiretrovirals. I should be OK."

"Yeah, see?" Jack said to the soldiers. "She's going to be fine. Come on. Let's go."

"Dr. Cann, you've made the fact that you don't like us crystal clear. But we're not idiots. Some, maybe all of these folks that just dropped dead around us, were on antiretrovirals. They don't work. I don't give a damn if she takes a boatload of antivirals four times a day. She's not coming."

Riley saw Jack's head bow in thought. Then he said, "We could take her in reverse isolation. We can put her in MOPP for the flight home. We'd be protected from anything she's picked up." Riley appreciated Jack's advocacy. The soldier simply shook his head. She saw Jack's shoulders slump, defeated.

"Please—Please take me with you," she said, level-toned, no hint of desperation, the kind of half-hearted plea associated with a predetermined defeat.

"No, ma'am. I'm sorry," said the soldier. "I really am."

Jack turned to her and walked closer.

"What's your name, again?" he said.

"Riley Mills. I work for WNN."

"Anyone, you want me to call?" Jack said.

"No one I can't call myself," she said.

"You'd better do it today. The networks here will go down soon if it's like everywhere else in Africa. There won't be anyone left to run them," Jack said.

"Yeah. Thanks for the advice," Riley said, smiling weakly at Jack. "I appreciate your attempt to help me, even if your goons won't let you." She paused and then said, "Besides, you know they're right."

Jack shrugged. Riley watched as he turned to leave. Jack paused and, without looking back, said, "For what it's worth, keep taking the antiretrovirals. You never know…"

She watched as the armed men escorted Jack down a small alley and disappeared. She looked around the market, littered with dead and crying children. She felt numb. She couldn't bear the pain of the children around her, much less the collective pain of Africa—her heart was ready to explode in agony on their behalf. Millions of orphans. Numb was good. Numb was necessary. *Hell, numb is all I got left.*

She took a step. It was a struggle to get her legs to comply with the desire.

Movement finally came with conscious effort. She headed for the alleyway leading back to her room. She paused at one of the vendor stalls, aimlessly looking around. Only crying children. She opened her floppy handbag, filling it with fruits, vegetables, and a few eggs, carefully placing them so they wouldn't break. She knew—eventually—she'd need to eat, even though food was the last thing on her mind. *It isn't stealing if they're dead.*

She walked back to her room in a disembodied, nonchalant manner, stepping over dead as if they were trees across a hiking path in the Rocky Mountains. Her brain had disconnected from the horror, and she could feel the chasm between the rational and emotional brain. She was consciously holding them apart, knowing that if she didn't, she would collapse from paralyzing fear and the ache of compassionate grief for orphaned children so powerful it would surely stop her heart. She sat on the bed, motionless.

As the sun slipped below the horizon and darkness came to her room, she reached over and flipped the light switch. Nothing. *Is the electricity already gone? That didn't take long.* She flopped the thin blanket to the side, laid down, pulled it over her head, and, caught between a state of exhaustion and numbness, fell into a fitful sleep.

The girl was half asleep, but she felt eyes watching her— angry eyes. She thought she smelled the alcohol-laden cigarette breath of her mother hovering in the air above her. She winced unconsciously, arousing from the murkiness of unrestful sleep. Hearing the creaking footsteps of someone going down the wooden stairs—a deep, prolonged creaking of wood scraping like a piston up and down on the loose nails holding each plank in place, she looked at the clock. 2:30 a.m. The front screen door was opening, the sound of the spring stretching as it swung open wide. The spring started to recoil, and she expected to hear the slam of wood on wood, but instead, there was the muffled sound of flesh against wood, a hand catching the door, gently letting it return to position.

She climbed out of bed and walked to her window. Below, she watched her mother open the car's back door and throw in a suitcase. She closed the car door carefully, using enough force to shut it, intent on being quiet. The girl watched as she reached into her purse, pulled out a cigarette, and put it between thin, tightly drawn lips. The match's flame was so bright compared to the ambient light that it almost hurt the girl's eyes, and she temporarily couldn't see her mother. The twinkling stars from the sudden stimulation of her retinas subsided quickly, and she watched as her mother climbed behind the wheel and started the car.

The car door started to shut but then stopped just short of closing. It opened again, about halfway. Her mother's head appeared, looking back at the house. The red dot of the cigarette brightened from a long drag. She reached up, pulled the cigarette from her mouth, and blew the smoke toward the house as if spitting on it. Slamming the door in contempt, she pulled out of the driveway. The girl watched as the taillights disappeared into the darkness, like a cigarette that had burned down to the filter, tobacco spent. A tear developed, so scant that it dried before it was able to roll halfway down her cheek. The corners of her mouth were slightly, perhaps unconsciously, curved up in a smile.

Riley awoke, shivering, tightly clutching the pillow in her arms, with her legs curled up, trapping the pillow as if it were trying to escape. She swung her legs over the side of the bed, still clutching the pillow, and rocked back and forth, tears in her eyes. Why she felt guilty had puzzled her since that night. She wasn't the one who had left. She wasn't an alcoholic. She didn't put out her cigarette on another person when she was stupid drunk. She looked down at her forearm, feeling the intense heat of an approaching cigarette. She had always told her teachers the circular burns were just infected mosquito bites—*I just can't stop scratching them*, she would lie, and intentionally, for emphasis, scratch the unhealed, raw burn, bravely holding back a cry from the agonizing pain.

She sat for a while, and slowly the tears stopped. She walked over to the small table by the window and picked up her notebook. She took the picture out and stared at the face of the little boy from Mto Wa Mbu. There was just enough light from the moon to see the details. She smiled gently, kindly. Lovingly? She put the photo back in the notebook, went back to the bed, and laid down. She knew what she needed to do—what she must do. She lay awake for a bit, smiling, before falling into the deepest, most restful sleep she'd had since she was 15.

At 0600, Jack was on a military jet, headed to Atlanta. Despite his trip, the team was no closer to knowing what they were dealing with and had no idea how to treat it. Their best guess had been wrong.

Before the sun had set yesterday, hundreds of thousands of adult men and women had dropped to the ground, dead, creating chaos on a massive scale. Jack recalled the TV images from his Lawrence lab. It was horrific from Kansas—the pictures of eastern and southern Africa were nothing short of mind-boggling. To listen to TV anchor, people talk about the challenges or to sit in Washington talking about theories and solutions all seemed so ineffective, insignificant, detached. But to be in the middle of it? His head was filled with images of the market—mass death, right in front of him. It wasn't on the TV or radio or internet. *It was happening all around me. I could touch it.* Words could not capture his feelings, the emptiness, the sense of hopelessness. It was impossible to comprehend how millions of people could die within a week. Even with massive support from North American and European countries, humanitarian efforts were laughably insignificant to the magnitude of the disaster. And now, western Africa...

Adding the rest of Africa to the list of dead wasn't like declaring a state of emergency after a tornado. Even the worst tornado only tore up a couple of miles. It couldn't be compared to an earthquake or even a tsunami. The entire continent of Africa was a disaster zone—11,608,000 square miles of death. *Hell, COVID didn't even prepare us.*

The adults populating twenty percent of the earth's total landmass had vanished in the geological equivalent of a nanosecond. An unfathomable number of children had been orphaned and were at risk of death from neglect—not because no one was trying, but because there was no way to help them all. It was the worst kind of triage—deciding which children had the greatest likelihood of survival and tending to their needs, knowing that the decision was a death sentence for others.

The world's impotence and sense of grief at the mercy of an unidentified assailant were impossible to quantify. The only thing more significant was their fear.

CHAPTER TWENTY-ONE

Riley sat at her computer, studying the route from Jos to Mto Wa Mbu. It wouldn't be easy to travel across a continent where most of the population was dead. She scanned the map. *Jesus. I must be nuts.* She decided to take a longer route with better roads instead of shorter but riskier ways. She would be crossing Nigeria and a sliver of Cameroon, then crossing Chad and entering Sudan—not precisely the place an American woman would generally be welcome — but this wasn't normal. If she survived that, into Ethiopia, across Kenya, and just over the border of Tanzania to Mto Wa Mbu. She would find him there, hopefully.

Even though she had picked the safer route, the unpredictability of electricity, gas, and GPS made her anxious. She printed two copies of the map, picked up her backpack, and headed downstairs. She walked the streets, eventually finding an SUV that appeared to be in one piece. She opened the door and flipped the key to check the fuel level. Only a quarter tank. She repeated this twice more until she found a Toyota FJ Cruiser with a full tank. It was about as far as she had thought through the journey. She recognized the lunacy of it all, but the mission and its meaning were more important than safety now. Maybe more important than her life at all. Besides, survival wasn't a given, regardless of what she did.

She wasn't stupid about the whole thing despite her nihilist thoughts. She stopped at an abandoned convenience store, little more than a shanty, and stocked up on drinks. It was mainly Coca-Cola, but she decided to take some beer as she got ready to leave. *You never know when you might need a little buzz.*

She climbed behind the steering wheel, buckled the seatbelt, and headed down Murtala Mohammad Way toward Chad.

CHAPTER TWENTY-TWO

The president was never happy about urgent calls to the Situation Room. It invariably was terrible news — not some catastrophe that had been averted or an unexpectedly happy story. No, always bad, always dire.

He paused, straightened his suit coat, and tightened his tie before opening the door and stepping into the room. Everyone stood as he entered, a chorus of *Good afternoon, Mr. President* greeting him.

"Good afternoon, everyone," the president replied. He sat down at the head of the table, and before his backside had hit the chair, he said, "All right. Let's get to the meat of the issue. What's going on?"

The national security advisor was the first to speak. "Mr. President, the situation in Africa is, as you know, both dire and tragic. The pattern of death is consistent with person-to-person transmission, much like the flu, but of course, this is a deadly malady." He paused and shuffled some papers, clearly concerned about his next words.

"Mr. President—I'll get right to the point. This doesn't appear to be an accident of nature. It appears to be a novel, weaponized biological agent that was being tested and, to the best of our knowledge, simply got out of control."

President Lopez listened intently, an elbow on the table, hand under his chin, index finger pressed to his lips. He didn't say anything but gestured for the NSA to continue.

"Mr. President, the data we've collected seems to make any other possibility remote, at best," said the NSA.

"Jesus, just spit it out. What's the bottom line, man?" The president disdained the advisor's predilection for theatrics. His abruptness caused the man to fumble some papers awkwardly.

"Well, Mr. President, we believe the North Koreans have created this mess, and the events in Africa are the result of a small-scale test against the Tanzanian village," he said.

"Go on," said the president.

The NSA and the chairman of the Joint Chiefs of Staff continued the presentation, showing evidence they'd amassed in their case against the North Koreans. The president felt increasingly agitated with each new bit of information while maintaining an unruffled external demeanor.

"So," the president said, "What are the recommendations? Have you thought that far ahead?"

The commandant of the Marine Corps, a four-star marine general, took over. "Mr. President, we need an interdiction team in North Korea as soon as possible. The goal would be to break into the lab—covertly—and recover the biological stock and any research materials. It would be essential to understand if they have an antidote for this hellish creation of theirs."

President Lopez thought for a moment, considering the recommendation. "Who would you be sending in, General?"

"The Navy SEALs, Mr. President. We have already developed a plan for their insertion and are working with our allies in Asia to put it into place," he said. He went on to explain the mission at a high level.

The president leaned back in his chair, elbows on the armrests, fingers interlaced. He looked around the room, not seeing anyone. He felt uneasy in a way he couldn't define. Was it the recommendation he was uncomfortable with? Or something else? He recognized the cognitive dissonance, two sides of what seemed like the same coin, battling incoherently in his head, not hearing either side with clarity. *What's bothering me? The evidence is pretty damn clear.* As his thoughts dissipated, his focus became more present as the general abruptly spoke.

"Mr. President, we all appreciate the difficulty of this situation. Biological warfare is an awful business. The reality, Mr. President, is that the proverbial cat is out of the bag. This shit, pardon the French, is spreading like wildfire. It's out of control. We need you to make a decision, now. Not tomorrow. Not next week. This is getting worse by the minute. We need to confirm that the North Koreans are responsible, and if so, whether they have an antidote," said the General.

The president didn't move or blink as the general delivered the message. He looked intently at the general, knowing he was correct. Acting now was not even the question. The president was asking himself, *Will it make a difference?*

"General, I agree, and wholeheartedly so, but do the SEALs have the expertise to know what the hell they're looking at in a biological warfare lab?" the president asked.

Anticipating the president's question, the general said, "No, sir, they don't. But we know someone who does. And with your permission, Mr. President, I'd like to call Director Montoya at the CDC."

CHAPTER TWENTY-THREE

Jack's cell phone vibrated. He pulled it out of his pocket and looked at the number. Jet lag and death had exhausted him.

"Hello, Catherine. What's up?" He hadn't been at the hotel more than 30 minutes, just enough time to shower but not shave the three-day-old beard.

"The president wants to see you," Catherine said.

"By *The President*, I'm assuming you don't mean the chancellor at KU?" Jack said, hoping it wasn't the other one.

"Yup. The President of the United States. As in Lopez. A car is waiting out front for you now, and the Secret Service is meeting you in the lobby."

"Do you have any idea why?" Jack asked.

"Not to be smart-ass or anything, but I suspect it's related to Africa," Catherine said.

"Ya think?" Jack said. He was pissed. "I didn't ask for all this crap, Catherine. I really didn't. I just wanted to slow down, do a little research at KU, sit on the damn porch with Marla."

"No one asked for this, Jack. Certainly not the poor folks who are dead. Not their children. But we're sure-as-shit knee-deep in it, so pony the fuck up and get down to the lobby. I doubt the Secret Service has much of a sense of humor right now." Jack appreciated Catherine's ability to let go of the propriety of her position and speak frankly.

He threw a couple of things in his backpack and headed for the lobby.

As the elevator doors opened, two imposing figures of identical height, military haircuts, and wedge-shaped, muscular bodies joined him. The seams on their black suit coats strained against bulging shoulders. He wondered how they didn't rip them to shreds just by walking. They walked shoulder to shoulder at a forced pace out of the hotel to a black sedan where a third figure opened the back door, silently motioning Jack to get in. He felt safer in West Africa than in this moment.

The Georgia state police escorted the car to the Fulton County Airport, where a Citation jet was waiting. They pulled up to the jet, and he was escorted into the aircraft, feeling more like he had been arrested than summoned for help by the highest authority in the country. He felt an ominous finality as the jet's door closed.

"Well, I know where we're going, but how 'bout telling me why?" Jack said.

The agent closest to him said, "We aren't authorized to speak to you," his face expressionless. He didn't even look at Jack.

"I think I have a right to know what *fuck* this is all about," Jack said, somewhat testily. Nothing. He decided he'd just be wasting oxygen if he persisted.

Ninety minutes later—a silent eternity—the jet landed in Washington. A helicopter bearing the presidential seal was waiting. It whisked the small group off. Intimidating, but Jack admired the efficiency. They were flying low to the ground, and Jack distracted himself from reality by noticing how beautiful the city was with the sun in the west. A few minutes later, they landed on the White House lawn. Jack looked at his watch as the doors of the chopper were opening. 6 p.m.

Jack was escorted from the helicopter, again between the two bookend agents, walking quickly from the landing zone to a door leading into the White House. He felt awed by the whole thing. They walked through a long hallway and down a flight of stairs, finally coming to a door with an engraved metal plaque. SITUATION ROOM. Jack felt hot in the chest. *Jesus... what's going on?*

One of the agents opened the door, and Jack walked into a 5,000 square foot room, with people sitting around an impossibly long table. Flat-screen TVs and computer monitors lined the walls. Everyone in the room stopped talking and turned to look at him. In another situation, he might have laughed. It was like a scene from a sitcom.

At the end of the table, a man stood and walked over to Jack. The man, in his mid-50s, was over six feet tall, with jet black, perfectly combed hair, and gray eyes. He was wearing a dark blue suit and red power tie. He reached out and shook Jack's hand. "Dr. Cann, I'm President Lopez. I'm pleased to meet you, although I wish it were under different circumstances. I've known Catherine Montoya for years. She speaks of you with high regard."

After a brief pause, Jack said, "Mr. President, the honor is mine. Please call me Jack." He paused, wondering if he should say what he was thinking. "No disrespect, sir, but I have no idea why I am here. I mean, I suspect it's related to the African catastrophe, but beyond that, I'm puzzled."

"Take the seat next to me, Jack," the president said, walking back to the head of the table. The national security advisor currently occupied the seat. Looking miffed, he moved, and Jack sat down.

Jack looked around the table, recognizing many faces—the vice president, the NATO commander, and the Joint Chiefs of Staff chairman. Those he didn't know, he could figure out from the brass plates on the table bearing their title.

"Jack, we aren't going to waste time. You know about Africa. We know you witnessed the whole thing in Jos firsthand. In talking to Director Montoya, she said, it's your opinion this is most likely a viral entity. Is that accurate?" the president said.

"Pretty much sums it up. Whatever it is, it's transmitted very efficiently and is lethal. The MOPP suit gas masks seem to filter out whatever it is—although that's now in question because I've heard there've been some U.S. soldiers of African descent in MOPP that have died. That certainly adds to the puzzle. The bacterial cultures have all been negative. It seems the most likely explanation is a new type of virus originating in Africa, a ramped-up COVID or something."

The president looked at the chairman of the Joint Chiefs. "General, please take it from here."

The general looked more like a fit grandfather than a four-star Marine Corp veteran. Horn rim glasses and the classic marine haircut gave Jack a vision of the general behind the wheel of a 1957 Buick on a Sunday drive—right up until he spoke. It was more like a bark than speech.

"Dr. Cann, let me be crystal clear that everything you hear from this point forward is classified as top secret. Should you have the misfortune of discussing this information with anyone outside of this room, you will be arrested and tried for treason. Do you understand?" The general glowered at Jack.

"I understand," Jack said, glowering back. His opinion of the military wasn't improving. *What the hell do they know that I don't.* He wanted to tell them, *Thanks... not interested,* and leave. He was about to be given a responsibility he didn't want.

"Dr. Cann, the U.S. Government, including the Armed Forces, believe you are correct in attributing what is happening to a virus. What we disagree with is that it spontaneously originated in Africa," the general said.

Jack's eyes narrowed, partly in confusion and partly in concern. "Where do you think it came from, then? Outer space?" Jack knew he shouldn't have said it, but he couldn't stop the comment, and being a smart ass to the Joint Chiefs of Staff carried for him a particular pleasure in the moment. He noticed the president's half-smile.

The general, not used to being questioned, tilted his head forward. "North Korea, Dr. Cann. North Korea."

"So you hypothesize that this is like COVID, somehow escaping from North Korea? Can you explain why the North

Korean people don't seem to be dying?" Jack said, more serious.

"Dr. Cann, we don't think this originated in nature. We don't think it's like COVID. Our intelligence suggests this may be a genetically modified virus created by the North Korean military for biological warfare," the general said. "We think they tested it on the people of Mto Wa Mbu, and it got out of hand. We think they underestimated its virulence."

Jack slumped back in his chair, stunned, feeling like he couldn't breathe. He straightened up and looked at the general. "What evidence do you have?"

The general nodded to a captain standing at the back of the room. The video monitors around the room came alive, displaying satellite images, maps, timelines, faces of Asian men. He stood and walked to a screen across from Jack.

"We began seeing increased North Korean military chatter the week of the Mto Wa Mbu disaster. It's encoded, and we don't have a complete translation yet, but the word virus is prominent in the communications, and Africa is mentioned multiple times." The general moved to the next monitor.

"The communications have also allowed us to identify a previously unknown North Korean military site that we believe is a biological weapons lab. It's in some extremely rugged terrain, close to Baekdu Mountain at 9,003 feet above sea level, right on the North Korean-Chinese border. It's primarily underground." He pointed to a satellite image showing a concrete box nestled between several mountains. The general turned to the captain again and said, "Go live." The screen transformed into a real-time image. "Captain, have Space Force zoom in, please."

"Yes, sir, General, sir."

A satellite camera peered into the compound with remarkable clarity. Jack could see people moving.

"Focus on one of the sentries, Captain," the general said. The picture zoomed in, showing a North Korean soldier guarding a massive iron door, North Korea's red star emblazoned on his hat.

"The location of this facility makes an operation extremely sensitive—not just because it's inside a rogue nation, but because of its proximity to China. I could stand on the top of the wall of this compound and piss over the Chinese border," the general said.

"I see it's a North Korean facility, but how do you know it has anything to do with biologics?" Jack asked.

The screen changed, projecting new images.

"Dr. Cann, this series of videos will show you why we believe this is a biological lab. Captain, speed it up." Jack watched as a truck left the mountain facility. The video was playing in fast forward, but he could follow the truck's path. A four-hour trip took just a few minutes to view at the accelerated rate. "The truck drove about 200 miles, ending up at this warehouse." The general pointed to a drab, two-story, windowless wooden slat building. "Looks fairly benign. The sign says Kim's Restaurant Supply. We kept the satellites focused on this facility and tracked every vehicle leaving it. We found a series of trucks going from this facility to this one," he said, pointing. "The sign clearly shows it's the Democratic People's Republic of North Korea Hospital Supply. So we watched the hospital supply warehouse and found loaded trucks returning to Kim's, where we believe they off-load supplies for the lab onto another truck—the same truck we tracked to and from the military facility. Our North Korean operatives have confirmed all of these events. And Dr. Cann, one of the main items on the bill of lading for these trucks are things required for human cell cultures," the general concluded.

The room was silent. Jack felt every eye in the room staring. He looked from the general to the president and said, "So you're concerned that the Africa thing is some rogue virus created by the North Koreans?" He felt stupid even asking the question. The details compiled by the general and his crew were impressive. Jack's edge of disdain for the military was softening, if for no other reason than their incredible technology.

"In brief, yes, Dr. Cann. We think they have been working on this for years. They refused to sign any of the biological weapons non-proliferation treaties. We know, for a fact, they have had a biological weapons program since the 1980s."

"But why?" Jack asked. Silence in the room prompted him to say continue. "Why would the North Koreans develop such a biologic? What would be their goal? They already have enough nuclear weaponry to make everyone nervous, right? I mean, you can control where you send a nuclear bomb, and sure, there's a little fallout, but if this is a creation of theirs and they can't control it, what's the end game? Why would they release it if it's so contagious that it can kill a continent in a couple of weeks? Eventually, it'll land back in the homeland, which would be an unpopular political decision, even in North Korea. It's worse than sending a bomb into Pyongyang."

"We appreciate your perspective, Dr. Cann," the general said, "but our intelligence tells us that is exactly where this came from. This isn't a government known for making decisions constrained by logic."

"And what about our guys dying in MOPP?" Jack asked.

"We've determined that those episodes were likely due to defective MOPP mask filters," the general said.

"Worn only by American soldiers of African descent?" Jack pressed.

"I know it's hard to believe, Dr. Cann, but that seems to be the case."

Jack shrugged his shoulders and leaned back in his chair. He couldn't put it together in a way that made sense. He wanted to tell the general the meeting was over, at least for him.

"So, why am I here? If you've already concluded that the North Koreans have manufactured this super-virus, what do you need me for?"

The general again nodded to the captain. The lights in the room dimmed, and all monitors synchronized to the same picture. Jack sat up when he saw his face on the screen, his name in the corner of the screen, *Cann, Jack SSN: 158-98-6547.*

"Dr. Cann, you were a collegiate wrestler, correct?" the general said. The monitors were playing footage from the University of Kansas wrestling archives, and Jack was the star.

"Apparently, you know that," Jack said, anger rising at this invasion of his privacy.

"Do you still stay in good physical condition, Dr. Cann?" The video seamlessly transitioned to show a satellite image of Jack running, as clear as the North Korean guard. "Captain," the general commanded, "how fast does Dr. Cann run a mile?"

"Sir, he averages a six-minute, fifteen-second pace on a five-mile run," the captain said.

"Not bad, Dr. Cann. Not bad at all," said the general, nodding with mock approval. Jack's anger was morphing into nervousness. He thought about Marla and wondered exactly how much they knew about him. *What do they know about her?*

"Wow. You folks have been doing some homework. Gotta ask you again, though," he said with an edge in his voice, "Why am I here?"

"Dr. Cann," the general said, "have you ever been to North Korea?"

CHAPTER TWENTY-FOUR

A door at the far end of the room opened, and five men dressed in black, skin-tight uniforms entered the room, lining up shoulder to shoulder beside the general.

"Dr. Cann, meet your escort into the North Korean lab at Baekdu Mountain: the Navy SEALs, team Two," the general said. Jack felt a wave of nausea. "They operate out of Virginia Beach."

"What the *hell* are you talking about, General?" Jack asked.

The general started to speak, but the president cut him off. Jack could tell the president sensed his anger and rapidly approached reluctance to cooperate.

"Dr. Cann—Jack—Dr. Montoya and I have known each other for years. As I mentioned, she has limitless respect for you and says you're the best virologist on earth... *on earth,*" he emphasized. "For her to say that means something to me. We're looking at a global crisis on a scale not seen since World War II, and Catherine's telling me you're the one to figure out what the North Koreans have done."

Jack looked the president straight in the eyes and squinted as if it would help him discern if the president was telling the truth.

"Are you as smart as Catherine thinks you are, Jack?" the president asked thoughtfully. His tone was authentic.

"I've had my successes. I've failed too. Catherine must have been excessively complimentary." Compliments, even if deserved, made him feel self-conscious. He had always been wary, back in Boston, when he was complimented. It always felt contrived, inauthentic, driven by jealousy or competition.

The president smiled. "Your successes weren't exactly small, Jack. HIV. H1N1. COVID. Impressive track record," the president said.

Jack paused. "So, what do you want me to do, exactly?" Jack said, looking back at the general.

"We need you to get inside the lab and figure out how they've done this, so you can figure out how the hell to stop it," the general said.

"Well, that's great, and all, but I don't read Korean, and I doubt that they'll happen to have a translated copy of their research log on the workbench," Jack said, edgy again.

"That's why we've paired you with team Two. Half of them are fluent in Korean—written and spoken. They can translate for you."

"Why not just send the SEALs in, steal the goddam lab book, and bring it back? Why do you need me?" Jack asked.

"Because, if possible, we don't want them to know the United States Navy has been in their lab, Dr. Cann," the general said. "That'd be an act of war."

"So take pictures of the book," Jack said.

"We could do that, but we feel that having a knowledgeable virologist along will be more—ahhhh—productive. You can look at the lab understand things we can't. We could miss something, even something obvious, if we don't have an expert who knows what he's looking at or for," the general said. "Frankly, we think your physical condition is reasonably good, and you won't be a liability to the operation. Except..."

"Except what?" Jack said.

"You had an ankle injury your senior year in wrestling, didn't you?" the general queried.

"Yeah. What about it?"

"Could it be a factor in the mission? Does it ever bother you?" the general asked.

"I haven't had trouble with my ankle since college. I run every day, play hoops, and still wrestle a little. No issues."

"Good. So you're in?" the general asked.

"Do I have a choice?" Jack said.

"Of course you do," said the general. "You can go to North Korea, or you can sit in a secured compound until this whole thing is over. Now that we've shared our most sensitive national security information with you, you aren't going anywhere without a SEAL on your butt."

"Some choice," Jack said, his look unmistakably communicating disgust. "Guess I'm in. So, what's next?"

"Well, Dr. Cann, we need your body to be as fit as your mind is smart. The SEALs have never left a man behind, but we've never had to take a civilian along either. We don't want to be changing that just because you're along. We need you not to be a liability, Dr. Cann," the general said. Jack felt his irritation billowing. He just wanted the general to get to the bottom line.

"OK, OK! I understand. So, what's next?" Jack asked impatiently. "Just tell me what the hell I need to do!"

"Lieutenant, why don't you take it from here?" the general said.

"Dr. Cann, I'm Lieutenant Bob MacKinsey," said the man standing closest to the general. He was shaped like a bodybuilder, with brown eyes and a nose that must have been broken three times and never set. "I'm the team leader. I'm fluent in Russian, Arabic, and Chinese—multiple dialects—and Korean. I've been a SEAL for seven years. I'm also a Navy aviator—I fly fixed-wing aircraft and choppers. I'll be leading this team of five, and my job is to incorporate you into it in the next couple of days before we head out. It's also my job to make sure you don't end up dead, so we need to be clear right now that you'll listen and do whatever you are told at all times. Can you do that, Dr. Cann?" The lieutenant's eyes were fixed in a blinkless stare. Jack was still trying to get his head around the enormity of what was happening. He had a sense of disembodiment like he was watching a movie, not his life.

Jack narrowed his eyes. "Yeah, I can do it," he said. "Did you say we only have a couple of days?"

"Yeah," the lieutenant responded. "I'm going to be seeing how tough you are, Dr. Cann. The entire team needs to know your capabilities, at least physically, so we can plan accordingly," the lieutenant said.

"I'd at least like to be able to say goodbye to my wife before we take off," Jack said.

The general stepped forward. "We've already taken care of that, Dr. Cann."

"What the hell does that mean?" Jack demanded angrily.

"She's been told you've been urgently sent back to Africa and that you'll be out of contact for the next week or so."

"You lousy son of a..." Jack didn't finish.

"Dr. Cann, we appreciate you're upset. I'd like to be sensitive to that, but I think you need to appreciate that if you and the SEALs aren't successful, there won't be anyone, anywhere, to say goodbye to in the not-too-distant future. We're not just talking about national security, young man. We're talking about what we believe to be an issue of global survival," the general said, his voice dark, ominous. Jack took a deep breath, his anger fading as logic took over. He knew the general was right.

"OK, general. I get it. I'm in. When do we start?"

CHAPTER TWENTY-FIVE

Jack's iPhone went off at 04:30 a.m., harp strings of the alarm paradoxical to the starting a day of training for a mini-invasion of a rogue foreign power. He never had trouble getting up early, but the fact that he and SEAL team Two hadn't arrived in Virginia Beach until 10:30 p.m. after a day full of surprises—and fitful sleep—had him moving more slowly than usual. He rolled over and groped for the light switch. He sat upon the cot, rusty bedsprings scraping against each other in a screeching, fingernails-on-chalkboard way. The sound woke him fully.

He was in a small barracks on a remote part of the Naval Amphibious Base. No one knew where he was except the five SEALs, the captain, and the members of the National Security Council. All information was provided on a need-to-know basis. The facts made him feel uneasy. He could die, and no one would ever know, much less why.

Someone knocked on his door. "Dr. Cann?" a voice said.

"Yeah, I'm up. Come on in," Jack said.

Lieutenant MacKinsey walked in. "You'll wanna stretch out before our run, Dr. Cann. Then a big breakfast. We have a long day ahead of us."

Jack looked up at the man. "Lieutenant, I'd prefer it if you'd just call me Jack. I have a feeling we're going to be spending some quality time together over the next week." The lieutenant smiled.

"Sure, Jack. The guys call me LT. While we keep the line of command when needed, we're really a team for the most part. Not a lot of hierarchy."

"Well, that's a step in the right direction," Jack said. He was too tired to kick-start his skepticism of the military.

"Roger, that. Get stretched and be in front of the barracks at 05:00, sharp."

Thirty minutes at 04:30 seems to go a lot faster than at three in the afternoon. He saw the SEALs lined up as he walked out of the door. He couldn't believe how cold it was.

LT was looking at his watch as he walked up. "Doc, let's get one thing straight right now. 05:00 means 05:00— not 05:01! Got it?"

"Yeah, I got it..." Jack said. *Jesus, this is happening.* An ember of his dislike glowed brighter.

"Here's what's up today, gents. We're going to do five miles this morning as a nice warm-up. Then breakfast and a briefing on the North Korean lab, at least to the extent we know anything. We'll plan ingress and egress points. Transportation in and out has already been set. More on that later. Captain Warren will be dropping by after that to meet Doc. He's the CO for this little operation, which they have code-named Safari. I guess some sick fuck in planning is referencing the African thing and the fact we're hunting down the cause.

"Any questions?" LT asked.

"No sir!" the regular SEALs shouted.

"OK then, let's see you kick this five-mile run's ass. Shark, lead us on the gauntlet course—plenty of hills to see what 'ol Doc is made of." Shark nodded. The six of them lined up. LT clicked the timer on his watch and said, "GO!"

The entire team was impressed with Jack's run. He beat two of the SEALs. It helped his confidence — and the SEALs' confidence in him.

Jack quickly stopped in his room to splash his face and grab a towel. When he walked into the dining room, the five Navy men were already eating, talking loudly, with lots of backslapping and guffawing. He pulled up the remaining chair and sat down, marveling at the amount of food on the table. It looked like a buffet table at an all-night diner.

"We expectin' another 15 folks?" Jack said, gesturing toward the food.

"I told you, Jack, we have a full day ahead of us. You won't be sitting down to lunch, so you better tank up!" LT said, his mouth working a strip of bacon.

John Tubman, a Seaman, picked up a platter mounded with sausage and ham, passing it to Jack. "Pile it on, Dr. Cann." An African American man, Tubman stood 6'2" and had green eyes. His nickname was Bugger because he was an expert in electronic warfare and could wreak havoc on a foe's electronic infrastructure with his Pandora's box of DoD-developed viruses, worms, and other malware. Part of his weaponry was carried on his dog tag chain: a jump drive. As Jack took the plate from him, he noticed huge keloid scars on the man's hand. Bugger was at once handsome and frightening. Jack imagined what it must be like to run into him on the wrong side of a mission, to have the last thing you see be those emotionless green eyes. Jack wondered how he was still alive, with so many black people dead.

"Thanks," Jack said. He took some ham. "Seaman, what is your role on the team?"

"Whoa, Jack. Everyone, let's all get something straight right now. We're a team, and that includes the good doctor here. Dr. Cann asked me to call him by his first name, Jack, so

I think, with his permission, we should all be on a first-name basis," LT said.

"Ohhh, LT—he ain't Jack—he's Doc!" said Jesus Menendez, another Seaman. He cackled in a near-maniacal manner. Manny, as his teammates knew him, was the shortest of the team. He had black hair and a wicked scar from ear to chin, a result of someone trying to cut his throat on a mission he claimed he couldn't talk about. He was the group's weapons expert. Everyone at the table nodded in agreement as Manny cackled on. He seemed a little unstable.

"I'm good with that," Jack said. "You all understand I'm the kind of doc that can't help you if you get shot, right?" Everyone laughed. Jack took a bite of bacon. "Which one of you, besides LT, speaks Korean?"

"Me," said Shark. Shark, Tom Shelby, was a chief petty officer. Tall, sinewy, and blonde, he looked like an Olympic-class swimmer. He loved the water and knew everything there was to know about underwater operations. He was a legend, even by SEAL standards. Rumor had it that he was so good he could sneak up on a school of fish without being noticed. He once swam the English Channel—and back—for fun.

"And him..." Shark said, nodding toward Bugger. Jack smiled.

"You guys are full of surprises," Jack said. "I suppose half of you speak Farsi and Russian, too," Jack said, being a smart ass. LT, Manny, and Eddie Waxman raised their hands, grinning. Eddie had a penchant for blowing things up. He was the demolitions expert and had been anointed with the nickname of Greaser.

"Where did Greaser come from?" Jack asked.

"Because when I'm done, all that's left are grease spots," Eddie said, smiling. Repulsed, Jack managed a weak smile.

CHAPTER TWENTY-SIX

After cooling down from the run, stomachs full, they collected in a wood-paneled room in a building next to the barracks. There was a projector on the table, hooked up to a computer. A woman dressed in civilian clothes was waiting.

"Good morning, SEALs. I'm from the NSA, and I'm here to brief you for Operation Safari and the facility at Baekdu Mountain." In her late 30s, she had short-cropped brunette hair, and her head was held in a way that exuded federal officiousness. Jack immediately felt rebellious upon seeing her. He wondered if the SEALs felt the same way or if they just didn't notice. *No, they noticed.* They were just disciplined enough to hide their disdain. He admired their control. They sat down and opened the briefing booklets in front of them.

"Baekdu Mountain is in the northernmost part of North Korea and abuts against China." She used a laser pointer to show the team the geographic points, even though one step forward would have allowed her to use her finger. "It's the highest mountain of the Changbai mountain range to the north, the Baekdudaegan mountain range to the south, and the highest mountain on the Korean peninsula and Northeast China. Its name means ever-white, referring to the fact that it's almost always snow-covered. The temperatures can swing wildly, fluctuating by up to 50 degrees on any day." Jack wondered if the SEALs cared about this kind of information.

"Baekdu Mountain is about 320 clicks from Changchun, China, as the crow flies. Amazingly, the mountain's elevation is 9,003 feet above sea level—of course, this will be important in planning. The lab facility sits at nearly 8,000 feet, five miles to the southwest of Baekdu, here," she said, pointing to a small square on a satellite image. The following slide was a close-up of the facility, similar to the one Jack had seen in the Situation Room. She pointed to a dark rectangular spot. "This is the main door. We think it is the only door into the place. Our North Korean operatives have told us that this elevator leads to underground labs where the research is carried out. A keypad with Korean characters controls access to the elevator. They believe the lab is only one level, somewhere between 75 and 100 feet below the surface. The fact that it's only one level is both good and bad news, as you no doubt know." Jack looked around the room to see if he was the only one that didn't know what she meant. It was clear all others had made the connection. She took a breath, ready to move on.

"Uh—excuse me," Jack said. She turned to look at him. Jack thought the movement had caused her pain from the look on her face. "I'm not sure I know what the good news-bad news thing means."

"She means, Doc, that it's good because we won't be having to search multiple stories. It's bad 'cause if they figure out we're there—well, let's just say it complicates us leaving quietly," Manny explained.

"Oh," Jack said. He wasn't sure any of it was particularly good news.

"May I continue?" the NSA hardbody asked tersely. Heads nodded.

"The walls around this place are virtually impossible to scale. They're 30 feet high, 12 feet deep, and made of poured concrete, so there are no handles for you to use. Even a grappling hook would be unlikely to catch, assuming you could even throw it 30 feet up and 12 feet inward, without, of course, making a racket and having the North Korean Army kill or capture you before you got to the top."

Jack reached into his pocket and subconsciously pulled out his keychain Rubik's Cube. Glancing down at it briefly, he returned his gaze to the woman and continued listening as his hands worked away. He looked over at Tubman, who was watching his hands, brows furrowed. Jack neatly aligned the colors without looking down again.

"Do we know anything about what's actually below the deck?" LT asked.

"Unfortunately, very little. It is too deep to tell much, but we think there are two main crossing corridors based upon infrared satellite feeds. No details beyond that," she said. "We think from the footprint of the courtyard that the facility is around 7,500 square feet in size. It's not huge, but you can't expect to be out of there in five minutes either unless you just get lucky. We still have operatives trying to get into the facility. North Korean security is paranoid to the second power."

"Well, gents," LT said, "it looks like our ingress and egress point isn't going to be a big decision. There's only one. Bugger, thoughts?"

"Yeah. I'll bring my screwdriver," Bugger said. The SEALs cracked up. Jack couldn't believe they found this funny, given the situation.

"Doc, what's on your mind?" LT asked.

"I sure as hell hope you guys know what you're doing because this all sounds pretty goddam impossible to me," Jack said.

"Doc, I've broken into tons of things like this. I carry all sorts of gizmos with me for exactly this purpose. If I can't get 'er done, Greaser here'll take care of it, and we'll repel down the shaft. Quiet if possible, loud if necessary, but the job gets done," Bugger said.

"OK, Bugger, thanks. Just make sure you bring the right key. So, fellas, after we get in, then what?" LT asked.

"Let's assume the infrared is right and plan to take the thing by quadrants," Shark said. "We'll leave Manny up top to welcome visitors while the rest of us are down below. We can pair off, Doc going with one of the teams, cover the closest two quadrants first, meet up, and if no one finds what we're looking for, we'll hit the last two quadrants. 'Course if anyone finds the lab cooking the virus crap, just give a holler, and Doc, you and your team need to skedaddle over there ASAP, and the rest of us'll cover the six."

"I like it. Nice and simple," LT said. "Any other thoughts, guys?" The SEALs were nodding in agreement with Shark's plan.

Jack thought they made it sound like going to the mall or walking down Massachusetts Avenue and window shopping in Lawrence.

"What'll I be doing? Just following you all around?" Jack said.

"Doc, you'll go in with an empty backpack, and you'll be leaving with it full. You pick up every damn notebook and piece of paper you find, and if you see cultures that look interesting or unusual or whatever the hell you look for in a virus lab, grab it."

"Well, wouldn't they be keeping their records electronically? On a computer?" Jack said. "And it's more than just a little risky to be grabbing unidentified samples and stuffing them in a backpack, don't you think? I mean, if our intelligence is right, this stuff is lethal," Jack noted. "Kinda an issue, fellas."

"Don't worry about computer notes. Bugger will have everything uploaded from their system directly to the NSA in a matter of minutes, then give their system one helluva virus of our own. And as far as the infection stuff, we'll all be in a special MOPP gear—lightweight, damn near impervious—so, Doc, you can collect with reckless abandon and not worry. Grab it and wrap it in some of the special shit the Bethesda folks gave us, and we'll be good to go," LT said. Jack's brows furrowed. It verged on the cavalier.

"You seem—ahhh—concerned," Shark said.

"Fuck, yeah! You guys aren't? I mean, I don't know what concerns me more—your lack of concern or the insane plan!" Jack said.

Tubman jumped in, "Doc if you're smart enough to solve that goddam Rubik's Cube while not even lookin' and carrying on a conversation with the NSA, even if things don't go as planned, you'll help us figure it out." Jack looked down at the Rubik's Cube in his hand, all six colors perfectly aligned. He didn't recall pulling it out. He smiled. *These Navy guys are OK.* Jack refocused when LT spoke.

"Look, Doc—Jack—I know this seems like we're rushing into this. Well, come to think of it, we are. It's a goddam emergency. But try to understand that *this is our job.* We do this stuff day in and day out. We've never lost a man and never come back without achieving our objective. Never. And I'm not about to let our North Korean brethren ruin that record," LT said. Jack felt mildly better. His confidence in the plan was elusive, but trust in his teammates grew.

"OK, LT. I'll shut up and just get with the program," Jack said. "Just one more thing. How do we get into the compound?"

"We'll talk about that later today, Doc," LT said. "But now, we need to go meet up with the Captain at the beach."

"What're we going to the beach for, LT?" Greaser said.

"Not really sure. Guess we'll see when we get there," LT said.

A short jog later, the team was standing on the beach of the training grounds. Waves were coming in at a good clip, the tide inbound. Captain Warren and his administrative officer walked toward the group, both dressed in Navy whites. It seemed out of place on the beach.

When LT saw the Captain, he shouted "ATTENTION!" The SEALs snapped into position, saluting.

Jack, wondering what the commotion was and not seeing the Captain, said, "What's up, LT?" He turned and found himself nose to nose with the Captain. "Oh, hi," Jack said nonchalantly.

"So, Lieutenant MacKinsey, this is Dr. Cann, I presume?" the Captain asked.

"Yes, sir, Captain, sir!" The Captain stepped back and looked at Jack with raised eyebrows. This anal-retentive stiff certainly didn't help Jack's skepticism with the military.

"Uhhh, there a problem, Captain?" Jack said.

"Well, Doctor, that's what I'm here to find out," the Captain said. "I want to make damn sure, Doctor, that you don't get any of my SEALs killed. I want to be clear that I'm against this cluster-fuck, ill-conceived plan, but the president and Joint Chiefs seem to have a bee up their ass on this thing and demand that Cann go along. Personally, I think it will get everyone killed."

"Sir? So what's up?" LT said.

"I gained agreement from the Joint Chiefs that if the good doctor can't handle 20 minutes of surf torture, he's done," the Captain said, smiling. Jack thought he looked sadistic.

"Captain, all due respect, sir, but we won't even be in the water on this mission," LT said.

"Lieutenant, I appreciate that. It isn't about being in the water. It's about toughness—mental and physical. Operation Safari isn't some goddam weekend warrior affair. The world depends on results—and I'm responsible. I'm not going to fail because some pansy-assed civilian professor can't hack it." Jack was officially pissed. He was standing right in front of the Captain and being talked about like he wasn't there. It stoked his competitive urge and his ire for the military—or at least, for the military brass.

"What's this so-called surf torture, LT?" Jack asked, glaring at the captain, making it clear he was up for a challenge.

"It's also known as cold water conditioning, Doc. It's part of SEAL training. You lay in the sand at the edge of the water with your buddies, arms interlocked, head toward the incoming surf. As waves come in, they roll over your head, and ya need to hold your breath until it rolls back out. Waves get deeper and stay longer, and, of course, it's cold as hell because you're wet. It weeds out about 15 percent of the SEAL candidates," LT explained.

Jack liked to swim, and this didn't sound fun, but he sure as hell wasn't going to let Captain Warren intimidate him into quitting.

"Well, when do we start, LT?" Jack said, rubbing his palms together, welcoming the challenge and smiling tauntingly at the Captain.

"In three minutes, Dr. Cann," said the Captain. "Lieutenant—a private word?" Jack watched the Captain and LT walk down the beach about 20 yards. They talked for about thirty seconds out of his earshot. He continued watching until LT said an abrupt Yes, Sir, turned and walked back to the group.

LT pulled Gunner, Bugger, Shark, and Manny together and gave them the instructions away from Jack. It made Jack nervous.

The four men walked to the edge of the surf, joining Jack, two on each side. They interlocked their arms. "One minute," LT said. "OK, sit down, backs to the water. Thirty seconds. OK—lay down. Twenty minutes to hot showers, gentlemen!"

The first wave rolled in, the coldness hitting Jack like he was naked in the Arctic. It didn't even cover his head. It was bearable but certainly not enjoyable. Another wave came in, and as soon as Jack felt it on the top of his head, he closed his eyes and held his breath. Water shoved at his head and shoulders, but he didn't move, anchored firmly to the bodies on either side, fine sand beneath them. The water washed a thin layer of sand out from under his back, and as it receded, it created a vacuum-like space underneath him, sucking him down. Water was over his head, but just barely. This might not be too bad.

The next wave was more prominent, perhaps marginally deeper, and colder. He didn't open his eyes under the water, but the fact that it covered his body to his belly button led him to guess it was six inches over his face. It receded more slowly than the last wave. He noticed his SEAL companions were taking deep, full but rapid breaths between the waves. They were hyperventilating. He emulated their breathing pattern, figuring they had done this before. Another wave, deeper, longer. And another. The waves were beginning to pick up the mass of entwined bodies, shoving them toward the beach as they rolled in. Feeling the sand under his feet, Jack instinctively dug his heels down and into the sand to prevent being swept out with the receding wave.

Fifteen minutes into the drill, an unexpectedly big wave crashed down on the five men, lingering longer than all the others combined. Jack's lungs were searing—like he had just been forced to inhale campfire smoke and was required to hold it in. His initial impulse was to let go and stand up, but a flash of the Captain's arrogance gave him strength. A little longer— that's all I need. The lack of oxygen was making him see stars. He could feel the wave start to recede, but it was pulling them with it, and he couldn't feel the sand. Shit! Now what? He felt the arms on each side of him relax just a little, and he sensed the bodies on each side of him start to float upwards. Against his instinct, he relaxed a little too, letting his legs rise as if he were learning to do the back float. The five men popped up to the surface, taking deep, gasping breaths. They bobbed on the surface for a few seconds when Jack, through water-clogged ears, heard LT's shout, "Twenty minutes! You're done, guys."

He stood up, dizzy, cold to a depth he had never experienced, waist-high in the Atlantic. He pondered giving the Captain the middle finger salute but understood his success was a bigger insult than an obscene gesture.

Standing by the Captain, LT asked, "Anything else, Captain?"

"Well, I gotta give it to him, Lieutenant. He's a tough son of a bitch for an academic pinhead. Good luck, Lieutenant," the Captain said as he turned and walked away.

Jack, displaying an unusual hue of purplish-blue skin, walked up to LT. They stood for a moment watching the Captain walk away.

"LT—just what did he tell you in that little chat before the fun group exercise?" Jack asked.

"He told me 'I don't care if the shit drowns,' Doc. I think that's exactly what he expected," LT replied as he slapped Jack on the back. "He's a son of a bitch, Doc, that's all I got to say. A real mother fucker."

CHAPTER TWENTY-SEVEN

Riley had been lucky, covering over 1,300 miles in just two days. She found fuel in Cameroon just before entering Chad and three times in Chad.

The Toyota began having the bucking sensation of an engine caught between gulping fuel and sniffing fumes 80 miles down Route 3 in Sudan, and for the first time on the journey, Riley had a sinking feeling. The FJ sucked fuel with the enthusiasm of a college freshman at his first kegger, but it was as good of a ride as she could have hoped for, so she stuck with it, despite passing thousands of abandoned vehicles on her journey. And gas was free—when there was a station.

Three minutes later, the Cruiser coughed to a halt and died, exsanguinated of petrol. She climbed out and, squinting against the brightness, reached back in the FJ, grabbed her wrap-around sunglasses, and put them on. The drive left her as stiff as she could ever remember, but she suspected she was on the front end of a long workout. After stretching a bit, she opened the back of the vehicle and emptied her pack of clothing and other non-essentials. As she tossed the soap aside, she wondered how a hot shower could be considered non-essential. She could smell herself, and while she was no girly girl, it caused her to grimace. *Jesus.*

She filled the pack with as much liquid as she could carry, and as she slung it on her back, she saw her camera. She hesitated for a moment, pondering if the extra weight would be worth it. She decided it would be, especially once she got to Mto Wa Mbu. She strapped the camera case around her waist.

She looked around and noticed a small shack about 50 yards off the road from the SUV. It didn't appear that anyone was around, and if there were, they would only be children. It was the worst time of day to be on foot — about 100° and would only get hotter as the day progressed — so she walked off the highway, down the embankment, and over to the shanty. There was either no door, or it was swung wide open, the cool, dark interior inviting her in. Riley didn't think a swimming pool could be better at the moment.

She stopped at the edge of the doorway and slid the pack off her shoulders, letting it half fall to the ground. She stepped into the darkness of the small building. Her sunglasses made it too dark to see anything. As she reached up to remove the sunglasses, she heard a shuffling noise. *Maybe a kid playing in the dirt?*

She reached up and partially lowered her glasses, peering over the top and reflexively stiffening when her eyes connected to what she had heard: a cobra at eye level, less than three feet away, in the corner of the shack. Her mind went blank for a moment, her heart beating as if it were about to gallop out of her mouth. She took a slow step backward. She noticed the black band around the serpent's neck—it was a black-necked spitting cobra, recognizable from the jet-black head and throat that abruptly transitioned to the tannish color of the body. Before WNN deployed her to sub-Saharan Africa, she'd taken a course on African wildlife, a primer of sorts, the type of thing that is typically useless to people. But then, most reporters don't end up trekking alone through the Sudanese high-dessert en route to Tanzania.

She remembered the tall, scruffy, blonde-haired, twenty-something from the local zoo that had taught the course. He was one buff kid. She'd thought about getting his number after the course but figured she was headed to Africa. *What's the point?*

The zoo guy made a big point that the black-neck could bite but preferred to spit its venom, resulting in the victim's blindness. *I'm screwed if I'm blinded out here in the middle of goddam nowhere.*

She had not lowered her hand from the bow of her sunglasses, so she slowly raised them back into place but realized she couldn't see the snake at all now. *A fucking catch-22: glasses down, it blinds me. Glasses up, it bites me.*

She continued backing up slowly. The edge of the doorway came into her peripheral vision. *Just another foot, and I'm free to run.* As she raised her left heel and continued to move backward, she noticed the cobra's head cock ever so slightly back and up. She lost all interest in slow movement, jamming the glasses over her eyes as she felt a spray of warm venom bathe her face and arms. Her back slammed into the side of the doorway and a nail head sticking an inch out of the wood punctured her flank, the pain shooting deep, radiating up to her shoulder. She turned and ran, the nail ripping her flesh, creating a jagged opening from her flank to her ribs as she exploded into the sunlight. The venom running down the eyepieces obscured her vision. As she ran in the direction of the road, she ripped the glasses off her face, the sudden brightness clawing at her retinas, making it impossible to see anything but the gross outline of the Toyota. She tripped and fell over a short shrub, screaming as she imagined the snake descending on her. She scrambled up and continued to the Toyota. Climbing in, she slammed the door.

She was out of breath but safe inside the SUV, which was as hot as a sweat lodge. She sobbed, trying to catch her breath, consciously willing herself to be quiet. Calming somewhat, she looked out across the short, brown stretch between her and the shack. Until now, she hadn't appreciated that the SUV's windows were tinted, and it seemed odd to her that it had escaped her notice. She squinted in concentration, scanning the land between the shack and the Toyota, anxiously looking for signs of the snake. There was no discernible movement. She slumped back into the seat, not recalling it being this comfortable in the 1,300 miles leading up to this moment.

She leaned back against the headrest and contemplated closing her eyes when she realized the Toyota's tailgate was still open. As she glanced in the rearview mirror, she heard a hiss and saw the snake's head appear.

Riley's flight response kicked out adrenaline, resulting in near panic. She frantically groped for the door handle, clumsy with terror. The snake struck with frightening quickness. She didn't see it but heard its neck slam into the top of the SUV's seat, just missing her left shoulder, too far away for its fangs to enter her skin. Crying and screaming, flailing at the door, her hands finally found the door lever as the snake positioned for another strike. The latch disengaged, and Riley kicked with both feet, causing the door to fly open violently. The snake lunged, again and again, was thwarted by the headrest as Riley scrambled out. The door rebounded hard against its hinges, the bottom edge slicing across her shins. She felt the impact, but the terror allowed no pain to register as she sprinted down the highway, looking over her shoulder as if a pack of African wild dogs had been loosed after her.

Riley had no idea how far she ran before slowing to a fast jog and eventually a walk. The door had opened the skin of her shins in wide, surgical-like incisions, and blood had filled her shoes, the red liquid coagulating around her feet. The clots made it feel like she was walking in warm mud and made a squishing sound with every step.

As her pace slowed, her objective mind returned, taking an understandable leave of absence during the reptilian encounter. She realized how hot it was and how profusely she was sweating from running in the heat for the first time. Then she remembered the backpack filled with yummy wet things to drink on the ground back at the local herpetarium. *Crap.*

Riley stood in the middle of the road for a few minutes, pondering her predicament. *I'm in the middle of the Sudanese desert in 100-plus degree heat and no living adults on the continent. I have nothing to drink, there's not a vehicle in sight, and the sun will be up at least another six hours. Perfect. What a way for a rescue mission to end.*

CHAPTER TWENTY-EIGHT

Jack was being shaken awake by LT. He squinted from the light streaming in from the hallway. He looked at his watch—4:30 a.m.

"Doc, you gotta come see this," LT said. "More shit's hittin' the fan."

"Huh?" Jack said, half asleep.

"The Middle East is goin' down now," said LT.

Instantly awakened by the comment, Jack pulled on his jeans and accompanied LT to the kitchen. Bugger, Shark, Greaser, and Manny were glued to the TV. The banner at the bottom of the screen said, DEATH IN THE MIDDLE EAST.

"Turn it up, Bugger," Jack said.

"No one can remember the last time there were so few worshippers at morning prayer in Masjid al-Haram, the largest mosque in the world, the very heart of Mecca, in Saudi Arabia," the voice of a British female reporter said, sounding like she was reporting from a bathroom stall. "Usually, several thousand people would be here on their knees at sunrise, and, depending on the time of year, as many as one million would show up for prayers. But the square is nearly devoid of life. With the sun now up, you can see devotees are lying face down in odd positions, and most aren't moving." The camera focused on a worshipper who paused and looked down at a kneeling man as if he recognized the fellow. He reached down and put his hand on the man's back, gently shaking him as if he thought him asleep. The body toppled onto its side, the camera zooming in to focus on the man's eyes, fixed in a death mask.

"As the sun has continued to rise, the fear that the African infection would arrive in Saudi has now become a reality." The camera panned back, revealing hundreds of worshippers frozen in position. "This small group of men found themselves surrounded by death. The heart-wrenching sound our viewers hear in the background are groans of agony—grief on a wholesale scale. It has grown louder in the short time I have been on the air with you, not because it is coming closer, but because new voices are joining the painful chorus, people waking up to death. Just days after an unknown pathogen annihilated western Africa, death has laid siege to the Middle East." The camera focused on the reporter dressed in MOPP.

"It's a familiar pattern: death, mourning, and a public health disaster on a scale that every citizen of the globe is now well versed. It's now clear that those beyond Africa—all of us—are no longer safe." She pauses.

"Many scientists hoped whatever this is would be like COVID, only this time it was going to stay put, where it originated. There had been hopes that NATO's fastidious use of MOPP gear in cleaning up the mess would stop the disease's transmission at the water's edge of Africa, and the CDC's rapid response team's recommendation of antiretrovirals was going to work." She paused dramatically and looked over each shoulder. "Now this, the end—*Yawm ad-Din*—Judgment Day in Islam, without Allah, without trumpets, no earthquakes crushing mountains, the sun isn't dying. Only people," she said as she swept her hand in a circular motion in emphasis.

She continued, walking tentatively among the dead bodies. "The only plausible explanation is person-to-person transmission, and many are blaming the African governments, the world's health authorities, for reacting sluggishly — especially in the aftermath of the recent pandemic. In the global confusion and stunned inaction that followed the early reports of mass death in Africa, the borders to the Arabian peninsula were not closed to travel—they remained open for a week, and the ferries from Eritrea and Somalia to Yemen ran uninterrupted in the days following Mto Wa Mbu. Death ascended north and eastward, and infected adults surely traveled to Saudi Arabia, or throughout the Middle East, for that matter. Jumping off the ferry, they could wander around Aden, a Yemen city of nearly one million people, spreading the infectious agent in the densely crowded open-air markets. Any number of asymptomatic, infected individuals could have dispersed throughout the peninsula, creating a huge number of illness vectors from a single African ferry rider."

Another pause, her hand reaching to her ear as she listened to her earpiece. She looked back at the camera, "We are receiving reports that, curiously, there are fewer deaths in Israel and that most of those deaths are of Middle Eastern origin. It's important to note that Israel closed all borders on day one, the government quickly isolating Palestinians to prevent spread."

The reporter droned on, "Global paranoia is palpable. With the Middle Eastern oil supply under NATO control, China, Japan, the Koreas, and much of the old Soviet empire are understandably anxious. If NATO, under U.S. command, wanted to, it could cut off oil to the rest of the world. It's diplomatically sensitive, but the controlling parties have thus far understood not only the political necessity of continuing to supply the world but the practical realities. There is an understanding of the interdependence that has grown between countries, and it's in no one's interests to have a war over oil, especially when so much chaos is already permeating the world."

While the reporter spoke, banners scrolled at the bottom of the screen:

Assistance to 300 million Middle Easterners spread thin; NATO Troop supply running low.

Smoke from funeral pyres reminiscent of Desert Storm and Saddam's burning of oil rigs; odor described as "horrific."

Saudi Arabia's massive oil tanker Ab Qaiq, crew dead, runs aground near the African Cape; 20 miles of De Hoop Nature Reserve coastline oil-covered.

Again, the reporter paused, putting a hand against her gas mask, listening.

"Ladies and gentlemen, a new development. We are getting reports of widespread deaths around the Grand Mosque of Paris and throughout the Arab community in that city. The French government suspects recent immigrants have carried the disease into these communities. The relative segregation maintained by these immigrant subgroups may be protecting the rest of the citizenry. To ensure they remain isolated, French troops in MOPP gear similar to what I am wearing have quarantined the area in the hope of preventing further spread. The ease of global travel is threatening the entire world."

"Goddam North Koreans! I hope they're fucking sweating about this. At least it's headed their direction instead of ours," Greaser said.

LT said, "Coffee's ready. Anybody want some?" His lack of concern was at once reassuring and unnerving to Jack.

Jack stood up. "Yeah, I do. No sense in going back to bed. What's on the training slate today, LT?"

"Skydiving," LT said, deadpan.

"Skydiving?" Jack said. "For real?" Jack had always wanted to skydive.

"Yup. You're going to get a crash course in HALO, Doc," LT said.

"HALO?"

"High altitude, low opening." Jack didn't like the sound of those words used in the same sentence.

"And would that lesson be didactic?" Jack asked.

"Yes, this morning is didactic," LT said.

"Meaning?" Jack asked.

"This afternoon is practical. And yeah, I mean you'll be jumping with all of us. And unfortunately, you need to get it right in one try because we're on our way to North Korea tomorrow. You'll be in the lab the following night," LT said. Jack knew his blood pressure was rising from the pounding in his head. He looked around at his teammates. They looked bored.

"How high? And how far do we free fall?" Jack asked.

"Oh, 35,000 feet is where we're gonna be jumping from, and we'll open the chutes at 3,500 feet. We use gliding chutes to hit the landing target on the ground," Manny said. "It's awesome!" His tone was gleeful.

"Is this another surf torture thing—to see if the professor can hack it? Or is this important to the actual mission?" Jack said.

LT looked down, scratched his temple, and said, "Jack, this isn't just important to the mission. The whole damn thing depends on it. If we can't drop into the research compound, there's no mission."

Suddenly, skydiving seemed less thrilling to Jack. "So we're going to skydive into the compound? A compound that's in the mountains? In North Korea?" Jack said.

"Yeah," LT said.

"Goody. I've always wanted to do that," Jack said, shaking his head. "OK. Any more surprises?"

"Nope. That's the last one, Doc. She's a doozy, though, huh?" Manny said. "We'll teach you all ya need to know this morning, and we'll jump this afternoon. Smart as you are, Doc, it'll only take one jump for you to get 'er down. Promise." Jack looked at Manny skeptically.

"Look, Doc, you hadn't ever done surf torture either, and you handled it. This'll be a cakewalk for you," LT said. "We have the best equipment there is — the gear is warm, the oxygen bottles we use are state-of-the-art, and the chutes are easy to steer."

"Jesus, I'm glad Marla doesn't know about this," Jack said. "She'd kill me. Assuming, of course, I don't end up as a bloody splotch first."

Jack spent the rest of the morning learning about HALO jumps—double- and triple-checking equipment, turning the O2 on, hyper-oxygenating before the jump, how to steer the chute. He could recite the steps of the process by lunchtime.

"But why does it have to be high altitude? I mean, can't we jump right over the compound or have a helicopter drop us in or—hell—anything but..." Jack said, tilting his head toward the video screen looping HALO technique.

"Doc, it would give us away before we ever hit the ground. Choppers are noisy. And, believe it or not, a regular 'ol low altitude parachute opening can be heard from a long ways away, as would a plane dropping us. Gives up the element of surprise," Greaser said, the one in the group most excited about jumping.

"Doc, you're a smart man. Most of what's involved is intellectual— learning how to do it. You can learn this stuff easy, compared to what you do for a living! And later today, you'll practice with us," LT emphasized.

"Anything else?" Jack asked. "If we aren't going to jump right over the compound, then where do we jump from?"

"Ya saw in the video that the chutes we use are gliders. We're going to glide in, Doc," Greaser said.

"From how far away?" Jack said.

"Don't know. They'll tell us when we're on our way. The chutes will let a guy go about 20 miles from the drop, though, and since you travel at 50 to 60 kilometers per hour, it don't take long to get where you wanna be," Greaser said.

Several hours after lunch and one last quiz, Jack and the SEALs walked up the back of a C-2 Greyhound cargo plane dressed in specialized, skin-tight, black MOPP suits. The rest of the gear was already aboard the plane. They buckled into bench seats and were soon gently circling upward like a falcon on a hot air current. They started putting on their gear about 15 minutes after take-off, checking themselves, then doing buddy checks.

LT motioned for Jack to come closer. "Doc, see this?" LT was pointing to what looked like a small black button on one of the chest straps of the parachute.

"Yeah," Jack responded.

"This is an infra-red beacon. It isn't visible unless you use night vision goggles," LT said. "There's an identical beacon on the back of the parachute pack."

"OK," Jack said. "But we're jumping in broad daylight. Why are you telling me this?"

LT hesitated. Jack sensed this couldn't be good. "Because, Jack, we're jumping at night." Jack's expression didn't change. Nothing could surprise him at this point.

"Well, this just fuckin' keeps gettin' better, LT," Jack said, giving up and just grinning.

LT slapped him on the back. "That's the spirit, Doc!"

Speakers crackled alive, and the pilot announced they were five minutes from jump altitude—35,000 feet. When Jack thought of skydiving, he imagined 5,000 feet. He was going to be jumping, for the first time, at a height seven times that. He put on the jump helmet. It looked like the head of a praying mantis.

"We're going to be jumping seven miles off the target, Doc. We'll show you how to free fall to get within a couple of miles of the landing zone before pulling the cord and gliding the last two miles for an easy touchdown," LT said.

"Three minutes," the pilot said. "Doors opening." As the back of the aircraft began to open, the men grabbed onto the bar running along the length of the plane's fuselage. Jack could feel the drag on the aircraft, caused by the rear platform dropping down from the plane's belly.

"Thirty seconds," the disembodied voice said. Jack looked at LT, who gave him the thumbs-up sign. Jack returned the gesture more confidently than he felt. His stomach had butterflies the size of condors.

"Five...four...three...two... one... GO!" the voice said.

Manny was the first one out, followed by Greaser and Bugger. Jack was intentionally fourth. There would be three SEALs in front of him and two behind him if he got into trouble during the free fall.

Jack dove off the plane's platform as if jumping off a dock into Clinton Lake outside of Lawrence. Initial terror morphed into fascination and curiosity. It wasn't as cold as he thought it would be, and the view was stunning. Looking down at the earth from 35,000 feet in a 737 window seat was one thing. It was life-altering to see it while free falling. *This is fun!*

After a few moments of wonderment, Jack looked to his left and saw Shark, who gave him the two-fingered sign to keep his eyes on the two SEALs below him. Jack acknowledged with a thumbs-up. He tilted his body downward and accelerated down toward Manny and Greaser. Shark and LT did the same, slowing to hover in formation just above Jack to each side. Dropping from seven miles above ground at the terminal speed of 126 miles per hour, they rapidly closed the seven-mile gap to two as they approached the 3,500-foot mark. At 4,500 feet, Manny, below everyone else, held his arms out in a T indicating everyone should spread out and prepare to open their chutes. Jack glanced at the altimeter on his wrist. He couldn't believe how fast it was twirling.

Manny's chute opened. Jack pulled his ripcord. The chute flew out of its pack, and he went from 126 MPH to about 20, jerking his torso violently, causing momentary disorientation. He was surprised the boots didn't fly off his feet from the deceleration. He saw two SEALs in front of him, about 500 yards to his left and below. He steered toward them, lining himself up to follow them to the landing zone. After minutes of gentle gliding, he relaxed, and it became enjoyable again, at least until he remembered why he had to learn this in the first place. He thought about what LT had told him on the flight up. *We're going to be jumping over North Korea at night.* Jack immediately appreciated the challenge this added to the mission—to his survivability. *I won't be able to see anything — or anybody. Shark can't tell me to focus. Manny won't be able to warn me that it's about time to open my chute. Jesus...*

The ground was swelling up toward the jumpers, their target a 50-square-yard patch of dirt at the edge of the base. Manny was already down. Jack had lined up reasonably well behind Bugger, but he could see he was still to the right of the landing zone as he approached. He pulled the left cord and aimed for the center of the dirt patch. The landing zone, which had been the size of a postage stamp just seconds before, was growing at an alarming rate, and Jack was still pulling hard, trying to line up for the middle. He quickly realized he was too low to continue correcting his path, so he straightened up for touchdown. He touched down, hard, on the far right corner of the landing zone. Had it been a walled compound, he might well have smashed into the wall.

He stood up, brushed himself off, and started gathering up his chute. Manny walked over to help.

"Doc, not bad for your first jump!" he said. "Lemme help you with this today. When we hit the ground in Korea, you'll just unbuckle and leave the whole mess for the North Koreans to clean up."

"Thanks," Jack said. He was wondering if he would survive to unbuckle the damn thing. "Manny, how big is the landing zone in North Korea?"

"It's the same size as this, Doc, maybe a little smaller. You're gonna do fine," Manny said. Jack wondered if he was just blowing smoke up his backside. He figured he was, but he was appreciative of the encouragement. He was beginning to understand why they never lost a man. *They really are a team. These nail-tough men care about each other.*

Half an hour later, the incursion force was back at the barracks, debriefing. "OK, guys, not bad," LT said. "What went well?"

"We all hit the mark," said Greaser.

"Yes. Excellent job, everyone," LT affirmed. No one else seemed to have much to say. "What needs to be better next time?" Initially, there was silence.

Shark raised his hand. LT nodded at him. "Doc, you need to be focused the whole time, buddy. I know it was your first jump and all, but our next jump is at night over North Korea. A few seconds could mean the difference between making it down alive — or not. I mean, I don't wanna be an asshole or anything, but..."

"No, Shark. You're right. I wasn't focused. At least not the whole time," Jack said. "I'll be focused tomorrow night. Promise." The group was silent. Jack knew they were wondering if he could do this if he would lose focus. If he didn't make it, it would put the entire mission—hell, maybe the whole world—in jeopardy.

"OK, then, let's grab some chow," LT said. "I want you all to take it easy after dinner and hit the rack early to be ready for tomorrow."

After a hearty, protein-heavy meal and the single beer they were each allowed, Jack felt a hard, sound sleep ahead. He felt particularly thankful for this luxury and savored the bubbly bitterness against his grilled steak. The meal made him feel like he was becoming one of the team. They even joked a bit. He marveled at this group of exceptional individuals who seemed nonplused by the mission they were about to embark upon. He knew, in their way, they must surely be nervous. How could one not be? Nervous, maybe, but ultimately, totally confident in their abilities. It gave him a sense of comfort in his role. He had gained a new perspective on the military in just a few days. These men, professionals in their work, had not only welcomed him in but had befriended him and were doing all they could to protect him—to help him survive.

He was about to turn in when there was a knock on his door.

"Yes?" Jack said.

Bugger stuck his head in the door. "Hey, Doc, let's go play with the night vision stuff! Bet you've never seen anything like our toys!" His love of cool technology trumped his tiredness.

"Sure, I wanna hit the hay soon, but I'd love to see what you got," Jack said. "Besides, it sounds like it isn't just a 'let's go play with this toy' bonding experience, considering we're jumping into North Korea at night."

"Yeah. This is your private tutorial, Doc. If you don't know how to use these things by tomorrow night, you'll end up in a North Korean gulag—if you survive," he said, handing Jack night vision goggles as they walked out into the darkness.

LT gathered the SEALs together in his room after Jack was asleep. "All right, guys, I need to know where your heads are regarding Doc. I want honesty."

"He has a snowball's chance in hell of making it down alive, much less landing in the compound," Manny said, brows creased in concern.

"I'd have to second that, LT. He spaced out after we jumped. If he loses sight of us in the daylight, how the hell is he going to keep track of us at night?" Shark said.

"You're being pretty harsh on him, guys," LT said. "He's taken everything we've thrown at him. And he's smart. He'll be focused, make it down, and complete the mission."

"And just what the hell do we do if we end up there without him?" Bugger said.

LT paused. He pursed his lips, looked down, and shook his head. Looking up, he said, "Ya just grab as much shit as you can and bug out."

CHAPTER TWENTY-NINE

Marla woke up exhausted. If she didn't know better, she would have thought she was pregnant, but that wasn't possible. She was on birth control, and she and Jack had agreed before they even moved in together that children weren't something they wanted.

She dragged herself out of bed with dramatic emphasis, enjoying the moment as if she were playing for an audience, or at least for Jack, had he been home. She stretched, stood up, and walked to the kitchen. She picked up the mug she had set by the Mr. Coffee, programmed the night before, and poured a cup. After adding milk, she glanced out the window, pausing to listen to the sounds of the morning through the open window. A meadowlark was sitting atop a small lilac bush, just feet from the window, chirping merrily, oblivious to the issues crushing down upon the human world.

Given the state of the world, she was confident the news would hold no surprises. *How could it get worse?* She picked up the iPad, and it sprang to life.

She tapped on the news app. The headline was predictable: MIDDLE EAST CHAOS. She shook her head in compassion for unknown victims. She didn't read beyond the fact that millions had died in the past 24 hours. Over a billion in the last month. It was similar to headlines she read daily— only the numbers and places were different.

Scanning the article, she noticed a diagram thumbnail titled, *Map of the Infection's March.* She tapped it, and it enlarged, illustrating the timeline of death from Africa to the Middle East, with black dots marking death's path, numbered in the order in which the areas were infected. She started to close the diagram and stopped, her heart accelerating. She felt weak, dropped the iPad on the table, and stood up, hands on either side of it, looking down. Her eyes quickly scanned the map of the sequence of the affliction, slapping her hand to her forehead. *Jesus...*

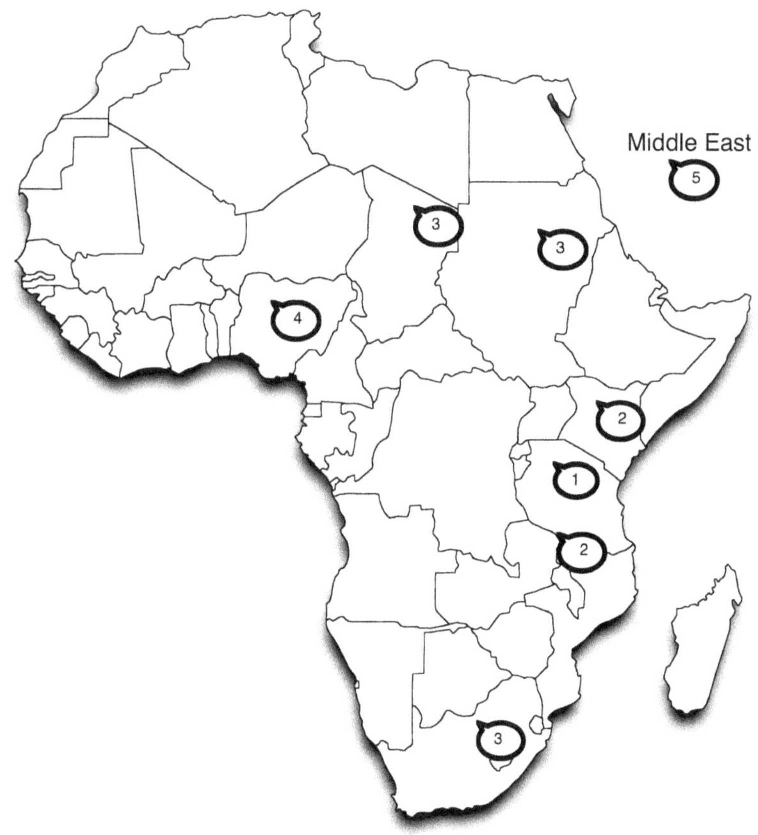

Her first instinct was to call Jack, but she had no way to reach him. *I've got to call Catherine.* She scrambled to find the number and dialed Catherine's cell phone. It felt like it rang an infinite number of times before Catherine picked up.

"Hello?" Catherine said.

"Catherine! It's me, Marla—you know, Jack Cann's wife."

"I know who you are, Marla, but I'm kinda busy here..." Catherine said.

"I'm not sure, but I think I have some information—or at least a theory—that I need to bounce off you," Marla said. "At the very least, it's a huge clue, that is, if you haven't already figured it out."

"What the hell are you talking about, Marla," Catherine said edgily.

"I saw a map in the news chronicling the sequence and locations of the infection. It's identical to the path of early human migration out of Africa."

Catherine was silent. Marla didn't know if she was pissed or pondering.

"Keep going, Marla."

"OK. The first deaths were in the Olduvai region of Tanzania, right? Mto Wa Mbu was followed by deaths up and down Eastern Africa. Two weeks or so later, it was all along western Africa: Sudan, Chad, Niger, and Nigeria. And yesterday, it hit the Middle East," Marla said. "Catherine, the infection—or whatever the hell it is—is following humanity's evolutionary migratory path out of Olduvai."

"Jesus..." Catherine whispered. "So, you mean..."

"Yes, Catherine. We may be able to predict where death is going to strike next if I'm correct."

"Jack sure picked a shitty time to be out of contact," Catherine said.

"What do you mean, Catherine? You sent him back to Africa two days ago, didn't you?" Marla said. The silence told them each that they had no idea where Jack was. Marla felt instantaneously nauseous.

"Marla, I'm sending a plane for you. You've just been appointed to the RRT as an emergency member. Pack your bags. They'll be there in four hours."

CHAPTER THIRTY

The RRT members were sitting around the table, new faces intermingling. Catherine had informed the President of the new theory, and he had sent the Health and Human Services secretary, the surgeon general, his chief of staff, and the deputy chairman of the Joint Chiefs of Staff to the meeting.

There were other men and women in the room, some in military garb, including a two-star general. They all were very serious and severe-looking as if they had never heard a joke in their life. If there was a more intimidating audience, Marla couldn't imagine it. The chrysalis dangling in her stomach hatched, blossoming into a full-fledged butterfly. It felt like a giant swallowtail. Mild nausea washed over her.

Catherine was not intimidated. "Good morning, ladies and gentlemen," she said as she walked without pause to one of the end seats. She leaned forward slightly, put her hands on the table, and looked around the room.

"You all are aware that Jack Cann, a virologist, has played key roles in the development of H1N1 and HIV research. More recently, he made critical discoveries leading to the COVID vaccine. He has been on my consultant panel at the CDC and a rapid response team member for years. Beside me is Dr. Marla Qui, a Ph.D. physical anthropologist, who, either out of desperation or just poor judgment, married Jack." She nodded towards Marla and smiled. The humor helped Marla relax a bit.

Catherine continued. "I have invited Dr. Qui to join the RRT." The other RRT members looked at each other in surprise, not informed of this new development. Catherine continued. "Earlier today, Marla noticed something extraordinary about the situation in Africa and the Middle East. Marla, please take it from here." Catherine motioned for Marla to come to the front of the room. A large screen TV was on the wall behind her, and Catherine flipped open a laptop and clicked the mouse. Marla's first slide displayed the world and the migration paths of humans outward from Olduvai in Africa.

"Thank you, Dr. Montoya. Could the lights be dimmed a bit, please?" A middle-aged woman leaned back in her chair and flipped two switches, and every other light in the room darkened. "Thank you. Here we have a map of the world. Homo sapiens originated about 200,000 years ago, here, in Olduvai Gorge, in what's now Tanzania." She pointed to the area on the map. "This is also where the first wave of deaths occurred." She paused and looked up, facing a room full of unflinching faces in dim light. It wasn't like a class in Lawrence where you could see from the students' faces if they got it or not, and it sure as hell wasn't the Freestate Brewery.

"From the Olduvai region, the humans spread out along these lines," she said, pointing to northeastern and southern Africa. "Then, about 70,000 years ago, humans migrated into western Africa, the second major migration wave. About 50,000 years ago, humans made it to the Middle East. During that period, they moved down through Southeast Asia, including India, Pakistan, Myanmar, Thailand, Cambodia, and so forth, all the way into Australia. They migrated into China, Mongolia, and what used to be the Soviet Union about 30,000 years ago. Man hit eastern Europe about 20,000 years ago and made it across the Bering Strait during the last ice age, about 12,000 to 15,000 years ago, populating North and South America last."

"Very nice anthropology lesson, sweetheart," a voice said from the back, raspy from years of tobacco abuse. "But what's the point?"

Marla recoiled at the condescending tone of the man's voice and the word *sweetheart*, anger rising in her chest. Her fear of being in front of a strange audience evaporated. She responded without even a hint of anger.

"Sir, please don't call me sweetheart. It's unprofessional, so let's all agree that we won't be using that kind of speech moving forward." Marla noticed Catherine smirking in the darkness. *She must love a good smackdown when she sees it.* Marla looked around. The faces were still stern but nodding in agreement.

"Good," she said. Her confidence solidified, and she continued in a much more authoritative voice.

"The point of this is that the order in which populations are being affected by the infection — dying — is following the same path of early human migration. The first deaths were reported here," she said as she pointed to the Olduvai region. "From this point, death spread south to South Africa, and east and north—into Kenya, Ethiopia, Somalia, Sudan—covering every place in Africa except the west. There was a brief pause in the deaths, and then, a little more than two weeks after the last deaths in the east, western Africa was hit, millions more dying."

"But would the delay simply be due to the time it takes for an infected individual to get over to western Africa?" one of the military women asked.

"Well," Marla said, "that's possible, but if whatever is happening was only because of an infectious agent, I would have expected the Middle East to have been infected before western Africa because of proximity. It's closer to the epicenter where this started." The woman nodded in understanding.

"Now we have the Middle East, millions more dead. Now, here's the really interesting part of the theory," Marla said. "The Middle East was affected within the two-day timeframe I would have predicted it to have been."

"What the *hell* do you mean that *you* predicted? How on God's green earth could you predict something like that?" challenged a middle-aged man with gray hair in a marine haircut. He was ex-military, now part of the CIA's biological warfare intelligence group. "I mean, people are dying. How could you possibly predict when they will die?"

"What's interesting—as well as terrifying—about this is that not only are the deaths following the migratory path of early humans, but the time frames are similar, proportionally, to the original migration dates. In other words, there was a bit of a delay in death between East and West Africa, just like there was a delay in the original migration. There was another delay —a really short one—between West Africa and the Middle East, but it is proportionally correct—to within about a half-day," Marla explained.

"Is this good or bad news," asked a woman with a remarkably squeaky voice in comparison to her broad, stumpy body.

"It's good news because we can roughly predict *where* the next wave of death will occur and possibly *when* it will happen," said Marla.

"Young lady, how could you possibly figure out when the next wave would come? It sounds impossible," said an older gentleman, who was wearing a sharp-cut blue suit, white shirt, and a red power tie.

"It is just a simple calculation. Man first showed up 200,000 years ago, in eastern Africa, right? The migration to western Africa happened about 70,000 years ago, 130,000 years after man developed in Olduvai Gorge. The next major migration to the Middle East from northeastern Africa was only 20,000 years later. The period between eastern and southern Africa being wiped out and the spread of the entity to western Africa was 13 days. If we make the assumption—and it is an assumption — that time today is relative to time between human migrations in the past, then all we have to do is calculate how many days 20,000 years translates into." Marla grabbed a marker, walked over the dry erase board and wrote out the math, the onlookers slack-jawed.

20,000 years = 7,300,000 days
130,000 years = 47,450,000 days

47,450,000/7,300,000 = 13/x where "x" will be the predicted number of days between western Africa and the Middle East

x = (13 x 7,300,000)/47,450,000
x = 2 days

"In other words, the Middle East was affected when the equation would have predicted," Marla said, circling the two days on the board.

Seeing the math agitated the audience. They were beginning to understand that this physical anthropology professor from Kansas knew what she was doing.

"So the calculation was accurate," Marla concluded.

The general asked, "Dr. Qui, do you think we can rely on these calculations?"

"Well, general, we are dealing with assumptions—but they seem pretty accurate so far, considering we are extrapolating from tens of thousands of years down to days in present time. Of course, there may be some inaccuracies with the predictions, moving forward," Marla said.

"Based upon your model, Dr. Qui, where should we be focused next?" the general asked.

"It is likely to affect India, Pakistan, the Pacific Rim countries, maybe even Australia."

"When? How long do we have to prepare for that?" asked the squeaky-voiced woman. Marla swallowed hard. She didn't even want to hear the answer she was going to give. "If the current evolutionary migration theories are accurate, these areas were all populated about the same period as the Middle East. It is unlikely that people were in each of these areas exactly 50,000 years ago. Rather, they likely took years, hundreds, maybe thousands of years, to spread across these geographic regions. So, it should be..." Marla took a deep breath, "Any time now."

The hum of the laptop was suddenly abnormally loud. Life on earth is imploding.

A slender man with Asian features spoke. It was the president's Chief of Staff, Thomas Nakamoro. "Dr. Qui, if this is correct, then you're telling us that, in a matter of weeks, the United States is likely to experience the same thing as these other regions?" Marla nodded her head in affirmation and said, "We're already seeing it, Mr. Nakamoro. African immigrants, as you and everyone else know, have been dying for weeks."

The general, a take-charge kind of guy, boomed in, "Well, goddamit!' What do you know that's helpful? Any ideas as to what it is?"

"We have some theories," Catherine said. "The first is the most obvious and, we think, the most likely. An infectious agent originated in the Olduvai region and has simply been spread by human-to-human transmission. Certainly, this wouldn't be the first time a new disease has cropped up in Africa. COVID is a pretty fresh example, and the spread pattern is strongly suggestive. However, as you all undoubtedly know, the researchers have not yet identified an infectious agent. Specimen quality has been poor." She paused and looked around the room. "We do know that whatever it is, is not responsive to antiretrovirals or the new COVID prevention meds. If it was, we should've seen a positive outcome in western Africa."

"Great! So we know a few ways *not* to treat it," the general said sarcastically.

Catherine continued. "The second theory is that it's infectious, but that susceptibility is somehow genetically pre-determined, and those having the closest roots to our African forefathers are most susceptible. That's why related ethnic populations in other countries may be dying while other races are spared. We're unsure why kids are spared, but it may also be related to genetics, in combination with an immature immune system. You are all familiar with our Stanford expert's theory on SIRS?"

A woman with short curly red hair and intensely green eyes asked, "What other theories are you considering?"

"Frankly, there are no other theories. Our main focus is to identify the infectious agent causing this. It's our opinion, as well as the opinion of many of our expert colleagues that this is viral." The room fell silent yet again.

The first person to stand was the general. "We have to get talking with Asian-based operatives. With everyone's permission, I would like to leave," he said as he stood. Everyone understood that his asking permission was rhetorical.

"Certainly, General. Is there some way we can stay in touch?" asked Catherine.

"I know where to find you, Dr. Montoya, and Colonel Surrey will be by your side, keeping us informed. Thanks for the consideration." He turned and quickly exited, dialing his cell phone as he walked out the door.

The remaining crew members milled about, talking in low voices for a few minutes, leaving in ones and twos. The room was empty except for the RRT. They sat in silence for a few moments; then Rick spoke up.

"You know what we need to do now, don't you? We need to set up shop in India. We need to be there when people start dying. We need specimens that have just dropped dead," he said.

"I know, Rick," Catherine said. "When Marla first told me her theory, I contacted the Indian prime minister. They already have what we need, so we're leaving in four hours."

Catherine picked up her briefcase, paused, and, turning back to the team, said, "Pack like you're never going to see home again."

CHAPTER THIRTY-ONE

Riley walked all night, motivated by the coolness and prodded by the fear of lying down on the same earth the snake had crawled upon. The moon provided just enough light for her to follow the highway, and she stayed dead center, fearing what might be lurking at the edges.

Her body hurt from the toenails up, including an incessant pounding in her head. Her tongue felt like moss drying in the August sun of Texas, and she was worried that even if she did find something to drink, it would never recover full function.

As the sun inched up over the eastern horizon, predictably, the temperature rose. She was surprised how rapidly it became unpleasant as she continued her trudge forward in a zombie-like state, only occasionally conscious of her thoughts. She hoped she would come across a village before it became so hot that the waves of heat rising off the asphalt obscured the distant horizon. It was still cool enough that the road in front of her was sharp, distant objects distinct. Unfortunately, it appeared to be an unbroken expanse of evermore sand and scrub brush, split down the center by a black ribbon leading deeper into hell.

Her wish came and went, the sun beating the pavement into giving up the heat it was absorbing, rising like waterless geysers. Her vision was no longer sharp, and she gave up trying to see down the road.

It wasn't just the pavement being pummeled by the sun; Riley knew she was getting seriously close to heat sickness. Dehydration made her lightheaded, and she began seeing things in front of her, but they disappeared as she approached. When she started hearing things, she thought she might as well just sit down and wait for the end. She heard the horn of an approaching vehicle, rubber tires whining against the blacktop. She giggled to herself—it was an irrational, high-pitched, cackling laugh. She wondered if she had lost it, deciding that the ability to ask the question indicated she had not. She sat down in the center of the road, facing east on Route 3, the direction she needed to go to get to Mto Wa Mbu. The pavement burnt her through her shorts, but she didn't care. She closed her eyes, hoping the auditory hallucination would disappear, but it kept getting louder and closer. The sound of the wheels stopped, but the engine was still audible, real. She just sat, rocking to and fro, wishing for it to stop.

She jumped up with incredible energy when she felt a tap on her shoulder, fearing a cobra had just bitten her. She couldn't see clearly, having had her eyes shut for some time. The mid-morning sun was suddenly flooding her eyes, but she was sure she saw a figure—a man, or rather a teenage boy. And a pickup truck, with kids standing in the truck bed peering over the cab and older kids leaning out the passenger's side window.

The boy that poked her spoke in a language she didn't recognize. He managed to communicate well enough with gestures for Riley to understand he wanted her to get in the truck. She shook her head in enthusiastic acceptance and asked him for water using her thumb and hand to illustrate a bottle with a neck, held to her cracking lips. He went to the truck cab, pulled out a waterskin, filled tight, and handed it to Riley. The vessel produced a welcome cool sensation as she cradled it in her palms, a preview of the sweet water that would rehydrate her tongue. She greedily glugged the water, sucking nearly a quarter of the skin's contents before lowering it from her lips. The boy reached for the skin, but Riley hoisted it again. After a few more gulps, she gave it up freely, suddenly conscious the children were watching her greedily dispose of their water supply. Her stomach felt full, and her body cooler. She climbed in the back of the pickup and sat down with the young children.

Eight hours of bouncing around a pickup bed on a rough African road wears on the soul, but Riley was inexpressibly joyous. The kids were very resourceful companions, finding water and Coca-Cola and other wonderful things to drink along the way to Wad Mandi on the west bank of the Blue Nile. The Sudanese city of nearly 350,000 had been reduced to a putrescent, above-ground cemetery. The odor of rotting humans was so thick that it was challenging for Riley to breathe, even with a handkerchief held to her face.

She signed to the driver, a wide-eyed teenager with a toothy smile and scar-pocked face, to let her off. He stopped, and Riley jumped out in a section of town close to a sign she saw pointing south and labeled Ethiopia. The children bid her goodbye in their language, and a flurry of arm waving and wide grins as the pickup continued on its journey.

Riley again went from car to car checking fuel levels— with the hope of finding one with air conditioning. She was about to give up when she saw a 1990s BMW painted an odd shade of pea green. It might have been a vintage auto, but it had been abused past any value other than essential function. It had a full tank and, blissfully, a functioning air conditioner. She pocketed the keys to prevent someone else from absconding with it and walked across the street to gather provisions for the remaining trek to Mto Wa Mbu, still 2,100 miles away. Riley piled rations into the front seat, got in, and headed south down Route 3.

CHAPTER THIRTY-TWO

Marla woke as the jet touched down, just before the sun was up at Mumbai's Chattrapathi Shivaji International Airport. It seemed like a lifetime since she left Lawrence, but it was only two days after the invisible assailant had rocked the Muslim world.

She huddled close to the small group of Americans as they were shunted through diplomatic security channels, avoiding the masses in the international arrivals terminal. The dreamlike sense Marla had was compounded by jet lag. The black stretch limousine, sent by the Indian prime minister, seeming bizarrely out of place, enveloped by poverty. She watched out the window as they whipped past slum after slum on the way to Breach Candy Hospital & Medical Research Centre in south Mumbai.

Icy cold air surrounded her as she walked into the hospital, leaving the humid Indian morning behind. She was handed an ID badge and then followed the group, led by an Indian Army captain, through multiple long hallways and many turns, finally heading down a dimly lit, dead-end corridor. About two-thirds of the way down the hall was an elevator, with security guards on each side, both armed with sub-machine guns. She stepped into the elevator with her colleagues. Always the anthropologist, Marla noticed that the eye-contact-avoiding-discomfort associated with elevators translated across cultures.

The doors closed silently, and they descended into the basement, the ride stopping with a lurch that made Marla's stomach flip. The doors began opening before the car had come to a complete stop.

Standing three feet from the door, arms crossed, was a hulking figure of a man with a broad, toothy grin and fire-red, curly hair as coarse as the fibers of a steel wire brush. Marla watched as he stuck out a hand the size of a child's baseball mitt, grabbed Catherine's hand, and shook it vigorously. This was repeated with Marla and the rest of the team.

"Welcome, y'all!" the man said with a Texas accent. Marla was surprised to hear the drawl in Mumbai and wondered if jet lag was already getting the better of her.

"My name's Ted. Ted Wright. I'm sort of a glorified project manager for y'all, with a scientific background, but probably pretty dense compared to y'all." There was a brief uncomfortable pause.

"Uhhh... anyway, it's about time you guys got here. I was getting a little worried that all our preparation here would be for not. It seems like the whole friggin' world is upside down, and the situation's spiraling way out of control. It feels a bit like all the shit's coming down on me. Well, probably you too, I 'imagine. Washington seems to think I walk on water from the get-things-done perspective. Hell, all they need to do is look at what these Indian folks did, and they'd relax a smidgen. Their lab is ready for damn near anything."

They followed Ted down a corridor, footsteps echoing against the cinderblock walls. Ted's cowboy boots made a ker-plopping sound that he seemed to particularly enjoy. Guards lined the hall, spaced about 20 feet apart, gazing unblinkingly at the wall on the opposite side.

"Ted, how did all this come about? I mean, if this complex is what you say it is, how is it that it came to be fitted to our needs," asked Rick.

"Well, boss, Dr. Montoya pretty much pulled a bunch of strings. You can do that as the head of the CDC, I guess. Anyway, I got my orders and was here in Mumbai two days ago to make sure stuff was gonna fit the bill. Maybe the good doctor could fill you in a bit."

Marla silently followed as they stepped through the doorway into a room the size of an oversized double-car garage. There was one door to the right with a sign over it reading: TO QUARTERS. The remaining wall space on each side of the room was lined with large lockers, each containing a full MOPP suit and NBC mask. There were *How to put on MOPP gear* diagrams every two feet above the lockers.

Ted said, "I think I should show you the quarters first." He pushed a red button, and the door slid open. "I think you'll be fairly comfortable here. Ain't no windows, and that kinda stinks, but all in all, 'most everything you need is here."

He pushed open another door that opened into a large room. "This is the commons area." A kitchen of near-industrial size and quality opened to a living area, complete with a large, flat-screen TV, ping-pong table, a bank of computers, and a long dining table and chairs. There were several sofas, easy chairs, and a wet bar with stools. "The bar is off-limits until 5:30 every night. Your meals will be prepared for y'all. Just tell them what you'd like." He continued walking toward a door across the room. They entered another hallway, about 50 feet long, with eight doors, four on each side. "These are your sleeping quarters. Each room has a complete bath, a desk with a computer, and a TV. Dr. Qui, I assumed you'd wanna stay with Dr. Cann when he gets here, so there's a double bed in the first room on the left," Ted said. "Now, why don't y'all check out your rooms for maybe fifteen minutes, then meet me in the commons area.

"Jack's coming here?" Marla asked, surprised, hopeful. "Where is he?"

Ted looked surprised. "Uh, I just assumed he was gonna be showin' up soon, Dr. Qui. Ain't he?" Marla knew the look of puzzled concern on her face told Ted everything he needed to know.

"Sorry," Ted said, avoiding her eyes.

"It's OK, Ted. I just thought you might..." Marla stopped.

Catherine said, "Wow, Ted. This is amazing. Thanks for your help." Marla appreciated her interjection. "Let's do as Ted suggested and freshen up a bit."

CHAPTER THIRTY-THREE

❝ Mr. President, we need a green light—a GO—for Operation Safari. I don't want the SEAL team getting on the damn plane only to end up aborting the mission and having them rot in a Chinese prison for the rest of their lives," said the general.

The only people in the room were the Joint Chiefs, the NSA Advisor, and Elaine Morrow. They were sitting, the president looking out the window at the Washington Memorial. Only the general seemed relaxed. This was his game. The NSA was fidgeting like a first-grader waiting for the end-of-school bell.

There was a knock at the door. "Come in," the president said, turning to look. A woman dressed in a black dress with a white apron entered, carrying a tray holding a sterling silver coffee pot, four coffee cups, and saucers. The general frowned as if this were a violation of a major military treaty.

"Ahhhhh... Ms. Sarnoff! Thank you for bringing the coffee," the president said.

"My pleasure, Mr. President."

The president waited for her to close the door. "Coffee, anyone?" he said with a nonchalance that seemed odd, considering the situation. He looked around. "No takers? Well, I need a cup," he said, pouring for himself.

"Mr. President?" said Elaine, as the president lifted the cup to his lips and took a sip.

"Boy, does the kitchen make a great cup," the president said.

"Mr. President, the SEALs are sitting in a box on the tarmac in Hyderabad waiting to be loaded onto a flight headed for Chinese airspace. I need your decision now. Is it green light—a GO? Or NO GO?"

The president took another sip of his coffee and thoughtfully, slowly, set the cup neatly into the saucer's groove. His smile faded as he put his hands together, index fingers pointing, and pressed them against his pursed lips. He picked up the cup, took another sip, and, as the cup touched the saucer, emitting the delicate clink of china against china, he said, "Operation Safari is a GO."

CHAPTER THIRTY-FOUR

Powan's black caterpillar-like eyebrows were furrowed in puzzlement. He flipped the paper on the clipboard back and forth several times, checking and re-checking. He loaded crates of cotton on the Changchun-bound Air India flight every day, but he had never loaded such a large crate before. One more look, and he climbed on the forklift, skewered the pallet underneath the huge wooden box, and pulled back on the hydraulic lever. The forks lifted the crate several feet off the ground with ease. It was taller than usual, so Powan had to peer around the side of the box to see where he was going.

He pulled up to the middle of the 747, the cargo hold gaping like a mouth ready to take a bite out of an oversized burrito. He lined up and simultaneously raised the fork to just above the floor level of the hold as he inched toward the plane. Skillfully, Powan lowered the pallet onto the rollers in the hold, and several coworkers pushed it deep into the belly of the aircraft, lashing it with thick nylon belts to metal rings on each side of the oversized box. As he pulled away, he thought these larger crates might be a good thing—fewer trips to load the plane.

Oddly, the next crate Powan approached was normal size, about a third the size of the one he had just loaded. He sighed, wondering why the company had decided to ship in the bigger crates, hadn't just switched all of them at once instead of complicating his life by mixing sizes. He shrugged his shoulders and kept loading.

An hour after the crates and 400 passengers were loaded, Powan watched flight 1129, engines whining, accelerating down the runway, and pulling away from Hyderabad's Rajiv Gandhi International Airport. He silently wished he could, someday, take the direct, eight-hour flight to Changchun, Jilin province's capital city, sitting among India's business elite while sipping a Taj Mahal lager and eating curry.

Jack wondered how the hell he'd managed to get himself into this mess. He wanted to kill the guy who'd loaded the crate. He wondered if the others were thinking about how nuts the whole damn thing was. He guessed not. The entire scene was surreal. It would have been even more bizarre had he known about the chicken tandoor and booze served a floor above them. The strangeness was compounded by the tiny, bright LED lights the SEALs had set up inside the crate, producing an odd luminosity.

When they took off from the Naval base, the team had only a vague idea about the plan. They were given the dirty details en route. Air India flight 1129 was a direct flight to Changchun, China, and just happened to fly directly over the Chinese-North Korean border before angling north, just 10 miles southwest of Baekdu Mountain. *We're going to jump out of a goddam commercial jet over remote mountains along the Chinese-North Korean border? At night?* The wave of nausea that came over him while hearing the plan was mild but unequivocally real, and while the lurching of the Navy plane could have caused it, he was pretty sure it was the implausibility of the mission. After a bit of introspection, he figured he was lucky: At least he wasn't feeling worse. The mission might result in his death—he figured he had a 30-70 chance of survival, just from the jump. If he did die, no one would ever know because none of them had a single piece of identification on themselves in case they were killed or captured. Still, he figured a 30 percent chance was better than the 100 percent likelihood of death if whatever the North Koreans had loosed on the world infected him.

For Jack's benefit, the team again went through all of the gear and how it worked. He knew how to shoot a rifle, but he was issued a handgun. They taught him to use a gun-shaped, battery-powered tool to remove the rivets from metal panels. They all had one. It seemed an odd bit of equipment for the SEALs. Jack thought they were all in trouble if he needed this in the North Korean lab.

They were dressed in pressurized, black, skin-tight, specially developed MOPP HALO jumpsuits. Each jumper had an oversized altimeter and GPS with luminescent dials lashed to their right wrist and synchronized atomic wristwatches on the left. They put their parachutes on and double-checked them before being packed into the crate, complete with oxygen canisters. Since they were jumping at night, their dive helmets had specialized night vision shields. Flip it down; it was on. Up, off.

The items needed for the mission had been divided between them, so they all were roughly the same weight—they all needed to descend to earth at approximately the same speed so they wouldn't be separated. They all carried a 9mm SIG Sauer P226 pistol with a suppressor—a silencer, in lay terms, as Jack was told when he asked what a suppressor was—and extra 9 mm clips. Jack had what seemed like a ton of clips for the SEAL's M4 assault rifles. Bugger was so damn big that the only thing he could carry and still not outweigh the others was a virus-loaded jump drive on a chain around his neck. No matter what it was, at least two of everything existed on two different bodies, including a second jump drive carried by LT. Jack and Shark each carried a specialized, temperature-regulated container of live tissue culture media for viruses and a self-contained incubation chamber for bacteria, each about the size of an eyeglass case.

Jack noticed a piece of equipment on LT's shoulder harness that none of the others had. He pointed to it. "What's that thing?"

"Just before we jump, I arm this little gizmo by pushing this button," LT said. He lifted a small, hinged plastic cap to reveal a black button. "It lets the NSA know it's time to point a satellite at the compound and fuck-up their electronics. It blinds them."

"It'll take out their monitors or something?" Jack asked.

"Exactly," LT said. "Didn't you see the little black boxes on the compound walls when we were looking at the photos?"

"Nope. Glad I didn't. You guys need to work on your communication! I mean, damn, fellas! This just seems to get more and more complicated the closer we get to Baekdu mountain," Jack said.

LT grinned. "Hey, we're paid to think on our feet and make shit up as we go," he said.

"Any other little minor details you've left out that might be important for me to know?" Jack said.

"Not that I can remember right now," LT said, still beaming in a manner Jack thought bordered on inappropriate, given where they were sitting. "Just remember to steer your fall toward the GPS—you're on track as long as the LED is green—if it isn't, the arrow will point you in the right direction."

Jack noticed LT constantly checking his altimeter. He figured it was because the cargo hold wasn't pressurized, confirmed when LT's altimeter read 10,000 feet, and he said, "OK guys, time to put on your helmets and turn on your oxygen — just about one-third of the way. Right now, you only need a little supplement — we need to save all we can. And turn on the helmet communicators."

Jack unhooked his helmet from the clip on his chest pack and put it on, again thinking about black praying mantis heads. He unclipped the top of his chest pack and turned the small black knob on the oxygen tank, and re-clipped the pack. He felt a cool breeze on his face inside the mask as the oxygen began flowing.

Again, Jack saw LT looking at the altimeter on his watch, so he looked at 35,000 feet. Cruising altitude.

"Time to go to work!" LT said, pointing at his wrist.

The SEALs untied their make-shift seat belts—metal rings bolted to the bottom of the crate and ropes—and opened a couple of black bags. Out came two black, battery-powered impact wrenches, and in a matter of moments, the team was standing in the hold of the 747. Even though Jack had trained with these guys for a few days, he was amazed at their deftness. Surgeon-like efficiency and focus; no wasted motion, no wasted energy. They headed for the back of the plane and stopped where the fuselage began inclining, indicating they had reached a point of significance to Jack.

"What's up?" Jack said.

"This is our egress point," Manny said, pointing down.

"Huh?" Jack said.

"This is where we jump from, Doc," Manny said.

"OK, all, do one last check of your gear, and then do a buddy gear check after that," LT commanded. Jack noticed the tone of LT's voice was different; it was officious, crisp, focused. Jack and Manny checked each other's gear. Jack was thrilled Manny was looking at his, as clearly he was the expert among the experts for HALO. Manny thumped Jack's chest, nodded his head once, and gave a thumbs up.

Shark pointed, "This is it, LT."

The group crowded closer, looking down. He was pointing at a riveted seam that began at the incline of the tail section, holding a rectangular panel in place that was about as wide and long as a Volkswagen Beetle.

"OK, fellas," LT said. He looked at his watch. "We need to have this thing open not much more than 10 seconds before we jump. Too early, and the pilots will be thinking about where to do an emergency landing. Too late, and we'll parachute into the middle of nowhere." Jack appreciated LT's honesty, but sometimes he wished he would just tell him what to do without editorializing.

"We have about twenty minutes until we reach the jump zone, so let's get busy," LT said.

The SEALs went to work, two on each side of the panel. They drilled a hole the size of a dime in each corner of the middle panel and a mirror image hole on the adjacent panel for twelve holes in total. LT then produced 12 metal bars about eight inches long. One half of the bar was grooved such that a cable, attached in the middle of the bar, and almost half the width of the bar, could lie flat in the groove, making it appear like it was one long piece. The cable stuck out about four inches longer than the actual bar. The end of the cable was looped, like a bike chain for a paddle lock. The cable could be pulled out of the bar, forming a T, with the loop of the cable at the bottom of the T. Working in twos, they placed a bar through the hole until the entire bar was outside of the plane, but the loop of the cable still within, held by the SEAL. Then they pulled up the loop, disengaging the cable from the groove and allowing the bar to be pulled up tight against the outer wall of the fuselage. They then used a mini-winch with a J-hook on each end to connect the cable loops and cinch them tight. Within five minutes, they had placed all the fasteners.

Jack watched with amazement."So this allows us to remove the rivets well before the jump but hold the panel in place so as not to tip our hand?" LT shook his head in affirmation.

"Yeah, we'll pop the winch handles all at once, and the panel will fly off. The captain will know something is wrong almost immediately, so we'll all need to be out of here in 30 seconds or less. If he even initiates a turn, it could leave us somewhere we don't wanna be."

With the T-bars in place and the panel secured, LT ordered the team to remove the rivets. The rivet drivers rat-tatted alive, the clatter adding to the already intolerable noise. Jack was amazed at how easily the rivets seemed to come out. The SEALs were a lot faster than Jack, but he quickly got the hang of it. They were done in just a few minutes.

When the work was done, LT watched his watch intently. "Three minutes to jump, gents," LT said. "Activate your infrared strobes. We'll line up in the same order as the jump the other day. Jack, you're fourth. I'll be jump master and leave last."

LT directed one man to each of the six winches. "We'll do a visual count from five," LT said. "The four SEALs gave enthusiastic acknowledgment. Jack shook his head with all the confidence he could muster. LT, watching the time, raised his left hand, right hand on the winch release. He flipped the switch on his harness to initiate the NSA's satellite jam, and fingers began counting down. "Remember—track toward the coordinates on the GPS. We need to close the four-mile gap between here and the compound."

Jack's heart was hammering its way up to his throat. *Jesus... just let me die now!*

LT's last raised finger morphed into a fist, and six men simultaneously pulled their winch release, and the plane's panel was ripped away, immediately disappearing into the dark. The men seamlessly moved into jump position, LT standing beside Manny, the first jumper. Greaser and Bugger were in front of Jack, Shark behind. LT looked at his watch one last time. "GO! GO! GO!"

Jack watched Manny, Greaser, and Bugger disappear. He wanted to hesitate but knew if he did, he might just say screw it and surprise the Chinese airport workers in Changchun. He took three running steps and was consumed by darkness.

CHAPTER THIRTY-FIVE

He couldn't see a damn thing. *Where the hell is everybody?* Jack felt a real sense of panic. He centered, gathered his wits, reached up, and pulled the night vision shield down. Ahhh! He could see three of the infrared—IR—beacons below. He thought it was odd that he couldn't see any lights on the ground, but he had never jumped at night before. *Maybe that's just the way it is from up here.*

He glanced at his altimeter. He was falling in the direction the GPS was pointing. He needed to pull his chute at 11,500 feet—Baekdu mountain was slightly over 9,000, giving him just over 2,000 feet to get his chute open, but 1,500 feet less than his practice jump. He'd had plenty of time the other day.

He focused on the three beacons below him, glanced back, and counted two more. Everyone was out and in a good position. He looked back down. *Wait a sec... There are only two lights. One. None! OK... Where'd the fucking lights go?*

A second later, Jack knew where they had gone. Water covered his face shield. He couldn't see a thing. He was in a cloud! *Nobody talked about this!* He couldn't even see his altimeter. He flailed to wipe his visor—good enough to see he was at 20,000 feet. He looked back. No lights. *Dammit!* He wiped his visor again. 15,000 feet. At 126 miles per hour, covering 5,000 feet sure doesn't take long. He focused on his altimeter, wiping the face shield intermittently. He wiped again in time to see the altimeter shoot past 11,500. He grabbed the ripcord, caught it in his right hand, and pulled. He heard, then felt, the chute open, again impressed by the deceleration.

He couldn't see a thing, but at least he hadn't splattered into a mountainside—yet, anyway. He strained to see the beacons. Nothing. He checked the GPS. The arrow was pointing slightly right, so he adjusted the chute and came in alignment.

He looked at his altimeter: 10,900 feet. Only 1,900 more feet until I hit something. 1,000 feet. *Shit. I'm screwed...*

Jack had resolved to die 900 feet from impact when he broke through the bottom of the clouds, and three beacons suddenly became visible. His elation was short-lived when he realized they were not far below and in front but significantly further right than he. He looked up and found that two more beacons had emerged from the cloud cover but were almost directly above him. His GPS said he was on track, but surely the SEALs knew what they were doing.

I pulled the ripcord too late! I'm too low to the ground. I'll never clear the compound wall.

He pulled hard on the handles and glided into alignment with the lights in front. His GPS directed him to steer back left. He still was too low compared to the lights. He pictured slamming into the side of the compound's wall. If that didn't kill him, the fall would, and the noise from his plowing into the wall would get the others killed, too.

He set his jaw and focused on the beacons in front of him. They were starting to drift left. *Wait a sec... now they're going right. What the hell...* Jack was getting closer by the second. He could make out the dark forms of his companions now. Seconds later, the compound came into view. The SEALs had come in too high and were circling so as not to over-shoot! By dumb luck, Jack was at the perfect height to clear the wall and land without chute manipulation, the GPS perfectly aligned. But he sure as hell didn't want to hit the ground first. If he aroused the North Korean guards, he wouldn't know what to do. *Guess I just try to shoot them.*

It quickly became apparent he didn't have to worry about landing first. He saw a muzzle flash come from one of the silhouettes descending into the compound, moments before his boots scraped against the top of the wall. *Damn, that was close.*

He saw more flashes as he careened down to the courtyard, his feet hitting a great deal harder than on the dirt back at the Naval base. He tumbled several times, getting wrapped up in the chute like a bug in a spider's web. *That was graceful.*

He scrambled to his feet, flailing to get free of his inanimate captor when he felt a strong hand grab him. He expected to hear an angry Korean.

"Doc!" It was Bugger. "Shh!" He pulled Jack down into a crouch and helped him unbuckle from the chute.

Free from entanglement, Jack ran, in a crouch and behind Bugger, to the nearest wall, disappearing into the shadows. Jack watched as the other SEALs secured the courtyard with his night vision shield still on. There were several irregular mounds on the ground, which Jack knew must be dead North Korean sentries. He couldn't help but feel bad about their deaths.

Bugger and Jack remained motionless while watching the rest of the team take out the surveillance cameras. The satellite would only block the monitors for another 10 minutes before it moved out of position, and they didn't want to be caught with their proverbial pants down when the jamming signal disappeared. No doubt the soldiers on the other end of the cameras already knew there was a problem. Still, hopefully, they were working on the assumption there was a system issue, not a covert assault by the U.S. military, deep into North Korean territory.

After cautiously surveying the situation, Bugger tugged on Jack's sleeve, and they ran to join the rest of the team, which was standing tight against the wall on either side of the stainless steel elevator door they had seen less than a week ago in the White House. The keypad was flush with the wall, with no visible way to access the electrical guts. Bugger reached into his fanny pack and pulled out a device about the size of an iPod. He pulled his gloves off, held it within a few inches of the keypad, and poked buttons on his gizmo. Above the Korean-character push buttons, the LED strip sprang to life, a glowing, muted blue light penetrating the blackness. The SEALs, night vision engaged, were temporarily blinded. Instinctively, the Navy men flipped their night vision shields up as the elevator doors opened. Bright light and North Korean soldiers flooded the courtyard.

The brightness completely blinded Jack. As Bugger forcefully shoved him to the ground and against the wall, they heard the staccato firing of suppressed weapons. Jack groped for the button to retract the night vision shield, finding it after the gunfire had stopped. His eyes adjusted, and he saw bodies lying in abnormal, crumpled positions, bathed in fluorescent light that extended out of the elevator in a broad V-shape as if spotlighted at the close of some tragic opera. He felt no fear but was mildly disoriented until Bugger lifted him to his feet.

"Doc, you OK?" Bugger said.

"Yeah, I guess," Jack said. "Is everyone else OK?" he said, looking around. There was no response, but he counted five upright figures.

"Well, I guess it ain't a secret were here," Greaser said. "Ya s'pose that's just the first wave?"

"I dunno," LT said. "I figure they don't have too many men here—maybe a couple of platoons on rotating shifts. Don't matter, though. We need to get going." The LT's words seemed almost prescient as the doors to the elevators started to close. LT put his arm out, stopped the doors, and stepped halfway into the elevators to hold them open. "OK, boys, let's execute."

Shark and LT unclipped their chest packs and tossed them at the feet of Manny, who immediately opened them and began unpacking a variety of what Jack assumed were explosives and other weapons, setting up his perimeter of one. The other four clambered into the brightly lit box, and LT stepped in. As the doors closed, Jack couldn't help but wonder if someone was waiting at the bottom. He was pretty sure he knew the answer.

"Jack," LT said, "You need to stand with your back against the elevator wall here," as he pushed him up against the short front lip of the elevator. "It is pretty well protected, so don't move until one of us tells ya to, got it?"

"Yup," Jack affirmed, no interest in debating. It was clear that the SEALs were focused on the mission and keeping Jack safe.

LT and Bugger reached into a pocket on the side of their legs and pulled out what appeared to be a can with a handle. "Turn your O2 on about a quarter-turn," LT said.

"What's that?" Jack asked, nodding at the canister. "Seems a bit unwise to be tossin' grenades into a biological lab. Won't that spread stuff all over?"

"We aren't that stupid, Jack. It's tear gas and a concentrated form of an anesthetic—halothane. It'll first temporarily blind them, and then it'll put 'em to sleep or at least incapacitate them long enough for us to take 'em out. Tear gas alone, and they'll be able to fire their weapons down the hall at us blindly, and I don't know about you, but I ain't interested in trying to dodge random bullets bouncing between the walls of a narrow hallway." Jack nodded his head enthusiastically in agreement.

An electronic jingle signaled that the door was about to open. LT stood pressed against Jack on one side and Bugger on the other, his massive frame at least partially protected by the front lip of the elevator. Shark and Greaser knelt behind LT and Bugger; their M4s leveled toward the door. The two SEALs popped the pins on their canisters, holding the striker lever tightly.

Jack felt the elevator slowing, then stopping with the characteristic bounce — a universal sign indicating the ride was over.

CHAPTER THIRTY-SIX

L T and Bugger threw the canisters out as soon as the elevator doors opened a crack. The sound of the clanking told Jack it was a long hall with a hard floor. Before the canisters had finished their noisy dance, automatic weapons fire erupted, and bullets pummeled the stainless steel doors, holes erupting in the back of the elevator. Jack was happy the North Korean bullets were powerful enough to penetrate the steel; otherwise, they'd be careening around like marbles in a bathtub, making life unpleasant. Thankfully, the outer wall, combined with the double layer of the inner and outer elevator doors, was too thick for the bullets to penetrate completely.

Shark and Greaser intermittently returned fire, although they couldn't see through the white cloud filling the hallway. The 90 seconds that passed between the release of the gas and the cessation of the firing seemed like millennia. The two kneeling SEALs cautiously peered around their standing counterparts. No movement. The gas had cleared enough for them to see that there was no place to hide between the elevator and the first cross hallway, where they could make out a couple of bodies on the floor. Once they stepped out, they would be completely exposed. They waited another minute, during which time they pulled the pins on two more gas canisters, ready for the next wave.

They stepped out and moved heedfully down the hall, followed closely by LT, Bugger, and Jack. Six North Korean soldiers lay motionless, three on each side of the crossing hallway. Four of the six were dead. The halothane had knocked them to their knees, right into the counter-fire laid down by the SEALs. Shark and Greaser pulled zip ties out of their pockets, tied the two sleeping survivors' hands behind their backs, and lashed their feet together. Jack was impressed by this intentional sparing of the two survivors. They could have easily put a bullet in the base of their skulls and not had to worry about them again. They were the U.S. military's ultimate killing force, but only when necessary.

"All right," LT said, "Greaser, jam the elevator, so our ride home doesn't get co-opted, then get back here pronto. No doubt if anyone was sleeping down here, they aren't anymore." Greaser headed back down the 50-foot hallway, a spotless, bright white concourse, shooting out camera lenses as he walked. He was back moments later, giving LT the thumbs up.

"Great. Now, let's secure these two corridors," LT said, looking at his watch. "Shark, Greaser, take that side. Doc, you hang with them. Bugger and I will take this one. Be back here in five. If anyone hears firing, move to the sound and help out, and pray we don't both hear firing at the same time. Got it?" Thumbs up all around.

Jack crossed over to the opposite hallway with his teammates, who positioned him between them. Greaser, in front, crouched with his M4 raised in his right hand, the unpinned canister in his left. Shark, similarly crouched, had his back to Jack, protecting their flank. They approached two facing doors about a third of the way down the hall. The SEALs lined up on each side of the door, backs against the wall, Jack emulating them. Greaser leaned over, looking at the base of the door, checking to see if there were lights on. It was dark. Reaching down, he turned the knob and pushed the door open wide. Shark and Greaser erupted into the room, weapons leveled, laser sights scanning. Light from the hallway was enough for them to see that the stark room was barren of human life. They motioned Jack and signed for him to turn on the light. When it was fully illuminated, Jack could see a lab facility. Although refrigerators were jammed full of culture media for bacteria and viruses, there were no incubators.

Shark walked over to Jack. "Anything here, Doc?"

"Nothin' too impressive. A prep lab—they probably keep this as sterile as possible to avoid any chance of contamination of their base media," Jack said.

"Move on," Shark said, motioning Greaser and Jack to leave the room. He then pulled a small black box out of one of his pockets. It had a silver clip attached to a short wire hanging off one end and a recessed button on the other. He peeled a paper off the back of the box, the way a kid pulls the paper off the back of a sticker from the dentist and stuck the box to the wall at the level of the doorknob. He then pulled the wire out of the box and fastened the clip around the wire, creating a loop. He pulled the door until just his hand was still in the room. Through the crack, Jack watched as he looped the wire around the doorknob and snugged it up. He carefully closed the door, activating the black box. He took out a black marker and drew a tiny dot in the upper left-hand corner of the door, communicating to the SEALs that the room had been cleared — and booby-trapped.

Jack gave Shark the *What in the hell was that look.* "C-4, Doc. It'll warn us if someone is playing games with us, moving from room to room. They'll only move once..." Shark said.

They secured the room across from the first and moved on down the hallway, clearing additional rooms in the five-minute timeframe. They hooked back up with their counterparts at the hallway intersection.

"Anything down there look interesting?" Jack asked LT, tipping his head toward the rooms.

"Na. Just storage, I think. I ain't a microbiologist, but I know what an incubator looks like, and I didn't see nothing like one," LT said. "Oh, and Doc, don't be goin' in any door with a small black dot on it. Upper left. It's—"

"Booby-trapped," Jack said, finishing his sentence. LT nodded.

LT led the group down the main corridor toward the remaining two wings. The entire group was feeling edgy, knowing in their guts it couldn't be this easy. Fifteen yards from the corridor intersection, there was an explosion behind them from the hallway that Shark's team had cleared. They all turned and instinctively crouched, weapons ready. They heard the tink of metal hitting metal in one of the corridors they hadn't cleared in front of them. LT and Bugger turned to protect their flank, and as Bugger lobbed a gas grenade into the right-sided hallway, a rush of North Korean soldiers appeared from the left, firing at the SEALs as they ran. Bugger, in front, was downed by the fire. LT returned fire immediately, taking out the first two, and Shark, who had rolled to the opposite side, took out the next two, their momentum carrying them to land on top of the first bodies. The SEALs low-crawled to the body pile, using it as cover, as two more North Korean soldiers rounded the corner. Greaser popped off two rounds, nailing each in the head, dropping them in seconds. Still holding his weapon on the level, he reached into his leg side pocket, extracted a gas grenade, pulled the pin, and hurled it at the far wall of the left corridor as he hit the deck just in time to duck machine gun fire from two soldiers that materialized at the end of the corridor. The grenade hit the wall and bounced down the hall, spewing white, opaque gas.

LT and Shark picked off the two recruits while Jack and Greaser pulled Bugger behind the makeshift North Korean soldier barricade. Bugger had been hit, and though his flap jacket stopped the bullet, the force had knocked him off his feet and sucked the air from his lungs. He was OK—and pissed.

"Just gimme' my goddam weapon," Bugger muttered to Greaser. "I've about had it with this shit."

"Settle down a sec, Bug. Let the sleeping gas do its work," Shark said. The firing had stopped. They cautiously peered over the pile of dead bodies. Blood was pooling into an ever-larger lake from the human sandbags, which had been riddled with bullets from both sides.

The SEALs lined up, two on each side, Jack with Shark and Greaser, and they inched toward the hallway intersection. Hearing nothing, the leads peered around the corners and, seeing nothing, proceeded. Shark's team encountered an identical physical configuration—four doors, two on each side— and began the process of clearing them.

LT and Bugger rounded the corner and paused, facing a short hallway with a single, glistening silver door at the end a keypad on the wall to the left. "Uh oh," LT said. "Bugger, I need you to crack this thing."

"No sweat, LT." Bugger rummaged through his chest pack and pulled out a small calculator-like instrument. Holding it up to the keypad, he punched a few buttons and watched as the display came alive, numbers flowing across the screen so fast they couldn't be read. LT crouched, weapon pointed down the hallway in the direction they had come from, covering their six. Bugger keyed in a few more instructions, and, moments later, they heard the electronic locks retract. Bugger stowed his toy and, with M4 pointing forward, cautiously pushed the door open. Entering the room back-to-back, they found themselves in a small, square, windowless room suffused in purplish-blue light, another security door in front of them.

"Must be a clean room," LT said. "These are UV lights. They kill bacteria and stuff on you before you go into whatever is behind the next door. I'm betting it's the lab."

Bugger extracted the same apparatus used moments before and had them inside the next room in a matter of seconds. When the electric locks clicked, the UV lights automatically shut off. They found themselves in a vast, white-walled room. Incubators lined the walls, and lab workbenches filled the middle of the room. There was elaborate glass equipment, machines the size of small cars with flashing multi-colored lights, and sterile hoods.

"Shark, Greaser!" LT said into the communicator. "Clear out that side ASAP and get Doc over here. We're in the lab."

"Roger that!" Shark's voice crackled back in the team's headsets. Bugger went to the entry point of the lab to cover and meet the three men. LT continued exploring.

A few minutes later, Shark's team appeared at the end of the hallway, opposite Bugger. They moved quickly, pausing at the hallway intersection to ensure no surprises, and crossed over to join up with LT and Bugger.

Bugger escorted them into the lab. Jack noticed the UV lights as they walked through the anteroom.

"OK, Doc, time for you to do your thing—whatever that is," LT said. "What do ya need from us?"

"Just pick up every bit of paper you can carry, especially any bound journal sittin' around," Jack said. "Have ya found any computers?"

"Yeah, over there," LT pointed.

"Well, sic Bugger on that and have him download as much as he can," Jack said.

Shark replaced Bugger in the anteroom to watch for unwelcome visitors. Bugger sat down at the computer and pulled out the tools he needed to torture the electronic enemy into giving up critical information.

"What else?" LT asked.

"Well, Greaser is already taking pictures of everything. Now I just need to nose around." Jack walked around the room once. He counted the number of incubators: six. He stopped at one of the larger machines. Pointing at it, he said, "This is a sequencer."

"So?" LT said.

"So," Jack said, "It means they have one of the key pieces of equipment to manipulate genes. And if I'm not mistaken, this is one of the more advanced sequencers available. It uses chain termination technology."

"Uhhh—English, Doc?" LT said.

"It's the newest technology. Only a few research facilities in the U.S. have it. It makes sequencing DNA and RNA not only simpler but faster. How the *hell* they have this is beyond me," Jack said, shaking his head.

"Doc, the North Koreans are always in cahoots with someone, and they don't just do military espionage. They have folks embedded in our businesses and universities, too. The fact that the North Koreans have this doesn't surprise me a fucking bit," LT said, somewhat disgusted.

"Well, we're in the right place. They have everything they need to manufacture a new infectious agent. I find this whole goddam thing frightening," Jack said.

"Just focus on getting what we need, Doc," LT said. "We'll make sure they don't get to use any more of the stuff in here; I damn well guarantee that," LT said.

Jack pulled out plastic test tubes, half with growth media for viruses and half for bacteria. He went from incubator to incubator, transferring a small amount from each unit into one of his tubes, carefully labeling it with the lot numbers attached to the unit. He could quickly tell the difference between viral and bacterial cultures and guessed roughly 15 different bacterial strains and ten or so viral strains.

LT walked up and handed him a thick, black-covered lab book. "I think this is the mother lode, Doc."

Jack flipped through it. It was in Korean. "Why do you think so, LT?"

"Because it says something in the first few pages about an experimental virus. I haven't read the whole thing, of course, but it sounds bad to me," LT said.

"I agree, but Jesus, I hope you're wrong. I got what I needed. Can we get the hell out of here?" Jack said. He paused. "Wait a sec—just how are we getting out?"

"Don't worry about that. We got a taxi up top. We're about ready. Just waiting on Bugger to finish his job. Bugger! How's it goin'?

"Just about there, LT. I downloaded the whole damn shootin' match; now I'm just uploading one helluva virus into their military IT system. Should mess them up for a while. It'll even screw up their flight control and tracking system and allow us to hack into them for the next 48 hours or so," Bugger chuckled. "Done. Let' go!"

LT nodded to Greaser, who took out yet another black object about half the size of a shoebox. He punched a few buttons and waved for the group to head for the lab exit. He placed the box in the middle of the room and pushed one last button. Concomitant with a high-pitched beep, LED numbers appeared: 120. 119. 118. He sprinted to join the others.

The group moved quickly but cautiously, pausing at intersections before turning down the main hallway. They sprinted to the final corner, again pausing, before running toward the elevator door that had been propped open. With ten yards to go, they heard footsteps behind them. They piled into the elevator, two SEALs and Jack standing behind the door edges and two flopped prone, M4s pointing down the hallway. A dozen North Korean soldiers filled the hallway. The SEALs fired first, dropping the first few soldiers as the doors to the elevator closed, and they felt the pull of the car moving upward.

Greaser quickly unzipped his chest pack and pulled out another black box like the one he had left in the lab. He quickly punched in some numbers. As soon as the doors opened and the SEALs confirmed no hostiles were waiting, Greaser flipped the last switch on the box, placed it on the elevator floor, and pushed the down button before stepping off. "It'd be a terrible time to have company now," he said.

CHAPTER THIRTY-SEVEN

The elevator doors opened, SEALs crouching, weapons open for business. Two dark figures were visible in the light of a quarter moon, cloud cover gone. Jack was confused. Why didn't they fire on them?

He flipped the night vision shield down and clicked it into place. The silhouettes were identical to the other SEALs. Behind the men was an outline of a strange-looking aircraft—stumpy, short wings jutted out from the mid-body of what was a helicopter, rotors whirling on top. The tail rotor was not visible, concealed by what looked like oversized '57 Chevy hubcaps.

The two new players were friendly, urgently beckoning the six men to come. LT and Shark bolted from the elevator. Bugger reached back, grabbed Jack's chest pack, and pulled him forward. "Get goin' damn it!"

That was all the invitation Jack needed. He sprang from the illuminated box, followed by the remaining SEALs. He emulated the two in front, running hunkered over. As he approached the strange aircraft, he became suddenly aware that something was missing: the rotors of the chimerical bird were whirring—in fact, visibly speeding up as they approached—but there was no sound. It was the famed stealth helicopter purportedly used by the SEALs, but whose existence the lay press had never actually confirmed.

LT and Shark arrived first, turned, and knelt to cover the others as they leaped into the helicopter. Seconds later, they lifted off, pulling upward from the compound with such momentum it threw the soldiers to the floor. Jack felt the movement shift forcefully from up to forward, telling him they had cleared the compound's high walls. They quickly reached a jet-like cruising speed, and as the flight smoothed, Jack and the SEALs buckled into their seats. The simple act of sitting down after the intensity of the last half-hour seemed blissfully luxurious to Jack. He glanced at his watch. Jesus... That was only 30 minutes!

He leaned his head back against the side of the aircraft and closed his eyes. He wanted to go to sleep and wake up with Marla, but the vibration of the rotors, transmitted to his skull through his helmet against the fuselage, denied him the thought for more than a few moments. He shook his head slowly.

"Doc? You OK?" LT said.

He opened his eyes, looked at LT, and took a deep breath, shrugging his shoulders.

"I'm exhausted," Jack replied. "I haven't been this spent since—well, ever."

"Whatcha got in your little bag, Doc? Anything that's going to help us?" LT said.

"There's a little of everything in here, LT. If they had the bug in that lab, we have it," Jack said, patting his chest pack.

"I hope you're right, Doc, 'cause I sure as hell ain't going back!" Bugger said, slapping Jack's thigh so hard it hurt.

"I hear that," Jack said. "No offense, fellas, but I'm not a fan of this kinda work. Prefer the lab, by far." The team chuckled.

"Well, Doc, you'll be in the lab tomorrow morning. We're headed directly to Mumbai via Seoul to drop you off at some fancy-ass lab there," LT said.

"It's nice to know you guys are planning out my life. When the hell were you going to tell me?" Jack said.

"Just did, Doc. We had orders, Jack, and we followed those orders. The moment you stepped on this aircraft, our mission from the lab and protecting you changed to just protecting you. You're our sole mission now, Doc. Now our only job is to make sure you and the specimens get to Mumbai in one piece," LT said. "After that, we sit tight with you and your team there — your security detail."

"Don't we have to stop somewhere to pee and get gas? I thought helicopters couldn't fly too far on one tank?" Jack said.

"Well, assumin' we don't have our ass shot out from under us by a Chinese or North Korean fighter before we get to the South Korean border, we'll land in Seoul in about 30 minutes, board a transport jet, and besetting down at the hospital where the lab is in about eight hours," LT said. "An NBC decon crew will be waitin', and we can get outta these monkey suits."

"I'm for that," Jack said, leaning his head back and closing his eyes. Not even a North Korean fighter threat could keep him from sleep.

CHAPTER THIRTY-EIGHT

Riley's determination had served her well, and, other than the close encounter with the cobra, the trip had been remarkably smooth. When needed, she found fuel, and few gas stations required a credit card. Pull up, fill up, drive on. She never drove past a potential fuel point, even if she still had half a tank. That's how she had ended up in the middle of Sudan with an empty gas tank and a spitting cobra.

She approached Addis Ababa, an Ethiopian city of 3.1 million people before the plague, hopeful that she might find a place to stop and rest for the night. She pulled up to what appeared to be a hotel. She opened the door, got out of the car, and stretched. She took a step, and a burst of automatic weapon fire—a machine gun—split the air. She ducked and covered her head with her arms. Simultaneous to the end of the staccato burst, a teenage boy, multi-colored shirt tied around his head, began shouting at Riley. She understood the language of the machine gun. She looked up at the boy, who was standing over her on a second-story balcony. He had fired into the air as a warning. Three doors opened on the lower level, multiple boys stepped out, each brandishing an automatic weapon of their own. Riley figured they were between 12 and 15 years old.

Riley slowly raised her hands over her head, a gesture that the boy on the balcony found funny. His laugh prompted the other boys to join in. Riley felt like she was in a bad spaghetti western, except she was scared shitless. The laughter stopped as unexpectedly as it had erupted, the boys simply staring at her. She was unsure what her next move should be or if she should move at all, so she stared back.

Riley understood that these boys, mere children, had no idea what to do next. They had probably organized into some loose alliance after losing their parents; their survival on the streets enhanced being in a group, a gang, of sorts. She wondered if they were brothers or cousins or just friends. Whichever, she was sure they were as afraid as she was, maybe more. Her fear retreated, giving way to a sense of compassion— the same sense that was drawing her to Mto Wa Mbu.

She slowly put her arms down and let them hang at her side, pausing, an attempt to show them she meant no harm. The boy on the balcony scrunched up his nose and narrowed his eyes, fading back to a flaccid face. He tipped his head slightly to the side in a single nod, righting it again as he lowered the barrel of the weapon and pointed it at the ground. *He's telling me to go.*

She climbed in the car and drove away, looking back in the rearview mirror. She wondered how long they would survive.

The brief episode made it clear to Riley that things had gotten more dangerous in the past few days, as older children began to understand that they were in charge. Access to weapons was easy, especially in rural areas. Cities provided too many variables, too much possibility for chaos, and well-established rivalries and prejudices. *I need to avoid cities. I've got to be more careful, more thoughtful.*

She drove as fast as she could safely maneuver through the streets of Addis Ababa. She was shocked at the number of armed children she saw. The extent of what was happening in Africa—to the African people—was more evident to Riley the further she drove, but she still couldn't comprehend the magnitude. *The adults are all dead. The children... my God! The poor children. What will happen to them?* Was it a blessing or a curse that they've been spared? The gnawing feeling that she had fought in Dar es Salaam stabbed at her innards again, as if she were digesting her own body from the inside out.

She drove on, staring down the road, just enough awareness to stay on the asphalt. Her mind was numb again, each additional trauma increasing her ability—no, her need—to shut out the reality pressing in at her on all sides. By the time she woke up from her trancelike state, she was well beyond the city limits of Addis Ababa, again in rural territory.

She flipped the headlights on as the sun slipped behind the western horizon. She couldn't get the children out of her mind and couldn't forget the realization she'd had back in Dar es Salaam: *You can't save them all.* It reverberated in her head like her ears were playing ping-pong with the thought. It was all accumulating. The trip. The stress. The thoughts. The exhaustion.

She pulled off to the side of the road, locked all the doors, and climbed into the back seat. She curled up for desperately needed sleep. *I can't save them all, but I can save one.* She saw the face of the little boy in Mto Wa Mbu, and, as sleep tugged successfully at her consciousness, a soft smile appeared on her face.

CHAPTER THIRTY-NINE

Dhanesh Mehta, a handsome lad with thick black hair, parted neatly on the right and a soft, photogenic face, knew he was lucky to have a job at all, much less at Indus Cocktail Bar & Tandoor, a hopping place located in the Hotel Diplomat, one of the premier hotels in south Mumbai. It was a favorite of tourists and ne'er-do-well locals, so he made good tips. While not genuinely upscale, it had a friendly atmosphere, and at night it rocked to music played by its in-house DJ. Ganesha had blessed him.

In English, his name—Dhanesh—translated into "lord of wealth." He found this humorous, but anyone following him home after work would see it did not reflect any financial reality. He lived in a hovel in the Dharavi slums. The caste system in India was, as a five-minute tour of this impoverished area would clearly show, alive and healthy. His wife, Falguni, took care of the family with his meager income, including their three small children, which Dhanesh considered wealth beyond measure. He had two boys, Kalyan, five, and Gagan, two. The eldest was a beautiful eight-year-old girl, Edha, meaning sacred, which was how Dhanesh treated his entire family.

Despite working for Indus, Dhanesh barely made a living wage. He appreciated his job, though, and never complained, at least at work. He was a trusted employee and highly valued at Indus. His primary responsibility was waiting tables in the bar. He would carry appetizers from the kitchen to the patrons in the bar while they waited for a table in the main dining room. Customers liked Dhanesh, often tipping him more for delivering a single drink than he would make in an hour from Indus. He appreciated these gestures greatly, and when he recognized a repeat customer who had previously tipped well, he made sure the barkeep accidentally spilled a bit more gin in their drink.

He showed up to work about an hour early, hoping to have a bite to eat before starting work at 8 p.m. The bar was already noisy with customers talking loudly, the air thick with smoke and the pungent smell of dried gin. He sat in the cramped back room while eating a piece of naan and some day-old tandoor lamb. The management always left uneaten food from the night before for the staff — another thing Dhanesh was thankful for. He finished nibbling the last few morsels of meat off the rib bone and tossed it into the garbage pail next to the door. He grinned at his NBA-like skill, stood up, and walked to the sink to wash up. He put on his stiff white shirt and black waistcoat, ready for the eight-hour, noise-infused shift. He turned and walked out of the room with a sigh through swinging doors. As the doors opened, his face morphed into a broad smile that any of his friends would have known was forced, and he walked into the bar. The noise of the place slapped him in the face as hard as the hand of a jealous lover, and, had one been observing, she would have seen him wince. He paused, surveying the panoply. Before he was even able to take a breath, a male patron six feet to his left motioned him to come over. Dhanesh responded immediately, striding to the round table where two young men sat, he presumed, with their dates.

"Boy, get us another round," said the man, with a heavy British accent. He was dressed in a business suit and had the appearance of someone important.

Dhanesh smiled and bowed and said, "Yes, sir! Immediately! What are you having?"

The man, looking irritated, said, "Boy, just ask the waitress who served us earlier and don't bother us with such details. Now go on..."

"Yes, sir," said Dhanesh compliantly. He navigated to the bar, searched through the open tabs, identified the table number, and put in the order. The barkeep, working with the efficiency of a nuclear clock, poured the drinks and put them on a serving tray. Dhanesh hoisted the tray of drinks with a slight grimace and resumed the pleasant faux demeanor common to him and his coworkers. He knew this same scene would play over and over throughout the night.

It was just before midnight, and the bar was buzzing with semi-soused patrons— Indian, British, Korean, and American—all swilling some form of gin, for the most part. The wine drinkers had abandoned any hope of deep, meaningful, quiet conversation hours ago. Above the din, Dhanesh thought he heard the engines of motorcycles outside. He paused, listening. The riders had shut them off; the sound was gone. As he completed that thought, there was a muffled sound of cracking wood behind the bar, coming from the back room where he had enjoyed his lamb about four hours earlier. Seconds later, the two doors of the break room crashed open, and two men wearing black ski masks and brandishing 9 mm Rugers in one hand, and sawed-off shotguns in the other hurtled themselves into the bar. The shorter man pointed the shotgun skyward and pulled the trigger, the blast reverberating throughout the room. A hush immediately followed screams. Pieces of loose plaster fell from the ceiling and skittered and bounced across the floor to the background beat of disco music. Smoke from the gun temporarily obscured the two men, creating an even greater sense of fear.

"You!" screamed the taller of the two men at the DJ, leveling the 9 mm at his chest, "Turn off that music, now!" The DJ, hands shaking, managed to find the volume knob. "Everybody, get away from the bar! Get over there!" The bar patrons, fear visible, pushed each other hurriedly to the end of the room opposite the bar.

The screamer said, "Put your hands behind your head and keep them there!" The shorter, more violent intruder was busy having the barkeep stuff money into a small backpack while his accomplice was holding the crowd at bay, pistol and shotgun sweeping back and forth. When the barkeep finished stuffing the bag, the shorter thief turned and looked menacingly at the crowd. He strolled toward the frightened group, holding the money in his left hand, shotgun leveled in the right. A woman standing next to Dhanesh in the front of the huddled crowd slumped forward onto the floor, fainting from fear and alcohol. Her momentum snapped her head forward, banging it hard against the floor. Dhanesh looked down. Blood was pooling quickly, running out from under cover of her long hair. He quickly bent down to help the woman.

"Get up!" shouted the short man, glaring at Dhanesh.

"She's hurt!" Dhanesh said emphatically.

"I'll show you hurt, you fuckin' Kutta!' said the thief, leveling the shotgun at Dhanesh and pulling the trigger without hesitation. A loud bang accompanied a bright flash, followed by a smoke plume that was eerily accentuated in the subdued dance floor lighting of the bar. Dhanesh, the good Samaritan trying to help someone he didn't even know, someone he had been waiting on all evening, was forced down by the blast, landing on top of the woman he was trying to help as if the very hand of God had reached down and shoved him. In the mêlée of screams and smoke, the two men backed quickly out of the room. Moments later, the sound of motorcycles erupted, fast fading into the distance, leaving only the sounds of whimpers from frightened revelers.

The disappearance of motorcycle engines coincided with the eeee-awww of the Mumbai police, who arrived within minutes. As they entered the bar with weapons drawn, the barkeep informed them that the perpetrators were gone. Holstering their weapons, they moved to the two bodies on the floor. They rolled Dhanesh off the young woman and onto his back, just as she started to stir. Dhanesh was unconscious, bleeding profusely from head and chest wounds.

Twelve and a half hours later…

The two nurses had never been in the section of the hospital where they had been instructed to take the injured man, now stable. They could see a lighted area up ahead and stainless steel, restaurant-like swinging doors with small slit-like windows fashioned out of mirrored glass. They had been instructed to push the red button to the right of the doors when they arrived and leave the patient on the gurney with his IVs, monitors, draining chest tubes, and a portable ventilator puffing away at 12 breaths per minute. They did as instructed, each having an odd sense about leaving a critically injured patient unattended in a deserted hallway. They nervously looked over their shoulders as they walked down the corridor, concerned for the abandoned patient—and a bit for themselves —in this odd, scary place.

An ICU nurse and trauma surgeon waited on the other side of the swinging doors, dressed in MOPP gear. As soon as the nurses had disappeared into the blackness of the long hallway, the doors were unlocked from the inside, opening with the hum of automation and accompanied by the hiss of an airlock being released. The two MOPP-clad workers pulled the gurney into a small anteroom and pushed a button, closing the doors.

CHAPTER FORTY

Jack awakened hours before hitting the outskirts of Mumbai. He used the time to filter through the lab notebooks with Bugger and LT. They were written in Korean, which was not a surprise, but Jack found it frustrating. He had to rely on his companions' translations, and he was used to double-checking things for himself. It wasn't that he didn't trust people. He was simply meticulous. It was a trait that had always served him well in the world of research.

There were no surprises. Anthrax. Ebola. Tularemia. Yersinia. Even smallpox—something that no one was supposed to have, but hardly a surprise that the North Koreans kept some on hand.

Bugger had cracked their computer files mid-flight. Again, nothing. Maybe they just needed more time to dig deep into the electronic stuff to find what the NSA was convinced existed: a novel, genetically-modified, highly lethal, infectious agent.

The jet slowed and angled earthward. In the hazy orange of the sunrise, Jack could see the landing strip in the distance.

The aircraft pulled up to a small hanger and powered down. Heavily armed soldiers in MOPP gear surrounded them. Tanker trucks pulled up, and it sounded like the jet was being put through a car wash, Jack recognizing the sound of liquid under pressure spraying the fuselage.

"They're killin' anything we might have brought along for the ride," Greaser said as if Jack didn't know.

The racket stopped, and the doors opened. The men hopped out. Even the SEALs were happy to have their feet on the ground. Each mission crew member was greeted by two soldiers and led to a detox station, where they were showered and scrubbed. Jack's pack was placed into a large, clear, plastic bag, sort of an oversized sandwich bag. It, too, was decontaminated.

They were then led down some stairs and into a smallish room where more MOPP-clad personnel met them and helped them out of their gear. It was as finely choreographed as a Christmas performance by the Radio City Rockettes. There were even clothes in his size hanging in wait for him.

After decontamination, the group was escorted to a humvee and arrived at Breach Candy after about a 45-minute drive. They exited and walked in, still with a military escort.

The group walked down a series of hallways and shuffled into a freight elevator. An Indian Army captain served as their attendant. He leaned over so he could swipe a magnetic card hanging around his neck, activating an unmarked button at the bottom of the panel. The doors closed, and they heard the hushing noise of hydraulics slowly losing pressure as they began to descend. The whole thing seemed increasingly bizarre to Jack—a tall order, considering that less than 10 hours before, he had been dodging automatic weapon fire in a subterranean, North Korean Army research lab.

The elevator's hissing got louder as it slowed, valves slowly clamping off the oil flow, ending with the down-up bump of the destination.

Jack looked at LT and asked, "Are we going to the lab?"

The doors chunked open before LT could answer, and he motioned Jack to get off. Jack turned and glanced down to ensure the elevator had lined up with the floor. It had, and as he looked up and stepped forward, he came face to face with Marla.

Jack blinked, confused. Marla stepped into him, giving him a full-body hug and a kiss.

"What? When..." Jack stammered, clearly confused. Marla put her finger to his lips.

"I got here yesterday, honey. Catherine asked me to come to Mumbai."

"Wow! What a great welcome-back present!" Jack said. "I can't believe you're here! I thought I wouldn't see you for weeks, maybe months!" Jack paused, then said, "Honey, I know it's hard to believe, but I was...."

Marla interrupted. "Jack, we all know where you were. We were briefed about an hour ago. I'm just glad you're safe."

"Ted, can we go see the research facility now?" Catherine interjected.

"Absolutely. I'm excited to show it to you. Welcome, Dr. Cann. Good to have you back in one piece."

"Who are you?" Jack asked Ted.

"I'll fill you in later, Jack," Catherine said. "This is Ted."

"There is one more thing I need to tell y'all," said Ted, as he reached over and shook Jack's hand. He paused, worried about what he was about to say. He ran his fingers nervously through his mop of hair, slicking it back into place.

"What is it, Ted?" Catherine asked.

"Well... uh... basically, y'all are stuck here for the duration," Ted said.

"What on hell do you mean, Ted?" Catherine said.

"Well, the Lopez Administration has decided that this will be the site of all research efforts, even if this thing hit India. We've already developed contingency plans for replacing personnel as needed. I mean, if the Indian folks start dropping, we'll need to replace them. The thought is that it would be too hard to keep any continuity in the research if we picked up and moved every time another region is hit. So, I guess what I'm tellin' ya is that this is home for you until this is over, one way or the other." The team knew what *one way or the other* meant, and each paused in brief reflection.

Jack followed as the team retraced their steps back to the locker room, each finding a locker labeled with their name.

"Y'all need to put your MOPP gear on every time you enter the lab. Just follow the instructions on the signs above the locker. Won't be too long before it's second nature, but I can't emphasize enough how important it is to make damn sure ya got it on right."

"Oh, goody. More MOPP," Jack said.

They dressed in silence, putting on everything except for their masks, and stood up to head into the research lab.

Ted said, "These masks have radio communicators in 'em. Gotta have 'em to talk to each other. 'Course, you have to be on the same channel. You switch it on here," he said, pointing to a knob slightly above the right eyepiece of the mask. "You can see what frequency other people are on by looking at the LED numbers on the front of the mask here," he said, pointing to the two small numbers on the forehead of the mask. "Turn it on and dial it to channel 23. Only the main research team—that's you guys—are to be on that frequency. There's a little heads-up display on the inside of your mask so you can see what frequency you're on." They each flipped the switch and dialed to number 23.

Stepping up to the door, they pulled on their masks. They checked each other's mask connections as the diagram instructed, giving each other the thumbs up.

"Oh, yeah," said Ted, his voice mechanical in the headset. "If you want to speak to everyone in the facility, like giving an update or somethin', switch to channel 50. In other words, whatever you say over channel 50, everyone will hear, so be damn careful if you use it. Don't need any more anxiety than there already is."

Ted looked at each of them and said, "OK, partners, time to saddle up!" as he reached up and pushed the ENTER DECON CHAMBER button next to the stainless steel door. The door opened with the hiss of a vacuum releasing, and Ted leaned in to open it and led the group inside a small rectangular room large enough to hold about ten people standing close together. Ted said, "Jack, shut the door and push the button on the left." A small label above a red button on the wall read ENTER LAB. Jack did as instructed, and as he pushed the button, the lights dimmed, and ultraviolet light suffused the room.

"The button Jack just pushed activates pretty powerful ultraviolet light, potent enough to kill any bacteria or virus that might be on the suits. Prevents us from contaminating the lab from the outside. The button down here," Ted said, pointing to a second red button at the lab end of the room labeled LEAVE LAB, "uses not only UV light but also sprays a mist of hypochlorite solution on your suit to neutralize any chemical agent, like sarin and the other organophosphates, from contaminating the clean dressing chamber. Until we know exactly what we're dealing with, or at least what we're not dealing with, you must activate each button on entering or exiting the lab. Everybody clear on that?" The six-team members indicated their understanding with thumbs up.

The UV light faded, and the overhead lights came back up, glaring brightly, as the gleaming metal door leading into the lab swooshed open, revealing a massive facility that was iridescent with halogen light. It was easily the size of any indoor football stadium without the seats. There was a hum in front of them, or maybe from overhead. Not loud, but of the sort that became irritating quickly. There were no fewer than 50 people, all in MOPP suits, scurrying about purposefully. The facility was partitioned into discrete areas with signposts like those over roads in a small city, announcing the purpose of the space. To the right, they saw signs marking the electron microscope. There were nuclear magnetic spectrometers, centrifuges, and machines measuring blood electrolytes and enzymes toward the middle. A little to the left was the road sign for DNA sequencers. They continued walking toward the center of the research stadium. There were isolation rooms, a CT scanner, and an MRI machine, each entombed in a small room made of thick, clear, leaded glass. Signs marked the microbiology labs, one for bacterial and one for viral studies. There were autopsy tables in the pathology lab in glass-walled, temperature-controlled mini-rooms, complete with tissue processors. It was as if an entire research lab had been manufactured for the very crisis they faced. Giant TV monitors hung on walls and ceilings, a worldwide scoreboard of sorts. And it was all under a hospital in India.

Jack, mouth slightly agape behind his mask, was silent.

Ted said, "We can even do HVEM—high-voltage electron microscopy—which lets us do a 3-D reconstruction of cells and their organelles. Dunno why in the hell that would be important, but we can do it!"

Marla, slowly turning from left to right, hesitatingly asked, "Where on earth did all of this stuff come from?"

"Well, Ted," Catherine said as she waved her hand, "it would probably be helpful if you could tell us more about this place. I can see now why the administration wants us to plant here. This would be impossible to reproduce somewhere else."

"I kinda figured you'd understand that once you saw the place. Do you want the detailed tour or the 30,000-foot thumbnail?" Ted queried.

"Let's split the difference. How about the 15,000-foot view? Everyone agree?"

"Yep. I'm sure I'll have a few questions," Jack said, as everyone else shook their heads.

"You got 'er," said the Texan. "About the only thing this lab can't do is bring back the dead." Ted chuckled but quickly stopped when he saw no one else was laughing. "We got about everything, really—from gross pathology down to electron microscopy and gene sequencing. You can run tissue and fluid samples through our spectrometer, looking for everything from heavy metals to novel, uncharacterized compounds. We have cryo-technology that allows us to rapidly freeze even the largest body with minimal crystallization damage at the cellular level. We can..."

Catherine held up her hand, palm out, cutting him off. "Got it, Ted. Thanks. Let's go."

Ted returned Catherine's favor, cutting her off. "Well, Dr. Montoya, all due respect, but I don't think you have all of it. At least not some of the more interesting aspects, I imagine."

Jack turned and stared at Ted and noticed that Catherine was looking at him quizzically, brows furrowed.

"What do you mean?" she said, concern in her voice. Jack thought she had probably had enough bad news.

CHAPTER FORTY-ONE

" Now jus' hold yer horses, there y'all. Don't be gettin' yer panties in a wad jus' yet," Ted said, holding up both hands. "The prime minister ordered that all victims of major trauma in all of India's big cities be immediately transported to centers where they can be cared for with advance life support." Ted paused and took in a deep breath. "We're waiting for a victim of trauma to have a spontaneous death, without any other identifiable factor for having caused the death."

"Yes. Yes," said Catherine tersely. "We know about that. It was the CDC that recommended this approach to the prime minister. Then as soon as that person dies, we immediately transport the body for study in a cryo coffin. This isn't news, Ted." Jack heard irritation building in Catherine's tone.

"Dr. Montoya, that isn't all the prime minister authorized me to do, and Washington pretty much gave me the green light to make modifications I thought would be helpful. So, I suggested some modifications to the plan, and the prime minister felt my suggestions were good and that the situation deserved some... err..." Ted struggled for the appropriate words, then continued. "More aggressive, shall we say, research support to streamline the process and guarantee success."

Jack was still staring at Ted, a look of puzzled concern pasted to his face. He didn't know Ted or his abilities, and his communication style wasn't helping to defuse his or any of the team's discomfort. It seemed they were about to find out something unpleasant, and Jack sensed it made Catherine particularly nervous.

"Ted," she said pointedly, "What in the hell did you do? Cut to the goddamn chase, OK?"

"Simmer down, Dr. Montoya," Ted said. "I'm pretty sure I made yer job easier." Catherine took a deep breath.

"OK, Ted. I'll ask the question," Jack said, breaking 15 seconds of tense silence. "Exactly what kind of support are you talking about?"

"Follow me," said Ted, motioning them to follow him. They walked about 30 yards further into the lab. A large, rectangular, stainless steel building rose above them, about a story high. It was large enough to shelter two large tour buses, with room to spare. Jack thought it looked like the largest AirStream RV he had ever seen. There were no windows but wide, swinging double doors on each end. Multiple insulated pipes ran down from the ceiling above the structure, intersecting with other, smaller lines of the same appearance that ran parallel to the unit's roof. From the parallel pipes ran multiple hoses that penetrated through the top of the stainless steel building, each glistening like frost on a wintery morning when the light refracted off of them just so. A wispy veil of smoke-like mist hovered just above the roof. On the far side, opposite the team, was a long, gently sloping, window-enclosed walkway, easily 200 yards long, entering the gigantic underground facility from the ground floor several stories up. It terminated in the back of the silver monolith.

"What in God's name...?" Catherine whispered.

"Let's go inside," Ted said as he pushed open one of the doors.

"Jesus..." Jack said. The building was lined with three rows—one on each wall and one down the middle—of small, self-contained, glass-walled ICU rooms the size of a large walk-in closet, each equipped with all monitors needed to care for critically injured patients. A small box, about 18 inches square, jutted out to the right of each cubicle's door. It appeared to be the room's climate control system.

Big red LED numbers read 23° Celsius. To the side of the temperature gauge was a variety of other numbers, including the time. The box was linked to the monitors within the room, so the patient's blood pressure, respiratory rate, blood oxygen saturation, carbon dioxide production, and body temperature could be viewed without entering the room. Beneath the line of digital numbers was a heart rhythm monitor, or ECG, for continuous monitoring of the patient's heart. Beneath the ECG tracing was a small TV screen, about 6 x 6 inches, transmitting a close-up of the patient's body from the chest up, thanks to a ceiling-mounted, closed-circuit video camera. A large metal tube entered the roof of each of the ICU rooms. Jack noted this and assumed the hoses they saw from the outside were connected to this tube, but he couldn't imagine what it was for. There was one nurse for each bed, the letters RN visible on the front and back of their MOPP suits. There were physicians, too, identified in the same way.

Catherine, Jack, and Marla strolled down between two rows, looking from side to side. Rick, Lucy, and Suzanne stood in place, trying to take it all in. Not all rooms had a patient. The group paused at one of the cubicles containing a patient. It was a male, probably in his mid-thirties. He was on a ventilator. There was an IV pole on either side of the bed, one holding a bag of clear fluid and the other a yellowish liquid. He was covered up to the waist by a blisteringly white sheet. A large bandage was on his head; an apple-sized stain of bright red blood was on the dressing. The observers could hear the ventilator cycling slow breaths through the glass.

"We decided that it would be more likely for us to be able to obtain the kind of sample we needed if we had the trauma victims here, on-site. As soon as they die, that metal pipe you see coming into the ceiling will dump liquid nitrogen over the body. Every patient on the ventilator has an NG tube—a nasogastric tube that goes in their nose and down into their stomach. Once the patient dies, an alarm will alert the nurse to connect the NG to a small spigot immediately—you see it coming off the metal pipe there," he said, pointing to a finger-sized tube hanging off of the larger tube in the ceiling. "It will pump the liquid nitrogen into the stomach and immediately freeze the core of the body. The external body surfaces will be frozen by spraying the body from spigots in the ceiling. If the patient isn't on a ventilator, the nurse will quickly place an OG or oral-gastric tube—the same as the NG, only it goes through the mouth instead of the nose. She has 90 seconds to complete it before the liquid nitrogen pours out from above, and she has to make damn sure the door to the cubicle is sealed. It isn't much time, but these folks have been trained out the wahzoo, and they've got it down."

Jack had been listening carefully."So, to be clear, this only happens if the patient dies, right?"

"Absolutely, Jack. No one is being killed. All of these patients are being treated to the fullest extent of modern medical and surgical intensive care. At least one of the doctors is a trained trauma surgeon, and the other is an intensive care specialist, and one of each is here all the time. Those who recover will be sent to a regular hospital for further rehab. In fact," Ted looked around, paused, and pointed, "look right there." In the next row of cubicles, a patient was sitting on the side of the bed, assisted by a worker with the letters PT marked on her MOPP gear. "That's our physical therapist helping the patient with strengthening exercises. He couldn't sit up by himself a week ago. He'll be discharged tomorrow."

"Impressive, Ted," Jack said. "I guess the question comes from still just a little edgy."

"Welp, I s'pose bein' part of a small North Korean invasion force will do that to a feller," Ted said, grinning. He then gave a long sigh. "Look, you guys, sooner or later, one of these injured patients is going to be stable, maybe even getting better, maybe, like that woman over there, getting ready to walk out of here. But instead of walking out of here, one of them will die suddenly, unpredictably. No warning, no nothing. Just like all the reports we've had from all over the world. And there won't be a damn thing we can do to stop it. But when it happens, we can get tissue that has only been dead for ninety seconds. Hell, most of the tissue will be frozen before the cells even have a chance to die. It will be like obtaining living tissue. None of this could be done if the patients were in a regular hospital. And it sure as hell can't be done in the field."

Jack felt a palpable release of tension with this revelation. He watched Catherine eye a chair, wearily walk over to it, and sit down.

"Well, Ted. I have to admit. This is more than I expected in India. Your modification is amazingly great. Now, let's hope we're smart enough to use what you have," Catherine said.

The moment of near-peaceful reflection was broken by the blurt of an alarm toward the back of the room. A bright red light was flashing over the door exiting the long sloping walkway that the team had noted entering the back of the ICU complex.

"What in the hell is that?" Jack asked.

"We have a new patient arriving," replied Ted. "They're brought into the ER upstairs and undergo stabilization and decontamination before they're brought down here. If they need surgery, they get it, too." Jack migrated closer to the stainless steel swinging doors, the others following. The doors opened with the hum of automation, revealing two individuals in MOPP, one RN, and one MD, pushing a hospital bed. An IV pole on the corner held a unit of blood that was dripping rapidly into the patient's arm. The RN had one hand on the bed's headboard, pushing, and one hand pulling a portable ventilator behind. The ventilator was running at a pace faster than normal breathing, with the familiar FOOOSH-HUSH, FOOOSH-HUSH cycling of the ventilator bellows. Several other MOPP-suited ICU workers descended upon the new arrival as they rolled through the doors, looking at the IV lines to ensure they were working and checking the endotracheal tube exiting the man's mouth to ensure it was securely fastened and wouldn't accidentally be dislodged.

"Put him in bay 22, over there," said an MD, pointing toward an empty room. The attendants complied by pushing the bed toward the room, with Jack and the team following. The process was amazingly smooth and efficient. Jack couldn't help but notice the man's chest and the head was heavily bandaged, bright red being more plentiful than the original white color of the gauze. Out of each side of the man's chest were tubes the size of a longshoreman's thumb, connected to longer tubes that ran to a rectangular box collecting blood and a bubbling blue fluid in a separate chamber. Another clear tube emerged from under the sheet, draining clear, yellow urine collecting in a bag suspended from the bed's railing.

Jack elbowed Ted while they were walking and said, "Ted, I gotta tell you, I am impressed with this. It's a bit overwhelming to get my head around it, but wow! It is amazingly well-designed, and your people seem to be all over it."

"Yeah, thanks. I do think this setup gives you folks as good a chance as possible to figure this thing out," Ted noted, glancing sideways at Jack.

The attendants paused as the RN opened the door to bay 22. The latch clicked, and there was a sound of a vacuum being released like that heard when opening a new can of coffee.

"Why does it make that noise, Ted?" Marla asked.

"Oh, yeah, I forgot an important point about the rooms. Each one of them is a negative pressure room. When the door is opened, air only flows into the room, not out of the room—in case it's infectious. We don't want it pushed out into this room. Everyone is wearing MOPP, but there's no need to take the risk."

The attendants lined up the bed with the door and guided it into the ICU bay. Jack, Marla, and Catherine were standing on one side of the bed, and Ted, Rick, and Lucy were on the other, as it was pushed by the RN and pulled by the MD head-first into the bay. Jack couldn't help but notice the man's face as he went by. It was calm, almost smiling. He was handsome, too, at least to the extent one could tell, given his injury. As the foot end of the bed passed by, he noticed a sticker pasted on the footboard: MEHTA, DHANESH; GUNSHOT WOUND TO THE HEAD AND CHEST. Once in the room, the nurse plugged the ventilator into a wall outlet and switched off the battery powering the unit. She again checked tubes and other lines, ensuring nothing had been inadvertently disconnected in the transport. Satisfied with the delivery, the two attendants walked out of the room and closed the glass door, sealing the patient to his fate. The doctor hung a clipboard on a hook beside the monitors outside the room.

Jack picked up the patient's clipboard and perused the face page. It was Mr. Mehta's personal information. Worn pictures from being carried for too long in a wallet—probably the victim's wife and three young kids—stared at him, smiling soft, loving smiles. Jack looked from the bloody body back to the clipboard. The faces looking back seemed to be silently pleading with him. Dhanesh might die of his wounds, or he might get better under the watchful eyes of the ICU staff. He might walk out of the complex with a new life. Or he could die suddenly, at any time and without explanation. But one thing was sure: It suddenly felt much more personal to Jack than it did just a few moments ago. Now there were faces. Names. Dhanesh Mehta, and his wife and kids. Something felt oddly different. *The poor bastard has kids.* The faces of his children... were now indelible in his brain.

"So, Ted," Marla said, with hesitation, "I have a question. The sequence of death has been predictable. Eastern and southern Africa, western Africa, the Middle East, and now we think it will be India and the Pacific Rim. If we have a lab full of native Indians as the research support staff, what happens when death comes to India? Won't we be screwed? I mean, if the staff starts dying, everything could stop dead, right? Uh...pardon the pun."

"Well, Marla, remember that contingency plan I told you about? Thanks to yer theory, I took the precautionary step of recruiting the research support staff mainly from Europe and the U.S., although there are some Asian folks and even a few Indians. I figured we might need people around a bit longer than... uh... the Indian folks might survive," replied Ted. "I thought we might need a few more rounds if you catch my drift before we nailed down a cause and solution." He paused.

"There are two requirements that all these folks. Of course, they have to be capable in their field and speak English. I also have a succession plan, if you will, for all researchers, based upon where they are from. So, for instance, I'm planning to replace our Asian workers next, so I have European, and U.S.-based replacements lined up. They can be here in less than 24 hours," Ted said matter-of-factly.

"Jesus. That's a little cold," Jack said.

"Yeah, but necessary," Ted replied, deadpan.

"Amazing," Rick sighed, shaking his head. "You have thought of everything."

"Yup. It's a whole lot easier to replace workers than build the first-class place like this somewhere else," Ted said, waving his arm in a semi-circle. "And, it doesn't just stop there..."

"Whaddya mean?" Jack asked.

"Well, it wouldn't just be a problem in the lab if the Indians start dying. It'll be a problem on a much bigger scale. If that happened, we would lose power in the research facility— we'd be dead in the water. So I have the U.S. Army Corp of Engineers manning backup at the power stations supplying Breech Candy and a whole oil refinery that can continue to fuel it, to boot."

"What happens if we're here long enough to deplete the refinery's reserves?" Rick asked?

"We'll divert oil tankers from the Middle East. The president has approved the whole plan. You all have become the Center of the Universe."

"Oh, goody," Jack said. "Nothing like a little pressure."

CHAPTER FORTY-TWO

Eleanor Davies had saved for her entire career, 25 years as a secretary, to afford this trip. She'd always wanted to see India, the former British colony. To her, it had the best of both worlds—the rustic and ancient, sprinkled with the refined legacy of the British occupation.

She was amazed by Mumbai's size. Massive by any measure, it made London seem like a countryside village, and she couldn't believe there were 14 million inhabitants. Her Blue Moon travel guide said that Mumbai, the capital of the Indian state of Maharashta, was home to many critical Indian institutions, including the Reserve Bank of India and the Bombay Stock Exchange. But what she noticed most was how abysmally poor the people were...almost all of them.

Eleanor's sister had begged her to cancel her trip in light of the fact it had been just under a week since a swath of death had cut through the Middle East like a Persian sword. Eleanor had waved off her concerns as an alarmist. Her doctor had started her on antiretroviral medication as a "precaution" before leaving London, even though it was unlikely to help. A quarter decade of yearning needed to be quenched, and now, she was going to drink it in by God.

Eleanor was well aware of the blight affecting the world, but it appeared to her that the Indian commoner cared little about what had happened in Africa and the Middle East. She didn't sense the palpable, society-level anxiety prevalent in England and was glad for it. She attributed this to illiteracy or perhaps the Hindu worldview but wondered how word of mouth hadn't at least spread concern.

She wandered most of the morning, meandering toward her goal, The Chor Bazaar—the thieves' market. She arrived just before noon. It was buzzing with the usual early-afternoon bargaining. She had read that the bazaar was a popular tourist destination in Mumbai, and she was excited to see the Indian art and antiquities.

Eleanor decided to purchase a small stone figurine of Ganesha, the Indian elephant deity known as the Lord of Success, from a curbside vendor, thinking it would be the perfect memento of her trip. She rifled through her purse and dug out 100 rupees. She was startled by the sound of ceramic breaking and looked up to see the vendor, a dark-skinned, thin Indian man of about 40 years, pass out across his cart.

Figurines flew in every direction, shattering into a mosaic of shards on the rough cobblestone street. Eleanor, stocky and probably twice the man's weight, hustled around the cart and laid him back onto the ground. His eyes, wide open, scared her. As people crowded around the man's body, staring down in disbelief, she could feel fear rise in those around her. Eleanor heard another scream ripple through the air from half a block away.

Just days after the Middle Eastern crisis had ended, a new one began. By sunset, Eleanor found herself amid millions of dead in Mumbai. She was numb, and as she sat in her hotel room, she wondered what the final tally of the dead would be in India, home to one and a half billion people.

CHAPTER FORTY-THREE

"Hello?" Catherine said, answering the phone.

"Catherine, it's Ted. Get over here. ICU patients just started droppin' like flies. Three, to be exact. And Catherine, they aren't dyin' of their injuries. Rick and Lucy are already here." Catherine clicked the phone off as she stood up. Jack and Marla instinctively knew what was going down from the look on Catherine's face.

They sprinted to the locker room, suited up in MOPP, and went through the decon procedure. The door to the research complex swung open, exposing a hornet's nest of activity. Ted was waiting for them, with Rick, Lucy, and Suzanne clustered around him, all in MOPP.

"Follow me," he said, turning and walking rapidly toward the stainless steel ICU. He pushed open the swinging doors, turned left, then right, and walked directly to bay 22. The casualty was the injured person they watched being brought in during the facility tour, Dhanesh Mehta. They could see the outline of Dhanesh's body through a light fog, coated in a thin, smoking crystal blanket. The mist was being slowly sucked out of the room by the negative pressure system. A digital thermometer to the right of the door read -20° Celsius.

After a moment of silence, during which Jack's brain struggled to grasp the totality of the scene, he asked, "So what happened, Ted?"

"Mr. Mehta was stable when he was brought here yesterday." Ted flipped through the paper on his clipboard. "He had a nasty brain injury, a contusion from a shotgun blast, and a few intracranial pellets; and had been in a coma until late last night. The docs did a great job with him. He could move his limbs, and they were slowly weaning him off the ventilator. He was responding to simple questions with eye blinks and head nods. Another day and he would have been taken off the respirator and probably been out of bed." Ted paused. "Then things went to hell in a handbasket before we even knew what was happening. Here. Watch this." Ted reached over and pushed a button on the monitor outside the room, beside the door. He held his finger on the button, the video running in reverse, slowly at first but accelerating. Simultaneously, the vital sign and room temperature read-outs dialed back too. Ted released the button and pushed PLAY.

"Here, at 14:33 today, you can see that Mr. Mehta's vital signs are perfect. A blood pressure of 124/72, pulse is 78, temperature is 98.4. All normal. Look here... you can see Mr. Mehta interacting with the nurse. Let me fast forward a bit," said Ted, the group's eyes glued to the small screen. He advanced the video until the clock read 14:42. "Again, everything is normal. Now watch what happens when the clock hits just after 14:44." As the time ticked down, Jack's epinephrine levels skyrocketed, and he could feel his heart pounding. The digital clock flipped over to 14:44. Five seconds passed. Ten. The patient's heart rate started to drop: 78...70...64...60...52...44...25...8. Zero. The blood pressure plummeted from normal to immeasurable. The nurse checked the IV lines in a panic. A red light started flashing simultaneously with the bleat of the warning horn that signaled the 90-second countdown until the release of liquid nitrogen into the room. The nurse was shocked into an erect stance and seemed paralyzed. The MOPP mask hid her expression, but her actions quickly demonstrated she realized what was happening. She quickly disconnected Dhanesh's nasogastric tube from the suction canister, then reached up and pulled the liquid nitrogen line down from overhead and connected it to the tube entering his nose with remarkable efficiency and the outward appearance of calmness. She then walked out of the video camera's view, with 50 seconds left on the timer. The 50 seconds playing in real-time seemed to drag on and on to Jack, but when the countdown turned zero, the camera showed the room filling with icy smoke. Dhanesh Mehta's dead body was frozen to the very core, 90 seconds after death. Ted reached up and stopped the replay. Jack and the others stood silently, looking through the mist at Dhanesh, realizing the salvation of the human race might be lying frozen before them.

Jack and the team stood in silence, staring at the frost-covered body through the mist. Jack couldn't suppress his concern for what would happen to Dhanesh's kids; their smiling faces had haunted him since he had seen their photos. *Had their mother already died?* If not, how much longer would the children have a parent? What would happen to the kids when she was gone? The personalization of the crisis, having seen Dhanesh the day he came in, lingered at that place in Jack's head between the conscious and unconscious.

"What's next, Catherine?" Marla asked.

"Collect samples of all tissues, beginning with Mr. Mehta, and process them for, well, everything. You name it. Bacterial and viral cultures, toxicology, light and electron microscopy. Any other ideas?"

Silence.

"Well, let's get at it then, folks," Ted said. "It's time for you to earn your keep."

CHAPTER FORTY-FOUR

Just 30 minutes after Dhanesh's death, samples from every organ had been taken, and processing initiated. Results, however, were still days away.

While interested in the viral culture results, Jack was more anxious to see what the electron microscope might elucidate. Clues to viral activity could be gleaned using microscopic examination of the cytoskeleton, the cell's interior support structure. The long process of getting specimens through the EM prep process raised his anxiety. It was painful. He couldn't remember the process in detail, so he sat down at the computer and opened the browser. He typed *preparation of specimens for electron microscopy* into the search engine and hit the RETURN key. A page of links appeared, and he clicked on the most logical descriptor, then was directed to a page titled "ELECTRON MICROSCOPY: SPECIMEN PREP." He glanced down the page. "Jesus..." he muttered under his breath, disappointed that he had correctly remembered how long it took and how complicated it was.

He used his finger to add up the time needed to finish the prep phase, line by line. *Sixty damn hours.* It was 18:15. Hardly three hours had passed since the deaths, and he was already anxious. The tissue wasn't even through the first prep step. The next 56 hours would be a bitch. *Damn.* The rest of the world could die in that time.

ICU deaths in rapid sequence. Flash-frozen bodies. Deaths had been reported all over the city within the same timeframe as the ICU deaths. The events of the Chor Bazaar were all over the news, of course. A WNN news helicopter had been filming the aftermath at the Bazaar. It crashed when the Indian pilot slumped over dead on the stick, pushing it forward and sending the craft careening into the mass of already-dead bodies peppering the Bazaar. The fire that resulted swallowed up the dead in a ready-made funeral pyre fueled by high-octane aviation gas. It was bizarre enough to be science fiction.

The team sprawled on chairs and sofas in the commons just after midnight exhausted from the day's events.

"I don't understand why the periods between death are so screwy," Catherine said. "I mean, western Africa was hit about twelve days after eastern and southern Africa. Then there were only two or three days between western Africa and the Middle East. Marla's calculations for the Middle East were right on target. The calculations made sense to me—to all of us. It made sense that the time between episodes would shorten because the time between ancient migrations from one area to the other became shorter and shorter, right Marla?"

Marla took a sip of her soda. Jack could tell she was pondering the question.

"It's driving me nuts," Marla finally said. "One thing we know for sure is the path of the migration. It's not just theory anymore. But the timing's off, or... or... something." Seemingly perplexed, she put her finger into the top of her soda and swirled it as if mixing cream in coffee. Suddenly, she slammed her hand down on the coffee table, startling the group with the un-Marla-esque maneuver. "I know! Genetic drift."

"What?" Catherine said.

"Genetic drift. We must be seeing the results of genetic drift across millennia. Not only does it explain the visible physical differences between the peoples of the Middle East, India, and Thailand, but it may explain the unpredictable slowing of the timeline."

"I understand what genetic drift is, honey, but I'm not following where you're going with it," Jack said.

"Genetic drift played an important part in the development of physical characteristics of the people populating the earth and may explain why people migrated. If you were born with skin that was darker or eyes that were narrower than the rest of your clan in the Middle East, you might have been viewed as abnormal and ostracized. The maternal instincts of even the earliest humans were probably really powerful. Some groups likely just killed the baby that looked different—infanticide." Jack noticed Catherine wince at the thought of killing babies.

Marla continued, "Some mothers would have invariably protected their children, perhaps leaving with the father to a location far enough away from the main group as to be safe. They reproduce again, and the same difference — another dark-skinned or narrowed-eyed child is born — stabilizing the change. Then other couples in the same situation run into the first couple, stay together and develop a larger clan. The dark-skinned kids grow up together and have offspring of their own, making more kids that look like them. Before you know it, the Indian subcontinent is populated with dark-skinned people—in just a few generations."

"Sure, that makes sense. But what does it have to do with the screwed-up time frame we are dealing with?" Rick asked.

"We only know of differences that we can *see*," Marla replied. "There are — without a doubt — *differences we cannot see*. Some of the changes peoples of India and Southeast Asia and the Aboriginals may have fixed into their genome by genetic drift were an enhanced resistance to whatever is now causing death. Their bodies may be able to fight it off longer. I mean, we know that HIV is uniformly lethal if not treated. But some individuals do much better for much longer without any treatment. They still die—but the process is delayed, for whatever reason. And some individuals can resist HIV infection altogether.”

“So the unanticipated delays between regional deaths are due to the same genetic process that led to different phenotypes, the physical, visible differences of the people?” Catherine said.

“Exactly,” Marla continued. “It makes sense that mutations of genetic drift affected not just physical appearance, but also physiological function—the way their bodies are reacting to whatever is going on. Some aspects of how their bodies work are different, perhaps including the immune system. If I’m correct in this logic, the deaths will continue. Maybe it won’t happen as fast between populations. Unfortunately, according to the migration theory and genetic drift, we don’t have any way to predict how long we have before the next round of death, China and Russia. And, I think, now that we’ve confirmed that Macaulay’s migration theory is correct, we can be certain of that.”

“Great!” Jack said excitedly. The entire room looked at him as if he were nuts. He looked around at his colleagues, who were all staring at him as if he had lost his mind. “What?” Jack said, puzzled.

“What the *hell* are you so excited about?” Rick said. “I hate unpredictability.”

A door opened, and Ted slipped into the room, unnoticed.

“What do you mean? *What am I excited about*? Isn’t it obvious? It means we may have more time than we thought to figure out what this is—and how to treat it! I hate unpredictability too, Rick, but this could be unpredictability in the right direction.”

Ted cleared his throat, and the room turned to look at him. “We may not have as much time as you think,” he said in a depressed tone. Jack frowned at Ted, who, he had learned, had a penchant for dramatics. Ted picked up the TV remote and clicked on the set. The text at the bottom of the WNN screen read:

NORTH KOREA DECLARES WAR ON THE U.S.

CHAPTER FORTY-FIVE

Jack had been up for half an hour. Even while lying in bed, he sensed the 24/7 hum of the lab, and it was downright irritating. The elusiveness of a solution intensified his intellectual focus. He knew he wasn't the only one that recognized the urgency of the situation, but it felt that way to him sometimes, with the entire human species depending on finding a cause and solution.

The most challenging times for Jack were those mandated by process: The time needed to process the tissue for light and electron microscopy and the time spent waiting for cultures to incubate. The time required for extracting tissue fluids for the spectrometer. All there was to do was wait.

He got out of bed and ambled quietly from his room to the kitchen. As he made coffee, he wondered if there had ever been such an abused coffee machine. He poured probably his 15th cup in the past 24 hours.

He sat down and began surfing the internet. No surprises. The news was uniformly depressing. An estimated eight million dead in Mumbai alone. He suspected that by the end of the day, death in other cities around the country would result in such disarray that there would be no way to know, much less confirm, how many had died.

Dawn came while Jack sipped his 16th cup of coffee. He knew it was dawn only because the clock read seven. He missed seeing the Kansas sun. *Hell, any sun.*

A door opened behind him, and Marla walked into the kitchen. Considering what had transpired in the past couple of days, the fact that Jack was able to notice how damn sexy she looked in her low-cut, V-neck tee-shirt and running shorts was an impressive example of how effectively one can suppress bad things in one's mind given the right stimulus.

"My God, Marla," Jack said, "You come out looking like that, and there isn't any place where we can go where people won't know exactly what we're doing?" He chuckled.

She gave him a fake frown and turned to the coffee pot so Jack would not be able to see her expression morphing into a sly smile. He walked over, put his arms around her waist, and pulled their bodies tightly together from shin to neck. He loved the way she smelled. He slid a hand under the tee shirt and caressed her belly, reconnecting to the softness and warmth of her physical being.

"God, Marla, I've missed this. It's been so hectic, so stressful, that I've forgotten to take care of you. In a way, it's times like this that I should be connected to you, not further away. I'm sorry."

She turned and kissed him gently, arms around his neck. They smiled tenderly at each other, eyes softening. Jack's hands migrated, one downward and one to her face, each caressing that which was willingly offered. He pulled her lips to his in a deeper kiss. The heat was building — and parts hardening — Jack temporarily forgetting where they were. He picked her up and sat her down on the counter, hands caressing her backside, neck to butt, while Marla's hands trapped each side of Jack's face in ever-deepening kisses.

"Come on. Right here..." whispered Marla.

"Jesus!" Jack and Marla jumped at hearing a voice that wasn't theirs. "Why don't you two get a hotel room, for God's sake! You're blocking access to the coffee." Catherine had walked into the room unnoticed. The heat dissipated more quickly than it had appeared, and the situation partially deflated in a manner of speaking.

"Morning, Catherine," Jack said, somewhat dejected.

"Morning, Jack. It appears as if you have been up for a while," Catherine said, grinning, tipping her head toward the bulge in his sweatpants. He turned away, his face red, generating the heat this time. "And good morning to you too, Marla."

"Hi, Catherine," Marla responded. "I hope we didn't wake you."

"Not at all." Catherine paused. In a more solemn tone, she said, "Seriously, you guys, if you want some time, I understand."

"Thanks, Catherine. We appreciate it. We'll take a rain check this morning. Too much to do—you know, working on saving the world and everything," Jack said with a grin.

Twenty-four hours had passed since the bacterial cultures had been put into the incubator. The entire team and a bevy of other interested parties collected in the microbiology lab, nervous anticipation visible. Jack watched as the lab technician bent over, peering into the glass-topped Petri dishes. Each dish was labeled with the tissue specimen origin: BRAIN, LUNG, HEART, KIDNEY, BLOOD, LIVER, SMALL INTESTINE. Glancing through all specimens, she shook her head, saying nothing. The tech pushed the top shelf back into the incubator and pulled out the bottom drawer: COLON, MUSCLE, BONE,

PANCREAS, ADRENAL, ARTERY, VEIN, TESTICLE, PERIPHERAL NERVE.

"Sorry, everyone, nothing here. All negative."

The group's hopeful anticipation, palpable a few moments ago, devolved back to their baseline of anxiety. Word spread quickly that the cultures were negative.

Jack attempted to inject some optimism, saying, "Sometimes it takes 48 hours, even for the aerobic bacteria to grow. If it's a fastidious organism, it may be picky enough to require more time."

The tech chimed in, saying, "Yeah and the anaerobes are over there. They can take up to a week to show." Jack could see that wasn't what the group wanted to hear. Another week without answers, and all of Asia might be face down.

Dinnertime, always late, was a precious, rare time for unwinding and no-holds-barred brainstorming, despite the team's exhaustion. They revisited what had been done to date and dissected out what might be more successful moving forward.

Rick and Lucy recounted their experiences and frustrations from Bethesda, right up to the disappointment of the cultures earlier in the day. Each team member filtered what they heard through their area of expertise, trying to connect the dots. Theories flew around the room, revisiting many of the ideas proposed back in Washington.

The NSA, still not having found any damning evidence in the North Korean lab materials, left Lucy and Jack thinking it was infectious, and like COVID developing in Chinese wet markets, hypothesized that whatever this was had started in an African animal vector, jumped species, and was now infecting humans. The migratory path the organism was following was related to population-based susceptibility—an unfortunate genetic Achilles' heel.

Jack, leaning back in his chair with his hands behind his head, realized that his wife had said nothing. She was a textbook picture of considered patience, even in the face of exhaustion, listening to each scientist, in turn, silent through the entire conversation. He knew—*no, was certain*—she had thoughts she was not sharing. Everything they were dealing with was unbounded by any known scientific or anthropological parameters—pure conjecture. There was a short pause in the discussion as they all contemplated sleep. Jack used it to pull her into the conversation.

"Marla, you haven't said a word all night. Something's bothering you. None of us know what the hell's going on, so I don't think your opinion could be any less helpful than any one of ours," Jack said, prompting her.

Marla leaned over, folded her arms on the table, took a deep breath, and softly said, "What if it's genetic?"

Catherine said, "That's what Jack and Lucy are suggesting, based on your theory Marla—that an individual's resistance to this is genetically determined."

"No, that's not what I mean," Marla replied, pausing. She took a deep breath, then said, "I mean, what if it isn't a genetic susceptibility to infection, but *only* genetic? What if this is a sort of genetic self-destruction of the human species? Like our genes have been set actually to cause our annihilation?"

The room felt instantaneously much cooler to Jack. The thought of a genetic predisposition to self-destruction wasn't something he wanted to consider, not out of impossibility but out of fear. It was foreign, the possibility terrifying. He could understand bacteria and viruses. They could eventually treat those things. But to think their cells had a built-in self-destruction mechanism? An internal time bomb? Unfathomable.

Marla continued, "I know it sounds crazy, but there are analogies. The dinosaurs, for example. The widely held theory of their disappearance is that a meteor struck the earth and created a dust cloud that blocked out the sun and killed the vegetation that the herbivores required. Once the herbivores died off, the predators followed." She paused. "But there are paleontologists who believe the dinosaurs evolved to a point where, genetically, they were unsustainable. They were too large to live, requiring too much to sustain themselves. In essence, their genetics made them into the most fearsome creatures ever to walk the earth. But those same genes may well have sealed their destruction." More silence.

"What if," Marla said, "the human genome evolved with a sort of suicide gene, set to go off at some future point — at a time when the Earth's population had grown to the point that would threaten the very survival of the species?" Marla paused again. Jack watched her, motionless, contemplating the possibility. She continued by saying, "What if the intent of the gene was to self-limit the human race at some point in time to ensure the future survival of the species?"

Marla's eyes narrowed as she started to speak again. "I mean, maybe we are looking at a point in human evolution where we've become the genetic equivalent of lemmings careening over a cliff and swimming out to sea, only to drown? I know that's a myth, but it seems apropos in the current setting."

Jack, noticing everyone staring at his wife, finally broke the silence, to Marla's noticeable relief. "Jesus, honey, glad you got that off your chest," he said, nervously chuckling.

As wild and implausible as they were, Marla's comments added a new dimension to his and the group's thinking—one that scared Jack well beyond anything he had felt before.

The clock hands migrated to midnight, and Jack suggested that sleep was a commodity they needed. Exhausted, the group broke off to their sleeping quarters—except for Catherine and Rick. Jack looked over his shoulder at them. "You two kids better get some rest too," he said with a smirk.

"We're just going to stay up and chat for a few more minutes, Jack," Catherine said. Jack disappeared down the hallway, hoping to pick up where he had been forced to leave with Marla that morning.

Rick and Catherine stayed up another half hour, watching TV and talking. Catherine turned the volume down on the TV and cocked her head toward the hallway, listening. She didn't hear any sounds emanating from the sleeping quarters.

"I think they're all asleep," she whispered, leaning over and kissing Rick gently, then more passionately. She reached for his hand as she stood up and escorted him to her room. She shut the door behind her and slid out of her clothes in a striptease. She noticed Rick smiling in appreciation—and anticipation.

CHAPTER FORTY-SIX

Rick walked to the pathology lab with Ted. "It's been two days since that Mehta guy died," Rick said. "Kinda ironic that a poor man from a Mumbai slum may be making the most important contribution to the world's salvation."

"The light microscopy samples should be done processing any minute," said Ted. "There will be enough to keep you busy until lunchtime." Rick noticed that Ted's good ol' boy Texas accent occasionally seemed to disappear.

"I have no doubt I can keep busy," Rick said. "The question is, will I find any clues. The samples we had back in the States were always too far along the decomposition curve for me to make heads or tails of things. Too much degradation. If the bodies were frozen as quickly as they seem to have been, and if there is anything that can be seen by light microscopy, we'll find it today." There was optimism and resolve in Rick's voice.

"Here are the first 50 slides, Dr. Matthews," a lab tech with a thick German accent said. Rick reached over with a deep, deliberate sigh and picked up slide #1, labeled MYOCARDIUM; LEFT VENTRICLE. He put it on the microscope's carriage and dialed the lens to 500X, knowing that a lower power would not reveal any secrets before he looked. He peered through the binoculars. "Yep. It's heart," he whispered to himself. He dialed the lens through 750X and up to 1500X. Twirling the microscope's knob, he brought the tissue into focus. He could only see a few cells in the field at this power, but the magnification allowed him to see the muscle cells clearly—sarcomere striations within the muscle cell. *Check.* The cell nucleus and nucleoli are sharp, well-defined membranes. *Check.* There had been no degradation of the heart sample.

The tech set down a second slide tray. BRAIN: FRONTAL LOBE, said the label on the first slide. Rick placed it on the microscope carriage and twirled through the magnifications. The brain cells' nuclei were crisp; the nucleoli, intact. *Bingo.* At least for the light microscopic exam, the rapid freezing strategy had worked. This was important enough to relay to the rest of the team, so he pushed the button on his communicator, notifying the others to turn on their MOPP headset.

"Hey, it's Rick. I have some good news. My quick review of the heart and brain shows that the nuclear structures and membranes are intact. The rapid freezing approach worked beautifully. We're on our way, folks. If there's something that we can see by structural exam of the tissue, we'll find it. I'm betting on EM to show us what we need."

Everyone responded at the same time. Rick couldn't decide who said what, but the cacophony was upbeat. "I'll keep you posted," he said.

Before everyone had signed off, Catherine said, "Anyone else finding anything? Jack? Lucy?"

"I've looked at about 60 percent of the bacterial specimens, and there've been a few things growing, but I think they're contaminates," Lucy said. "I'll have a better idea when I can see a smear of them under the microscope."

Jack chimed in, "The tissue cultures are alive and well. Every last one of them, damn it. Not a single sign of viral infection. Sorry to disappoint."

"Hey, we can only act on what we find," Catherine said. "I'd have to say that we have some very positive information—finally. Rick, keep us in the loop. Have the techs told you when the EM samples will be available?"

"At five a.m. tomorrow, almost 60 hours to the minute after samples were harvested," Rick said. "I'm hopeful EM will be our ticket."

The team met outside the decontamination room door at noon as they'd agreed to, stripped off their gear, and met in the kitchen for lunch and mental decompression. Rick and Jack were sitting at the table when the four women walked in.

"Jeez, even in MOPP gear, you guys stick together. Why can't women ever go to the bathroom by themselves?" Jack said, smirking. Marla gave him a look of pretend anger, then a pout, fading into a broad grin. Catherine's early morning interruption the day before had sustained their flirtatious mood.

Back in MOPP gear and the lab by 1:30, they broke off into their workgroups. The afternoon would be a repeat of the morning, save Rick's finding. No additional information was gleaned from hours of tedium. Rick couldn't believe that the glum group at dinner was the same group who, just eight hours earlier, had been upbeat, even optimistic. He collapsed with the rest of them on couches in the commons area and watched the movie Groundhog Day. It was an apt metaphor for what he felt as the team retired to their sleeping quarters, exhausted, unsure of what tomorrow would bring.

CHAPTER FORTY-SEVEN

"Wow, you're up early," Jack said, walking into the kitchen and finding Rick already there.

"I had trouble sleeping, knowing that the EM specimens would be ready this morning," Rick said. "I finally just got up at four and came to the kitchen for coffee."

"Well, I hope today's the day," Jack said.

"You and me both," Rick said. "If it keeps goin' like this, death might be preferable." They chuckled uncomfortably.

"I'm ready to go home, but I'd rather it not be in a box," Jack said.

Jack watched as the entire team assembled at 5 a.m., bleary-eyed and edgy. He knew if they didn't find something soon, it was likely they would all die. Despite trying to hold a stiff upper lip with him, he sensed Marla was increasingly worried. Her Asian heritage made her more likely to be affected sooner than others in the group.

Jack followed the group to the lab. He and Lucy began examining the anaerobic cultures. Although both knew it wasn't where the money was, they applied diligence. If the pathogen were bacterial, they would have had a clue weeks ago. After finishing the entire anaerobic Petri dishes, they re-examined the cell cultures for viral activity. Nothing.

Rick was energized when he entered the EM lab, the morning's coffee having taken hold. He greeted the techs and asked, "Are the EM samples out yet?"

The female tech responded in her thick, German accent, "Ja. We have set the ones that are ready by the scope."

"Fabulous," Rick said. Sitting down, he opened the vacuum chamber of the transmission EM and surveyed the samples in front of him, picking up BRAIN: BRAINSTEM. He placed it into the vacuum chamber and pushed a couple of buttons that turned from green to red, accompanied by the WHUMP-WHUMP-WHUMP of the vacuum pump sucking the air out of the chamber. He sat back. His thoughts were in Brownian motion but always returned to how sick he was of the damn MOPP suit. He couldn't help but watch the timer on the instrument panel of the scope, counting down from ten minutes. Indeed a situation of the watched pot that never boiled.

The shrill beep of the vacuum seal being complete sliced through his random thoughts, causing an epinephrine surge from deep inside his guts. His heart, racing well above its average rate, lapped itself as he reached over and pushed the SCAN button on the scope. The screen fluttered white-to-black and back-to-white as it slowly revealed an image. The smaller EM screen of the scope was linked to a 42" monitor suspended from the ceiling in the corner of the room.

He reached over and twirled a dial. The specimen came into view, magnified at 500X. He could see a matrix of glial cells, the girder beams of brain tissue, and neurons, akin to power lines that transmit messages throughout the brain, typical of the brainstem in network-like formation. He dialed up the magnification to 1500X, adjusting the specimen to focus the scope over a single neuron. His head was pounding. He realized he was holding his breath. He sat back and consciously took some deep breaths. The pounding in his head faded. He focused the cell's nucleus in the center of the screen. He dialed the magnification up to 50,000X. He examined the nucleus in detail, starting at the 12 o'clock point on the circular structure and moving toward the center in a deliberate pattern that ensured complete visualization. He moved to 1 o'clock, repeating the pattern. He did this until the entire nucleus had been examined. Good news: the specimen was perfectly preserved even at the subcellular level. Bad news: it was normal. He studied two more nuclei, randomly selected. Also normal.

He decided to take a different approach, quickly scanning several entire neurons at lower power to see if anything jumped out at him. He dialed the magnification down to 3000X. Nucleus, OK. Nucleoli, OK. The cytoplasm, the cell's blood equivalent, appeared normal. Within the cytoplasm floated the organelles, the cell's internal organs, each with their specific function. The endoplasmic reticulum, the protein factory: OK. The Golgi apparatus, a specialized manufacturing system that packages and ships the cell's products to other places in the body: normal. Cytosolic tubules, the train tracks along which cell organelles move from place to place within the cytoplasm: OK. Mitochondria, the energy production plant of the cell, the organelle that produces the cell's energy... Mitochondria... the...

"Holy shit!" Rick shouted, reflexively straightening his legs and coming to an erect position. He looked away from the tiny screen and closed his eyes. He opened them and looked at the screen again, focusing hard. He looked over at the big screen TV. It looked the same there, only about ten times bigger. He urgently scanned the next neuron and identified another mitochondrion. And another. And another. He scanned over, moving as far away from the first neuron as he could get within the specimen, making damn sure that what he was seeing wasn't just in a small section. Same thing. *Bingo!*

He pushed the communicator button on his MOPP suit. "Get down here. I think we have our first major clue." Within minutes, five more people were crowded into the EM lab, each huffing from the MOPP-suit challenged run, mask eyepieces fogged.

"Whatever this is, attacks the mitochondria of the cells, or at least the mitochondria of neurons. Look at this," Rick said, pointing out a jellybean-shaped structure with wart-like protuberances dead center on the screen. His coworkers turned to look at the monitor in the corner as Rick used a broom handle to point out the areas of interest on the large monitor. "The membrane looks like it has exploded from the inside out."

"You mean that watermelon-shaped thing? The thing that looks like a high-speed photo of a bullet blowing through a watermelon? That?" Ted asked. Rick saw everyone nodding in agreement with Ted's Texas redneck description. It did look like a transparent watermelon with little office cubicle-like dividers on the inside and the rind blown outward, like it had been shot by an assault rifle from the inside, frozen in place by high-speed photography. It had been frozen into place by liquid nitrogen at the time of death.

"Exactly. And look..." Rick stepped over to the EM control panel and adjusted some knobs. The image jumped to another mitochondrion. Same thing. "This isn't an isolated finding in one mitochondrion or one cell. I found this all over this specimen. I didn't take the time to confirm this by looking at another specimen, but this is real, and I'll bet dollars to donuts that other highly metabolic tissues will have this same characteristic—heart, liver, peripheral nerves, even kidney and the lining of the gastrointestinal tract." The group, Rick thought, seemed more puzzled than pleased.

Rick focused on yet another cell, homing in on a mitochondrion that looked like the others. "Look," he said, "the cristae is this membrane that folds on itself and makes little compartments like a honeycomb within the mitochondrion. You see here... they've lost their structure. I know you can't tell because I can't show you any normal mitochondrial structure here for comparison, but these look pale swollen. There are these blebs, these little balloon-like swellings on the outside of their membranes. Some of them have ruptured here, see?"

Rick, scanning the faces of his colleagues, said, "Here, look here." He grabbed a textbook, *The Microscopic Anatomy of Cells*, from a bookshelf behind him. He quickly looked up mitochondria in the index, turning to a full-page photomicrograph of a typical mitochondrion. "Look at this. This is what they are supposed to look like."

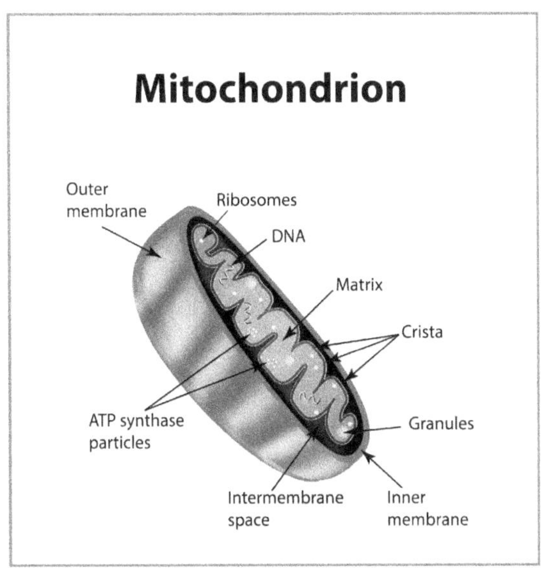

The mitochondria from Dhanesh Mehta had, on a cytological level, been blown to smithereens from the inside-out.

"OK. I'll bite," Ted said. "So what? So the mitochondria are messed up. Why's that important?'

"Mitochondria are, in the most elementary sense, the power generators for the cells of the body. They're like the lungs of the cell. They make ATP—adenosine triphosphate, the cell's fuel. It's like gasoline for a car or electricity for a light bulb. Our bodies need sugar in our diet to produce energy. The sugar we eat ultimately gets to the mitochondria, and it's there," Rick said, pointing at the book photo, "in the most elemental sense, that our body's energy is produced," Rick said.

"Oh. Well then, I guess that's a problem," Ted said, raising his furry eyebrows.

"Mitochondria do more than that, though, Ted. They function in different ways depending on the tissue," Rick said as he continued to work. "Mitochondria are organelles. Organelles are like organs within a cell. But what's critical to understand is that mitochondria are the only organelles in the cell that has its own DNA— mitochondrial DNA— or mtDNA."

"The mtDNA is inherited only from the mother, though, Ted. It isn't like the DNA in the cell's nucleus," said Marla. Rick stared at her like she had two heads. "Hey, I'm a physical anthropologist, remember? This is pretty basic stuff in my line of work. How do you think my profession figured out the pattern of human migration? It was by analyzing mtDNA."

"Excellent!" said Rick. "Yes, Marla's correct. And mtDNA helps regulate the synthesis of proteins and even *heme*—as in hemoglobin, the basic building block for our red blood cells. Without heme, no oxygen gets to the cells of your body. Anyway, Ted, if you haven't figured it out yet, without mitochondria... You get it."

"So, Mr. Mehta and over a billion other people have died from some form of mitochondrial defect?" Ted said.

"In a manner of speaking, yes, assuming I'm correct that this structural damage will be found in other specimens. It makes sense now as to why we could not see this in the earlier specimens. The mitochondria are significant—and quickly—degraded after death. Even a delay of half an hour would have been enough to have missed this," said Rick. "But, Ted, in answer to your question, yes, this is the metabolic equivalent to cyanide poisoning. Cyanide works by suffocating mitochondria." There was a pause as the group pondered the findings.

Rick watched as Jack looked intently at the screen, then walked closer, slowly and deliberately.

"What's this?" Jack said.

"What?" Rick replied.

"This," said Jack, pointing to a small, circular structure that was within the cristae of the mitochondria—the convoluted, folded membranes within the organelle. "Is this a viral inclusion body in the crista?"

"What's an inclusion body, Jack? And what in the hell is a 'Kristy?' It's like y'all speaking a foreign language," Ted said.

"A viral inclusion body is usually found in the nucleus or cytoplasm of the cell. It can be seen with a microscope, using special tissue stains. Inclusions are almost always proteins. More importantly, they represent viral replication or multiplication. The proteins are collections of viral capsid proteins, the building blocks of the virus's outer shell, so to speak," Jack explained. He continued, "And the cristae increase the surface area within the mitochondrion for the creation of energy and other important chemical reactions."

Rick squinted and cocked his head, processing what Jack had just asked. "Wait a sec..." Rick scanned to different mitochondria in the same cell. Sure enough, there was the same small round structure. A different cell, different mitochondria, same structure.

"You're right. I was so focused on the mitochondrial explosion that I completely missed that. Great catch, Jack!" Rick said.

"So this confirms we're dealing with a viral condition?" asked Lucy.

"It seems it's a strong possibility now, based upon this new evidence," Jack said. "I don't think we should stop looking at other avenues, but this is amazingly encouraging."

Rick said, "I'll look at other tissues from Mehta and the other victims when the specimens are ready. I want to make sure we aren't barking up the wrong tree. We'll need to take more samples and isolate mitochondria to culture for viruses. We also should look at sequencing the mtDNA."

Lucy looked uneasy. "I guess," she said with a compassionate hesitation, "at least the victims don't feel anything if it's as quick as cyanide."

"Yeah. Whoopee for us," Jack said.

The team worked until 11 p.m. before wolfing down some food and flopping into bed.

Jack looked at the clock. Two a.m. He couldn't sleep, and the sheep he had been counting all looked like wool-covered mitochondria. He went to the commons room with his cellphone and sighed as he dialed the number.

"Hello?"

"Burchill, it's me," Jack said. Burchill Smyth was a close friend of Jack's back at KU, a cellular biologist he trusted implicitly, professionally, and personally. He looked professorial — grey hair, short-cropped goatee, and glasses that were too big for his narrow head. Jack loved him for many reasons, but primarily for his ability to explain complex biology in simple terms. Jack's brain hurt from everything going on. It was being pushed to its cognitive limit, and he was in dire need of simplicity if he couldn't get sleep.

"Well, well, Jack. How's it goin'? You making any progress?" Burchill said.

"Some, but not enough and not fast enough. I need you to give me a quick mitochondrial tutorial—a *Mitochondria for Dummies lesson*, Burchill. I mean, I remember some of that stuff, but cell biology was a long time ago."

"That's a pretty bizarre request, Jack. Especially at— what, midnight or something over there?"

"Two a.m. Please, can you just give me some highlights, starting from the beginning, so to speak?" Jack said.

"Sure, Jack. Sure. Ahh... from the beginning, huh? Well, mitochondria are thought to be the descendants of an early bacterium that developed a symbiotic relationship with another cell about 1.5 billion years ago. It probably created a survival advantage for both cells. It's been hypothesized that these small, free-living bacteria were engulfed—not eaten and digested, but engulfed—by larger cells. For whatever reason, the smaller cell, the bacteria, was able to resist the digestive enzymes of the bigger cell. The two cells developed a symbiotic relationship over time, the larger organism providing, the smaller one with nutrition, and the smaller organism providing energy in the form of adenosine triphosphate—ATP—to the larger one," Burchill said.

"Yeah," said Jack. "I remember that, across time, the larger cell developed into the eukaryotic cell—a cell whose DNA is contained in a nucleus—and the smaller, engulfed bacterium became the mitochondrion."

"Exactly," Burchill confirmed. "And since the mitochondrion was originally a free-living bacterium, it was controlled by its own set of DNA, which was important for its reproduction. Mitochondria still contain DNA, mitochondrial DNA, or mtDNA. The mtDNA has become greatly simplified during evolution and the diversification of life across a billion and a half years. As you would expect, mtDNA has taken different paths as life diverged along different lines. Plant mtDNA genes, or genomes, are different from amphibians, which are different from mammals." Burchill paused. "Jack, you still there?"

"Yeah. Just taking it in. Anything else I need to know?" Jack said.

"Well, you probably learned that mitochondria were the energy factory for the cell, right?" Burchill said.

"Yup," Jack said.

"Well, that's a gross oversimplification of the mitochondria's role. They control most major metabolic pathways used by a cell—they build, break down, or recycle its molecular building blocks. Cells can't even make the RNA or DNA necessary for normal growth and function without mitochondria."

"In light of what's happening, that's pretty damn scary," Jack said.

"Well," Burchill said, "I don't know what the hell's going on, Jack, but if it involves the mitochondria, it's indeed scary."

CHAPTER FORTY-EIGHT

From the mood at the breakfast table, Jack could tell that he wasn't the only one who hadn't slept well. The team ate cold cereal in silence, except for the clinking of spoons on the edges of bowls. As caffeine stirred him to life, Jack wondered where death would strike next. One way or another, it was likely to be a big day somewhere, and he hoped it would be in the lab.

The techs had worked all night to isolate the mitochondrial inclusions, using a tedious series of tissue morcellation techniques and high-speed centrifugation, followed by a rapid preparation technique. The method enabled the team to isolate cell parts by their weight, but separating something even smaller than a tiny part inside a cell was challenging.

Jack walked Lucy into the EM Lab, and the EM tech greeted them. She pointed to five boxes sitting beside the EM specimen chamber. Taking a seat, Jack watched as Lucy began the slow process of going through each of the specimens.

Sighing, Lucy said, "Here goes nothin'." She placed it in the EM chamber, closed the door, and turned on the vacuum pump.

The next ten minutes evaporated in conversation until a beep and a green light on the EM's control panel indicated that the specimen was ready to examine. Magnification of 100,000X revealed small fragments of what appeared to be thin, long tubes. "Microtubules," Lucy uttered. "The skeleton of the cell. The inclusions would have to be heavier than this."

"Well, I guess I didn't expect to find it on the first pass," Jack said. "Ready for number two?"

"Yup," Lucy said as she punched a few more buttons, releasing the vacuum. She placed the second sample into the vacuum chamber and repeated the button-pushing sequence. The vacuum kicked in, humming. Ten minutes later, the green light blipped on. They were peering at a larger structure within seconds, measuring 450 nanometers.

"What is it?" Jack asked.

"I think it is part of a Golgi apparatus—the protein factory of the cell," Lucy said. "See this? It's the cisternae of the Golgi, and these little tiny balls are ribosomes."

"Well, dammit! We're not exactly getting any breaks, are we?" Jack said. "Slide number three, coming up!" The upbeat tone of his voice belied the tension he felt.

Jack watched as Lucy repeated releasing the vacuum, removing the specimen, and replacing it, sample after sample. His impatience became apparent as his fingers strummed on the table in rhythm to the whump of the EM vacuum. There was no more idle chatter between specimens, tension building, and ten minutes seemed like two hours. Another spherical structure appeared on the screen. It was larger and appeared to be filled with rope-like material.

"I'm guessing it's the nucleoli of the cells," Lucy said, squinting as if it would help magically transform the image into the inclusions they were now desperate to see.

"Mother f—" Jack said, completing the word in his head. He took a deep breath.

Jack had a sinking sensation as Lucy silently placed the final specimen into the vacuum, knowing what it meant if there were no inclusions in the last specimen.

The black-and-white screen glowed to life. More balloon-like structures. Pieces of mitochondria. Lucy panned around the specimen desperately, erratically. More pieces. Jack shook his head in disbelief as she slumped back in her chair.

Jack stared at the screen, numb. He started to look away, but a structure at the edge of the screen, about half the size of the other debris, caught his eye. "What's that?" he said.

"Huh?" Lucy said, straightening up.

"Right there. What's that?"

Lucy manipulated the dials, centering the structure. As she did so, more came into view. She scanned around the specimen methodically.

"Bingo!" Jack shouted. It was the same round structure he had seen within the mitochondria on EM the day before—with hundreds of inclusions. "We have it."

CHAPTER FORTY-NINE

Riley could see it in the distance. Nothing looked familiar. She'd never seen it from the ground. The last time she was here — 22 days ago — was in a WNN chopper, and she had only seen things from above. Twenty-two days. The world was a different place.

The irony of reaching Mto Wa Mbu on April Fool's day had not escaped her. She was sure there was meaning to this, but what? *Am I a fool for doing this? Is the joke on me? Is the little boy long gone—dead or moved to a city where supplies are more accessible? What the hell was I thinking?*

She pulled into the village and snaked through narrow alleyways. She soon found herself in the town center by the well. She got out and stretched her arms over her head. *Jesus, I'm tired of driving.*

She looked around, shading her eyes from the sun's intensity with her hand. She noticed an irregularity in the perpendicular line of the edge of a house facing the well. It vanished as soon as it had registered with her, but the sun's glare made it impossible for her to perceive its identity. A dog? A kid? Or my imagination?

"Hello?" she said, loudly but not shouting. *As if they will understand me...* She repeated it a bit louder. A small girl, maybe three, waddled out of one of the doorways off to Riley's left, arms raised, giggling with joy at the sight of an adult. An older girl, perhaps her sister, ran out after her, catching her before she reached Riley. The older girl was dressed neatly in a bright yellow dress with green streaks, and the look on her face was the antithesis of the toddler. *She's terrified!* The girl hoisted the smaller child onto her hip and backed away. Riley tilted her head, smiling kindly.

"It's OK," she said in a lilting tone. "Really. It's OK. I'm a friend," she said, holding out her hand, palm up. The older girl stopped her retreat, eyeing Riley. The toddler was struggling to free herself from her sister's grip, who was struggling equally to prevent her escape. Riley was impressed with the girl's skill at managing the smaller child. In that instant, the toddler arched her back, and with a simultaneous half-twist that morphed into a forward lunge. The girl successfully prevented the child from landing face-first on the hard dirt, but she was free and ran to Riley, who knelt, welcoming the child into her arms.

The child wrapped herself around Riley, who reciprocated, and they melted into each other. Riley could not recall a sweeter feeling—a more complete, instantaneous sense of love — than the hug of this child in this instant. She closed her eyes, wanting to freeze this moment as a profusion of tears —not of pain, but pure joy— pushed past the pressure of closed lids. She held the little girl, rocking her back and forth, comforting herself as much as the child.

She released her clutch and opened her eyes to gaze at the cherub's face. They smiled at each other in genuine happiness. It was then that Riley sensed children surrounding her. In her bliss, she had not heard them pad upon bare feet, each trying to get a closer look at this white woman, an adult, who appeared from nowhere. She looked from face to face, her heart swelling from pent-up compassion accumulated across a lifetime of pain. She wanted to give it all away, right now, to love and save — yes, *save* — these children. Not just one, but become the mother to forty, fifty, sixty kids, all of whom needed her, all of whom wanted her. She was going to be the mother she'd never had but had wanted, deserved. And at that moment, she realized something profound: By being a mother to them, they would be saving her.

When she stood up, she saw him: the one. *It's him.*

She made eye contact with the boy. He cocked his head, not sure why this white woman was singling him out. Riley smiled, walked through the sea of children to him, and knelt. She reached in her bag and pulled out her notebook, flipping to the back. She pulled out the photograph and held it up beside his face, looking from the photo to his face, her smile broadening. She focused on his face, still screwed up in puzzlement.

Riley flipped the photo around to show him. After a moment, he gently put a hand on Riley's arm and pushed it down so he could study her face. He smiled and took the photo from her, alternating looks from the photo to Riley.

"I came back for you," Riley said, pointing from her chest to his. "I'm Riley," she said, pointing to herself. She repeated Riley over and over.

Still smiling and clutching the picture, the boy looked at Riley, pointed at his chest, and said, "*Abasi.*"

CHAPTER FIFTY

While Jack and Lucy were busy chasing the inclusion bodies, Rick and Catherine labored away in the DNA sequencing lab. DNA sequencing, and certainly the sequencing of mtDNA, was not a core skill of Rick's, so they decided they would call an expert.

"Marcus, this is Rick Matthews. How are you?"

"Rick! I'm fine! How the hell are you? Where are you? You sound like you're talking from inside a bathroom stall," the voice said. Marcus Wetherby was a geneticist who attended the Naval Academy with Rick and now lived in LA.

"In Mumbai, working on the global thing. I'm sitting here with Catherine Montoya. We need a crash course in sequencing mtDNA. Can you do that?"

"Sure thing, Rick. Is that something you are working on?"

"Yup, and I don't have a clue about it," Rick said.

"Not much to it. mtDNA is always compared to the Cambridge Sequence, the normal mtDNA sequence in humans, and is structurally a simple circle of DNA containing 16,569 base pairs. You'll remember from basic biology that a base pair is made up of a combination of thymine paired with adenine or guanine paired with cytosine. Each is abbreviated by their first letter, so T for thymine, A for adenosine, and so on. The way these pairs interact with each other results in the formation of the classic double helix coil we're all familiar with, thanks to Watson and Crick," explained Marcus.

"Does the mtDNA code for anything useful, Marcus?" Catherine asked.

"You'd better believe it. It's more complex than just the whole ATP thing you learned in high school biology. mtDNA's genetic code is complex enough to build thirteen different proteins and 22 different types of transfer RNA or tRNA."

Catherine said, "I remember tRNA. It's one of the coolest things — a genetic sequence that attaches amino acids in a string, ultimately resulting in a protein molecule. I always thought of tRNA like the process of knitting a scarf. Every time the knitter puts a throw of the yarn around the knitting needles, the scarf grows."

"Yes, Catherine. In a way, tRNA is like the needle, and the amino acids are like the yarn. In other words, not only does mtDNA make some proteins of its own, it contributes key elements to other important proteins the cell needs for normal function," Marcus explained.

"Jesus, Marcus, you aren't giving me a warm fuzzy here," Rick said. "So this is going to be like looking for a knitting needle in a haystack?" making a play on Catherine's words. "How can we possibly track down what's causing the mitochondrial failure, infection or otherwise, with all of these variables?"

"Ahhh. So mitochondrial failure is part of the issue?" Marcus said. "And you think it's a mutation?"

"We aren't sure, but we're looking into it. We have evidence that points to a viral infection," Rick said. "Anything else we should know?"

"I wish I could tell you it doesn't get more complicated, but it does," Marcus continued. "When the mtDNA from any person is sequenced, several variations to the Cambridge Sequence can be identified. Many of the variations don't cause any change in function. One region where change is often found is called the Control Region. While there's no clinical significance to changes in the Control Region, it is useful in forensic investigations. It is the DNA fingerprint that you've heard about used in crime investigations."

"So, can this segment be helpful in our investigations here?" Catherine asked.

"Maybe," said Marcus, "but you won't know until you sequence the mtDNA from some of the victims."

"What do you think we're looking for?" Rick said.

"Beats the hell outta me," Marcus said, pausing. "There's more that might be helpful to you. A whole series of mtDNA mutations that cause disease has been cataloged, and there are some important nuances about mtDNA mutations that you need to understand. If a cell has a mutation in its nuclear DNA, that mutation will be inherited in every daughter cell produced by reproducing the original cell. But mtDNA mutations can vary from cell to cell—even from tissue to tissue. What's more, just the mere presence of an mtDNA mutation doesn't necessarily lead to disease. That's important because, frankly, if you start sequencing the mtDNA of our victims, you may run into lots of red herrings. If you find a mutation, it could be meaningless—or it could be the genetic defect that leads to the disease susceptibility that you have hypothesized exists. I read about your theory in the Times."

The first step in isolating the mtDNA progressed smoothly, and things were on target for initiating the sequencer about lunchtime. They were just about ready to put the first specimen through its final centrifuge when they received Jack and Lucy's good news. The mood in the entire complex visibly improved.

"Sounds like Jack and Lucy may have us close to finding the viral culprit," Rick said. He gave Catherine a furtive look and smiled.

"Yes," Catherine said, "It seems things are finally coming together. I must admit I've had my doubts about all of this." There was a pause as the centrifuge clicked off, and the machine's hum started a nearly imperceptible slowing. It would take almost 30 minutes for the device to stop, spinning at 9,400 times gravity.

"So you think it's viral, Catherine?"

"My intellect continuous to tell me it is." She paused. "But some of the things that Marla said keep me awake at night. What if it isn't viral?" She adored that she could have a scientific conversation with Rick in one moment and be incredibly intimate with him in others.

"You mean you think it could be bacterial?" questioned Rick.

"No. That's not what I mean," said Catherine. "What if it's neither?"

"What do you mean, 'neither'?"

"Exactly," Catherine said. "That's what bothers me."

CHAPTER FIFTY-ONE

The inclusion body samples had been in the mass spectrometer for an hour, and data was just beginning to spew out of the machine as Jack and Lucy returned from lunch. In 15 minutes, Jack could run the specimen results against the computer's database catalog of known proteins — over five million — to check for a match. The protein would clue them into a family of viruses. As Jack had explained to the group several days ago, the inclusion would likely be a known capsid component, a protein subunit that makes up the outer shell of a virus. Once they had that information, finding a path to a solution would be straightforward. The wait didn't seem as bad now that they had full bellies and the apparent success of the morning. Jack and Lucy were more relaxed and felt confident when the timer notified them that the process was complete.

The spectrometer spit out a paper copy of the results. Jack examined the computer tracing of the molecular footprint with Lucy peering over his shoulder. It looked like the wild scribble of a seismograph during a 7.0 earthquake.

"Thank God for computers," Jack said as he sat down at the spectrometer's keyboard. He navigated through several screens, clicked a few times, and hit ENTER.

"Well, now it's up to the computer," he said. He watched the screen as the sample's molecular fingerprint was compared to almost three thousand proteins every few seconds. Jack sat back in the chair and interlaced his fingers behind his head. Lucy sat on a desk to the side. Within half an hour, the machine had cranked through the catalog of five million proteins, as indicated by an electronic beep when it finished. Jack leaned forward, his hopeful look devolving into confusion. The protein was caspase 8, according to the spectrometer.

"What the hell?" Jack stammered. "What the hell is caspase 8? I've been in virology the better part of my adult life, and I've never heard of it."

"I have no idea," Lucy said in a confused tone.

Jack turned back to the computer and pulled up a search engine, typing in caspase 8. He clicked on the first hit and watched the page load. He'd never understood how the speed of the internet always seemed inversely proportional to the urgency of the needed information. He read the first paragraph. "Jesus..." he whispered, looking up at Lucy.

"What?" said Lucy, looking over his shoulder to read the screen.

> Caspase is a combined term that stands for *Cysteine-ASpartic ProtASEs.* The caspases are a group of intracellular cysteine enzymes that, upon activation, destroy essential cellular proteins, leading to controlled cell death. There are two tiers of caspase activation during apoptosis. *Initiator caspases* (caspases 2, 8, 9, and 10) are activated through the apoptosis-signaling pathways and activate the *effector caspases* (caspases 3, 6, and 7), which, in an expanding cascade, carry out apoptosis. Caspase cascades are initiated through the assembly of multi-protein complexes that trigger activation of the initiator caspases, which are then released and able to activate the downstream effector caspases. *Collectively, the caspase' are considered death effector proteins.* Caspases are produced by the cell and result in the death of that cell.

Jack sat back in his chair, numb, the enthusiasm of just moments ago sapped. He pushed the communicator on his MOPP. "Everyone, we need to meet now." Jack's tone was serious, washed out, and unexpected.

"What is it, Jack?" Catherine responded.

"Is everyone on?" Jack asked. Everyone in the group affirmed electronic presence.

"It isn't an inclusion body. Or if it is, it's something new. The protein that I was calling an inclusion body is caspase 8."

"What's it do?" asked Rick.

"Lucy and I did a quick search. It is an intracellular protein that initiates apoptosis — the cell's death sequence. It's part of a group of proteins known as death effectors," Jack said. "I hate to say it, but from what I've found out in the last few minutes, once the sequence is started, there ain't no stopping the chain reaction. It sets off an irreversible sequence that leads to cellular death."

"Wait a sec... Jack, did you say the caspase is intracellular?" Rick said.

"Yes, that's what I said," replied Jack." The caspases are intracellular—in the cytoplasm of the cell. Now you see my confusion? These inclusions—the crystals of caspase 8—are in the mitochondria. Yes, the mitochondria are intracellular, but that isn't where caspase eight is supposed to be."

"Jack, I'm not sure I understand why you're so concerned. Caspase 8 is in the mitochondria. I get it. But what's bothering you?" Catherine said, puzzled.

"Viruses don't attack the mitochondria, Catherine. They attack cells and replicate alongside the cell's organelles, all floating in its cytoplasm, like the mitochondria. Viruses don't get inside the mitochondria—or any other organelle for that matter."

"Oh my God," gasped Catherine. "So are you saying—after all this time—you don't think this is viral?"

"Either it isn't viral, or we are looking at an entirely new form of the virus with a novel replication cycle. I'm putting my money on something other than viral as of this moment," Jack said. "Now it's even more important to know what's in the mtDNA."

Jack glanced up and noticed a calendar on the wall. He silently counted, then added, "We've already been at this for four days. Time is not our friend."

CHAPTER FIFTY-TWO

Rick was just sitting down at the computer with Catherine at his side when Jack and Lucy arrived. Marla and Ted were already there.

"Perfect timing. I just uploaded the sequences into the computer," Rick said. The group collected around Rick at the terminal. He typed and clicked, and a diagram of a circular mtDNA strand appeared on the screen.

"We obtained ten different circular mtDNA sequences from the brain sample," Rick said. "Worst case is we'll know if there are any weird mutations in roughly an hour. The sequence-matching program will only grind out one analysis at a time, but they only take about five minutes each."

He sat back and sighed heavily. Rick was sick of MOPP. Sick of Indian curry. Sick of the sunless basement research facility. And he was sick of just *five goddam more minutes*. The days since Dhanesh's death had resulted in significant progress, progress that he was—as any lab anywhere would have been—proud of — if only death were not hanging over his head like the Sword of Damocles.

"Here we go," Rick said as the first mtDNA match was made. An identical strand of mtDNA was pictured beside the sample, matching the Cambridge Sequence identically. "No mutation here," Rick said. "Goddam normal. You would think just once in this fucking flail of a project we would get lucky on the first go."

Rick felt Catherine's hand squeeze his shoulder gently, "Patience, Rick." He relaxed a bit.

"I'm with ya on that one, buddy," chimed Jack. "The cosmos is not making it easy on us. Put the second sample in. Get on with it."

"Absolutely. I want to drink heavily tonight. Sooner we're outta here, the better," he said, as he served the computer the next mtDNA sample. A few minutes later, the computer cranked out the second sequence match.

"Crap. Specimen two is Haplogroup L1. It says in the notes with the analysis that's the African specific type, whatever that means," Rick said.

"It means," Marla said, as Rick turned to look at her, "that Mr. Mehta carried one of the oldest known segments of mtDNA, originating in Africa. It's, in fact, the oldest mtDNA strand in human existence—from the 'mitochondrial Eve,' the maternal ancestor of all living humans. Haplogroup L is subdivided into L1 and L2. They're ubiquitous, especially in this region, Africa and Asia."

"Uhh, thanks, Marla," Rick stuttered. "So by that, I assume this is normal?"

"Yes. A copy of it is probably in all of us. I hate to be a smart ass, but it's part of the catalog of sequences, so by definition, it is a known mtDNA strand."

Rick frowned the I'm-an-idiot-and-should-have-known-that look. "Of course. Duhhh. Batter three, you're up! On deck, mtDNA four." As Rick loaded the third sample, idle banter kept the group busy and their minds off the gravity of their work. Rick suddenly became very interested in the computer screen. "Hey! Hey! HEY! We may have something here." The group crowded up to the screen. The dead man's mtDNA was shown on the right-hand side of the screen, but the left-hand side was empty, a black box where the picture of a matching mtDNA sample from the catalog should have been. Instead of an mtDNA sequence, the words NO MATCH IN DATABASE were slowly blinking in bright green.

Rick, while typing, said, "I just asked the program to match the specimen to the closest catalog specimen."

In seconds, the computer pulled up the Haplogroup L1 subtype. "I'll be damned," said Rick. "I'll ask it to show us the differences between the two." A few keystrokes and a click, and the mtDNA strands on each side of the screen magnified a segment of mtDNA. The Haplogroup L1 specimen illustrated mtDNA segment 9541 as taggagggca ctggcccta acaggcatca ccccgctaaa tccctagaa gtcccactcc. It was a list of the nucleotides of that segment of the gene. The dead man's mtDNA showed segment 9541 as taggagggca ctggccccat acaggcatca ccccgctaaa tccctagaa gtcccactcc.

"I don't see a difference," Rick said.

"Rick, copy the letters of the sequences and paste them into a text document, one right underneath the other. It'll be easier to see a difference," Lucy suggested. Rick diligently obeyed.

"Okay, here you go," said Rick.

L1 specimen: taggagggca ctggcccta acaggcatca ccccgctaaa tccctagaa gtcccactcc.

Mehta specimen: taggagggca ctggccccat acaggcatca ccccgctaaa tccctagaa gtcccactcc.

With the team members looking over his shoulders, Rick focused on the screen, silently trying to find the needle in the genetic haystack.

"THERE!" shouted Marla. "Look at the second grouping of letters—the last two letters from the end in the second string. The T and A are flip-flopped. The base pairs are switched. That's the mutation." Rick bolded the letter.

L1 specimen: taggagggca ctggcccc**ta** acaggcatca ccccgctaaa tcccctagaa gtcccactcc.

Mehta specimen: taggagggca ctggcccc**at** acaggcatca ccccgctaaa tcccctagaa gtcccactcc.

"Well, it's a mutation, but it raises at least two questions. Is it a mutation that matters? And if it is, what does it do?" Rick said. "Remember our little mitochondrial educational session? Most mtDNA mutations don't result in any illness. We shouldn't jump to conclusions. We need to run the other seven samples."

Rick ran the remaining specimens over the next two hours. The same unidentified mutation was found in two other mtDNA strands of the seven remaining specimens. All others were matched to known samples in the database.

Rick scratched his head in puzzlement. "What's bothering you, Rick?" Jack asked.

"There are three different haplogroups of the mtDNA with the same mutation: L1, L3, and M subtypes. The segment where the mutation occurs is highly conserved between the haplogroups, at least according to what I've read. In other words, the mutation is occurring in a part of the mtDNA that is the same in all haplogroups — except in the Mehta samples. It bothers me, and I don't understand it."

Before the day was out, Rick found three mtDNA copies in every specimen taken from four different victims, as well as multiple other mtDNA haplogroups containing the mutation.

The team had found the defect, but they had no idea what it did or how it functioned.

CHAPTER FIFTY-THREE

"I know who can help answer what the gene defect might mean," Catherine said, dialing Manuel Jimenez, the mitochondrial disease expert who had helped educate the team earlier. Catherine pushed a button, and the team huddled around the speakerphone.

"Hola," Manuel answered sleepily.

"Manuel, this is Catherine Montoya of the CDC."

"Catherine, darling," he said in a thick accent. "What is the pleasure of your late call? Aren't you busy with the crisis?"

"Manuel, it's about the crisis. We've identified an mtDNA mutation that may have something to do with what's happening. I was hoping you could help Dr. Matthews and me understand a little more. We know that not all mtDNA mutations cause disease, but we don't want to be looking for the wrong thing—we don't have time for mistakes," Catherine said.

"You are correct that mtDNA mutations don't necessarily cause disease. Interestingly, mtDNA mutations can build up—accumulate—in the mitochondrion. Even if the original mutation does not cause a disease, it's possible that the build-up of the mutation across time could result in a threshold effect. In other words, at some point, the total number of mutations in the mtDNA accumulates to such a degree that mitochondrial disease begins to become inevitable— the threshold is met, tipping the cell from not having the disease to being diseased. Once the number of affected mitochondria reaches a certain level in a critical number of cells, the host organism will show signs of disease. This phenomenon is called threshold expression," Manuel said with great precision.

Manuel continued, "The conversion from a non-diseased state to a diseased state seems to occur when more than half of the mtDNA copies are defective, causing the mitochondrial disease to become unavoidable. The threshold for these defects can build for thousands, perhaps tens or hundreds of thousands of years; at least, that's the theory. It may be that the accumulation of some defect across time has resulted in the immunologic susceptibility to the virus you have hypothesized."

"We used to think that the human race arose from a single female and a single male, but it is more likely that the first female gave rise to female offspring, and their mtDNA mutated or somehow was altered in the early stages of the evolutionary process," Marla said.

"Yes, the lady makes good points," Manuel said.

"It's also important, given the information about inclusions in the mitochondria, that we keep in mind the evidence regarding viral-induced alterations of our mtDNA during our evolution," Marla continued.

"Well, while it is true that viruses have been documented to insert a small strand of their DNA into the host's nuclear DNA, causing mutations or disease," Manuel said, "I don't think it's ever been reported to happen in mitochondrial DNA."

"Yes, that's correct. I'm unaware that viral DNA has ever been identified as incorporating into the mtDNA genome," Jack said. "This could be a first."

"Wow. This just gets more and more interesting... and I don't mean that in a good way," said Lucy.

"There are other things about mitochondria that we haven't discussed—normal things that are important," Manuel said. "While the whole topic of mutations is interesting, it is important to understand that mitochondria play a critical role in normal cell death. They initiate apoptosis."

"What's a-pop-whats-iss?" Ted said, face contorting in attempted pronunciation.

"It's pronounced A-pop-toe-sis," Manuel said, ironically teaching correct pronunciation to a native English speaker.

"Apoptosis is programmed cell death. It occurs at certain times in the life of multicellular organisms," explained Rick, "and it's thought to play a role in weeding out abnormal or aging cells."

"Yes. That is correct, Rick. Programmed cell death, or PCD, involves a series of events that lead to cellular death. PCD is a series of biochemical steps that result in various morphological—that is, structural, physical—changes, including blebbing of membranes, changes to the cell membrane causing leakiness of the cell, cell shrinkage, nuclear fragmentation, and the destruction of DNA. Your specimens — the mitochondria that appear to have exploded, as you say, have many of the characteristics of apoptosis. Once the pathway to cell self-destruction is activated, it is impossible to stop it. In essence, the mitochondria die, stopping cellular respiration. It quits making ATP, and the cell has no energy source. This is exactly what happens in cyanide poisoning." Catherine noticed everyone shift uncomfortably in their chairs.

Manuel continued. "Now, what's encouraging about all of this, my friends, is that Jack's discovery of the inclusion bodies seems to make a great deal of sense in the scheme of things."

Everyone perked up. "Why?" asked Lucy.

"Because," Manuel said, "a viral infection may well trigger the mitochondrial PCD pathway. There is evidence that infections can lead to the production of cytokines—substances that switch on the cellular signals that lead to PCD. It's a highly evolved process designed by the body to kill infected cells to spare their healthy neighbors. We may simply be witnessing apoptosis that's out-of-control."

"That certainly makes sense," Rick said. "One of our U.S. team members hypothesized that we might be looking at an infection that results in SIRS—systemic inflammatory response syndrome, set off by uncontrolled cytokine production that leads to total body failure. Maybe the PCD pathway is being set off so suddenly by a viral infection in so many cells that SIRS is the answer, via PCD."

Manuel went on, "Certainly, there are situations we know of where mtDNA defects cause disease. But most of the diseases don't result in such rapid death. They kill slowly."

"Like what, Manuel?" asked Jack.

"In at least some of these mitochondrial diseases, the apoptotic process—PCD— backfires and begins killing certain critical cells, like neurons in the brain. If it happens in enough neurons, it leads to neurological problems. An example is the *MELAS Syndrome*. MELAS stands for Mitochondrial Encephalopathy, Lactic Acidosis, and Stroke-like episodes. An mtDNA mutation results in disturbed function of their cells' mitochondria. Affected patients develop brain dysfunction like encephalopathy, seizures, and headaches. Lactic acid, a waste byproduct of muscle activity, builds up in the blood and wreaks havoc on the body. These poor individuals have temporary paralysis of their arms and legs and often develop dementia. They are so mentally affected that they don't know they're still alive, and they die slowly."

"My God..." Jack said, shaking his head. "Not a happy story."

"Sorry, my friend," said Manuel. "Mitochondrial diseases are pretty horrible."

"It seems that we're likely dealing with a viral illness that stimulates apoptosis in critical organs, resulting in a cascade of rapid organ failure and death," Catherine said, more a question than a statement.

"It is possible, but it seems very odd," Manuel said.

"Well, let's get back to work, then," Rick said as he started to stand up, the others following suit.

"I'm confused," Marla said, stopping everyone's exit. "If this is viral, why haven't the cell cultures shown anything?"

CHAPTER FIFTY-FOUR

As compelling as Marla's theory was — that they were confronting some form of genetically-based self-destruction — Jack and the rest of the team couldn't get past their belief it must be a viral infection.

Two bits of new information taunted Jack, and he put it to the team. "So, this is seemingly a chicken and egg sort of thing. We're well beyond run-of-the-mill research," Jack said.

"What do you mean, Jack," Catherine asked.

"The questions I have are these: Does the caspase eight get turned on by a bizarre viral entity that somehow infects mitochondria? Or is the newly found mtDNA mutation causing caspase eight production and activation? Or is the mtDNA mutation simply lowering the resistance of the victims in such a way that a virus can initiate apoptosis?"

"Wow," said Rick, "You're right. Could be any of those things."

"Our days hold as much anxiety as promise lately," Lucy said. "The next wave of death—Russia—can't be very far away."

"I have to tell you; it's looking to be more and more like a genetic drift phenomenon. There just doesn't seem to be any other explanation that makes sense. Each of these geographic areas were populated by humans across time, and genetically humans became increasingly different enough to not only look different but to have a more robust immune response to the mitochondrial infection—if it's an infection at all," Marla said.

Jack continued to push everyone to work, almost without breaks. He had everyone sleeping in shifts. He only slept when his brain was indeed at the point of shutting down from exhaustion.

Jack walked into the EM lab. Rick looked up.

"Hey, Jack, by using a fluorescent antibody to stain the mtDNA mutation, we've been able to estimate that 40 percent of all cells in deceased victims contained the mutation. The techs developed an antibody to the mutation with a heavy metal tag, and we're just getting ready to look at a specimen. We're about to count the number of copies of the mutation within each mitochondrion.”

Jack watched as Rick took a tagged specimen and loaded it into the EM. The rest of the team lurked in the background, hoping to witness something encouraging. Ten minutes later, the silvery EM image appeared, and the search began.

“Here are some normal cells, guys,” Rick said, pointing with his finger. “You can tell because the mitochondrial and cell membranes are all intact, no blebs, no deformity. I would guess that... ahhh... about 70 percent of the cells are unaffected.” He continued scanning the specimen. “Here, you see cells undergoing apoptosis. They’re dying or dead—let’s see what the mitochondria look like in these cells.”

He increased the power, and a mitochondrion came into focus. “This is a normal mitochondrion—no markers here.” He dialed over to a different mitochondrion within the same cell but had clear bleb formation. “Here are Jack’s inclusion bodies or caspase eight or whatever. Now, let’s see... Here we go! There!” Rick said, pointing out a black blob stuck to a circular mtDNA. “Our tag works!”

“How many copies of the mutation in that mitochondrion?” Catherine asked.

“Gimme a sec. One. Two. Three... In this one, there are three copies out of a total of six circular strands,” Rick replied.

“What about another mitochondrion in the same cell?” Catherine said.

“The only mitochondrion in this cell that has blebs and signs of cell death is this one,” Rick said.

“Do me a favor, Rick, and check a normal mitochondrion in the same cell... just for peace of mind?” Catherine said in a pleading voice. Jack watched, wondering what Catherine was thinking.

“Sure.” Rick scanned the other six mitochondria in the cell. “Nothing.”

“OK. Find another cell that has been affected,” Catherine said.

“OK. Here’s one. Let me see... Seven mitochondria in this cell, one has blebs. Again, three copies of the mutated mtDNA in the blebbed mitochondrion, but the other six are clean.”

“Do another, please,” Catherine instructed, Jack, shaking his head in agreement.

“Five mitochondria, two with blebs.” Rick, counting out loud, found at least three copies of the mtDNA in each of the affected cell's abnormal mitochondrion.

“Rick, scan all of the mitochondria in a single normal cell—one that isn’t dying. Do any of them have the mutation?” asked Catherine.

"What's the point?" Rick asked. Jack thought he sounded irritated with Catherine's commanding tone.

"Just do it, please," Catherine said, softening her tone and squeezing his shoulder tenderly.

"Whatever. OK. So, here's a healthy, unaffected cell." He dialed up the magnification. "Nope, five copies of mtDNA in this mitochondrion, and no marker."

"Another mitochondrion, the same cell, please," Catherine insisted.

Rick heaved a deep breath. "Sure. Here is a mitochondrion that has a normal appearance. It has six strands of mtDNA and..." his voice trailed off. "Uhh, and one copy of the mutation." He quickly scanned other normal cells and other normal-appearing mitochondria.

"Shit, Catherine..."

"Yes, Rick, we have just determined the *threshold effect* for our mtDNA mutation. One copy of the mtDNA mutation—no problem. Two copies and the mitochondria are still healthy. Three copies of the mutation and the mitochondria explode from the inside out. Three copies of the mutated mtDNA within any single mitochondrion sets off the caspase cascade within that cell, leading to cell death. *Game over.*"

"So let me get this straight. If you're right, Catherine, we should see the mutation in some of the mitochondria of normal cells, but we should never see more than two copies in any mitochondrion if the cell is healthy, right?" Ted said, trying to follow the logic.

"That's correct, Ted," Lucy said. "We should at least check a few other specimens to see if Catherine's observation bears out."

"So, if I am interpreting this the right way, what we're seeing is the slow accumulation of the mutation in the mitochondria, that the mutation is inevitable, but it doesn't do anything until that third copy switches on," Jack summarized.

"That's about it," Rick said. As Jack listened, he subconsciously put his hand deep in his pocket. There was a slight twist on the downside of the Rubik's Cube. He tweaked it back into place with a flick of his wrist.

"Sweet work, everyone. Sweet work," Catherine said.

"Yup. I agree," Jack said. "But two questions remain," he said as he pulled the Rubik's Cube from his pocket. "Is a virus the cause of the mutation? And, more importantly, what is the threshold effect turning on?" He looked down covertly at the Rubik's Cube in his cupped hand; a single layer of red lined up neatly with two rows of blue. *It's wrong?*

CHAPTER FIFTY-FIVE

The team worked through the night with no further breakthroughs. They were exhausted and having a cup of coffee while discussing the mtDNA mutation. Theories of what it did were flying around the room when a tech burst into the room.

"Dr. Cann! Dr. Hermans! Come now!" the tech said, out of breath. Startled, Jack and Lucy clumsily scrambled out of their chairs, slowed by their own MOPP suits, with Marla, Ted, Catherine, and Rick on their heels. They ran the 30 yards to the Protein Lab. The tech was standing by a computer terminal located adjacent to the protein sequencer, a complex-looking machine about the size of an oven. The tech pointed at green capital letters on the screen.

PROTEIN ANALYSIS: SYNTHESIZED PROTEIN CONSISTENT WITH CASPASE 8

Jack looked confused. "How the hell could this be?" he said. "The mtDNA mutation is coding for caspase 8? It has to be a mistake."

"No, Dr. Cann. There's no mistake," the tech said as she handed him a computer printout. Jack looked at the paper.

PROTEIN ANALYSIS: SYNTHESIZED PROTEIN CONSISTENT WITH CASPASE 8

"I know this, dammit!" Jack said, wadding up the paper and throwing it on the floor. Jack was not prone to tantrums.

"No, Doctor. Look here," said the tech, picking up the paper and unwadding it. She pointed to the time on the report. It read 06:53.

"Six-fifty-three this morning?" Jack said. "So what?"

"Doctor, what you are looking at on the screen is *a second sample*. We didn't believe the first one either, so we ran a second one to confirm it. There's no mistake. The mtDNA mutation is the code to produce caspase 8."

Jack looked from the computer screen to the tech and back to the screen, mouth open, fog rhythmically clouding his mask eyepieces with heavy breathing. He turned and looked at the others. No one moved—no one could move—and no one spoke.

After a few minutes of dead air, Jack spoke in realization. "My god. How could this be? It isn't viral. It's bad genetics."

There was a long pause. Jack was clawing his brain in search of any logical answer but the truth—anything but the words he had just spoken.

"Holy shit," Marla said, looking at the floor. Jack saw an expression of horror visible through her mask. "It really is a built-in population control mechanism. It's been in our mtDNA since Olduvai Gorge first birthed our species."

"What are you talking about, Marla?" Catherine said.

"I mean this... this... the Death Effector Gene, or whatever you wanna call it, was programmed hundreds of thousands of years ago to switch itself on at some point in the future — automatically. The genetic timer was set to go off about 200,000 years from the time of mitochondrial Eve." Jack and the team stared at her. What she said made perfect sense but was too horrific to believe.

"You mean this disaster has been pre-programmed to happen? Our species was set up by God or Mohammed or Buddha—who or whatever—to become extinct?" Ted said.

"*Exactly,*" Marla said. "Every one of us carries mtDNA from the common ancestor known as mitochondrial Eve—at least one copy. But it seems from the sequencing of the victim's mtDNA that regardless of whether or not there is a predominance of mitochondrial Eve's original mtDNA strand, all strands that evolved from her original strand conserved the ability to trigger the Death Effector Gene. You follow?"

"Sorta," Ted said unconvincingly. "And who's Eve?"

"Mitochondrial Eve is how anthropologists refer to the most recent common female ancestor of all currently living anatomically normal humans," Marla said. "She came from Olduvai."

"Oh," Ted replied. "And so, this means?"

"No living human will be spared," Marla said with glum realization. "Does that help?"

"Yep, and I'm not likin' what I am hearin'," Ted said.

"The path of death has followed the pattern of human migration out of Africa. The reason for this pattern relates to mtDNA diversification from mitochondrial Eve's original mtDNA strand. The Death Effector Gene turned on, became active, or whatever it did, in the people carrying the oldest mtDNA strands first— mitochondrial Eve's original mtDNA, the most highly conserved, unaltered of all mtDNA. It turned on later in mtDNA strands that have evolved since her. Genetic drift is why there have been delays in the timeline that we didn't predict. Without the drift, the wave of death would already have swept across the globe, consistent with the original timeline of human migration. Think of it like this: with each migratory step since the Middle East was populated, the population gained some time on the Death Effector Gene. On an evolutionary scale, the populations along the path of migration have, in effect, younger mtDNA," Marla said.

"Is that why new immigrants coming to Europe and North America from Africa or the Middle East either have died or are dying, while there is sparing... least for now... of the lighter-skinned folks?" Ted asked.

"Right again," said Marla. "But don't misunderstand, Ted. This isn't a racial issue—it isn't about being Black or Asian or Latino or any color or race—*it's about being human.* It's pure Mendelian genetics. It's only a matter of time before the Death Effector Gene is turned on in every human's mtDNA. That segment has been highly conserved across time, which is why Rick and Catherine found the TA base pair switch occurring in the same segment of all mtDNA strands, regardless of haplotype. A small mutation from Eve's original mtDNA is enough to slow down the switch, but not enough to stop it or prevent the mutation's ultimate expression."

"Why in God's name would Mother Nature be doing this to us?" Lucy asked.

"Why do lemmings drown themselves? I know the whole suicide bit about them is folklore, but the result is still population control," replied Marla. Her responses had become less emotional, more objective. Jack could tell she was masking her fear.

"Why are kids spared? What's going on there?" Lucy posited.

"It's all conjecture at this point," Marla said, "But I'm guessing that the gene can't switch on until the person has reached a certain level of maturity. It's likely to be hormonal, related to maturity. I think we can conclude that the switch turns on at some point after the age of 17 or so, based on the patterns of death and the sparing of children into their late teens."

"But if that's the case," Rick said, "it isn't an extinction gene, right? I mean, the kids can re-populate the earth, no?"

"Doubtful, Rick," Marla said. She continued in her professorial tone. Jack was amazed by her objectivity — he felt like he could burst into tears at any moment. What she was saying was horrifying repulsive. "The survivors aren't going to magically become immune to the mutation, either."

Marla was silent for a few minutes and then said, "Do you think 17-year-old kids are going to be able to help those younger than themselves survive long-term? And what about reproduction? I guess the girls could become pregnant as soon as they start having periods at age 12 or 13, but I'm not convinced they can care for their offspring. If the Death Effector Gene turns on around age 16 or 17, most kids would be three or four when their parents die. Who is going to take care of the toddler-aged orphans? No, I think human extinction is likely— probably within two, three, maybe four years. It's leaving the young to die of starvation, disease, poor sanitation. The entire earth's infrastructure will collapse, just like we've seen in Africa, the Middle East, and China. At some point, no adults will be left anywhere to run the existing infrastructure, much less teach young teens how to run the equipment. The Death Effector Gene is cruel and efficient. Evolution is ruthless."

"So...what the hell does this all mean?" Ted asked, the incomprehensible keeping him from seeing the obvious.

Jack, still stunned by the fact this was not viral, reached up and slowly disconnected his MOPP mask, took it off, and set it on the table. Everyone noticed his action, a symbol of defeat and the associated powerlessness. The mechanism of death wasn't infectious. It was genetic.

"It means, Ted, we're all going to die... unless we figure out what to do about it," Jack said, looking at his feet. Looking up, he added, "And the way it looks right now, we're dead."

When Jack looked up, there was a tear in his eye. He watched as, one by one, the team broke down, some sobbing, others silent with tear-filled eyes, as they realized there might not be a solution — they, too, were going to die, just like the billions before them.

23:30 APRIL 2, THE WHITE HOUSE, WASHINGTON DC (09:00 APRIL 3, MUMBAI)

The president felt seasick as if he were careening to and fro on a narrow-gauge railroad, his stomach about to lurch. He wished it would go away. He needed a wastebasket in case he needed to puke.

The shimmying feeling persisted until he heard someone calling, "Mr. President! Wake up, sir! Mr. President?" He opened his eyes. One of the aids had a shoulder in each hand, shaking him. He sat up, dazed and momentarily confused.

"Mr. President, Dr. Catherine Montoya is on the phone. She insisted we wake you. She's calling from Mumbai."

"Oh, yeah. Dr. Montoya. Maybe she has some good news," the president said as the fog cleared. The aid handed him the cellphone.

"Hello? Dr. Montoya, this is President Lopez. What have you found?" He listened for a half-minute before he said, "Yes, I'll keep it to myself until after your press conference. Thank you, Catherine." He slowly lowered the phone from his ear and hung up.

CHAPTER FIFTY-SIX

Explaining the concept of mitochondria, much less a process of mitochondrial self-destruction leading to death to a room full of multi-national reporters and their interpreters, is akin to explaining the detailed inner workings of the space shuttle to a class of third graders. It's possible, but it requires answering many well-intended but misguided questions, using nothing short of hyperbole and simple, illustrative analogies that aren't spot-on accurate. It might require days, and days were one thing in pretty short supply.

The researchers filed into the hospital's pressroom, led by Catherine, who settled in at the podium. There was the usual barrage of camera clicks and flashes against a din of loud mumbling. She was clearly in charge and comfortable in the setting. She was not, however, comfortable with the topic.

Catherine said, "Please, everyone. Take your seats." There was a shuffling of feet and screeching of metal chair legs on the concrete floor as reporters scrambled to their seats.

"First, a statement. Yesterday, our research team, working in close collaboration with the Mumbai lab group, the residual Indian and United States governments, the CDC, and experts from all over the world, identified the cause of the sudden deaths that have been occurring all over the world." The camera clicks and flashes did not slow. "We initiated our research immediately following the death of an Indian man who provided us with the first viable specimen for study. The results of our work allow us to communicate to you that the cause of worldwide death is not infectious. I repeat, it is not an infection." Catherine reminded herself that she shouldn't use too much complex medical terminology. "It is, to be more clear, not a bacteria or virus, the two things that cause infections. This condition cannot be spread from person to person. You can't catch this from being around other people." Now the clicking stopped, and a collective sigh of relief around the room.

A reporter shouted, "So this means it's safe to travel and go out in public?"

Catherine took a deep breath. This was not exactly where she thought the questioning would go.

"There's no reason for people to abandon their homes. No need to leave cities or towns. You cannot catch the condition. This is both good and bad news." Catherine paused and looked around the room. She wondered which member of the audience would die first. She noticed several dark-skinned reporters toward the front and instantly decided it would be them. They're closest to mitochondrial Eve. A twinge of sadness, imperceptible to those in the audience, arose. She quickly suppressed it to maintain composure.

A man wearing a maroon turban toward the back of the room shouted in a heavy Middle Eastern accent, "Then what is causing this plague on humanity? Why is this 'good and bad,' as you say?" She wondered when his pure bloodline had been tainted. It was the only explanation for why he was still alive.

Catherine swallowed and looked down at the podium. As she slowly looked back up, she said, "It is good because, as I said, it can't be transmitted from person to person." Another deep breath and a pause. "It's bad because it's genetic. It's caused by a mutation in the genes of the people who are affected." Catherine, not prone to emotion, felt tears close to erupting. She looked down again, successfully blinking them away.

She continued after a hard swallow. "And it is likely—even probable—that every human on earth has the mutation inside of them."

The room fell silent—no camera clicks, no background buzz, no note-taking. Now actively blinking back tears, Catherine looked down as if to check her notes. Standing in a line behind Catherine, the other team members alternated, staring at their feet and looking at Catherine. They were afraid to look into the audience, full of people who had just heard what amounted to a death sentence for humanity.

The silence seemed eternal. Catherine looked up. Members of the audience, the majority of whom had remarkably blank stares, were peering back at her. *Didn't they get it?*

Catherine knew she needed to open the door for questions. She had to make sure the world understood — at least a little — about the complexity of the science and the dire consequences of what confronted humanity, even if the reporters were slow to pick it up.

"Are there any questions?"

Every hand in the room shot up. Catherine pointed to a young Caucasian woman with an English accent, who asked, "Can you explain what genes are?"

"Of course," Catherine said. "Genes are like the...the... uhhh... control center of the cells in our bodies. A cell is the building block of life. Our bodies are made of billions of cells, all working together to make us the living creatures that humans are. Genes run the cell's life—regulate their energy and determine what each cell does. For example, the cells that line our stomach make acid to help break down our food—the genes in the cells that line the stomach control the acid secretion.

There are genes in every cell in our body, and the genes are unique, special to that kind of cell. The cells in your brain have genes that do different things from the genes in your stomach cells. That's why it all works." Catherine saw that most faces in the crowd showed understanding. She felt like she was lecturing a Biology 101 class.

She continued. "Genes also control the cell's growth. Cells grow by dividing, so one can divide and become two identical cells. They will divide based on the body's need to replace cells that have died. Many cells in our body, once mature, don't divide anymore, like brain cells. Genes in the brain are mainly for making chemicals that allow the brain to work."

An Italian reporter, his accent classic, said, "I'm not sure I understand what you mean. Can you explain differently?"

"Sure..." Catherine replied, closing her eyes, searching for an analogy. "It's like the control center in a manufacturing plant. For the plant to function, build its product, package it, and send it to its customers, there needs to be some way to control everything. So control over the entire plant is in a single control center that coordinates when and how certain things happen to ensure the plant is working correctly. Genes are like the control center of the cell. Does that make more sense?" The man nodded in affirmation.

"What's a mutation? What does it do?" asked a man with mixed Asian features in the middle of the group.

Catherine could see that some in the group understood, and others still had a look of confusion. "If we go back to the example I just gave about the manufacturing plant and the control center is the genes, imagine what would happen in the plant if a new manager came in and didn't understand the workings of the plant. He starts making all kinds of changes without understanding what he is doing. It causes an important part of the plant's production to stop, and suddenly, the entire manufacturing plant is out of commission. The lights are on, and the machines all can do the work, but nothing is being made because one change caused the entire system to fail. The new manager in this story is the gene mutation." The *Ah-ha look* was now seen throughout the room.

A black-skinned woman dressed in a brightly multi-colored dress raised her hand. There were living paradoxes all around Catherine. It made her feel dizzy. *How can she be alive?* She knew there had to be genetic exceptions, cosmic hiccups that confounded everything they understood. Catherine nodded to her. "So what is the new manager doing in our plant? What is the mutation? What does it do?"

"The mutation occurs in a cellular structure called a mitochondrion," Catherine began. "It gets a little complicated at this point, but I'll do my best to explain. Most of the cell's control is in a structure called the nucleus, which is like the central control center of the manufacturing plant. Mitochondria are separate structures found outside of the nucleus, and they are essential to the normal function of the cell. They provide the cell with energy and make some proteins that allow it to work correctly. Imagine if the manufacturing plant were completely self-sufficient, had its power plant, and used generators to make its electricity. The control center is in charge of the entire plant, but the generators scattered around the plant are critical to the manufacturing process. As long as the generators are working, the plant hums along just fine, producing everything it is supposed to make. But what if one generator in the power plant goes down and electricity is lost to a part of the plant? The plant would not function properly. Maybe it could be fixed, or a workaround could allow the plant to continue functioning. Maybe the plant's control center could re-route power from other sources when that part of the plant was needed to complete the manufacturing of their part of the product. It slows down the efficiency of the plant, but they still get the product out the door—they're still functioning, just not optimally. But if all the generators went down, the entire plant would come to a standstill. There would be no power to re-route and no workarounds. Is everyone following me?"

Catherine saw in their faces that they understood, and many were nodding. "Mutations can cause the same sort of problems for cells. A mutation can cause part of the cell not to work properly but still get along, like the manufacturing plant losing a single generator. Or it can be such a bad mutation that all cellular functions simply stop, like losing all the generators in the plant. If this happens in a cell, it dies."

A disheveled-looking older man with a long beard and a Yakima raised his hand. Catherine nodded to him. "Yes, sir?"

"So what kind of mutation is it in this mito... mito..."

"Mitochondria," Catherine said, saving him from the pain of not being able to spit out the five-syllable word.

"Yes," the man said, smiling in thanks.

"The mutation in the mitochondria is a bad one. The mutation is causing all generators to fail, resulting in the total failure of the manufacturing plant. It causes the plant to shut down. It results in the cell's death."

"But how does it do this?" persisted the man.

"The mutation results in the mitochondria initiating what is called the Death Effector sequence. The gene turns on after three copies of the mutation accumulate in the mitochondrion and produce a protein called caspase 8. It's spelled C-A-S-P-A-S-E and the number eight. Caspase 8 ultimately causes the cell to die. After this mutation is turned on, there is no way to shut it off. We estimate that once about

40 percent of the body's cells have the mutation, it results in a cascade of intracellular events that lead to rapid, irreversible cell death, killing the individual."

The faces in the press corps now reflected a horrified understanding. Breathing was the only sound until a woman on the front row started sobbing softly, head bowed. Catherine could see her tears falling onto her notepad, causing the ink to run like the notebook itself was weeping.

A young American reporter toward the front said, "You said earlier that it's likely that every human on earth has the potential for this mutation, correct?"

Catherine looked at him directly and said, "Yes, that is correct," again feeling the urge to cry. She fought it back again, understanding that if she broke down, the near panic already felt in the room would turn to overt, crushing fear that would spread as quickly as the AP wire could carry the story.

"So," the young man followed, "we are all going to die. This is the end of humanity?"

In the few seconds that followed, Catherine's mind exploded in uncontrolled thoughts and self-analysis despite having scripted talking points. She knew if she told them the truth, at least as the team understood it, it would assure global panic. The lawlessness that had already gripped many nations would only worsen. What would anyone have to lose if they knew their death was assured? If you are going to die, no consequences could change that. Murder, rape, pillaging. No consequence is worse than death, so what would inhibit anarchy?

Maybe I should lie. Should I tell them we know how to treat this? Isn't hope, even if it's based on a lie, better than knowing there is no escape? As a parent, would you want to know you will die, leaving your three-year-old to die of starvation or thirst, all alone? What is the kind thing to do? What is the right thing to do? Physicians are skilled technicians, armed with scientific knowledge, and can do amazing things not even imagined by our predecessors just 20 years ago. But at the core, isn't compassion the most important therapy in the absence of hope? Isn't relieving human suffering what we are supposed to do. However, we can? *If a lie can spare mental anguish on a global level—or even for a single human being—wouldn't that be a forgivable sin? Yes.*

Catherine crumpled the script in her hand, visibly straightened her shoulders, and lifted her chin, projecting confidence. "No, it's not the end of humanity," she said with believable authority. "These five individuals behind me are already working on a solution to the problem and have made significant progress in the past 24 hours." She knew the team members had picked up on what she was doing as she turned to look at them, seeing them change their posture and expressions, intuitively understanding they needed to play along.

"It is critically important — crucial — that you communicate to the world that now is not time for panic. It will not help anyone. We should be able to treat this very soon, but until that time, don't give up hope. Even though a solution is close at hand, everyone should prepare for the worst. Make plans. Put your affairs in order. Talk to your children and be honest with them. Make sure they know where to find food and water. Keep some cash for them at home. If you have young children, make a plan for the older children of friends or neighbors to care for them if the worst does happen. But keep the faith that it is going to work out, and have faith in us to solve this puzzle." Half of the hands in the room shot up.

"Thank you very much for coming," Catherine said, turning to leave and motioning the others to follow. The room erupted with questions, shouted after the exiting team.

Catherine walked quickly down the hallway, the din of the pressroom disappearing behind her. She led the team back to the commons area and walked straight to her room. She sat down on her bed, buried her face in her hands, and sobbed uncontrollably, mourning the end of the human race.

CHAPTER FIFTY-SEVEN

President Lopez made good on his promise to Catherine, sitting quietly while his national security team watched the press conference. He considered telling them, but decided against it, primarily because he didn't understand the science, only the impact. As the president watched the RRT's press conference end, the world now knew its fate. His entire cabinet was looking at him.

Tom Nakamoro, the Chief of Staff, walked into the room. The president cocked his head up to listen to a whispered message. Try as he might not to show concern, the president knew that he did, a subtle mistake that increased the pressure in the Situation Room to the point it could have pegged a strain gauge.

He turned to the Army major running the AV panel and nodded. The monitors around the room lit up; each monitor showed the same thing: A satellite image of the massive plaza at Kumsusan Palace of the Sun in Pyongyang.

"General," the president said, "Please explain what's going on."

"Yes, sir, Mr. President. In the last eight days, North Korea — the most militarized nation on earth — has amassed one million troops." He looked over at the major sitting at the computer, held up his index finger, and circled it in the air to indicate he was ready to move to the next satellite image.

"Here, you see the North Korean Navy, to the extent it exists, steaming toward the west coast of the U.S. Next, major," the General continued. "And their Air Force is moving transport planes to civilian airports that are adjacent to major military installations, especially around Pyongyang."

"What do we know about their plans, General?" the president asked.

"According to NSA intelligence, the invasion is going to come from Mexico and Canada in a pincer-like attack. The North Koreans consider these two countries as bumps in the road because their militaries will be quickly overwhelmed by the sheer number of troops they will put on the ground. Staging troops will drop onto Mexico's Pacific coast to capture the deep ocean ports of Lazaro Cardenas and Manzanillo in preparation to dock naval transports. That's when the real fun will start. And Mr. President, the North Koreans are strongly considering a nuclear strike against key U.S. cities—Washington, New York, LA, Chicago, and Houston."

"Well, it's reassuring that you seem to have such detailed information about their plans. Glad you cracked whatever code they were using," the president said.

The general paused. The president noticed the general's brows folding in and down. The general said, "Mr. President, while all of this is incredibly scary, the most chilling fact is the North Korean transmissions were not in code. They openly communicate their intent, understanding that their destruction is likely. This is...," he paused and cleared his throat. "This is the entire country of North Korea in a coordinated kamikaze attack on the United States," the general concluded.

"My god..." the president said as he leaned back in his chair.

"Mr. President, we suspect the North Koreans have concluded the infection they loosed on mankind is about to overtake their own country, and they have no intention of going down from their disease without first punishing the U.S. for their insult of the North Korean people," the general concluded.

The president sat quietly for a moment, then turned to Elaine Morrow and said, "Call the Chinese premier right now, please. We'll work through them—the North Koreans seem to trust them.

Elaine dialed the number reserved for direct communication between the two heads of state. "I'll put it on speaker, Mr. President," Elaine said.

"Yes, please do," the president said. Elaine switched on the speaker system, and the phone rang with a loud sputter. As it rang an eighth, ninth time, the president noticed the growing concern on the faces in the room. After two minutes of continuous ringing, President Lopez nodded to Elaine, who reached over and ended the call with the tap of a finger.

400 MILES DUE SOUTH OF PYONGYANG

Wei Zhou was as scared as he had ever been. As an undercover CIA operative based in China for the last 25 years, he had had several close calls, but this was different. Although he'd been born in America, a Chinese mother and Latino father, he closely resembled the Chinese people from the region close to the Mongolian border. Of all the challenges he had encountered, he had never been accused of not being a local. When he had served the CIA, he had become the most reliable conduit of information from China in the agency.

Wei was up early, walking along the streets of Shanghai, China's largest city. He considered the city to be a proud symbol of Chinese national and global commercial success, watching it grow to 20 million citizens over the years, becoming one of the largest metropolitan areas on the planet. Wei recognized that China's industrial success and affordable motorized transportation had helped propel China's accomplishments, but he cursed the auto exhaust. It resulted in a brown, low-hanging cloud that got trapped in the windless confines of skyscraper canyons, creating a significant number of days when it was virtually impossible for him—or anyone else—to spend more than a few moments outdoors without having a sense that he was being viscerally eroded in real-time. It caused severe burning in his throat and chest as the thick, choking, visible air seared the sensitive lining of his lungs. He could see the air he was inhaling. A daylong visit to the city was enough to cause him to cough up brownish-black lung cookies for days. He was schooled enough in biology to know that his lungs had efficiently cleansed the air he exhaled, tiny airborne particles depositing themselves neatly amongst the same critical cells that took in oxygen and gave up carbon dioxide in the normal process of breathing. He marveled at the fact that the Chinese people were, in an odd way, Shanghai's air filters, like so many snails in a dirty fish aquarium.

Wei noticed the morning was peculiarly spectacular. The sky over Shanghai was cloudless, smogless, a color of blue that he recalled from a less industrial time. The sun was bright and piercing. He imagined the expanding color hanging low over the Pacific strait, a beautiful yellow ribbon connecting him directly to Kagoshima, Japan, some 570 miles directly to the east.

The beauty of the sky was not the only thing that Wei noticed. Between the darkened cliffs of the skyscrapers and streets still hidden from the rising sun, he noticed a curious absence of traffic upon exiting his high-rise apartment building. At least, traffic that was going anywhere. There were many cars, but few were moving, and most sat motionless, engines idling.

Wei looked to his left, then right. He began to feel an intense dis-ease as the sun rose and the darkened streets became increasingly illuminated by a type of natural light that hadn't touched the ground in downtown Shanghai for years. Not only was the sun illuminating the streets, but it was also allowing Wei to see the reason for the lack of traffic and the sudden clearing of the sky. Dead pedestrians dotted the sidewalk like bundles of garbage set out the night before by the store merchants. Autos sat half in and half out of storefronts, primarily at the intersection of roads where one road dead-ended in a T-like configuration with a cross street.

He heard a collision of metal, rubber, concrete, and glass. He ran around the corner, encountering a shiny black Mercedes— clearly a wealthy Chinese merchant — that sat high-centered, rear wheels still rotating, engine idling, teetering on a knee-high stone wall, part of the storefront of a fashion boutique in Shanghai's high-rent district. The shattered glass of the store window, strewn in every direction, crunched with each tentative step, reminiscent of the sound made by walking on a frozen crust of snow. Wei paused, noticing a thin mannequin standing beside the car, its red designer dress fluttering gently in the morning breeze. The vehicle had nudged the display doll just enough to turn it so that it appeared to be staring at the car's dead driver as if the inanimate human figurine had been stunned into silence. The oddity of an impeccably dressed plastic human looking at a real dead one slumped over the steering wheel of a Mercedes struck Wei as rich material for Edvard Munch, the expressionist artist for whom he had a fondness.

Wei knew what it all meant. The plague had turned on China with a vengeance, just a little over a week after death had marched through India and the Pacific Rim. Though a spy against this giant country, Wei was fond of it. He felt sadness as he walked through the streets of what had become an enormous charnel ground.

The president looked at the monitor in disbelief as he watched North Korean soldiers drop dead—one here, one there—and he felt as if he were hallucinating or watching a bad Hollywood horror flick on mute. The satellite images of Kumsusan's Plaza now looked very different from images that had revealed the arrow-straight lines of immaculately uniformed, heavily armed soldiers just a few minutes ago. He could still make out a few living soldiers, scrambling over a carpet of tangled bodies and trying to reach the edge of the plaza, thinking they could escape the fate of their comrades. It was like watching the last survivors of a poisoned ant colony struggling futilely to reach some unseen salvation.

The plaza was lifeless in two short hours. The most powerful man on the face of the planet sat silently in the Situation Room, watching his national security team stare at their shoes or the papers in front of them—at anything but someone else's face. He knew they realized that death was coming for them—for all Americans. It just wouldn't be at the hands of the North Koreans.

CHAPTER FIFTY-EIGHT

"Eight days. It happened in eight days," Lucy said glumly, rearranging her scrambled eggs yet again, even though they were long past cold and an odd hue of greenish-yellow. "Will it slow down, Marla?"

"I don't know," Marla said, thoughtfully sipping her coffee. "We may have already gained all the time we're going to get. If the genomic changes reached some level of stability in the migrations between India and China, the timeline might start to shorten."

"Explain what you're thinking, honey," Jack said.

"Well, we've been operating on the assumption that genetic drift is what explains the relative lengthening of the time between episodes of death since the Middle East. The evolutionary differences in the mtDNA between the Indian and Chinese may be less dramatic than between the Middle Eastern and Indian peoples. A more dramatic change could have resulted in a longer delay before activating the Death Effector gene. If the changes in the DNA between the Indian population and the Chinese were minimal, it's conceivable that the delay would be shorter."

"So it's possible that we are going to see an acceleration of death cycles? Russia, for example, could be affected a week from now?" Catherine asked.

"Yes, it's possible, but it would seem unlikely. Based upon the timeframes we've witnessed, I don't think the cycles would shorten so dramatically. I don't think two days is likely, but a week or two seems more likely than three or four," Marla said. "It's all a guess, but we do have the prior cycles as a basis for making that assumption."

Ted said, "Well, there's always an upside, folks. Without all those Chinese factories and cars, I guess the greenhouse effect should lessen, and global warming should slow down." Jack and the other team members glared at the callous but accurate observation. Embarrassed, Ted said, "Hey, I'm just sayin'."

"Yeah, Ted, it's great that our parentless children will die breathing clean air shortly after they turn 18, if not before," Lucy said, her eyes wet as she left the room.

After a day of no progress, Catherine and Jack were alone in the kitchen. It was 11 p.m., and they were exhausted, but neither could sleep. The world was falling apart. Entire societies had collapsed, and it was rapidly approaching the time when the team members would be directly affected.

"Jack?" Catherine said quietly. He looked up from a magazine he was mindlessly perusing.

"Huh? Yeah?" he said.

"You have to be worried about Marla because of her Asian heritage. Is there anything I can do?" Catherine said, putting her hand on his arm.

"Pray that she's right about genetic drift and ethnic group mixing," Jack said.

"What do you mean?"

"Marla's only a quarter Chinese and a quarter Japanese. Her grandparents both married white folk—hearty Midwestern stock. And they're pretty sure that her Chinese grandmother was the product of a rape that occurred in San Francisco, where her great-grandmother lived. The Chinese side of her family had come over to work on the transcontinental railway," Jack said.

"Well, that's all good news, right? I mean, if she's a mutt, she may have as robust a set of DNA as the rest of us, late migrators." Jack nodded his head weakly in agreement. He looked up at Catherine, trying to smile, a tear rolling down his cheek.

CHAPTER FIFTY-NINE

The Cabinet was already seated when President Lopez arrived. His step's bounce and projected energy level defied his internal milieu. He felt weak, defeated—the most powerful man in the world felt powerless.

He looked at the agenda as he sat down. Looking up, he said, "Ms. Morrow, let's begin with you. I suspect you have the longest update."

"Thank you, Mr. President," she said. She filtered through some papers and glanced at the laptop screen in front of her. Elaine was one of the few Cabinet members that preferred a computer to paper. Compared to the other members, the president appreciated this as a sign of her relative youth. He inwardly chuckled when it resulted in an occasional snarl from the older, technologically illiterate male members.

"It's pretty ugly out there, sir. A little more than a week ago, the condition raced, as Marla Qui had predicted, sequentially through Bangladesh, Myanmar, Thailand, Cambodia, and Vietnam. In Bangkok, the khlongs look like logging flumes, clogged with bodies floating parallel to the banks, bobbing along."

"What the hell is a khlong?" the attorney general asked. He was the most conservative member of the Cabinet—a stiff-suited man with a fake-bake tan, ivory buck-toothed mouth frozen in a phony smile, and Brylcreem-soaked hair. The president loathed him and deeply regretted having appointed him, a mistake that would be corrected next term, God willing.

"Canals," replied Elaine. The president wondered if she was refraining from adding *you moron* to her reply. "Bangkok is known as the Venice of the East. She continued, "The Chao Phraya, the main river of Bangkok, is loaded with bodies floating downstream from upcountry, and it continues to be force-fed more waterlogged bodies from canals intersecting with the river."

"Gruesome," the secretary of education said softly. She was the squeamish one of the group. The president just listened.

"With China and the Koreas affected now, I think we need to be frank about the fact, Mr. President, that it's increasingly every country for itself," said Elaine, a tone of finality in her voice.

The president looked over at the secretary of defense and nodded to him, indicating he wanted his input.

"Mr. President, there are no more resources to send, no more personnel to lend a hand in yet another vast geographic region. The U.S. and European forces are tapped out. Supply lines are so thin that they're ineffective, and there's a global shortage of petrochemicals. Just getting enough fuel to keep the Indian research team up and running is a colossal challenge. At this point, we need to just forget about the entire Asian region," he said, pausing. He pursed his lips. The president knew he was about to say something that made him feel uncomfortable.

"Mr. President, at this point, I feel I must recommend that the western part of the world focus on maintaining our supplies of food, water, and fuel. This wouldn't be a decision made out of political paranoia, but the stark realization that self-preservation now needs to trump humanitarian efforts that could sap the ability of our own people's survival." His voice increased in volume and speed as he completed the sentence.

"What about Africa? Are things stabilizing there at all?" the president asked hopefully?

The Health and Human Services secretary chimed in. "Mr. President, I've been working closely with the Department of Defense. Unfortunately, anarchy is the rule of the day in Africa and the Middle East, despite the military presence. It's inhibiting attempts to help, and disease takes a huge toll on pre-teen children. They are dying in droves from dehydration. Those with access to water are dying from cholera, now epidemic."

Elaine jumped back into the discussion. "Mr. President, many of the surviving children, are panicked and are migrating into the cities, thinking they can somehow escape death. All it's doing is spreading sanitation-related disease more quickly in densely populated areas. Paradoxically, they are walking into death, not away from it."

"Jesus," President Lopez uttered. "There isn't anything we can do, for God's sake?"

"All due respect, Mr. President, but with whom?" said the defense secretary. "It isn't just that our military is tapped out. Global infrastructure is failing due to the simple fact that there aren't any living adults in the affected areas trained to run things. Most affected regions' petroleum, water treatment, and food production plants have shut down completely. The only oil facilities in the Middle East still manned are those run by NATO engineers. Plants that are functioning have limited abilities to distribute what they're producing. Tankers loaded with oil are aimlessly drifting at sea, with entire crews dead and rotting on deck, becoming chum for seagulls. NATO Naval forces are busy tracking down the pilotless ships, hoping to bring them into the closest U.S. port.”

“God knows, we don’t need to add oil spills to the list of global disasters,” the secretary of the interior said.

“Christ,” the president said, looking at the interior secretary. “We’ve got millions of orphaned kids at risk for death, and you’re worried about a goddam oil spill? I’m all for the environment, but let’s try to focus on making sure there are some *Homo sapiens* around to enjoy it before we worry about saving it.” He felt guilty as soon as the words left his mouth, but the point was necessary, and it emphasized his first-things-first approach. “Will having the tankers commandeered for U.S. ports piss off our allies? What about Russia?”

“It could, Mr. President, but frankly, we have the only navy in a position actually to do something about the situation,” said Elaine. “I guess we could divert some of them to European ports. The Russians are probably OK in the near term with what they produce for themselves.”

“Yes, let’s do that. Every other tanker will come to the U.S., and for every two that go to Europe, send one to Russia,” the president said.

There was an uncomfortable stretch of silence. President Lopez looked around the room, making eye contact with each of the Cabinet members. “Does anyone have any other recommendations for me? Let’s move from recapping the bad news and get proactive.” He looked at the defense secretary.

“Mr. President, I advise you to order all U.S. military reserves to active duty in preparation for the disaster that’s evolving in the U.S.”

“Aren’t a lot of them already busy cleaning up the ethnic enclaves that are already dead?” the president asked.

“Yes, sir. But it’ll be easier to keep them there than to demobilize them and try to get them back. We’re predicting reservists will go AWOL in mass once this comes ashore. We need to keep them in the field, busy.”

“Agreed. Do it,” said the president.

“Yes, sir.”

“Mr. President?” said the HUD secretary.

“Yes?”

“We are seeing mass migrations of citizens out major cities and toward the countryside. People seem to be hoping to avoid the contagion. The streets of New York haven’t looked so deserted since the days following 9/11.”

President Lopez looked at him with a degree of incredulity. “This surprises you?” he said. “The fact that it’s genetic should slow that. There’s nowhere to hide from yourself, is there?” he said with unusual intensity, causing nervous laughter, the kind where people know they should laugh but don't feel like it.

In a somber tone, President Lopez said, "Half of the world's population—nearly four billion souls—have evaporated from existence in the equivalent of an evolutionary blink of an eye. I think I can understand people's desire to do whatever the hell they think will help themselves, as long as it doesn't hurt someone else." He paused then asked, "What else?"

The HHS secretary said, "While it isn't a health threat itself, it's nearly impossible to avoid the putrid odor of rotting flesh. It's a constant, inescapable reminder of death—people think it could make them ill, like medieval evil humors or something. The global wind patterns have pushed the rancid smell of decomposing humans in India and Asia into the atmosphere and carried it to the west coast. It's bizarre being able to smell death from ten thousand miles away. It dissipates as it crosses the Rockies and the Midwest, such that, by the time it reaches the east coast, it is barely detectable. Europe is benefitting from geography."

"The point being?" the president asked, brows furrowed.

"It's created constant emotional distress. It isn't the odor itself creating the discomfort, but what it stands for: an unseen, elusive enemy—and no escape."

"Yeah, I suppose it's always easier to deal with a known enemy. Knowing you're at war with terrorists or Nazis or Bosnians at least allows you to know what to shoot at. It would have been preferable to have North Korea invade rather than deal with the genetic defect's anxiety and no known solution. Speaking of that, what do we know from our folks in Mumbai?" the president said, looking hopefully at the HHS secretary.

"I received an update just 15 minutes before the meeting," she said. "I'm afraid there's no progress to report." The president exhaled loudly and slowly through pursed lips as if he were doing yoga in his chair. He looked down at his hands folded in his lap in deeply troubled contemplation.

"Goddamit! Doesn't anyone have any good news?" the president asked. He knew the answer before he uttered the words. The Cabinet members looked sullen. He continued, "Well, then I guess just keep telling me what you think I need to know."

The defense secretary cleared his voice and then said, with no small amount of hesitancy, "Our few troops in China report an explosion of flies equivalent to the biblical plagues."

"Hasn't that happened pretty much everywhere death has hit?" the president asked.

"Yes, but not to the extent seen in China. At least some clean-up in the other countries, which partially controlled the insects. My folks are reporting the skies are overcast, not with cloud cover, but because the air is so thick with flies that the sun is obscured." The President winced at the vision: A single dead human body generating hundreds of thousands of the irritating, filthy insects, hatching from writhing masses of white maggots boiling up out of various body orifices and exploded cavities. "It makes the Old Testament's description of the locusts seem preferable—even tolerable," the defense secretary concluded.

The commerce secretary chimed in, "Chinese factories are still running, and no one is at the helm. Some more modern factories have automated safety systems, and the equipment is automatically shutting down. But there are huge numbers of less sophisticated Chinese manufacturing facilities with no modern equipment and no computer monitoring systems, and they're just churning away, producing nothing other than pollutants."

"We did send our troops to shut down nuclear power facilities, the defense secretary said. "We've also secured Chinese and North Korean nuclear armaments. In retrospect, it seems ludicrous since there are no native adults living with the knowledge to launch weapons."

"Christ..." the president said. "What else?"

"Asia produces about 92 percent of the world's rice crop," said the commerce secretary. "It's bound to affect food supplies. There are runs on grocery stores, and supplies are quickly being depleted stateside. Fear of starvation is driving people to panic. Fifty-eight folks—mainly women and children— were trampled to death in a London grocery store earlier today."

"Mr. President?" the energy secretary said in his usual timid voice. The bespectacled man was a pasty color, with eyes that appeared like they were suspended from floppy eyelids at the top of his eye sockets.

"Yes?" the president said. "What wonderful news do you have for me?"

"Oil production in Asia has been affected much more than in the Middle East. NATO forces are simply unable to operate the Chinese facilities due to a lack of manpower. There are many critical oil supplies just sitting in storage tanks along the coast of the mainland, but no trained tanker crews to load and transport the oil. The Russians and some Eastern European countries have mandated involuntary blackouts two hours after sundown to save energy. Violators are being imprisoned."

"Well, maybe we need to ration energy here," suggested the attorney general. The president would have immediately agreed if it were any other Cabinet member.

"I agree," said the energy secretary, "But we'll need to manage it well and communicate well ahead of time that we're doing. The World War II generation will remember food and gas rationing. To the other 95 percent of the population, it will seem an incredible hardship."

The president held up his hand, indicating to everyone to stop speaking. He lowered his hand after the room grew silent and said, "I've had enough for today." He stood up and, as he buttoned his jacket, said, "I can hardly wait for tomorrow's meeting."

CHAPTER SIXTY

Jack thought of the New World, the part of the globe that had dominated so much of human history over the past 300 years. He pondered the evolutionary history that led to North America's colonization 15,000 years ago. The question that preoccupied him now was *When will the Death Effector Gene turn on in Marla and me?* Now that the cause of the global catastrophe was fully elucidated, he wondered how much of the world's remaining population was aware of their potential fate. A mitochondrial scourge—a cleansing at the cellular level, eliminated the whole. The irony didn't escape him: The same sub-cellular organelle that had provided life to mitochondrial Eve at the dawn of human evolution over 200,000 years ago was now ravaging the very earth she had populated. That death was traversing the same path humans had used to settle the Earth's continents was both poetic and logical.

He was thankful for the upside of the new findings because everyone could shed the MOPP gear. After its prolonged use, the ability to see and touch each other seemed odd. The time spent working seemed more straightforward, less of a burden, in a literal sense. Not manipulating delicate research tools with bulky MOPP gloves sped up the work.

Three copies of the mtDNA mutation were required to initiate the Death Effector sequence provided Jack with additional information. The finding that some cells had no mitochondria with the mutation, while others had one or two mutated mtDNA strands, indicated that the mutation accumulated across time. One or two copies of the mutant mtDNA were harmless, but a third initiated a cascade of intracellular events leading to cellular suffocation. More puzzling to Jack was that this cellular kamikaze effect only took place once 40 percent of the organism's total cell mass was affected. Jack concluded that the Death Effector Gene was like radiation's effect on living tissues in many ways. Radiation is cumulative, resulting in genetic defects and mutations, ultimately causing death, but at some future point in time. As the damaged genes build up over time, cells quit functioning and die or transform into cancer. The radiation dose that can cause death is known. Sublethal doses don't kill immediately, but the organism may die of any one of a myriad of potential radiation-induced dysfunctions long after being exposed. With

Eve's mutation, the outcome was death from asphyxiation. The formula was simple: three mtDNA mutations plus forty percent of the human's cellular volume equals one result—death.

The findings confirmed Marla's suspicion that genetic drift had potentially provided them with an unexpected break. Jack and the team could now assume the rate of cellular conversion was slowing along the evolutionary migration path. The mitochondria in every living human would eventually be affected but at different rates. Tens of thousands of years ago, people had moved away from hostile relatives as a short-term survival strategy—and was now turning out to provide potential long-term survival benefits or at least a delay in death. The delay in the Death Effector switch provided the window of time needed to find a cure to a deeply embedded evolutionary challenge.

"So, I hate to ask this, 'cause for the first time in my life, I'm going to sound like I'm a racist. Will this affect my family? I mean, we're all on the Caucasian side of the fence," Ted said.

Jack said, "Well, Ted, I'm assuming you are referring to the fact that, at least to date, death has not been reported in white folks?"

"Yes, Ted. You have Eve's mtDNA too. So do your wife and children. I know Texans like to believe they're independent, but they aren't that independent," Marla said, grinning. In a more serious tone, she said, "No one will be spared. The Alamo will have no survivors for a second time. No racial battle lines will be drawn on this one. No Tuskegee Project. No internment camps. All will fall." Jack recognized a twinge of irritation in her voice. "There are no life rafts on this sinking ship," Marla concluded.

"Yeah, s'pose not. The question is, how fast?" Ted said.

"The fact that we haven't heard anything more since China is encouraging," Catherine said. "The next wave will hit Russia full-force, with Europe and North America not far behind. Right, Marla?"

"Pretty much," Marla said. "We do know that the switch for the Death Effector mutation has slowed down. That's good, of course, but we can only guess how much more it will slow."

"It would be nice to know how much time we have," Jack said. "I guess at this point, we do whatever it takes. The question is, what is that?"

"To find a solution, you mean, Jack?" Lucy asked. "Frankly, I don't see any way this can be fixed."

"We don't have the luxury of planning around risk. We go with the first reasonable idea anyone has," Catherine said.

"Rick, isn't there some nerve we could remove from a living human to see how many mutations he has and what percentage of cells are affected? Wouldn't that give us a relative idea of time?" said Jack. "I mean, if you took a piece of nerve tissue from me and there were no mtDNA mutations present, would that help us in projecting a timeline?"

Jack watched as Rick pondered. "Sural nerve biopsy," Rick said matter-of-factly. "We could take a segment of the sural nerve from the lower leg. If it's removed, it causes some numbness to the outside of the foot—it doesn't do anything related to movement, and no muscles are affected."

"What'd we do once we got the specimen? How would that help?" Ted asked.

Rick responded, "Just like Jack said, Ted, we could prep it for EM and see how many mitochondria have the Death Effector sequence and estimate how many cells in the nerve are affected. I don't know what we could conclude regarding time left for the individual, but it might be useful information."

Catherine said, "How long would it take?"

"The biopsy would take about 30 minutes for each person," Rick said. "But we would need a surgeon. It isn't something any of us would be able to do."

Jack stood up. "Marla, come here for a sec." They walked to the end of the room out of earshot of the group.

"Honey, I think we should do this. I want to see what is going on in each of us, even if it doesn't tell us how exactly how much time we have."

Marla looked down. Jack knew she was struggling with the reality that her Asian ancestry made it likely that her mitochondria were already morphing. He suspected she was benefiting from both sides of her Asian ancestors intermingling their genetics with Caucasians, but it was just a matter of time. "Jack, I don't know. I..." Marla broke down, burying her face in Jack's chest.

"Marla, honey. This isn't over. And I don't want you to give up hope. There's already too much despair."

She wiped her eyes with her shirtsleeve as Jack held her and looked into her eyes. "OK. Let's do it," she said.

The British surgeon entered and proclaimed, "The best place for doing the biopsy is in the ICU. It's clean and relatively quiet and has readily available nursing staff. Jack had found him in the hospital upstairs and talked him into doing the surgery.

Jack went first, with Marla sitting at the head of the procedure table, face to face with him and holding his hands. Lying on his stomach with his left pant leg rolled up, Jack watched as the surgeon donned a gown and gloves and then watched over his shoulder as the doctor painted his skin with an iodine solution, turning it reddish-brown. The surgeon carefully placed sterile towels in a rectangle, creating a picture-frame-like clean zone around Jack's left calf, at which point Jack stopped watching. He felt the surgeon poking around on this leg, finally finding the indentation in the middle of the calf, the landmark for the nerve. He felt him use a marker to draw a two-inch line on the back of his leg.

"OK, Jack, there's going to be a little pinch here," the surgeon said.

"Pinch, my ass!" Jack exclaimed, feeling the large needle puncture the skin at the outer edge of his leg. An intense burning sensation moved up and down his leg as the needle went deeper. Jack gritted his teeth so hard his jaw ached.

Jack could only feel pressure for the next few minutes as the surgeon took a scalpel and made an incision over the anesthetized, purple-marked skin. Jack, watching Marla, noticed her wince.

"What? Why the look?" Jack said. Marla looked away and didn't answer.

The surgeon answered for her. "Oh, there's just a bit of blood welling up in the wound. No worries!" He was nonplused, and all Jack felt was the staccato pressure blotting blood away with gauze.

Jack felt more intense pressure—nearly to the point of pain—when the surgeon picked up a Y-shaped instrument with large, outward-pointing teeth on one end and a scissor-like handle on the other, placed the teeth into the incision, and squeezed the scissor handle hard, spreading the wound wide open. "There now, that certainly helped the bleeding," he said as if it would also help Jack's confidence.

Jack glanced back to see what was going on. The tool hanging onto his leg looked more like a medieval torture device than a surgical instrument. He quickly turned his head, preferring to look at Marla. He felt a wave of heat spread up from his leg into his pelvis and gut, followed by low-grade nausea.

The surgeon picked up the syringe again and said, "This is going to hurt a bit. I'm going to anesthetize the nerve itself now, so when I cut it, you won't feel a thing." Jack felt searing, poker-hot, electrical pain shoot down the back of his ankle and into his heel, and outer side of his foot as the surgeon pushed the needle into the nerve and began injecting.

"Jesus!" he yelped. "If it feels like this with you trying to numb the damn thing, I can't imagine...aarggg..." He held his breath in pain, cheeks bulging. "I can't imagine what it would be like without the anesthetic."

A few moments later and the surgeon said, "There." He held up an inch-long piece of nerve. Jack thought it looked like the white twine used to hold hay bails together back in Kansas. Jack watched as he plopped it into the specimen container.

"Now, lets' just get you closed up, shall we?" the surgeon said cheerfully.

Even though Marla had not seen any of the procedure, Jack knew she had seen the pain on his face, and he squeezed her hand to the point of hurting her.

Jack traded places with his stoic wife, and the entire scene was replayed with clean instruments.

During the procedure, Marla looked at him and said, "You know, the paradox of this whole thing is bizarre. I'm not doing this to help cure some condition—take out cancer or whatever. I'm having a procedure whose only value is to predict the relative time of my own death." Jack felt numb all over.

A couple of days later, the biopsy results came back. Jack had one copy of the mtDNA mutation in about 20 percent of his cells. Marla, however, had two copies in about 10 percent of her sural nerve cells and one mutation in another 30 percent. The process was moving more quickly in Marla. Heritage can suck.

The results were of more than selfish value. While Marla's mtDNA was converting more quickly than Jack's, it was also clear that it was happening more slowly than native Southeast Asians, who had never left their original homeland. The implication was clear: genetic drift, as well as ethnic mixing, had slowed—not stopped, but slowed—the activation of the Death Effector Gene. It explained the sparing of some dark-skinned and Asian peoples who had emigrated from their original geographic region two or more generations ago, especially those in Europe and North and South America. As long as a solution could be found before the gene was switched on in the emigrant populations, the various ethnicities could survive. The survivors' mtDNA may not be pure, but no one would be able to tell that simply by looking at them. And they would be alive.

The results from Jack's biopsy were also significant. Jack, Ted, Rick, and Lucy were all American mutts in heritage. A little of this, a sprinkle of that. Even Catherine's family had multiple genetic lines from Caucasians and Native Americans.

Ted put it best without mixing words. "Great, we getta' watch everyone else croak first. Not sure that's better."

CHAPTER SIXTY-ONE

Jack was frustrated by the past few days. They had been unproductive, and the team was depressed. This morning, he had videoconferences with leading scientists, a sort of worldwide brainstorming event, and Ted had reconfigured a large room in a little-used part of the lab to be a sort of media center. Multiple large monitors hung from every wall in the room. Six video-enabled computers were evenly distributed around a large oval table sitting in the middle of the room.

Jack had worked until 1 a.m. coordinating the participation of experts in genetics, mutations, radiation, cloning, oncology, cellular biology, and mitochondria. He had Catherine arrange for the CDC, the U.S, DoD, WHO, and the European, Russian, and South American agencies to call in. Jack knew Catherine was pissed at the political correctness of the whole thing when she complained, "Even when the whole damn world is dying, we have to play politics."

Ted chuckled and patted her gently on the back. "Well, I'm glad yer here, Boss."

Jack logged the team into the forum, and participants worldwide began to pop into the conference. The monitors on the walls lit up with faces from every region in the world where there were survivors.

Jack nodded to Catherine to start.

"You already understand why you're here," Catherine said. "So I'm dispensing with introductions and hope nobody's feelings are hurt, but frankly, time is more important than protocol now."

She paused before continuing. "Now, you all received a packet of information from us via email. I assume you have reviewed it. I'll allow the team on our end to answer questions of clarification, but if questions are asked that demonstrate you haven't read the material, we'll not allow you to ask more questions. Again, in summary, everyone's time is valuable, so don't waste it." Jack could tell Catherine was in no mood to screw around.

"We'll start by reviewing the findings to date in a very abbreviated form," said Catherine. Jack listened as she described the history of the events over fifteen minutes. He suspected everyone would remember her closing sentence:

"Once switched on, death is certain, rapid, and probably painless."

There was a pause. Jack shrugged his shoulders at Catherine, and she started again. "You are all probably wondering why the rest of us haven't, ahh, been affected by the Death Effector Gene yet. Marla, would you share your theory with the group?"

Marla explained in detail and concluded by saying, "What we have found is our common female ancestor's mtDNA contains a population control switch that, at some point in the future, would turn on, and result in a culling of the human population. A suicide switch, if you will."

"Excuse me. May I ask a question? This is Dr. Vlad Ivanov in Moscow."

"Of course," said Catherine, moderating.

"Why in God's name would such a gene exist? This seems preposterous to me," Dr. Ivanov said.

"There are examples in nature of animals who exhibit behaviors that lead to them dying in mass. Lemmings, for example. They tend to over-populate about every four years, resulting in large numbers of the creatures being driven by a strong biological urge, no doubt a result of genetics, to migrate. As a result, they are forced into bodies of water, rivers, the ocean, where thousands drown. It's not suicide, but it's hard to argue that their genetics don't predispose them to behavior that virtually assures a certain number will die. The population manifests unconscious, genetically driven behavior that self-culls the animals to ensure the species' survival. And recently, 26 dolphins—highly intelligent mammals—beached themselves in Cornwall, England. Veterinarians, unable to find a cause of death, no infection, no pathology, suggested this was a mass suicide. The same thing happened on the coast of Iran the year before that; only it was 152 dolphins. No explanation. Is it suicide? I don't know, but something seems to have programmed them to engage in self-destructive behavior, virtually guaranteeing their deaths."

"This all seems very unlikely," countered Ivanov.

"Maybe," said Marla, "but the suggestions in nature and across time are hard to ignore. Some paleontologists have suggested that the dinosaurs' genetics resulted in their extinction. Their genetics certainly made them large, and those same genetics could have easily made them too large to sustain themselves in their environment. It's been suggested that genetic metabolic disorders may have resulted in eggshells that were too thin, resulting in the loss of eggs before hatching." Marla paused. Jack could tell from her face that she was frustrated at resistance to what seemed so obvious to her.

Marla continued, "Look, the fact is, the data confirms this to be an mtDNA mutation destroying our species. Whatever the real answer is, I know one thing for sure, debating whether my theory is right or not isn't going to help us find a solution to the problem. It is what it is. Catherine, I suggest we move on."

"Agreed. Thanks, Marla. OK, then, any ideas as to next steps? Is this a solvable issue?" Catherine asked. Jack heard a false optimism in her voice. There was no immediate response. The room was so quiet that Jack could hear the electricity's buzz driving the monitors. "Anybody out there have any ideas? Any at all?" Catherine asked. Jack wondered if the electronic audience heard the shift in her voice—it wasn't pleading but close.

"Good morning, my lovely Catherine," said Manuel Jimenez, the genteel Spaniard who had participated in earlier videoconferences, breaking rank with his silent participants.

"Good morning, Manuel," Catherine said, happy to see her friend. "For the group, Manuel Jimenez is a physician with experience treating mitochondrial disease, based in Madrid. Manuel, hopefully, you can offer some insight?"

"Insight, perhaps, but good news, I think not. I have been struggling with your remarkable findings and how to approach this peculiar situation. I must admit that the treatment of known mitochondrial diseases is in its infancy in many respects, limited to nutritional supplements like vitamin C, biotin, zinc, and alpha-lipoic acid. The success of these things is poor, even for non-lethal forms of mitochondrial disease. There is one experimental treatment at the University of Florida called dichloroacetate. It has shown promise but has many side effects and is hard to monitor. Some patients treated with it end up with debilitating numbness in their hands and feet. And most experts think it will require some form of gene therapy in combination. Hardly a large-scale solution."

"Dr. Jimenez, this is Michael McMillian in New York. I'm an oncologist at Sloan-Kettering. My specialty is blood disorders—leukemia, lymphoma, and the like. Is there any way that a bone marrow transplant would be of benefit here?"

"Nice to meet you, Dr. McMillian. I don't have much experience in your field, but it seems that the answer is no. There are many challenges with that approach that make it impractical, as you no doubt know. The most obvious is the need, if I understand the transplant process, to wipe out the recipient's entire marrow with chemotherapy and radiation, which is simply not possible on a large scale. But I think there are more important reasons such an approach would fail. First, the mtDNA defect is in all cells, so even those transplanted from currently unaffected individuals would retain the defect and develop the mtDNA mutation to the threshold point. The result would be the same. The mtDNA mutation affects cells in the entire body, especially the highly metabolically active cells of the brain, peripheral nervous tissue, and heart. A bone marrow transplant would not have any effect on these tissues. The marrow might be cured, but the remaining tissues would still carry on, so to speak.”

“So, Manuel, in essence, any treatment must impact all cells of the body?” Catherine asked, stating what Jack thought would be evident to all participants. He was losing interest in the small talk.

“That is correct. As the lovely Dr. Qiu has pointed out, every cell in every type of tissue carries mtDNA from mitochondrial Eve. We simply can’t escape the reality of this unpleasant fact,” Manuel replied.

“Shit,” muttered Rick angrily. Jack assumed he had forgotten that the audio link carried his voice over the world. “There’s no solution to this, is there? We’re going to go the way of the lemming—no, worse—the dinosaur. We’re going to disappear from the earth. From single-celled organisms invading each other to Homo sapiens and back again. Full goddamn circle of life.”

Jack had stopped listening and was twiddling with his pocket Rubik’s Cube. He picked up a few words and phrases here and there... Dinosaurs. Evolution. Single-celled organisms invade other single-celled organisms. As Jack unconsciously clicked the final blue square into place on the cube, all six colors perfectly aligned, he sprang upright from a disengaged slump and looked at Rick with a near-gleeful, broad grin.

“No, Rick!” he shouted. “ We have an advantage over the dinosaurs. We can manipulate our genes. Mitochondria started as bacteria. Now we need to use that to our advantage!” Jack bolted out of his chair and ran from the room.

“Uhhh... I think this concludes our videoconference,” Catherine stammered.

CHAPTER SIXTY-TWO

Jack knew the team would follow him as he headed for the virology lab. He beat them by 30 seconds, and when they burst through the door, he was already drawing on the large whiteboard. There was an oval on the board, inside of which Jack was drawing what looked like a lunar module. Inside the capsule of the module, he drew a smaller circle.

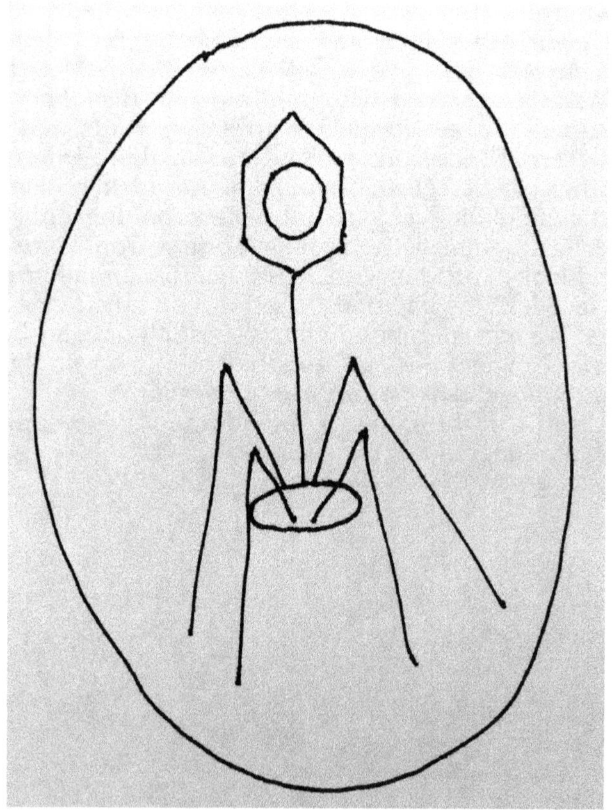

"Jack, what the..." Catherine gasped, out of breath, the last to arrive.

"Viruses may not be the cause of death, but they could be the treatment," Jack said excitedly.

"What the hell are you talking about, Jack?" Rick asked, puzzled.

"Guys, think about it. We think of viruses as causing disease—just causing infections. Adenoviruses cause colds. You get a runny nose, you cough, maybe get a little fever. Or HIV. It is a very different sort of infection, but it causes a known set of health issues for the person infected. In each of these cases, the virus gets into the body and attaches to certain cells. Once attached, the virus is absorbed into the cell and starts to replicate, ultimately causing illness by what they do to the cell." The group wasn't following his point.

"The virus's effect at the cellular level affects the whole organism," Jack said emphatically.

"Yes, Jack. Thank you for your Virus 101 course," Lucy said sarcastically. "I think we all know that."

Jack frowned and shook his head. "I know you know that, Lucy. You also know that viruses can cause things to happen more slowly. Like cancer. We know that there are cancers that originate from viral infections. Researchers estimate that ten, even up to fifteen percent, of cancers may result from a viral infection. The human papilloma virus or HPV causes cervical cancer. Liver cancer is caused by Hepatitis B, and even lymphoma is caused by Epstein-Barr virus or EBV."

Catherine said, "Jack, where are you going with this?" Jack knew he had intrigued her, and he noticed Marla was smirking.

"Each of these cancers results from slow transformation of the infected cells because the virus inserts a segment of its DNA into the host's nuclear DNA. The virus inserts what's called a proto-oncogene. Literally translated, it means *original cancer gene*. Once the proto-oncogene is inserted, it turns itself on, causing the cell to divide uncontrollably. Uncontrolled cell division is the very definition of cancer. Once the proto-oncogene is turned on, all of the cell's growth regulation abilities are lost, and it just grows and grows and grows."

"Jack, if you are insinuating that we somehow use viruses to alter the DNA here, I think you're fantasizing," Rick huffed. "Viral-induced cancers can take years to develop. Liver cancer can take two or three decades to develop once Hepatitis B infection starts. Same with lymphoma following EBV infection."

"Yes, you're right. But those are examples of slow transformation. There are two forms of transformation. Slow is only one of them. The other is acute transformation, or to put it another way, fast transformation. Some viruses can alter the cell's function rapidly. The infected cell is transformed as soon as the proto-oncogene is inserted and expressed. It doesn't take decades. It turns on as soon as it is inserted into the genome. Boom! A cancerous cell."

He sensed his team members were beginning to understand.

"So," Lucy said, her tone now that of curiosity, "You think we can somehow alter the mtDNA mutation using viruses?"

"Exactly," Jack said.

"It's a great idea, Jack, but it won't work," Rick said. "If the mutation were in the nucleus of the cell, I'd be with you. But the mutation is in the mitochondria. Viruses insert the proto-oncogene into the nuclear DNA. I'm not even sure if there is a virus that infects mitochondria. Or, for that matter, affects mitochondria."

"Correct again, Rick—sort of. In the medical world, Rick, you're taught Disease A treated with Drug B always results in Outcome C—the classic linear-logical medical approach. But we're going to change the game on nature. We do it all the time. In the virology lab, all bets are off. Our ability to innovate is only limited by what we can imagine and back up with known, or sometimes, unknown science. Bacteria ruled until we discovered antibiotics. and changed the course of nature." Jack paused and then said, "We're going to do the same thing here, only instead of treating an infection, we're going to treat a mutation... and of course, with luck, save humanity." Marla was smiling broadly.

Catherine, beaming, said, "OK, Jack. You've made your point. The suspenseful build-up is appreciated, but get on with it. People are dying to hear, literally."

"Three words," Jack said. "Chickenpox. Phages. Plasmids." He turned and wrote on his rudimentary sketch as he spoke.

He turned back to see Catherine's smile fade into confusion, along with the rest of the team. He'd lost them again.

Ted and Marla, in unison, asked, "What are phages?"

Jack didn't wait for more comments, ignoring the question for the moment. "Look," he said, "Rick is right that we are limited, to some degree, by the fact that viruses function by getting into the cell and doing their thing either in the cytosol of the cell or by inserting the proto-oncogene into the nuclear DNA. But what if we could insert a gene into the mtDNA? Think about what we know about the mitochondria. With tons of evidence to back it up, our theories suggest that mitochondria originated from bacteria. They are symbiotic organisms living within our cells. They have their own DNA." Looks of confusion still confronted Jack.

"We get all of that, dammit, Jack!" Rick shouted.

"Simmer down. It'll all make sense, but I need to go through this sequentially, or it'll be more confusing. So, not to be an ass, but sit down and shut up for a while," Jack said.

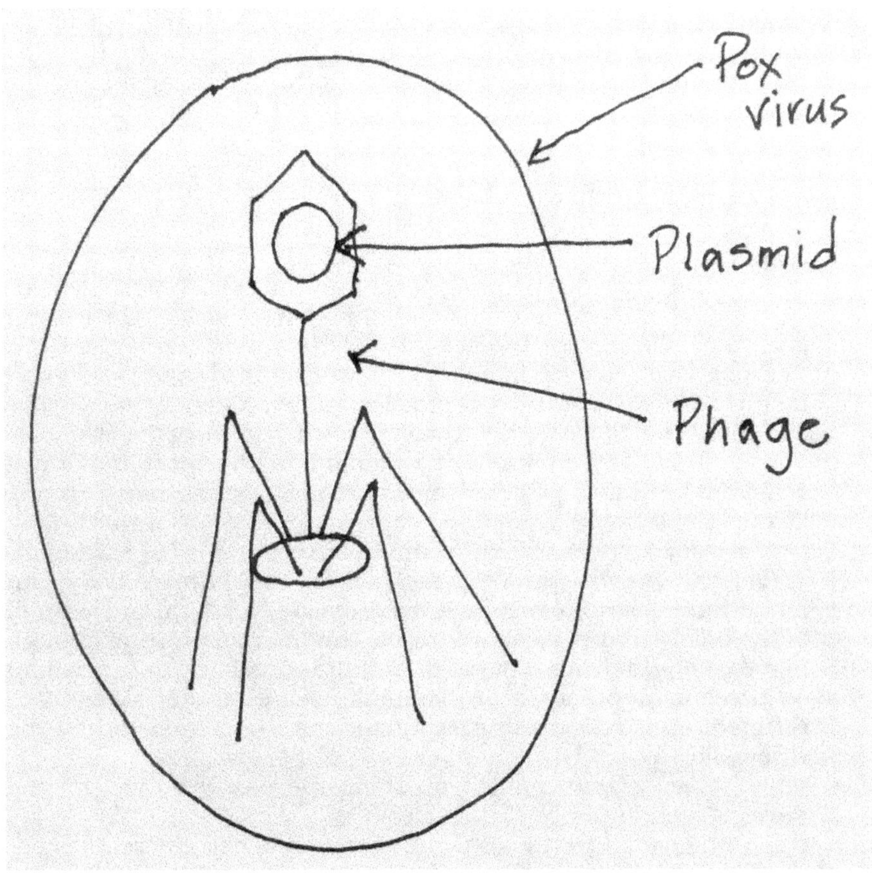

"I agree. Rick, just shut up for now," Catherine said. Jack showed he appreciated her assistance with a nod.

"We have to create an infection that will spread throughout the body by attaching to cells throughout the body, including nerves. Once the virus attaches to the target cell, it must release something that will get into the mitochondria and, hopefully, turn the Death Effector sequence off by inserting a different genetic sequence into the TA mutation region, disrupting its function." Jack walked over to his rudimentary drawing. He said, "Chickenpox..." pointing to the large, outer circle, "Phage..." pointing to the lunar module, "Plasmid..." pointing at the small, inner ring inside the hexagon. He watched their faces break into broad grins of understanding—and hope.

"Jack, what are phages and plasmids?" Marla asked for clarity.

"Phage is short for bacteriophage. Literally translated, it means *bacteria eater*. They look like little lunar modules. The phage attaches to bacteria using the tail fibers, the legs of the lunar module, and it 'sits' down on the bacteria so that the base plate—this flat part at the bottom of the capsule of the module—abuts the wall of the bacteria. It then injects its DNA into the bacterium. The phage's DNA uses the bacteria's resources to make more phages. Eventually, so many phages are reproduced that the bacterium explodes, killing it. The new phages move on to other bacteria, infecting them, and the cycle repeats as long as there are living bacteria."

"But how do the phages get into the cells?" Marla asked.

"We put them inside the chickenpox virus," Jack said, grinning. "We replace the pox virus' DNA with the phage's DNA. The pox virus is very infectious. It will bind to target cells and be absorbed, taken in by a process known as endocytosis. The cell eats the pox virus, not knowing it's a bad thing."

"How do you know it will bind to the most important cells, Jack?" Lucy asked. "It needs to get into the nerve tissue, at the very least."

"Pox viruses attach to the EGF receptor. EGF stands for *epidermal growth factor*. Every cell in the human body can make this receptor, including nerve tissue. It's a bit of a leap of faith, but I think we can count on the poxvirus hitting enough nerve cells to tip the scale of total mutations back to fewer than 40 percent. In other words, we don't need every nerve cell to be infected. Just enough to prevent the mutation from hitting the threshold."

"Jack, what makes you think the pox virus will hit the nerve tissue?" queried Catherine.

"Have you ever known anyone who had herpes zoster? Shingles? You know, the excruciating rash that occurs on the skin?" replied Jack.

Catherine grinned. "Yes. Brilliant, Jack!"

Rick had been sitting sheepishly with his mouth shut when Jack noticed him, hand raised like a kindergartner on the first day of class. "Yes, Rick?" Jack said, smirking.

"I understand that part, but how do we get the phage into the pox virus? I mean, we can't insert the whole phage as your drawing suggests, can we?"

"Nope. But we don't have to insert the whole phage. We only have to insert the phage's DNA. Once the Pox virus is absorbed, it will release the phage DNA, which will then use the cell's stuff to assemble whole new phages within the cell."

"But," Rick said, "phages continue to replicate until they burst a bacteria. That's how they kill them. What will prevent the phages from killing the human cells that they infect? That's no different from the mutation."

"We'll insert a STOP sequence into the phage's DNA so that after one cycle of replication, the process stops. It's a built-in kill switch," Jack said.

"This all sounds surreal, Jack. I mean, we're so far on the fringe with this, I don't even believe that we can do it," said Lucy. "I mean, come on, bacteriophages?"

"I understand the skepticism, Lucy, but phages have been used to treat patients with bacterial infections for decades. Phages have been used as a solution to antibiotic-resistant infections. Russian physicians have used phages therapeutically. A team of researchers at Strathclyde University in the U.K. are using phages to control methicillin-resistant Staph aureus, you know, MRSA, the so-called flesh-eating bacteria. And they're everywhere. Just a drop of ordinary seawater contains millions of tiny bacteriophages. And the beautiful thing is, they're harmless to humans."

"But you said they were used for bacterial infections. This is a mutation. Worse, it is a mutation in the mitochondria, not the nucleus. If it were in the nucleus, I might be more optimistic," Lucy said.

"Yes," Jack said, "but remember that mitochondria evolved from bacteria."

"So what?" said Lucy, shrugging her shoulders.

"The so what is that we simply have to tell the phage to target any residual bacterial receptor on the mitochondria. We need to trick the phage into attacking the mitochondria by altering its receptor target. It's standard DNA manipulation, used all the time."

Catherine intervened. "Jack, what receptor can be targeted?"

"Tom20. It is a mitochondrial receptor on the outer mitochondrial membrane. It's a protein receptor that imports proteins from outside the mitochondria to the inside, used for its health. We can find the information we need on the internet or through our colleagues and use it to build the sequence into the phage's DNA so that once the phage is assembled in the cell, it will attach to Tom20 and inject the mitochondria with its contents."

"What will be injected?" Rick asked, finally on board.

"That's the easiest part. A plasmid. All we have to do is create the phage so that the only DNA getting incorporated into the phage's head is the plasmid—not the entire phage," Jack said.

Marla again asked, "What's a plasmid, honey?"

"It's a circular strand of DNA that can insert itself into a DNA sequence. But it's extraordinary in that we can create it to insert itself into a very specific place in a DNA sequence. They've been used to get cells, especially bacteria, to do things they usually wouldn't. For example, you can insert a plasmid into a bacterium to produce human insulin. Plasmids are also how bacteria adapt to and become resistant to antibiotics. So, hopefully, you can see how this will work. We'll create what's

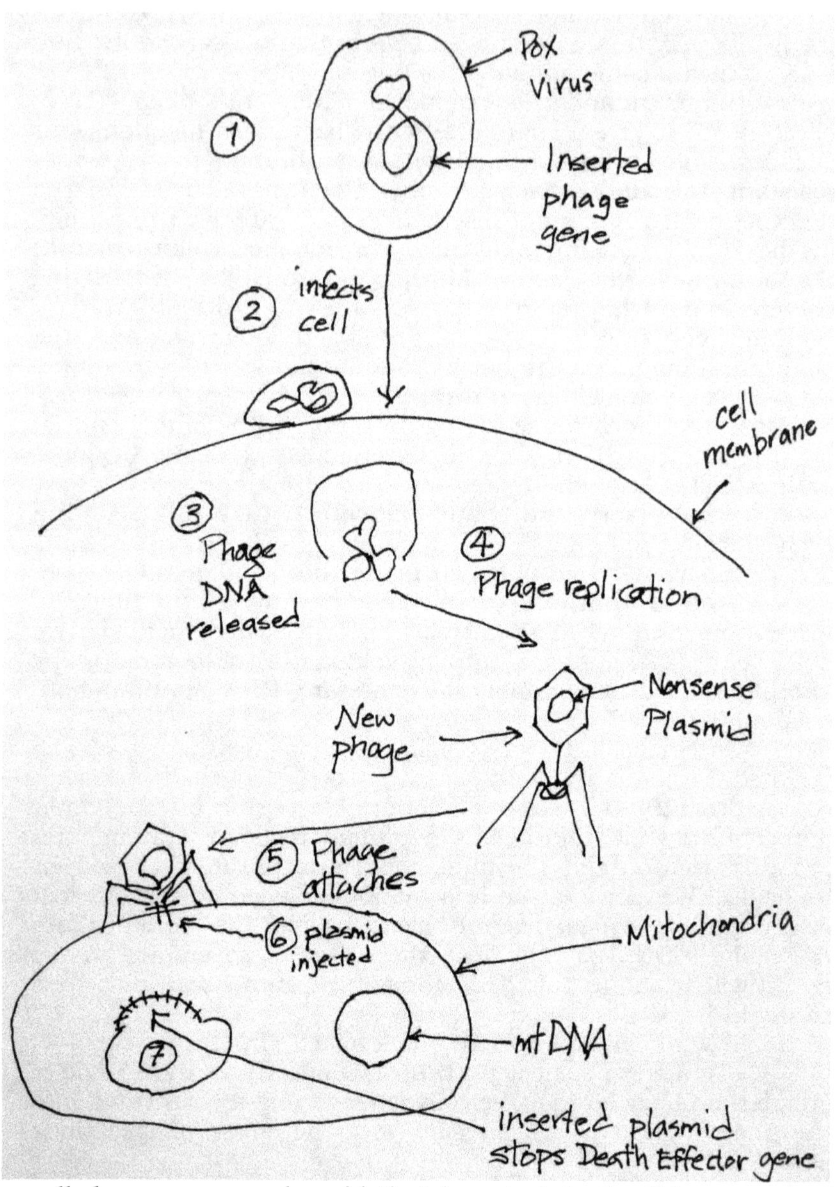

called a nonsense plasmid that inserts into the TA segment of the Death Effector gene sequence. A nonsense sequence is inert —it doesn't code for anything, so it disrupts or stops whatever process the gene would have coded for. In this case, we'll stop the Death Effector gene sequence from manufacturing caspase 8. By doing so, we'll stop apoptosis and, in short, save the human race."

"And all of this is possible?" asked Marla.

"Yes, in theory. Everything I have just described is something that has already been done somewhere... except the part about the phage attacking the mitochondria. I'm flying by the seat of my pants on that one," Jack said. "Whaddya think?"

Jack looked at his colleagues; each had an appearance of hopeful skepticism. "Look," he said, "it is pretty easy to conceptualize." He erased the whiteboard, picked up a marker, and drew in silence.

As he finished the crude artwork, Jack turned to see heads nodding enthusiastically and smiles on all faces for the first time in weeks. Hope had just arrived in the form of a hieroglyphic. It was theoretical, but having a plan was enough to create enthusiasm to carry them to the next level.

Catherine looked at Jack. "Can you write this down so we can get it out there and get people working on it?"

"Absolutely. I'll need a little time this morning, but I should have the details written up by noon," Jack said, standing up.

"I'll notify some key labs, so they know to expect this. Realistically, Jack, how long do you think it is going to take to get a useable vaccine?" Catherine asked.

"Useable? Well, we can have a reproducible process within three or four days if we're lucky. Then mass production can begin. We could be ready a week later. Vaccinating everyone will take time, and it could take several weeks for the vaccine to have its effect. Of course, hopefully," Jack said, recognizing that success depended on Marla's theory of genetic drift being correct and death cycles elongating rather than shortening, "there will be someone left to get the vaccine."

"Let's get to work," Catherine said. Jack noticed her tone was more upbeat than it had been in a long time.

"Jack, how'd ya get such a darn fool idea?" Ted asked.

"Back on the farm, we'd use non-traditional but obvious solutions for all kinds of stuff. For example, we could treat aphid-infested cornfields by releasing boxfuls of ladybugs, the aphid's natural predator. The fact that mitochondria are evolutionarily related to bacteria made me think of ladybugs and aphids. Phages are the bacterium's ladybug. The rest I just made up." Jack grinned as Ted shook his head in an *I can't believe it* way.

As they all prepared to leave, Jack said, "You all realize something important, don't you?" Five faces stared back at him. Each had many ideas about what might be necessary but wasn't sure what he was getting at.

Marla asked, "What, Jack?"

"We will have to assume this will work without any testing. No clinical trials to see if it's safe or if it works. No FDA oversight. This is going to be a global effort based upon the pure faith that we're right," Jack said in a dark tone, his enthusiasm of a moment ago now clearly serious.

"I think under the circumstances, Jack, the world's prepared to take a few chances," Rick said. "Is there something you are worried about, specifically?"

"Yeah. I'm worried about chaos theory. There are always unintended consequences. Always," replied Jack. "I just don't have any idea what they'll be."

"It's pretty clear that the increase in time between India and China reflects genetic drift," Jack said. "But there's no way of knowing with certainty if Russia is gonna be hit sooner or later."

"It seems to depend on the magnitude of the genetic change that occurred between populations tens of thousands of years ago," Marla said. "We have to be legitimately concerned that the benefit of genetic drift has already been fully realized."

Jack's face indicated unhappiness with this proposition. He knew it was impossible to know when the Death Effector sequence would reach the threshold in Russia or Europe. North and South America was a total crapshoot. He worried that South America might be hit before North America since it had a more direct genetic lineage from Europe. North America was full of human mutts—it hadn't escaped him that the genetic mingling of its population was unique, a veritable genetic alphabet soup — one from which his wife was benefiting.

Jack created a detailed recipe to guide research labs worldwide in making the complex vaccine. At noon that day, he had Catherine fax and email the recipe to every research facility worldwide — at least those with known living scientists.

MEMORANDUM

TO: GLOBAL RESEARCH LABS

The basic concept of the vaccine to the Death Effector Gene is as follows: A live, attenuated chickenpox virus in which the genome for the P4 bacteriophage, the smallest known phage, is inserted. The P4 phage must contain a nonsense plasmid that can insert itself into each of the following mtDNA sequences:

```
     1. taggagggca ctggccccTA acaggcatca ccccgctaaa
tcccctagaa gtcccactcc
     2. taggagggca ctggccccAT acaggcatca ccccgctaaa
tcccctagaa gtcccactcc
```

The P4 phage DNA must also have a nonsense code inserted into its DNA replication sequence to prevent uncontrolled phage replication after its first cycle and assembly of the phage. Unchecked, the phage will kill the host cell. The P4 phage must be altered to identify and attach to the Tom20 outer mitochondrial membrane receptor in human cells. Once attached, the P4 phage will inject the non-sense plasmid into the mitochondrion, where the plasmid will insert itself into the human mtDNA genome and disrupt the Death Effector Gene segment.

There are four research phases in creating this vaccine, and separate labs will be working on at least one of the four phases simultaneously. Once a phase has been completed and verified by at least one other lab, all labs involved will re-focus their work on another phase, or, if multiple phases have been solved, shift to working to combine the steps into the final vaccine production process.

Everyone reading this has expertise in one of the phases. Division of labor is critical, and all phases must be worked on in parallel. Please communicate your progress twice a day via email to our Command Center here in Mumbai. Dr. Catherine Montoya, the head of the CDC, will be asking all participating groups to choose one of the phases to work on, based upon documented experience and prior success.

To anyone without a background in science, Jack's recipe would seem to be lacking sufficient detail, but he knew those in the world of virology would understand it after a single read.

Jack was confident that combining them into a potent vaccine would be a piece of cake if each phase was solved. But he was worried there may not be a solution to trick the P4 phage into binding to the Tom20 receptor on the mitochondrial membrane. Nothing like it had ever been done. Everything else was pretty standard issue genetic manipulation.

Jack suggested that Catherine pull rank as the CDC head and begin making calls to drug companies that make vaccines. She called TransPharma, the U.S. pharmaceutical giant, and obtained their process for manufacturing the chickenpox vaccine. Commercial, private, university, and government labs worldwide were sent the recipe and asked to pass the process to all functioning labs within their respective countries. Of course, top labs in Asia and the Middle East were out of commission.

"So, all labs know they should devote themselves to only a single phase of the recipe, right?" Jack asked.

"Yes, Jack. For the hundredth time, *yes*," Catherine responded. "Everyone's playing nicely together, so relax." Jack couldn't hide his anxiety. He wondered if the world had seen this degree of global cooperation since Eisenhower's masterful coordination of the multinational forces during World War II.

To ensure each part of the recipe was worked on with equal vigor, Jack asked each lab to let him know which phase they felt most capable of solving. He received hundreds of emails within an hour of the recipe going out. While all were in English, many were barely decipherable, as the scientists writing them did not speak English as their first language. Many were simply constructed of several words, like "Tom20 reseptor." Despite the misspellings, Jack understood who was working on what. He compiled a list of the top 10 research facilities for each of his outlined steps. Most sites were renowned. The Salk Institute; the Viral Vector Lab and Laboratory for Neurovirology at UC-Irvine; the Victorian Infectious Diseases Reference Laboratory in Australia; the James Lab in Oxford, England; the Berkhout Lab in Amsterdam; and the Mesyanzhinov Lab of the Bach Institute of Biochemistry in Moscow, Russia. The Russians could be especially helpful with their expertise in phages. The list was a *Who's Who* of viral and molecular research genetics. In particular, Jack was struck by one name—the Molecular Virology Lab of Yong Seok Jeong of KyungHee University in South Korea. He wondered who was still alive in South Korea.

The virology lab in Mumbai was too rudimentary for Jack to do any of the research himself, and even if he had wanted to, many of the best research assistants in the lab were already dead. The lab was working with third-string, off-the-bench players. The nearest viral research lab was in Bangalore, a sixteen-hour drive from Mumbai on a good day, and the roads were clogged with rotting carcasses and sporadic clean-up vehicles. He didn't feel he could leave the group, and Catherine agreed.

"Jack, I know you probably feel like a second-string quarterback, but you're more valuable in calling the plays from the sidelines. The solution you designed needs to be coordinated now. If we don't execute your plan, it is all for nothing," she said.

Jack looked at her, pursing his lips in thought. "I suppose so, Catherine, but I'm a hands-on sorta guy."

"I know. But your brain is what solves these challenges, not your hands. Your solutions to COVID and SARS weren't because you were doing the grunt work in the lab. Your success was in what you conceptualized. You can take complex situations and boil them down to understandable, executable bits that trained monkeys like us can follow."

"I don't think you're giving yourself—or our global research colleagues—their due credit, Catherine," replied Jack.

"You know damn good, and well, I didn't mean that literally. I meant that what you do makes it easier for the rest of us to implement. You said it earlier—in essence, you've come up with a cookbook solution to a complex problem. Now I need you to run the show—to review the results we'll be getting from these labs to determine if they've accomplished what they've said they've accomplished."

"OK. I just was hoping to be in the lab. I'll play second string. Do I get a special jersey?" Jack said, grinning.

CHAPTER SIXTY-FOUR

"Ted, it's unbelievable what you've done to the place," Jack said, sweeping his arm in the air for emphasis. "This is like the NSA room at the White House. We can coordinate the global brawl from here, no problem!"

"Thanks, Jack. Never been in the NSA room, so I'll take yer word for it. I don't know if you know, but I have also pre-positioned U.S. and NATO Troops at key energy production sites. We need to ensure that the lab can function no matter what."

Jack was impressed. "Well, if I were guessing, I'd think it's one of the few remaining facilities in the near east with any consistent power."

"You know it, Jack," Ted said. "Pretty damn scary."

Jack walked around the converted media center where the team had held their video brainstorming session, with Ted quietly shadowing him. It had a background hum from the sheer number of computers in the room. He guessed close to 30 workers, elbow to elbow, sorting through the massive number of emails the team was receiving.

Jack had stayed up late the night before creating a streaming chat room that would allow the computer jockeys to communicate distilled messages to the team in near-real-time. He configured it to automatically forward each posting to each team member's cell phone as a text message. Flat-screen monitors on the walls relayed the same information in scrolling RSS messages. Similar large screen monitors had been placed throughout the lab. Jack thought it might help maintain the sense of urgency as if sudden death weren't enough of a motivator.

Jack paused to watch the impossible-to-miss digital numbers scrolling across the top of the screen, displaying the time that had passed since the research effort began. His eyes scanned down the left-hand side of the screen. In smaller, less visible letters was a list: Russia, Europe, North/South America. Jesus. *Time is not our friend.*

Jack leaned over and whispered in Ted's ear. "Well, one way or another, all research efforts will stop at some point, Ted." Ted frowned.

"Welp, when do ya think we'll get the vaccine?" Ted asked.

"The vaccine has to be in hand while there's still enough time for the virus to induce immunity, Ted. If it works like most other vaccines—chickenpox, specifically—it will take two weeks for immunity to develop," Jack said. He shook his head, pursed his lips, and then said, "To have a vaccine available to save Russia seems like a fantasy—in time to spare Europe, possible — but unlikely. The erratic timeline has made a prediction a ridiculous exercise."

Jack continued in a low voice. "What you've done here, Ted, is so important, because real-time information sharing is critical to accomplish what we've been asked to do—which is, basically, the impossible: To coordinate the production of a complex vaccine involving multiple production steps and over 500 labs scattered across the globe, each working around the clock on a different piece of a puzzle."

"Jesus, Jack. To hear you put it that way...." Ted's voice trailed off.

The door at the front of the command center opened, and Jack watched as Catherine walked over to them.

"Hey, Catherine," Jack said.

"Hey. It's unbelievable what these folks are doing, Jack. Each station in the command center receives forty to fifty emails per hour. They comb through each message, looking for information indicating progress. I created a mandatory, standardized communication process and sent it to all labs. The techs relay key information through the chat room in abbreviated form."

Jack grinned, then said, "Well, I guess the power of global technology is finally showing promise as a unifying tool for global cooperation, having previously demonstrated its usefulness in the January 6th attack and other terrorist acts, harassment, and identity theft." Ted chuckled. Catherine frowned.

Catherine plunked Jack down with a laptop in a high-back easy chair in the corner of the command center. From his position, he could survey the mêlée of the Command Center and keep tabs on critical advances. He was edgy, irritable, and wanted to have his hands in the actual research despite his joking. Even playing with the Rubik's Cube didn't help. Minutes seemed like millennia, and he grew weary of updates that communicated inertia. He suffered an odd form of boredom, matched only by the pitch of his suppressed anxiety. Messages filtered in, minute after minute, essentially confirming the obvious: no progress.

UPDATE

From: Molecular Virology Lab of Yong Seok Jeong

Phase III, No change in status.

The only interesting thing about some reports was their point of origin—areas where the Death Effector Gene had already manifested itself. *Was someone still alive in Korea? Genetic drift is screwing with us.*

Catnaps punctuated periods of intense attention. He knew he would have little real sleep in the days to come. He started dozing off, feet propped up on a side table as if he were sitting at home after a long day. His cell phone buzzed with an incoming text message for about the eight-thousandth time in the past 48 hours. Two days of constant updates of no progress resulted in near-complacency, with little urgency to look at messages as they popped in. He consciously kept his eyes closed, sleep pulling at him hard. Subconsciously, he detected a distinct increase in the amount of background noise. He opened his eyes just enough to focus on the closest monitor.

UPDATE

From: Salk Institute

Success in incorporating P4 Phage DNA into poxvirus. Success confirmed using EM, tissue cultures, and rapid sequence DNA analysis.

Simultaneously, email notifications appeared on computer screens of the Command Center workstations:

EMAIL COMMUNICATION

TO: MUMBAI LAB- CENTRAL CONTROL

LAB: Salk Institute

RESEARCH FOCUS: Inserting the genome for the P4 bacteriophage into the chickenpox virus.

PROGRESS UPDATE: We have identified a technique to insert P4 phage DNA into varicella (chickenpox) virus. Details to follow.

Jack sat motionless, his brain processing. The message hit the right set of neurons one breath later, and he bolted out of the chair, knocking over the side table. A cup of cold coffee with a surface skin of clotted cream splashed a chocolate-colored Rorschach pattern across the white wall. The laptop perched in this lap came down on the concrete floor, screen shattering, lettered keys skittering across the floor in every direction.

"Dammit!" he shouted. He took a quick step toward the center of the room, his foot coming down on one of the computer keys. The plastic key, under the force of his foot, slid along the concrete, slick as snot on a window, and he ended up on his back, falling hard, arms flailing. The fall knocked the wind out of him, but he was on his feet as quickly as he had lost them. Gasping for breath, his diaphragm temporarily paralyzed from the fall; he tried to speak to the gaggle of people that had rushed to assist. Catherine and Ted were the only other team members in the room. They had seen the message simultaneously and knew what had ignited Jack.

"Easy, partner," Ted said, easing him down into the high-back. "We saw it too."

"Jack," Catherine said, "as soon as you catch your breath, I need you to call the Salk Institute and go over their findings. We need to confirm them before we redirect the other labs working on the phase."

"O... K..." Jack said between shallow, ineffective breaths, his solar plexus slowly releasing its grip on his diaphragm.

With Catherine, Ted, Marla, Rick, and Lucy huddled around him, Jack hung up the phone twenty minutes later. "They did it," Jack said, looking up. "They really did it."

Ted slapped Jack on the back like he had just won a calf-roping contest. "That's great, partner! Good job, doctor!"

Marla caught Jack's eye, her face soft, warm, and loving. He noticed her shy smile and reached out for her hand. He hugged her tenderly for the first time in what seemed an eternity. She stood on her toes and whispered, "I knew you could do it, honey. I can't wait until this is all over. I miss you... I miss us." Jack kissed her cheek, then her lips. The warmth was familiar, welcome.

"Thanks, babe. I miss you too," he whispered back. "I'm ready to go home. You?"

"OK, enough already," intervened Catherine. "It's great we have Phase VI nailed down, but we still have three steps to go and no way to know how much time we've got until the next disaster. Save the celebrating until the rest of humanity is safe," she said.

"Right," said Jack, refocusing more quickly than his heart wanted him to.

"I'll have the crew notify all labs that the phase for getting P4 phages into the pox virus has been solved and divide up the labs workin' on it equally to get goin' on the remaining phases," Ted said.

"Excellent. Ted, make sure you obtain the detailed process from the Salk folks and distribute it to all labs. And make sure you get it to the vaccine companies, too. Oh, and Ted, make sure one of the research groups keeps working on the P4 phase Salk solved — I want to make sure we have a backup process for every phase," instructed Catherine.

"You got it, babe!" said Ted. Jack laughed as Catherine raised her eyebrows at Ted's babe comment. "Uh, sorry, Catherine. I was just excited about the news," Ted muttered.

Not more than an hour later, Jack watched as a young woman started jumping up and down, pointing at a monitor. "The virology lab at King's College in London is saying they've solved the phase they've been working on!"

Jack stood grinning at the monitor next to him. "Fabulous! So we need to get the Salk folks and the King's College folks talking, at least if the Brits' process holds up. I'll give them a call now," Jack said. Within ten minutes, he had confirmed that they had created a robust solution to insert a nonsense plasmid into the P4 phage's DNA to stop phage replication beyond one intracellular cycle. "Yep. They got it done, everyone. Ted, can you coordinate getting these folks together ASAP and disseminating their solution?"

"Good as done," Ted said.

"Catherine, can you contact the other groups working on this and focus them on the TOM20 receptor-phage phase? We gotta have it to combine the other phases," Jack said.

"Look at you! All full of orders for the head of the CDC! I guess coming off the bench isn't so bad, huh, Jack?" Catherine joked. "I'm on it."

The events of the afternoon had quickly drowned out Jack's morning gloominess. Optimism was palpable, and spirits were high, not just in the lab but worldwide. The pace of discovery was remarkable, and Jack increasingly sensed that maybe humanity might survive after all.

Jack recognized that the day's success had created the anticipation that the subsequent two phases would be solved just as quickly—that a text message must surely be out there, hovering in the ether, just ready to pounce on his and the team's cell phones with more good news. It made the passing of each subsequent hour seem never-ending. And as the hours accumulated, he sighed again and again, as messages again communicated, *No progress.*

CHAPTER SIXTY-FIVE

Nineteen hours after the King's College success, and just when the entire lab complex would benefit immensely from high doses of antidepressants in the water, Jack perceived the room's buzz shifting into high gear again. A few seconds later, he felt the buzz of his cell phone as a text message came in.

UPDATE

FROM: MESYANZHINOV LAB OF THE BACH INSTITUTE OF BIOCHEMISTRY, MOSCOW, RUSSIA

Solution identified to insert nonsense plasmid into the P4 phage that will insert into the mtDNA mutated sequence.

Jack latched on to the woman standing closest to him, a frumpy Indian woman dressed in traditional garb —one of the few inexplicably remaining native lab workers—and started country two-stepping with her. She, of course, had no clue what he was doing, much less how to two-step. He heard the room break into laughter at the sight of the cultural collision.

Jack repeated the routine of confirming the results and notifying the remaining labs. Labs were reassigned to the unsolved phase: getting the P4 phase to attach to the TOM20 receptor on the mitochondria.

"Catherine, contact the labs that were working on the P4 plasmid phase and have them see if they can combine their process with the others. If they can, we're one step further down the path when the last phase is delivered. All we'd have to do is incorporate it into the other phases, and we could jump to vaccine batch production. "

Jack had suspected that the TOM20 receptor phase would be the project's Achilles' heel but hadn't said anything. He didn't want to prejudice the researchers, and now it was the bottleneck. Altering the receptor target of a virus isn't the sort of thing you can accomplish by ordering a do-it-yourself-kit on the internet. One first needed to understand the receptor, Tom20, right down to its physical and chemical structure. That much information was off-the-shelf stuff, already known. Jack suspected the process would be complex, even if simplified by computer modeling of receptors and constructing DNA solutions backward. Knowing the protein structure of the receptor enabled one to create a DNA segment that could be placed into the virus's genome to alter the phage's binding site. Even so, he recognized that testing the phage's ability actually to bind to mitochondria would be a bitch. Somehow the researchers would have to show binding to the Tom20 receptor without taking weeks to prove it.

The other hurdle scared him—cobbling the phases together to assemble an active vaccine. He wasn't sure it had ever been done before. While the phases might all work well as stand-alone processes, trying to combine a series of complex steps may not work well in practice — maybe not at all.

The pressure Jack was feeling around the uncertainty of when and where the Death Effector Gene would next strike would have disabled most. The most difficult developmental phase of the vaccine was yet to be solved, and time was not on their side. Worse, if Russia was to be saved, they needed to get a functioning vaccine to the Russians now—a vaccine that didn't even exist yet—factoring in the time it would take to vaccinate millions of Russians physically. They needed months, not days. Quietly, he began to mourn the loss of people he didn't even know.

CHAPTER SIXTY-SIX

President Lopez sat sullenly at the end of the long dining room table, lost in thought. Global anxiety was approaching a different kind of threshold. Crime—murder, rape, theft—was rampant in the parts of the world where the genetic reaper had harvested his crop. Older men, a relative statement since the only individuals still alive were 18 and under, were preying on the younger. It was *Lord of the Flies* on a global scale.

President Lopez justifiably worried about what would happen to law and order in the Western world as time grew short. It seemed that when morality was most needed, it became least likely.

What if people begin to think there is no God, no Supreme Being. If no worldly consequence for behavior remained, and there were no police or military, the people would question the relevance and need for morality. What happens when people begin to think that there's no accountability for their actions? *We're all going to die anyway, right?* What happens when neighbors start thinking, *Now I can kill that asshole next door. I can't stand him, and he's pissed me off for the last time. Who's going to arrest me?*

His thoughts careened out of control: *If our days are indeed numbered, consequences for actions won't be part of the decision-making equation, right? Will the Jones family, with a 3-year-old girl, make a pact with the Sanchez, so their 15-year-old boy will care for the little girl as his sister? Will trust and faith and compassion—the very best qualities, qualities that enabled the successful evolution of our species—rule in the end? Or will we, on the brink of extinction, at the moment where we could showcase what has been argued to be the inherent goodness of humankind, regress into the darkness of chaos and evil?*

It was hard for him to imagine the lawlessness witnessed in Africa, the Middle East, and Asia could happen in London, Paris, Madrid, Toronto, Houston, Kansas City, or Seattle. *Darwin's survival of the fittest isn't in play anymore. The genetic die has been cast. Fitness has nothing to do with it. Death will come unless there's a solution from the Mumbai scientists.*

Even the President of the United States couldn't escape by getting on Air Force One and going underground. *It doesn't have to find me. It's in me.*

CHAPTER SIXTY-SEVEN

Catherine had Jack fielding calls from research labs seeking advice on TOM20 hurdles while managing the vaccine manufacturers' jitters regarding starting production. She felt their frustration—about the only thing to report to them was that another hour had expired.

She had just sat down to take a short break when the coarse vibration of her cell phone broke her near-meditative state. She reached for the telephone without even looking, expecting yet another meaningless update. She read the message, blinking in disbelief. She reread it, thinking she had misread it:

UPDATE

FROM: NORTH DAKOTA STATE UNIVERSITY, DEPARTMENT OF VETERINARY AND MICROBIOLOGICAL SCIENCES

Reporting a solution to altering the P4 phage's DNA so that it binds to the TOM20 mitochondrial membrane receptor.

I didn't even know there was a university in North Dakota. She started to text the rest of the team when Jack burst through the Command Center door, out of breath from running.

"OK, Jack," Catherine said, "Don't have a conniption. You need to find out if this is the real deal. I mean, I hate to be skeptical, but North Dakota State?" She watched as Jack's face switched from glee into a frown.

"Catherine, for Christ's sakes. I'm from Kansas. Not exactly the first university that pops into your mind when you think of world-class viral research is it? And I'm your point person. You grew up in rural New Mexico. Remember?"

"You're right.. Sorry. I'm just sick of the whole fucking thing and ready for the damn solution. Any solution," Catherine said, showing her frustration.

"And, I'll have you know North Dakota State's football team is amazing. The NDSU Bison. Undefeated in nine trips to the national championship," Jack added.

"I swear. The shit, you know…" said Catherine.

Jack began confirming the NDSU solution, and Catherine encouraged the rest of the group to wait as patiently as possible. Twenty minutes later, Jack returned, beaming.

"We're in the business of vaccine production, ladies and gentlemen!" Jack said. Catherine watched the room erupt with cheers and backslapping. After a few moments of jubilation, she watched as Jack tried to quiet everyone down, wanting to get going on the next steps.

Catherine tugged his shoulder and shouted in his ear over the din. "Let them celebrate for five minutes, Jack. We all need it." Catherine smiled at him. He complied.

As Catherine predicted, the excited chatter died down about five minutes later. Jack climbed up on a chair in the middle of the room and signaled silence.

"First of all, congratulations to everyone. Each of you has played a critical role in getting this project to where we are today. It's an amazing feat—you all helped create a one-of-a-kind vaccine in 85 hours. We need to combine the four solutions into a stable vaccine now, reproduce that process on a commercial, massive scale, and somehow distribute the vaccine to every living individual on earth. Not to be dramatic, but I doubt global cooperation of such a magnitude has ever happened. We may fail, but let's make sure it isn't because we didn't do our best." Jack paused. Catherine watched Jack closely. He was intentionally making eye contact with every person. She knew everyone realized his statement was not an exaggeration.

Jack continued, "We need to make sure the process for each phase is communicated to every functioning lab and manufacturing facility in the world. They must all work on combining them. The final step will be taking the modified P4 phage and inserting it into the pox virus.

"I have instructed North Dakota State to produce as much of the altered phage as possible. As labs work to confirm North Dakota's work, we'll be flying samples of their phage to labs throughout North and South America and Europe in hopes of accelerating the process. Hopefully, we're looking at no more than a day to a day and a half. In theory, we could be distributing the recombinant virus to vaccine manufacturers 24 to 48 hours after that — if there are no glitches. And that's a goddam big if. But… it's entirely possible we could have the vaccine in time to help Europe, maybe even the Russians. So, let's get to it!" The small crowd, energized by North Dakota's findings and Jack's speech, dispersed to their workstations, their enthusiasm evident.

Catherine noticed Jack beckoning her to the corner of the room, along with the rest of the team. In a voice just above a whisper, he said, "We need to keep at least one lab out there working on alternatives to each solution. If something goes wrong in combining the phases, we'll need a backup plan for whatever breaks down in the process. Catherine, do you have the list of sites continuing to work on alternatives?"

Catherine nodded as she motioned to her computer terminal. "I have two labs still working on different solutions to each of the phases' solutions. We have two alternative solutions that can be implemented for every phase, but the NDSU solution — it's the only one with no backup."

"I already called Fritz Halladay, a buddy at the U.S. National Bio and Agro-defense lab at Kansas State. They're already working on confirming the NDSU solution," Jack said.

"When did you have time to do... Never mind," Catherine said, shaking her head and smiling.

"I need to review all the other alternative solutions. Get them for me, please," Jack said. "And they need to be as detailed as possible. Oh, ask the labs who have developed alternatives to try and reproduce each other's results. Might as well keep them busy and get an independent confirmation at the same time."

"Will do," Catherine said, nodding in acknowledgment. She was glad she had called Jack for this crisis. His attention to detail and meticulous planning had made him so successful, and he was clearly in his element.

"Jack," she said, "you don't need to be in the lab to be great. You're showing everyone why you're the go-to guy, and you haven't touched a single cell culture."

"We'll see, Catherine. We'll see," Jack replied. "Now, let's quit yapping and get busy." Within 15 minutes, Jack had copied and pasted each of the four phases into a step-by-step recipe for vaccine manufacturing. Catherine read and re-read the printout, then passed it to the other team members for review.

Jack asked, "Are we good to go?"

Catherine said, "I am. Everyone? OK?" Everyone gave nods and thumbs-up. Catherine nodded to Jack, who swiveled back to the computer. Labs worldwide received the file with a mouse click, kicking off the next leg in the relay race.

Catherine walked over and stood by Jack as Ted turned to him, leaned over, and put his hand on his shoulder. "Nice shootin', partner. Now what, Jack? More waitin'?" Catherine, curious to hear his response, leaned in.

Jack, in a low voice, said, "Well, guys, being a firm believer in the fallibility of science, the challenges of reproducing results, and the chaos theory, I would say our time would be well spent praying."

CHAPTER SIXTY-EIGHT

Jedrek loaded breakfast onto the trolley. He always planned to be at least five minutes early, having seen servants executed in the foyer of the compound for lesser sins.

Jedrek was his name, but they called him Jester in Russian. He hated it, but what could he do? He worked for the Russian Mafia. He chuckled under his breath at the thought of the word, *worked*. He was enslaved. *What else could you call it?* He couldn't leave, and he wasn't paid unless you considered food to be a payment. Even if he could escape, he didn't think he could make it back to Poland.

He loathed working for Dmitry Zaytsev, a fifty-year-old man with coarse salt-and-pepper hair in a tight, military crop, piercing blue-green eyes, and a face deeply pitted from teenage acne. Jedrek, a devout Orthodox Christian, hated his boss, the man at the pinnacle of the most powerful of all Russian mobs.

Jedrek always listened to what was going on around him, even though he never appeared to be anything but busy with his duties. He learned through his ears, and his ability to recall, often exact detail, what he had heard, made him legendary in his village. While he was growing up, kids would plunk him in the middle of a circle, and each would blurt out a different word in rapid succession. Jedrek would then repeat the words back to them in exact order to their amazement. His record was 33 consecutive words.

Jedrek's quiet, seemingly disinterested presence allowed him to learn that Dmitry, his boss, personally took part in mob hits, unlike some of his contemporaries who outsourced killings. It gave Dmitry a sense of power, as well as the security of actually seeing his victim lying in a motionless, bloody heap. And he didn't like worrying if his henchmen had successfully carried out his orders.

Using his silent, subversive skill, Jedrek learned that Dmitry's empire was well-diversified, generating nearly a billion dollars in revenue every year. He owned oil and gas fields in Siberia and had an active arms-trading group in the Middle East. Jedrek was nauseated by the fact that Zaytsev controlled the child prostitution market in South Africa, as well as significant parts of Brazil and Argentina. *Those poor children.* But what most upset Jedrek was that Dmitry Zaytsev seemed as untouchable as feared.

The thing that kept Jedrek from simply giving up was very simple, and it gave him great glee whenever the thought traversed his consciousness. For all of the glitz and glamour, Dmitry Zaytsev was a hostage in much the same way Jedrek was. Dmitry rarely left the grounds, primarily because of concern for his safety. He had everything he needed to run the business from his mansion. It was an odd life. Rich and powerful beyond description, yet, in essence, living a life of confinement. Even a beautiful prison is still a prison.

Jedrek knew Dmitry's daily routine as well as he knew his own bodily functions. The crime boss rose at 6 a.m., exercised a bit, and had a shot of vodka before showering. He took breakfast in a nook off of his bedroom. He had the same thing every day, and Jedrek delivered it precisely at 8 a.m.: a huge omelet, a sandwich of salted meat, and a small bowl of kasha—a porridge Dmitry had loved since childhood—with a dollop of sour cream on top. Dmitry washed it all down with strongly brewed, hot coffee.

Jedrek began the trek to Mr. Zaytsev's room. He would wait until precisely eight to knock. It was rumored in the kitchen that the last servant who knocked on his door before it was eight o'clock had his right arm amputated, with no anesthesia, to remind him that punctuality—not too early, not too late—was valued by Dmitry. Jedrek had no reason to doubt the story.

Jedrek positioned himself in front of the door as the grandfather clock at the end of the long hallway began to chime, the first in the cycle of eight. Before the second tone, he knocked. The clock completed six more chimes, the final clong lingering for half a minute before fading to silence. Mr. Zaytsev unfailingly answered the door before the tolling stopped. Jedrek felt a sense of panic. Now what? He wondered if he should knock a second time. *Did he not hear me?* He never slept in.

With a sick feeling in the hollow of his gut, Jedrek reached up and knocked again, tentatively but loud enough that it should be heard. Another minute passed. He knocked a third time, harder, a bit emphatic. No response. Now, what do I do?

He decided that no matter what he did, it would be a bad choice. Call the cook, and he would be fired for being an unthinking idiot. Enter the room, and God only knows—but at least Dmitry might be inclined to generosity, an offering of food taming the beast. If he was shot, well...

Jedrek swiped his security card and, after hearing the electronic locks click, reached down, turned the doorknob, and slowly opened the door.

"Mr. Zaytsev? I have your breakfast here. May I come in?" he said timidly.

His question went unanswered. He pushed the door wider and rolled the breakfast cart into the room. "Mr. Zaytsev?" he said louder.

The broad, high-backed chair that Dmitry usually sat in faced the wall of windows looking out over his grounds. Jedrek could see Dmitry's legs dangling under the chair's seat; he was waiting for breakfast and simply not responding to the insignificant Jester. As Jedrek approached the chair, he saw Dmitry's arm resting on the table. He tentatively pushed the breakfast trolley forward and around the side of the chair next to the table. His master was crumpled over, head resting on the table, sleeping soundly.

Confronted with this new quandary, Jedrek wondered, *Do I wake him and risk his anger? Will he punish me for a cold breakfast if I don't wake him and simply leave his breakfast?*

He decided to shake Dmitry gently, figuring that an angry man with a full stomach would be less angry than a man waking up hungry to cold food. He reached out and gently grasped Dmitry's shoulder and nudged him. "Mr. Zaytsev?" He was oddly stiff. He shook him a bit harder. "Mr. Zaytsev?" The next attempt at waking him was a shove hard enough that Dmitry's arm accidentally flopped off the table, the weight carrying the rest of his body off the table and onto the floor. Jedrek shouted in surprise, his voice reverberating through the room and out the door.

He instantly recognized his howl was a mistake. It would bring people from all directions and seal his death. He already heard the rapid clunking of military boots coming from far down the hallway. *Think, Jedrek! Think!*

He looked around the room and took a tentative step. His shoe caught the wheel of the breakfast cart, and a crystal water glass bumped into the vodka bottle, resulting in a brief, high-pitched note. The musical tone triggered a simple melody in Jedrek's head, leading him to recall a series of tones he had heard before—in Dmitry's bedroom—one morning when he was delivering breakfast. He had just rolled the cart into the room. Zaytsev's back was to him, facing the wall to the right. Jedrek had asked him if he wanted him to wait outside. Dmitry had said no, as he poked numbers on a keypad. Jedrek, eyes intentionally averted but ears sharp, heard a different tone for each number...five beeps but only four tones. It's a five-number code with four digits. After the fifth tone, a paneled door, unknown to Jedrek, opened, and Dmitry disappeared. Jedrek had set up the breakfast, and just before leaving the room, from the corner of his eye, had seen Dmitry exit the little room and shut the door.

Now he ran to the bedroom area where he had seen his boss punching buttons. He frantically searched for a keypad and was stunned when he grabbed a small mirror in an attempt to take it off the wall, and it didn't budge—but instead pivoted flat against the wall, revealing a nine-digit keypad. He could hear the tones—the highest tone was first, lowest tone second and third, next to the lowest tone fourth, and the second-highest tone last. He quickly pushed the buttons in sequence, memorizing the sounds for each number, and then, as if he owned the mansion, reproduced the five tones he had heard Dmitry enter months ago. The panel-covered door clicked open. Jedrek flipped the mirror down over the keypad and disappeared into the wall.

He found himself in a panic room—Dmitry's hole for when he felt threatened or the compound was stormed. It contained a small arsenal as well as some food and vodka and was fully wired with video monitors and a computer terminal, and, with microphones, as he could hear running footsteps through tiny speakers jutting out from the back wall. The door contained a slab of one-way glass—clearly undetectable from the bedroom. He felt marginally safer—but if Denya or Yvan knew of this room, he was still dead.

Jedrek heard the disembodied running slow. He peeked out the glass portal, and even though he recognized the irrationality, he was still unconvinced he couldn't be seen. He saw a fellow servant, Kiril, appear in the room, breathing hard. He watched as Kiril tentatively walked over to Dmitry's body. He looked around the room, puzzled.

Jedrek heard more running—at least two people. Get out! he mouthed to Kiril, knowing it was a futile gesture.

The footsteps slowed and then stopped. Jedrek glanced back at monitors. Dmitry's two principal lieutenants were slowly approaching the bedroom, weapons drawn. Jedrek's head was pounding. He realized he was holding his breath and consciously released it and took several slow, deep breaths. The pounding receded.

He watched as Dmitry's two bodyguards, Denya and Yvan, charged into the room, their Stechkin APS semi-automatic pistols drawn. Kiril froze, not knowing what to do. Seeing their leader on the floor, the armed men simultaneously pulled their triggers twice, and four bullets exploded into Kiril's head, throwing him backward, dead before he careened through the plate glass window behind him. Jedrek clenched his eyes hard, the heat of nausea washing over him. He forced his eyes open and watched the men rush over to Dmitry. He could see them checking their boss for a pulse. The look on their face confirmed what Jedrek already knew: Zaytsev was dead.

Jedrek heard Denya say, tinny through the speakers, "Yvan, go get Boris. Run!" "Bring him! Quickly! And keep to yourself. We don't want the organization to panic." His black-clad partner disappeared, off to find Boris, Dmitry's second-in-command. Denya walked over to the door and shut it, engaging the electronic lock. Jedrek watched Yvan disappear from the video camera's sweep, the metallic clip-clip of his footsteps still audible.

He continued watching Denya, who was almost nonchalant, considering his boss' body was sprawled out in front of him. He holstered his weapon, looked down at Dmitry, shrugged, reached over, picked up the sandwich, and began eating.

Jedrek looked around the panic room, confident that Denya didn't know about it. He looked at the controls beneath the video monitor and noticed a labeled knob. He twirled the knob to Security—Boris' office. The screen showed Boris' desk, chair pushed back, the whitish glow of a bank of surveillance monitor screens backlighting the room. He was just about to twist the knob again when he heard the beep and click of the electronic door to the security room opening. Yvan's head came into view as he walked into Boris' office, the nerve center of the global operation.

Boris?" Jedrek heard Yvan say. Yvan called out again. All Jedrek could hear was the pervasive background hum of energy being sucked from the grid by the wall of high-tech computer gear in the little room. Jedrek held his breath as he watched Yvan walk closer toward the desk and pull out his cell phone. A cell phone rang through the speakers, muffled but definitely coming from the security room. On the second ring, he watched Yvan reach inside his black blazer and pull out his weapon as he cautiously walked around the desk. He watched as Yvan stared, standing erect for a moment, processing what seemed impossible. Calmly he knelt, and while Jedrek couldn't see, he assumed Yvan had found Boris. Yvan stood, Boris' security card in his left hand, and quickly left the room.

He's coming back. He wondered if the henchmen were as terrified now — the thought of an insider killing them off one by one. He flipped the video control to hallway #1 and watched Yvan face beyond mere concern, speed-walking toward Dmitry's room.

Jedrek switched the video to the bedroom entry. Yvan nervously looked in each direction as he knocked and waited for Denya to let him in. After a moment, he said, "Denya, it's me. Let me in." There was no answer. Jedrek chuckled under his breath. He observed Yvan reach into his pocket, pull out a security card, and swipe it. Yvan pushed the door open. Jedrek stepped over to the window to watch in real-time.

Yvan walked in, shutting the door in an almost lackadaisical manner. Jedrek was wholly focused on his face. Something else was wrong. He glanced over at the breakfast nook. Denya was lying on top of Dmitry, motionless. *Jesus!* Jedrek had been so focused on the video that he hadn't noticed what was going on 15 feet away. He held his breath again as Yvan drew his pistol and hugged the wall leading to the bathroom, slowly advancing. Jedrek watched as Yvon peered through the crack between the door and the hinges, then, weapon leveled, burst through the opening and disappeared. A moment later, a confused-looking Yvan reappeared and walked over to the two bodies. Yvan felt Denya for a pulse. He looked at the food on the table, picked up a hard-boiled egg, and took a bite.

Jedrek thought Yvan was starting to act drunk, but he hadn't touched the vodka on the trolley. Maybe he was perplexed by the events of the morning, struggling to piece it all together. *No... there's something else. He acts like his body is weighing him down. He can't take a normal step.* It appeared to Jedrek as if the force of gravity was increasing, sucking Yvan slowly toward the floor. Yvan stumbled toward the two bodies, terror on his face, crumpling on top of them. Jedrek watched unblinkingly.

He peered out of the panic room window for well over an hour. No one else came. He poured a glass of vodka—the good stuff—then slid to the floor of the panic room and preoccupied himself by trying to piece together what happened. It was like they had been poisoned. *What worked so rapidly? So completely? Cyanide? Yes! It must be cyanide.* It's instantaneous, easy to carry enough to poison a large group, and easily hidden in food.

Jedrek was feeling pleased with his cleverness until he remembered something important. Dmitry didn't even eat...

Jedrek looked at his watch. It was midnight. He hadn't seen any signs of life out the window, or any place else for that matter. He decided he'd make a break for it.

He opened the lock and poked his head out, listening carefully. Nothing. He stepped out and headed for the dimly lit hallway. Still no sign of Dmitry's brutes. He walked down the elegant staircase that overlooked the foyer. He had checked it on video many times over the last hours. There was no sign of life.

He got to the bottom of the stairs and had turned left toward the kitchen. Bodies littered the hallway. He squinted in the darkness, trying to make out faces. *Mafia guys.* He made his way through the obstacle course of rigor mortis, and just as he was stepping over the last body, the corpse reached up and grabbed his ankle.

"Shit!" He shouted in terror, easily escaping the grip. "What the..." One of the mobsters was still alive.

"Help me," he said weakly. Jedrek quickly grabbed the man's pistol and tucked it in his pants.

"What happened?" Jedrek asked, kneeling beside the man.

"I don't know. The comrades just all started dying. My legs... My legs just quit working, and now I am having trouble breathing. My arms are... are going numb." He was up on an elbow, and his arm gave way to the 180-pound body pressing down on it. He was now face down, pathetically struggling like a pithed animal, to turn his face to Jedrek. Jedrek reached down, put a hand under his chin, and lifted and gently turned his head, only to be greeted by a long, slow exhale and fixed, dead eyes.

He stood and walked to the servant's quarters to find only his non-Russian white colleagues were still alive, planning their escape.

CHAPTER SIXTY-NINE

66 The poor bastards. They didn't even have a chance to benefit from their contribution—assuming it all works when it's tossed in the salad bowl," Jack said, responding to news of the Russian calamity.

"Well," said Catherine, "While the information from Russia is bad, there are some interesting new developments. Death doesn't seem to be advancing as swiftly as in China."

"And it doesn't seem as quick or complete," Rick added. "Only about 40 percent of the adult population was dead in the first day. By that point in China, only children remained."

"That's good news?" Jack asked. He thought it was a little bizarre to interpret the news in a positive light.

"Very few deaths have been reported in western Russia," Marla said. "Maybe Europe and the Americas have more time..."

"There's disturbing news, too. The attenuation—or whatever—of the Death Effector Gene is causing sudden-onset of lower extremity paralysis," Jack noted. "I mean, did you see the photos of all the paralyzed people?" He referred to some video from the BBC showing people pulling themselves along with their arms, legs flaccid, trying to get off the sidewalk and into a building. "I'm sure they'll still die. But my God, the cries for help...I don't understand Russian, but, jeez..."

"Yup. That's strange," Ted said. "It's horrific."

"The BBC reporter said those not 'blessed with instant death' suffered an ascending paralysis. I think he said, 'like mercury rising in a thermometer on a warm day.' Once the diaphragm is paralyzed, they suffocate," said Lucy, shivering.

"Jesus. How awful. That explains the videos of gasping people. And the victims are fully aware as it's happening. Honest to God, they look like a fish on the dry dirt of a riverbank, gasping for air," Jack said, shaking his head.

"What do you think is going on, Marla?" Catherine asked.

"Beats the hell outta me... another genetic hiccup, no doubt," Marla said. "All I can think of is that there's some significant alteration in the mtDNA that occurred between when China was populated and the time when people migrated north into Russia. Genetic drift that affects the mitochondria on a much bigger scale must be at least part of the explanation.

Or maybe there is some nuclear DNA shift conferring some resistance to the Death Effector Gene."

"Whatever it is, I'll take it," Catherine said.

"I'm with you on that. What's becoming clear to me is the effect of genetic mixing between groups who migrated more recently—the more recent the migration, so to speak, the more protective their mitochondrial genes—if you consider slow death an improvement," Marla said.

Jack was aware that he was wearing his anxiety on his sleeve. It wasn't surprising. After all, he was the leader of a global effort with humanity's very existence at stake, so a little more epinephrine than usual—the fight, flight, or freeze hormone—was pouring out of his adrenal glands. He was exhausted, and he knew his fellow team members were too. He looked over at the mirror on the wall in the Command Center, wondering why it was there in the first place. *Jesus. I look awful.* The dark circles under his eyes defied his usual Midwestern boyish appearance. *And that damn clock!*

It was only a few hours since Jack had distributed the recipe. He wondered what he would look like if the process had taken longer. He was on to Marla's tactic of trying to lure him out of the Command Center. She would use any excuse. Lunch. Dinner. The mother-like, 'You need some fresh air.' Rarely did it work. Jack took meals in the Command Center, a good portion uneaten.

Jack worried the combination of the phases wouldn't be as simple as he had written. If one step in the process were off, the entire thing could fail. What worked as a solution in one Phase could fail the next—if the buffer solution were just a little too acidic or too basic, the phages would die in the process. There were a thousand ways things could go wrong, and only one way it could go right — and it was eating him alive.

Every time he looked up, another hour was gone. No reports of death in Eastern Europe yet, but the storm could land ashore there at any time.

Jack, the embodiment of patience and calm thinking, picked up a chair and hurled it against the wall as the clock changed to midnight, marking the 25th hour with no progress.

"Goddamn it!" He looked down at the splintered chair, breathing deeply as if he had just finished a half-mile sprint. He closed his eyes, intentionally slowed his breathing, mindfully relaxed his shoulders, and slowly turned to the Command Center staff. Catherine looked scared, something Jack had never seen before in this rock of a woman.

Breathing back to normal, Jack said, "I'm sorry to all of you. I haven't been handling the stress of this well, to say the least." He paused, took a deep breath, and said, "No more outbursts. I promise."

Moments later, Marla walked in. He was standing silently in the middle of wooden shards, a roomful of eyes pealing on him. Jack looked at her and walked to her slowly, then hugged her gently. "I'm sorry, honey. I completely lost it."

"I know, hon. I know," she said. "You know, Jack, my parents told me that worrying was a waste of time." Jack focused on her intently. He had great respect for Marla's parents. They had retained a good deal of their wonderful Asian heritage and philosophy of life, and more than once, he had found solace in its wisdom. Marla continued, "They would tell me that if you're facing a challenge that you can do something about, there's no need to worry. And if it's a challenge you have no control over, there's no need to worry. So either way, honey, you need to get a handle on your worry. It isn't helping you—and it isn't helping them," she said, tipping her head toward the staff. "You know that at any moment, we could hear from one of the sites, and the solution will be in our hands. It's research. You know better than most how it goes. And, besides, we have no idea what the timeline is for the rest of the world. It doesn't seem to be predictable now. We don't know, so just keep focused and let's create the vaccine."

"You're right, honey, as usual," he said smiling, his muscles palpably relaxing in Marla's embrace.

Catherine walked over to the couple and said, "You OK, Jack?"

"Yep, Catherine, I'm. Sorry."

"Don't worry about it. Watching your postal episode will probably keep me from doing it tomorrow," she chuckled. "I'm sure my blood pressure is at about stroke-level."

Jack's little episode, as it became known, resulted in a collective release of tension, creating renewed focus and patience for the entire group. He hadn't taken his frustration out on anyone. He had smashed a chair, something he imagined about two-thirds of the Command Center staff secretly wished they'd done.

At 8 a.m. on April 15th, Jack was sipping coffee when an email dinged into the system.

PLYMOUTH PHARMACEUTICALS IN THE U.S. HAS COMPLETED THE COMBINATION OF THE PHASES AND HAS OBTAINED A RECOMBINANT VIRUS FOR VACCINATION. REPLICATION STUDIES COMMENCING.

Jack joined the room in cheering and immediately sat down at a terminal, blogged the news around the globe, and then pasted it into an email addressed to ALL.

He climbed up on the chair and held up his hands for quiet. "OK, this is, of course, fabulous news. We need to wait to hear back from two other sites that the process works and that the recombinant virus will replicate in production-sized quantities. It's very exciting, but please stay vigilant and keep perspective, so we don't put the cart before the horse."

The communication from Plymouth was news that he needed—that the team needed—but the joy was short-lived. Just an hour later, two staff members who had been crewing an email station walked up to Jack with printed copies of emails in their hands. "Dr. Cann?" said a pretty young woman with a French accent.

"Yes? Oh, hi, you two. What's up?"

"Dr. Cann, Raphael, and I have noticed something quite disturbing. We have each been receiving emails from a variety of labs in different parts of the world asking if anyone has been reporting difficulty in combining the Russian phase into the process," the young woman said.

"What?" Jack replied, concern in his voice, eyebrows furrowed. "The segment... provided by the Mesyanzhinov Lab?"

"Yes, sir. We have no fewer than..." The young woman shuffled through the printed emails, counting aloud, "Seventeen research centers reporting they can combine all the phases of the solution except the Mesyanzhinov phase. The process breaks down."

"But what part is breaking down? Are they getting the nonsense plasmid into the phage, and it won't combine after that? Or are they not able to get the nonsense plasmid into the phage's DNA?" Jack asked in a pleading tone.

"It seems, sir, that the process of actually creating the altered phage is not working. Each of the labs reports that they tried to alter the buffer solutions, incubation temperatures, light conditions, and other manipulations, but nothing seems to work."

"SHIT!" Jack muttered, squinching his eyes and jaw. It was loud enough to get Catherine's attention.

"What's wrong, Jack? You have that *something bad has happened* look," Catherine said.

"That's because it has, Catherine. We have a major goddam problem. The Mesyanzhinov solution is not reproducible in other labs. Do you have the list of the labs that are still working on that phase?"

"Right here. They each have created a solution slightly different than the Mesyanzhinov group," Catherine said. Jack took the papers from her and studied the different Phase IV options. One solution was from the May Laboratory of Molecular Virology at La Trobe University in Australia, the other from Centro Nacional de Microbiologia, Virology Service in Madrid.

"Hell, they both look good. Just minor differences between the two, but some significant differences from the Mesyanzhinov process. Catherine, any thoughts?" Jack asked.

Catherine paused thoughtfully and said, "If you think they both look reasonable, why don't we send the Australian solution to half of the labs and the Spanish solution to the other half. Surely one of them will work."

"I agree," Jack said. He handed the recipes back to Catherine. "But if there is any sign of failure, regardless of where solutions came from, we march on with whatever other backup solution we have. Email the alternative recipes to the Command Center group and have them distributed."

Jack watched as staffers flooded the internet cloud with emails:

The Mesyanzhinov solution initially proposed has not been consistently and reliably reproduced in many labs worldwide. We are sending a new methodology for the phase. If you have already attempted to incorporate the Mesyanzhinov Lab solution into your process, it's essential to re-do the process with this new approach. Please see the attached recipes for the new phase processes from Australia and Madrid. As always, please keep us informed of successes and glitches in real-time.

Jack was standing next to Catherine. He heard her let out a heavy sigh, "Maybe Plymouth Pharmaceuticals knows something everyone else doesn't. Is there anything else you can think of, Jack?"

Jack, frowning, was tapping his fingers rhythmically on the tabletop. "Unfortunately, there is," Jack said, pursing his lips and looking intensely at Catherine.

"What?" Catherine asked.

"Call the SEALs," Jack said, pulling his cellphone out of his pocket.

CHAPTER SEVENTY

"I just don't understand. Why you? You're a goddam scientist. Hell—you're *the* scientist! You're running this whole freaking sideshow! Why do you need to go on another military mission?" Marla asked.

"Marla, it isn't a military mission at this point. The SEALs are my escorts. I'm mean, the Death Effector Gene just took out the Russian military. It'll be a piece of cake," Jack said.

"OK, great. Still, why do you have to go? Why can't they just go and get the shit you need?"

"Because the only thing they could do is find research logs or hack into computers and download the data—they can't interpret it—they can't find the error. And if there's a small error, we'll still be ahead of the game. I can call the lab with the fix if there is one. The Russians were the world's experts on phages. If we can't find the mistake now, we have to rely on a backup solution that may not be nearly as robust. We could lose days. And we don't have days," Jack said. He took Marla by the shoulders and said, "It took us 36 hours to uncover the error. We can't afford another 36." He pulled her against him, and she buried her face in his chest, weeping.

"Honey, listen to me." He took a finger and put it under her chin, lifting her gaze to his. "We both know what's at stake. You and I—are responsible for finding a solution. And honestly, I'm doing it as much for us as I am for the rest of the world. Hell, I'll admit that. If we save the world, we save us! If we save us, we save the world! There's no separation anymore. It isn't them and us. It's just us...all of us." She managed a weak smile.

"Very Zen, Jack Cann. Very Zen. You've spent a little too much time around my family," she said, hugging him tightly. "So get out of here," she said, swatting his butt. "Just don't forget to come back."

An hour later, the SEALs and their civilian partner were strapped into a B-1-B, taking off from a military airport not far from Breach Candy hospital.

Less than 30 minutes after the jet's wheels were up, Marla felt an unusual tingling in her feet and prickly heat with every step.

CHAPTER SEVENTY-ONE

Jack watched the ground approach as the B-1-B touched down at Sheremetyevo International Airport, northwest of downtown Moscow, just over five hours after departing Mumbai. He was surprised that the SEALs assumed there wouldn't be military resistance from Russian forces. He knew from LT that the White House had communicated the urgency of their trip to Russia in hopes of preventing any misinterpretation. However, it was unclear precisely whom they had talked to given the circumstances.

He felt the jet turn at the far end of the runway and pause. He watched as LT peered out the windows alongside the pilots. "Looks deserted," LT claimed. "There's some lights on in a couple of buildings, but I don't see any moving vehicles or people."

"What now?" Jack asked?

"Suit up," LT said matter-of-factly. Jack wasn't thrilled to hear this, nor was he surprised. Their gear was similar to the North Korean incursion but lighter in weight, not being as protective as MOPP.

"I don't think we're gonna have any resistance," LT said as the bomber taxied closer to the airport's hangers, stopping about 300 yards away.

Jack followed as the SEALs exited the bomber, weapons ready, jet engines still whining and ready, just in case. He surveyed the horizon. Nothing, and he assumed LT felt the same as he gave the pilots the signal to cut the engines. Jack was struck by how insanely quiet it was—no car horns, no loud jet engines.

"Jesus, I could get used to flyin' in this thing," Greaser said. "Makes everything else we get around in seem slow."

"It's one fast motherfucker, but not much for stealth,' Shark said. "Loud as my mother-in-law."

"All right, guys, focus. We need to find a bird or two. You three, check the hanger on the right; we'll check left," LT directed. Jack followed as his group took off on a sprint. Fifteen minutes later, he and the SEALs were aboard two KA-26 helicopters, headed to the Mesyanzhinov Lab at the Russian Academy of Sciences just southwest of the center of Moscow. Jack continued to be surprised by the versatility of his comrades, with LT piloting one, the other flown by one of the B-1-B pilots. As the choppers descended and touched down,

Jack saw a street sign: Leninskiy Prospekt. He recognized the name from the pre-mission briefing: The broad avenue adjacent to the Academy.

"All right, let's get to the lab and get Doc what he needs to fix the problem," LT said, taking off on a fast jog. Less than five minutes later, Jack followed the soldiers as they stepped over the bloated dead bodies of Russian security guards and walked through the unlocked doors of The Laboratory of Molecular Bioengineering. He noticed the SEALs were a lot less vigilant than they had been in North Korea—but then everyone here was dead. The jog made his leg throb—the nerve biopsy just over a week ago. The Death Effector Gene was always on his mind. Now his body was reminding him of it, too.

LT jumped over the reception counter as Jack looked around the lobby. "Bingo! Room 215. It's on the second floor," LT said.

Jack followed as they ran to the first stairwell and clamored up to the second floor. "You three, go left, we'll go right. It is a square building, hallways all connect, so we'll eventually meet back up. Radio as soon as you find 215. GO!" LT said.

Jack was with LT and Bugger. They were jogging, looking from side to side at the numbers. 110. 111. 112. 113. 114. They're all in the one hundreds. Jack stopped.

"Guys, we're on the wrong floor," he said.

"What the hell you talkin' 'bout, Doc?" Bugger said.

"We're on the wrong floor. They don't count the ground floor as level one. It's zero. The second floor will be the third floor in the US."

"Shit," LT said. "He's right." LT radioed the other group to meet them a floor up.

Jack's group made it to 215 before the others. The lab personnel was all dead; some slumped over their workstations. Jack noticed a dead researcher sitting on a tall chair, slumped over on the workbench, pen still in hand, her thick, long blonde hair draped over her face, flowing onto the black slate bench as if it were a white death shroud placed for burial.

Moving quickly along the bench, he found two lab manuals and began leafing through them. They were all in Russian.

"Goddamit!" Jack muttered. "Why can't anything be easy right now? Just once..."

"Easy, Doc," LT said. "Lemme see what you got."

"These are probably important. I'm guessing everything in here would have been geared toward the phage phase they were working on," Jack said.

"By God, Doc, you're right," LT said. "The title on this notebook is Death Effector- Phage Project. Then there's a '⅓' marked on it."

"What does the other one say?" Jack asked.

"Same thing, except there's a 2/3 marked on it," LT said. "What the hell do the one-third and two-thirds thing mean?"

"It means we're in a world of hurt. There's another notebook around here somewhere—those are notebooks one and two of three. Why the hell wouldn't the third be with these two?" Jack said.

"Translate the last page in the second book for me, LT," Jack said.

LT read it aloud, then said. "I may be able to read Russian, Doc, but what I just read to you sounds like mumbo-jumbo to me."

"It's the process for part of the solution, but it stops before the most critical information. And most researchers end with a summary of the entire process. We gotta find that third book," Jack said. "Bugger, can you start trying to hack their computers? That may be our only hope." Bugger nodded and immediately went to work.

Jack and the rest of the group frantically looked for the third notebook. Within 20 minutes, they had opened every drawer, cupboard, nook, and cranny in the lab. They found lots of notebooks, but not the ones they needed.

Bugger hacked the system, but searching for project information only turned up emails. Jack had LT translate the email subject lines for him. None of them contained enough information to be helpful.

"Doc, if we can't find what we need, we gotta get out of here. I mean, everyone's dead and everything, but you just never know. Besides, don't you have a backup plan or something?"

"Damn it!" Jack put his head in his hands. His mind was like an untamed monkey, racing randomly from branch to branch. He wondered how long Marla had left—her Asian ancestry had to make her remaining time short. He worried about her parents. He doubted that a vaccine could be completed in time if they went to the backup plan. The logistics of producing it, the... *It's too much.* His head was pounding. He closed his eyes, hands on his head.

"Doc? You OK?" Bugger said.

"Hell no, I'm not OK, Bugger! The world is dying, and it all hangs on a goddam paper notebook we can't find!"

"Doc... come on. We gotta go," LT said quietly, tugging on his sleeve. He opened the door and walked out, followed by his SEALs. Jack, limbs heavy, biopsy incision throbbing, stood up. He paused at the door.

"Wait!" Jack shouted, startling the SEALs, who immediately shouldered their weapons, ready to engage.

"Goddammit, Jack! Never yell at a SEAL, or you'll get shot! Scared the shit outta me!" Shark said.

Jack shrugged sheepishly, then said, "Oops..."

He turned and walked back into the lab with the SEALs following. He walked directly to the blonde corpse and swept her hair back like he was going to give her a ponytail, revealing the corner of a notebook that was pinned between her head and the bench. Manny grabbed her hair and pulled backward, rigor mortis fixed. The notebook was stuck to her face, postmortem fluids having oozed through her skin.

"Don't let it rip!" Jack shouted, noticing the tension between the piece of paper and her cheek and how the weight of the notebook threatened to rip the page. Shark grabbed the book to support its weight and then gingerly peeled the page away from her flattened half-face.

"Ewwww... Doc, you better hope she used waterproof ink," Greaser said. The comment caused Jack to grin despite the macabre scene.

"Believe it or not, Greaser, waterproof ink is standard in labs," Jack said, adding, "For different reasons, of course." Jack took the notebook and laid it down on the workbench, moving aside for LT to translate.

"Well, Doc, you got your summary pages. It starts two pages back and concludes on the page with goo on it."

Jack reached into his chest pack. He fumbled around and pulled out a piece of paper that was folded like a second grader's homework. Unfolding it, he said, "OK, LT, read what you got." As LT read, Jack followed along, comparing it line by line to the phase's solution submitted by the Russians earlier.

LT read in a monotone. "Then mix the C-A-C-L-2 solution with the denatured alcohol. Next, add 20 milliliters of 0.1 mM of M-G-S-O-4. Mix gently by..."

LT was reading literally. Jack was translating the letters in his head: C-A-C-L-2, calcium chloride, M-G-S-O-4, magnesium sulfate.

"Wait! Reread the last sentence," Jack said.

"Mix gently..."

"No, not that one, the one before that, LT," Jack said.

"You mean Next add 20 milliliters of 0.1 mM of M-G-S-O-4?" LT said.

"Yeah. Are you sure it says M-G? Not M-N?"

LT double-checked. "Yup, it's a G."

"That's it! That's the error! Their email transmission had a typo—a goddam typo derailed the whole thing! M-G is magnesium. M-N is manganese. It makes perfect sense, now," Jack said.

"Doc, what are ya saying?" Shark said.

"I'm saying, one wrong letter made a huge difference. None of us caught it, but we should've known! Magnesium is critical to catalyzing the insertion of the plasmid into the viral genome," Jack said.

Manny said, "What's it all mean?"

"It means all we have to do is a change to using magnesium instead of manganese, and the process works!" Jack pulled out his iPhone and texted Catherine. She immediately acknowledged understanding.

"Now we can go," Jack said. The SEALs slapped Jack on the back and guy-punched his shoulder as they headed out the door and started walking down the corridor, LT in the lead.

Without warning, Bugger shoved Jack behind him and drew his 9 mm, firing while running backward down the hall. Jack hightailed it toward the door. Fifty yards away, someone was firing at them from around the corner. Plaster exploded next to Jack's head, tiny shards slamming into his face, the bullet just missing.

Bugger went down, a bullet ripping through his left thigh. Jack heard him fall, turned, and drew his pistol, firing as the assailant's head intermittently peered around the corner, keeping him pinned down. He got to Bugger and helped him up.

The other SEALs fully engaged the attacker, allowing Jack and Bugger to clear the doorway into the stairwell. They continued down the stairs, Bugger leaning heavily on Jack. He was bleeding rapidly from a gaping exit wound on the back of his thigh. They heard a few more rounds pop off, then silence, followed by feet quickly descending the stairs.

Shark and Greaser relieved Jack, and Bugger put an arm around his team members.

"Who the hell was shooting at us?" Jack asked, winded from hauling Bugger's massive frame.

"Some goddam Russian equivalent of Barney Fife... looked like a security guard. Why he would give a rat's ass about us being here is beyond me," said Greaser. "Ya woulda thought he'd have gone home long ago, with everyone dying, but no, he had to stay and shoot us up for chrissakes..."

They made it to the helicopter, loaded Bugger, and Shark started an IV. A makeshift tourniquet slowed the bleeding. Jack was worried enough, but when Bugger lost consciousness en route to the airport, he felt a sense of panic. Bugger woke up just before touching down, 20 minutes later. The engines of the B-1-B were already spinning up as Jack, and the team boarded the warplane.

"You guys are treatin' me like a pussy," Bugger joked. Jack was deep in thought. He knew Bugger's unconsciousness was not a good sign.

"What, Bugger?" Jack said, unbuckling his restraint and moving to his side.

"Doc, I can't figure out something. If this is a gene thing killing everyone, and Africans were the first affected, why ain't I dead?" Bugger asked. "I mean, I may be dead before, for this flight is over, but not 'cause of the gene." He chuckled.

"We think that Africans mixed with other races may have gotten enough of the altered genetic code to slow the process down. Any white blood in your family?"

"Well, I don't know, but for the first time in my life, I sure as hell hope so!"

"Looks like you been shot up too, Doc," Manny said, pointing to a pool of blood collecting around his foot.

Jack looked down. He was bleeding. He rolled up the leg of the uniform, revealing an open wound. "Hell, guys—I just ripped my stitches out!"

"I think you'll live, Doc," Bugger said, his chuckle turning into a coughing fit.

01:00 APRIL 16, MUMBAI (15:30, APRIL 15, WASHINGTON, DC)

The jet touched down just 15 hours after leaving Mumbai. It taxied up to the private terminal, floodlights turning night today.

Jack was the first one off the jet, followed by LT and Shark. He walked, zombie-like, toward the hangar, stopped, and looked back at the bomber. His face was vacuous, gaunt, as he watched Greaser and Manny struggle to carry a sagging body bag down the gangplank of the jet. Bugger died three hours into the return flight. He had never been with someone when he died, much less while holding his head.

LT put his hand on Jack's shoulder.

"You OK?" LT asked quietly.

Jack turned his head, their eyes meeting. There was a long pause, each feeling their pain, as well as that of the others, hoping to find comfort they knew wasn't to be found. These rough and tumble professional killers had represented something he used to hate. Yet, he had rapidly come to admire them—to love them—like brothers. His eyes started to tear. "He saved my life," Jack choked out.

"Yeah, maybe, Jack. Maybe," LT said.

"Can it possibly get worse?" Jack asked. No sooner had the words come out of his mouth than he turned and saw Marla rolling herself toward him in a wheelchair, sobbing.

CHAPTER SEVENTY-TWO

Marla's lower extremity paralysis infinitely magnified the pressure Jack felt. He felt guilty for leaving her to go to Russia, returning to find her disabled, a sure sign of her impending death. It simultaneously made it more difficult and easier to focus.

Verification came that he had made the right decision in having all sites utilize one of the two back-ups to the Russian process when he received a new message from Plymouth Pharmaceuticals within minutes after returning from Moscow.

PLYMOUTH PHARMACEUTICALS REPORTS THAT THE RECOMBINANT VIRUS PRODUCED USING THE ORIGINAL PRODUCTION METHOD DOES NOT REPLICATE IN STANDARD INCUBATION MODELS.

"It's amazing, the difference one letter can make," Jack said. "The manganese must cause some phage replication defect. I don't even understand how Plymouth got as far as they did, considering the Russian process didn't result in a viable phage for half the rest of the frigging world."

Jack looked down, massaging his forehead vigorously as if his brain hurt. He looked up and said, "Catherine, if one of the two other solutions doesn't work, we're screwed. You know that, right?"

"I can't think of anything but that, Jack. Russians are dying in droves. Europe and North and South America are next, and we don't even have a process to make the damn vaccine. If something doesn't happen soon, and Marla's calculations about the Death Effector Gene's activation path are correct, most of Europe will be dead before a single dose of vaccine is produced, much less given." They stared at each other.

"Do you think the slowing of death in Russia is real? I mean, do you think it's a trend we can count on—that it'll continue to slow through Europe and the Americas to buy us more time?" Jack asked.

Jack looked to Marla, who shrugged her shoulders and looked at Catherine. He could tell she was trying to be fully engaged despite her increasing disability.

"Who the hell knows," Catherine said. "Half the time, I don't know what to think. Since this thing started, time has evaporated before my very eyes. I know we've come a long way, but right now, it doesn't seem like it." She paused, then said,

"With all, I feel like I have accomplished in my lifetime, you guys, smack dab in the middle of a global crisis, I have this odd sensation of completeness. It's the first time I have ever felt it, and I want it to last. I am not ready to die."

Marla's paralysis was a billboard to the team, announcing their impending death. It made the entire team more philosophical, thoughtful, and introspective. But to have Catherine Montoya become verbally introspective—well, that was new.

Jack recognized Catherine had just given him an opening to talk more personally. He took it with the enthusiasm of a shark in chum. "Catherine, this thing with you and Rick… it seems good for you." Jack saw Marla give him an *I-told-you-not-to-say-anything* look. Too late, his face communicated back.

"You know, guys, I've always been a strong woman, always felt like I didn't need anyone else, that I could do it alone. Before all of this, Rick was the same way, a male model of independence. He's in many ways the antithesis of what I would want in a man. I have always abhorred the frat boy type, with the good looks nice physique. But getting inside of his head has been an amazing experience—and unexpected. I'm sure you know we have been sleeping together, but what he does for me emotionally is indescribable. I've never had a man truly seek to understand me, to listen intently, much less take the time to connect authentically. I can communicate with him on any level, in any environment—whether professionally, personally, at a black-tie affair at the White House — probably even over a beer while eating shelled peanuts in a backcountry New Mexico bar. He astounds me with his ability to communicate with his heart. I mean, this is a strapping Naval officer, a linear-logical physician, who had no intention of a long-term relationship, yet his core is warm, tender, soft. Neither of us expected what had happened to happen. I don't know… probably makes no sense to you."

"It makes perfect sense, Catherine," Marla said. "You're in a hugely responsible position, under a great deal of stress, and half a globe away from home in a world that's turned upside-down. If Rick helps you, great. I don't think anyone here is losing any sleep over it. Except maybe you," Marla added, winking. Jack detected the gesture and was happy her deterioration hadn't left her without a sense of humor.

Jack looked at the message in disbelief. He had received it only 48 hours after the team had asked labs to retool with an alternate phage solution:

WE HAVE COMPLETED THE COMBINATION OF THE PHASES AND OBTAINED A RECOMBINANT VIRUS. REPLICATIONS STUDIES IN HEN EGGS DEMONSTRATE EVIDENCE OF REPLICATION IN LESS THAN 24 HOURS. WE ANTICIPATE CONFIRMING THESE RESULTS WITHIN 24 HOURS.

"Why the hell didn't they let us know they were so close?" a staffer asked Jack.

"The Salk folks are pretty cautious. Maybe they were unsure themselves and thought that being able to communicate one message of total success might spare needless pencil-tapping anxiety," Jack said, grinning. The staffer didn't seem to think it was too funny.

It didn't escape Jack that there was no loud celebration this time, just a twitter of acknowledgment. The staff was worried it might be another false start. He knew that another disappointment would put them all over the edge.

Jack, on the other hand, was elated. He had great confidence in the Salk researchers and knew most of them personally. He picked up the phone and called Catherine.

"Catherine, I'm guessing you already know, but Salk came through. I need to talk to you privately—now." Catherine agreed to meet him in an empty room off of the ICU. Jack arrived first, with Catherine arriving a few moments later.

"What's going on? Why the secrecy?"

"Nothing secret, I just wanted to talk to you. We need to move forward without further confirmation of the Salk findings. I don't think we can risk not trying something, even if we don't have confirmation by a second lab," Jack said.

"Wow. Jack, are you sure?" Jack knew what she was thinking—he usually played his cards close to his chest until his results were confirmed and reconfirmed by different players in his lab. But Marla, not the masses, was driving his urgency. His planning was now never without consideration for saving his wife.

"Absolutely. COVID taught us that much — go with the first viable option, but in the process of confirming it worked, so many people died while it cranked through the regulatory hurdles. We can't make that mistake," noted Jack. He continued, "I'd rather be giving some type of vaccine than have people dying because we never made it out of the gate. Europe's next. We need a vaccine now to have a chance, so we have enough time to administer it and let it work. Doesn't mean we can't let the other labs continue, and if they confirm success, we can be confident. Others can work on confirming that the recombinant virus alters the mtDNA. Either way, I think we need to move to full-scale production now."

"I guess you're right. Even if we had vaccine today, we're behind the eight ball. We'd be hard-pressed just to get it distributed. Even if we started vaccinating Europe today, many people would die before they ever developed an immune response from the vaccine—and many would never even get the vaccine. If there are manufacturing glitches in converting the process from lab quantities to production quantities, our timeline becomes even shorter," Catherine said. "Jesus, this is scary, Jack."

"So, we agree?"

"Yup."

"I'll go give the order. Get the Air Force to fly some of Salk's new virus to the vaccine manufacturers you lined up in the U.S. and abroad."

"Consider it done. I've lined up only manufacturers with bioreactors. We can have the vaccine in two days if we hit on all cylinders. Go, Jack. And I pray that we're making the right decision."

"You and me both, Catherine. You and me both." Jack paused and then said, "Catherine?"

"Yes?"

"Can I ask one more thing of you?"

"I'm already planning to have the vaccine flown directly here, Jack. I think the wife of the man who developed the solution should receive one of the first doses, don't you?" she said, smiling.

Jack smiled weakly. He had a massive lump in his throat, preventing him from getting out the *Thanks* he wanted to say. He looked away, then went to the Command Center and climbed up on his makeshift podium chair.

"Everybody, please listen." He waited a moment for everyone to stop and pay attention. "I'm approving the Salk process to begin vaccine manufacturing. Please do not stop any other labs currently working on vaccine production. They will, hopefully, soon be telling us they've replicated Salk's success, and this will be all the confirmation we'll need. Please, for now, no questions. Just communicate to your respective groups out there what is happening."

Catherine did her part over the next several hours without even pulling any strings from the Oval Office. She had, in essence, become the Chancellor of the World; what she wanted, she got. A few hours after their conversation, half a world away from Mumbai at Moffett Field in Sunnyvale, CA, seven F-22 Raptors lined the tarmac, ready to take off for bioreactor vaccine manufacturing sites in the U.S. Each fighter was carrying a payload far more valuable than weaponry: 24 vials of recombinant poxvirus from the Salk Institute — possibly the salvation of humanity. Within minutes, they were airborne, traveling at the speed of sound toward their destinations—New Jersey, Georgia, North Carolina, Houston, Phoenix, and Seattle. The seventh F-22 headed to Wichita, Kansas, with 240 vials to connect with twelve B-1-B Bombers at McConnell Air Force Base. They would immediately launch for vaccine producers in Mexico City, Brazil, London, Amsterdam, Paris, and Madrid. Seed virus was being sent to Stalingrad, Moscow, Mumbai, and Seoul, hoping there was enough personnel still standing to produce a vaccine for the children of the affected countries. Fueling tankers were strategically positioned for in-air refueling to maximize the speed of delivery. Less than 12 hours after Catherine gave the order, every major vaccine-producing facility in the world had the recombinant stock virus and began mass production. Each of the bioreactor sites outside the U.S. had been asked to identify other areas in the region that could manufacture vaccines and coordinate the distribution of at least one vial of the pox strain to every possible site. All functioning production facilities throughout the world were needed to meet the vaccine demand for the nearly two billion remaining souls, most of whom did not live in North America.

CHAPTER SEVENTY-THREE

Jack knew the vaccine solution had significant, built-in advantages that some of his colleagues may have missed. One was that the Pox virus is easy to grow, and the process for producing the chickenpox vaccine had been optimized for years. More important was the Pox virus' virulence. Miniscule amounts could cause rampant infection. Because of this, once the vaccine was available, it might not be necessary to give as much as usual, allowing for a relatively small amount of vaccine to treat a large number of people.

"The whole vaccine production thing is making me nervous," Jack said to no one in particular. The team was collected in the Command Center, the quintessential watched pot.

"Yup. It's pretty much going to be a challenge. I calculated that vaccinating every remaining living being on the planet with one milliliter of the vaccine would require producing two million liters of the stuff. And then those two million liters have to be packaged for delivery—in glass vials or pre-loaded syringes or something," Ted said.

"And," Lucy added, "The entire process will have to be carried out in a temperature- and light-controlled environment. No one knows if the vaccine will be stable if exposed to extreme heat or cold or even bright light."

"Well, aren't you two cheery?" Jack said sarcastically.

"Jack, the production facilities aren't taking any chances. They know there is only one chance to get it right," Catherine said.

Forty-eight hours after delivery of the seed virus, Markum Biopharm in San Francisco sent a message to the Command Center, simultaneously dinging Jack's cell phone:

BULK VACCINE PRODUCTION BEGAN TODAY AT 0544. IT'S CONFIRMED THAT THE PRODUCTION PROCESS WORKS WITHOUT ALTERATION. ANTICIPATE FIRST DOSES COMING OFF THE LINE IN 12 HOURS. SINGLE-DOSE VIALS.

Markum's announcement was the first in a chain reaction of communication.

ECCO PHARMACEUTICALS IN NEW BRUNSWICK, NEW JERSEY, INTO BULK VACCINE PRODUCTION. MULTI-DOSE VIALS ARE ANTICIPATED IN 24 HOURS.

Research Triangle Park, North Carolina, Houston, Phoenix, and Seattle all reported within three hours of each other. The Salk process was so well defined that following it resulted in highly predictable timelines.

Jack was elated by the news as he scrolled through the notes. "Hey! Better yet, the folks at Salk have confirmed that their mutant virus can insert the nonsense plasmid into the mtDNA of human cultured cells!" Jack exclaimed. "Look! They emailed beautiful EM photos of tagged mitochondria," he said, holding up his cell phone, the plasmid luminescent in the picture. Jack emailed the micrograph around the world.

Within two days, all manufacturers had begun their packaging process in every conceivable configuration—single-dose vials, multi-dose vials, even liter bottles. Jack was aware that Catherine had decided the vaccine should be accumulated for bulk shipping to increase efficiency and reduce the potential for riots as people scrambled to get vaccinated — it was something that hadn't happened with COVID. Still, then with COVID, there were unvaccinated survivors. If only enough vaccine could be sent to London to cover a third of the population, there would be fighting for those doses, no doubt. So, until there was enough to vaccinate the entire city population, it was to be held in warehouses. It wasn't a guarantee of avoiding conflict, but it certainly made sense to Jack and the rest of the team, who had discussed the sticky challenge. Jack figured that, based upon the timeline, planes loaded down with vaccine could hit Europe in the next 24 to 36 hours. Not everyone would benefit, but a considerable number would. And, of course, the vaccine was being produced locally in Europe, too. Things finally seemed to be working out.

More good news confirmed their luck was turning. Just before dinner, a new message hit the computer screens:

BERKHOUT LAB IN AMSTERDAM HAS REPRODUCED THE SALK PROCESS EXACTLY TO SPECIFICATION AND CONFIRMS ACTIVE VIRAL REPLICATION IN HEN EGG MODELS USING THE VACCINE PRODUCT.

Jack had his hand on the door when he heard a whoop of glee behind him in the Command Center. He turned to see the young woman who had given him the bad news about Mesyanzhinov. She was beaming, her beautiful white teeth visible across the dim room. "Dr. Cann! Berkhout replicated Salk's findings!"

Grinning broadly, Jack climbed up on a chair. "Folks, we've done our job. The vaccine is being produced, and we have confirmation that the process is robust and that the vaccine works in human tissue cultures. Fabulous job, everyone." He turned and walked out of the Command Center, his smile quickly dissipating, hoping there was at least one dose on its way to Mumbai.

CHAPTER SEVENTY-FOUR

R iley looked up from the sink and smiled. The sun was slung low in the west, an orange glow washing the plains. The laughter of children playing hovered in the air, a reminder of her newfound joy. She slowly dried the few remaining dishes and put them away.

Her life had been transformed in this little village. The pressures of WNN were in the past, and she had no intention of going back to that kind of life. Abasi was her life now, and she wanted to ensure that his childhood was as happy as hers was tragic, at least to the extent one could do that with a child who had lost his parents. She walked to the side of the room, pulled back the thin cotton veil separating Abasi's space from the larger room, and smiled at the little bed, a filthy old soccer ball smack in the middle.

A deafening roar came from the alleyway, shattering her blissful solitude. She was confused for a split second, but the shrieks of children immediately focused on her—more screams and then the yelling of older children, accompanied by a second roar. The melee of voices was uninterpretable, but the roar clearly said *lion.*

She ran to the sink and grabbed a butcher knife, then ran into the alleyway and found herself facing a male lion standing over a small boy, bleeding profusely from the neck. Children of all ages had poured into the alleyway, effectively trapping the lion. Riley knew this was not a good thing and screamed for the children behind the lion to move out of the way, offering it an escape route.

The beast had a giant paw on the child's chest and seemed unlikely to leave voluntarily. Riley had heard from some of the children that rogue lions were preying on humans, especially older males who had lost dominance in their pride. It had become an easy proposition since there were no adults to defend the children. It appeared this was one of those males. Riley could see that chunks of his were mane missing, either from fights or age.

Riley saw the boy's chest still rising and falling. *He's still alive.* She recognized that if he didn't bleed to death, the weight of the animal's one extremity pressing down could suffocate him. She turned to a teenage boy standing next to her, keeping the cat in the corner of her eye, and instructed him to get the rifle she knew was kept in the village.

The lion sniffed the boy, clearly preparing to begin the feast. Detecting this ominous gesture, Riley took several running steps toward the lion, shouting. His downed quarry endangered by Riley, the lion jumped over the boy and inserted himself between her and his prey. She succeeded at her goal of distracting him from the boy, but the carnivore now felt threatened.

The boy arrived with the rifle and a box of loose bullets. Riley grabbed the weapon, loaded two cartridges, and leveled the sight at the lion's head. The animal took a step toward her, and as the beast roared and pushed back on his haunches to pounce, she squeezed the trigger, dropping the lion with a single shot that entered his mouth, exploding through the back of its skull. She walked up to the furry mound and put the end of the barrel against its head, and pulled the trigger despite it being completely motionless.

She walked around the carcass to the boy—it was Mosi, a 4-year-old, the youngest of three remaining in his family. She knelt beside him, fighting tears. S

Riley surveyed Mosi's tiny body. The beast's teeth had punched huge holes in his neck and skull, and blood was everywhere. His little chest was still moving, but she knew it wasn't the kind of movement that was actual breathing. She scooted her arms gently under the limp boy, sat down in the dirt cross-legged, and cradled him close to her bosom, rocking slowly. The tears came now, in a torrent, and she tried to sing *Hush little baby don't you cry...* but the lump in her throat refused to let the melody escape. She let out an agonal cry and squeezed Mosi tight as his chest quit moving. Mosi's siblings gathered around, each sobbing, on the ground beside Riley and the dead boy, clinging to each other and touching Mosi's little body.

Riley felt spindly little arms encircle her neck, and she blinked through her tears as Abasi cradled her from behind, the caretaker being cared for. She marveled at the paradox of life at that moment: death in her arms, life clinging to her neck. She smiled briefly before her wails continued.

Mosi's body was cleaned, wrapped in a bright multi-colored blanket, and laid on a small cot. Riley didn't know what the burial custom was but knew there was a place outside the village that the villagers used for burials.

Just after sunrise, she supervised as the boy's body was put on a small wagon and everyone in the village followed it out to the burial site. Some of the older boys had dug a grave about two feet deep. Riley suspected it wasn't deep enough but was so exhausted that she said nothing.

She picked up the tiny body. She was surprised at how light the Mosi was. He was so full of life a day ago. She couldn't understand how so much had existed in such a small body.

She began to tear up again as she remembered him chasing after a soccer ball, his toothy grin almost arriving before the rest of him.

She set his body down in the hole as gently as she could. One of the tall village boys stood at the head of the grave, hands folded. He said something Riley couldn't understand, but there was a lilt to the voice and cadence of speech that was prayer-like. He finished speaking, and two other boys began shoveling dirt over Mosi.

They covered the body, and children silently filtered back toward the village. Riley stood beside the grave with Abasi's hand in hers for some time. She turned and started walking back to the village with Abasi. Her tears had stopped. She looked askance at the little boy holding her hand as she thought back to the early days of the African disaster when she was in Dar es Salaam. *I may not be able to save them all, but I can save one.*

CHAPTER SEVENTY-FIVE

Ted entered the commons room, grinning widely, and said, "The first ten million doses of the vaccine from Markum got to San Francisco. They're gearin' up to inoculate the Bay Area, just two days after production started. I hear vaccine's flowing from their new bioreactor like gasoline from a pump."

"That's awesome, Ted," said Marla. "How many people will the first round cover?"

"Well, the metro area has slightly more than seven million people, so the first delivery will pretty much vaccinate all of San Francisco—if it works beyond Petri dishes and hen eggs," Ted replied.

"That's great and all, guys, but it isn't quite smooth sailing there," said Rick, pointing at the TV.

"Turn up the volume, Rick," said Jack. A reporter's voice narrated a video shot in the Golden Gate city.

"As surely as the rising sun brought dawn and the possibility of salvation, the vaccine distribution process brought unwelcome problems. Despite best efforts, the distribution of the vaccine has rapidly turned into chaos. The National Guard has been activated to keep the process orderly, but it's clear that people simply aren't going to play nice."

The scenes could have been confused with a third-world riot, as the shot switched to a masked man wielding a pistol while his partner lugged boxes, presumably of the vaccine.

The reporter continued, "Caregivers at drive-by vaccination clinics were being held up at gunpoint and vaccine being taken from them in batches. The part-time soldiers couldn't be everywhere at once, and communication was sketchy as to who was to do what and when."

The scene changed again, this time showing a straight line of vaccine seekers erupting into a scrum of shoving, kicking, and flying fists. "Fights between those waiting for their turn were common as tempers flared from the exhausting monotony of the process. Standing in line for hours has resulted in toxic levels of emotional stress among the population. Tragically, guns have been drawn, and the targets of such anger will no longer have to wait for the Death Effector Gene. Shootings, not surprisingly, have created temporary calm through fear."

Another switch, this time to a line of military personnel with riot shields being over-run by civilians. "Solders are being attacked by mobs, each vaccination point a Boston Massacre-like re-enactment. Doing their best to avoid violence, the soldiers backed up and attempted to calm agitated crowds. Still, in several places around the city, citizens were shot dead by military personnel when things became overtly threatening."

The video switched from the U.S. to Europe, with the Eiffel Tower becoming the backdrop to burning cars and plumes of smoke. The reporter continued seamlessly, "Europe has fared no better. Parts of Rome are burning for the umpteenth time in history. The Spanish army is dealing with nothing short of civil war. Berlin, London, all variations on the theme. And, as you can see, by the Eiffel Tower in the distance, Paris is crumbling."

"Good God," Marla said, "Human behavior is devolving into something as sinister as the mutation the vaccine cures."

The room phone rang, startling Jack and everyone else in the room. He reached for it. "Yes?" A look of concern came over his face. "Catherine, it's for you," he said, handing her the phone. "It's the mayor of San Francisco."

Catherine took the phone and listened as Jack and the team watched. Her lips were pursed in concentration, and she spoke only in single syllables—yes and no—for the first few exchanges. Jack could see she was getting increasingly irritated. Finally, she blew up.

"Look, Mr. Mayor, there is no goddam backup plan!" Catherine almost screamed. She listened for a moment, then said, "Look, no team in the history of the planet has confronted the logistical nightmare we have. To have a vaccine at all is a fucking miracle! But when you take all that we've faced and compound it with penetrating fear and irrational behavior in an entire population..." she stopped dead, again listening, the mayor's voice audible to everyone. Jack knew Catherine had reached boiling point when she screamed into the receiver, "I know the vaccination program is failing, goddammit!" she said, slamming the phone down.

Days ago, Jack feared that Marla would prove right when she voiced her fears that anarchy would rule. Now it was real.

Jack had never seen this side of Catherine when she spoke again. "The vaccine program is failing, and the first day of vaccinations hasn't even come to a close yet."

Ted said, "Well, I was just beginnin' to think that maybe the Californians were just crazier than the rest, then the Europe thing came on." Jack at least appreciated his attempt to interject some levity.

"And it isn't just San Fran," Marla said, pointing at the screen. Along the bottom scrolled the words Riots in New York, Chicago, Miami, Atlanta.

Catherine said, "I'm afraid, ladies and gentlemen, that although we have a solution for a vaccine, it's doubtful that we'll save very many people if we can't vaccinate them, and the populous seems unlikely to calm down." She sounded more composed to Jack than she had earlier. "Trying to vaccinate people one by one is going to promote more death, more disaster. They're acting like animals from San Francisco to Warsaw."

Ted said, "Hell, I'm ashamed to be an American for the first goddamn time in my life. I mean, for God's sake, who would have thought my own countrymen would behave like that? It makes me wanna bomb 'em instead of vaccinate 'em!"

"I dunno, you guys. I think that maybe it's just sort of the first day jitters, so to speak," Rick said. "I bet the process will smooth out over the next few days." It was hard to know if he believed what he said or said it to calm his lover.

"Yeah. I agree with Rick," Lucy added. "I suspect people will calm down and think a bit more rationally after today. It'll go fine tomorrow."

Jack thought his teammates sounded overly optimistic, and the reality seemed very different to him. Capitalizing that Marla was the only social scientist in the group, he said, "Marla, what do you think?" He recognized the group had come to listen to her with great respect, even hopeful anticipation. Every theory she had offered had generally turned out to be correct.

Marla leaned forward in her wheelchair and put her arms on the table. She took a deep, cleansing breath and spoke slowly. "I would like to believe Rick is right." She paused, indicating the but was about to come. "But we aren't dealing with a small group of rational, educated people. Statistically, one in five Americans is illiterate. I think what we saw today is exactly what we can expect everywhere. We are seeing it everywhere. Between a lack of information, whether it's because people haven't been appropriately prepared, or simply a lack of the ability to understand what's being told to them, and sheer, bald-faced, fear-driven panic, I think we're looking at herd survival mentality. From a social science perspective, panic will rule, not logic. People's survival instincts have been turned on, and, paradoxically, they aren't allowing those trying to help them survive to do their job. From an anthropological perspective, Darwinian evolution is kicking in and trumping social and moral order. Even the illiterate understand the phrase, *only the fittest survive.*"

As had happened at several poignant moments over the past month, Marla's clarity cut to the quick of the issue. Jack didn't know how to respond, and from the look on everyone's faces, he figured they knew Marla was correct.

Catherine stood up and said, "Everyone, after listening to all this, I've made a decision that I want to share with you, and I want your input. I will let the process we've laid out operate through tomorrow—to see if people will be more levelheaded about participating in the vaccination program. After Marla's input, I have my doubts that it will work. If it doesn't, vaccinations will be behind by at least two days, and we'll have missed the opportunity to have about 25 percent of the North American population vaccinated."

She paused and looked around the room before continuing. "I have also given the order to protect the vaccine supply with deadly force, and earlier today confirmed this with the White House. They agree. We must preserve the vaccine from theft so, if necessary, we can figure out another way to administer it. If we don't have it, we can't give it. Any disagreements? Thoughts?" Jack and the others nodded in solemn agreement.

"OK then, we'll see what tomorrow brings. Goodnight everyone. If you pray, you might want to do it tonight."

05:00 APRIL 24, MUMBAI (15:30 APRIL 23 SAN FRANCISCO, CA)

Catherine awoke with a foreboding sense she had never experienced before. She prided herself on being an objective, linear, logic-driven person, but something about how she felt was powerful, unrelenting. A sense of doom permeated her entire being.

As Catherine rolled out of bed, Rick, already up, said, "Lordy, Catherine, you look like you didn't sleep a wink. You OK?"

"No. I feel like something terrible is going to happen. And I feel slightly nauseated by everything." She got dressed and went to breakfast, conversing politely but not present as she sipped coffee and watched her eggs get cold. She felt Rick squeeze her hand. She knew he was still concerned that she looked poorly as he stood up, walked to the TV, and turned it on.

"Please don't, Rick. It's too early. Please?"

Rick smiled kindly and said, "Sure, Catherine. No problem," and sat back down.

Catherine knew the others noticed this exchange, and she detected a general increase in the group's anxiety level by her simple request. Breakfast was finished in the absence of WNN.

Catherine stood up and polished off her coffee, resulting in even more significant gastric upheaval. She'd eaten nothing to shield the caffeine sloshing around her already-nauseated stomach.

"I'm gonna head over to the Command Center," she said, heading for the door.

"I'll go with you, Catherine," Jack said as he stood to leave.

They walked together in silence for a short distance before Catherine paused and gently grabbed Jack's arm, looking at him softly.

"Jack, you must be a mess. How are you holding up?" Catherine asked.

Her heart about broke as she watched Jack's eyes well up. She heard the ga-lump of Jack's hard swallow.

"She's getting worse, Catherine. It's progressed from her feet to her calves...no motor function and only some sensation. She only has control of her thighs now. She can lift them, but the leg below just flops around."

"I'm so sorry, Jack. We should have vaccine today, though, so that will help," Catherine said, hoping she sounded encouraging.

"Will it? I mean, we have no goddam idea if it will stop the Death Effector Gene once it initiates. Worse, what if Marla gets the vaccine, but the paralysis continues ascending, and it stops the process after she's become a quadriplegic? For her, that would be worse than death."

The pain in Jack's voice pierced Catherine's innards, causing an internal wince that exacerbated her own lurching sensations. She tugged his arm to get him to start walking again, not knowing what to say.

They walked slowly through a lab to the Command Center and pushed open the door. Each of the monitors had different channels streaming in from all over the world. They were all programmed to run brief captions of the narration, rolling across from the bottom of the screen like an NFL football game scores. They paused, looking from monitor to monitor:

MILAN — ERUPTS IN RIOTS

NEW YORK — STREETS ON FIRE; MILITARY SHOOTS 128 CITIZENS DEAD

PARIS — ANARCHY AKIN TO FRENCH REVOLUTION

BUENOS AIRES— THOUSANDS WHO MAY HAVE SURVIVED WITH VACCINE DEAD IN CLASHES

Catherine noticed Marla was just rolling up when dizziness rudely intruded upon her nausea, and she began to teeter. Jack steadied her, an arm around her shoulder.

"I woke up this morning, and I knew this was what we'd see. I felt it in my guts. Marla was right—again. The distribution process won't work. It can't work. There's too much fear and panic. The urge for self-preservation is taking more lives now than the Death Effector Gene. Death will surely come either way. It's like knowing you are going to die in one of two ways—either a cyanide-like death, quick and painless or the slow march of paralysis and death by exposure or suffocation. It's between a cyanide capsule you can take now or a loaded gun that you can fire only after you have nearly starved to death. Death is certain in either case, but it's the knowing, the waiting, that makes you want to swallow the cyanide," Catherine said, exasperated. There was a long silence. Catherine noticed Marla looking down at her legs and heard her utter a soft sigh of resignation.

"The vaccine has resulted in pure Darwinian survival: sheer, brutish competition for a valuable resource. And the frustrating thing is, Jack, the resource isn't limited. We can make enough for everyone, but no one can seem to wait for their turn. It's as crazy as the nuclear strategy of mutual self-destruction," Catherine said.

"Darwinian evolution created us," Marla said. "Now it's destroying us..."

CHAPTER SEVENTY-SIX

J ack helped Catherine to a chair. He knew her mind must be a blur, unfocused and confused. Marla rolled her wheelchair over and held her hand.

Catherine stammered, "The vaccination plan has failed. The simple act of sticking a needle in a person's arm and pushing one cc of vaccine into their body has failed after over 200 years of success. And the failure isn't that the vaccine doesn't work. We simply can't give it."

Catherine's simple statement elicited a stream of memories for Jack.

200 years ago...The simple act of sticking a needle in a person's arm...The simple act of sticking a needle in a person's arm.

Jack recalled the story of Edward Jenner, the army surgeon from London who, in the 1790s, discovered that people who contracted cowpox from milking cows were immune to the deadly smallpox virus ravaging much of Europe. Both were Pox viruses, but they had very different outcomes. Jenner coined the term vaccination from the Latin word *vaccinus*, or "from cows." He discovered that by taking a sharp object and rubbing it on a cowpox lesion, a zit-like, round, red bump on the skin of someone with the benign cowpox disease, and then using the object to scratch the skin of another person, the individual would get the gentle cowpox and be immune to the more lethal smallpox.

Jack loved the simplicity of Jenner's solution. Rudimentary, even crude, yet elegant in its simplicity. But Jenner's simple scratch inoculation was no less labor-intensive than a vaccine that required an injection. It was just as impractical as Catharine's original plan. The populace wouldn't wait for someone to give them their vaccine with a scratch from a sharp object any more than they would stand still for an injection. They want it now. *How do we get it to them now?*

He thought of the auto-injectors the military uses for organophosphate poisoning. In battle, every soldier has one of the cylindrical devices, which can be triggered by slamming it against the thigh, activating a spring-loaded needle that injects the antidote deep into the leg muscles. If we could just get the vaccine into auto-injectors and then pass them out, one per person. *No. It's impractical.* We can't stop the manufacturing process mid-stream and repackage. It would take too long. Besides, fear and greed would result in people stealing more than one auto-injector and giving themselves or their loved ones more than one dose. The public's mentality, at least related to medications, is based on the *If a little is good, more is better* philosophy. It wouldn't reliably maximize the number of people receiving the vaccine. *Think Jack... THINK!*

Jack looked back at Catherine. She was catatonic, immobile. Her hand looked pale and doughy in Marla's. Marla looked at him in a state of panic.

"Honey, she'll snap out of it," Jack said in as comforting of a voice as he could manage. It didn't appear to relieve Marla.

"She may," Marla said, "But what about me?" Jack noticed Marla's eyes clouding. She was having trouble holding her head up.

"Marla!" Jack shouted, taking her face in his hands. "What's wrong, honey?" She was losing consciousness.

Marla looked up at Jack and managed a weak smile. Just before losing consciousness, she whispered, "I guess we're not in Kansas anymore, huh, Jack?"

Marla's simple comment and sudden demise triggered a cascade of recollections for Jack. He saw himself back in Smith Center, Kansas — 11 miles from the center of the continental U.S. The increasing likelihood of Marla's death was playing with his mind, and he was having nostalgic, overly beneficent memories of how good things used to be, how carefree life had been as a child.

He reached into his pocket and pulled out the Rubik's Cube, his hand acting independently of the rest of his body. The cube was a mess, a cacophony of colors. As his mind raced, his hands worked the cube furiously, instinctively. He was tumbling down a grass-covered hill in the green of June, Marla toppling along after him, giggling with delight, the rasping call of cicadas echoing around them. Then he was at the farm, the smell of the dirt, the good times, and the outrageous chores. He was standing between waist-high rows of corn just north of the farmhouse, arms raised, a red flag tied to a two-foot-long stick, one in each hand. The crop duster, loaded with pesticide, was making an impossibly slow left-hand turn as the pilot eyed the two tiny red specks a hundred feet below, a quarter-mile in the distance. *How do they not fall from the sky at such a slow speed?* Jack always wondered. Descending to about 20 feet above the ground, the pilot lined up the tip of his right-wing on Jack's red flags. The corn, thick with aphids, was being slowly devoured, and Jack's boss had finally given up on the army of ladybugs set free in the middle of the field two weeks earlier. Either the field was sprayed now, or his Angus cattle would have to be sold before winter—a huge financial loss. He needed the corn for silage to feed his herd through the bitter winter months of the high plains.

The loud, guttural engine came closer and fast. It's not going so slow now! It was about 50 yards away when Jack sprinted to his left, just in time to avoid the cloud of organophosphate pesticide drifting slowly downward to blanket the rows of corn where he had just been standing. Jack mentally noted the row where the slowly descending toxic mist hovered and counted 12 rows over, keeping his gaze fixed to that spot. He walked five rows back toward the fog, stopping and standing between the 12th and 13th row. He raised his hands again as the pilot circled wide left, readying the chemical warhead for the entomological enemy, guided by his human mark. Jack's eyes, glazed over, unfocused during this brief visit back to Kansas, cleared, and he realized he had just found a solution to the worldwide vaccine distribution problem. He smiled a subtle smile of *knowing*.

Jack felt the weight of something in his hand and looked down. He was confused. The Rubik's Cube was in his hand, six colors in perfect alignment. Puzzled, he slid it into his pocket and turned to Catherine, eerily calm in the face of Marla's apparent deterioration.

"What?" Catherine asked. She appeared confused by his suddenly calm countenance.

"I know the answer. I know how to deliver the vaccine," he said calmly.

Catherine's glazed puzzlement seemed permanently fixed on her face. She didn't hear him. He reached over and put his hands on her shoulders, turning her toward him.

"Catherine, listen to me. I know how to vaccinate the masses. We don't need to give it by injection, and we don't need to do it one at a time. Do you hear me?"

Catherine began to arouse. "You... you... what?"

"I-KNOW-HOW-TO-DELIVER-THE-VACCINE," he repeated slowly, loudly, like an American in Paris, assuming if he speaks English louder and slower, the French-speaking waiter will understand. She sat up, now paying attention, a bit of the light back in her eyes.

"How?" she said, with a look somewhere between confusion and excitement.

"Crop dusters," Jack said, a boyish Midwestern grin plastered on his mug.

"Huh?"

"Crop dusters," he repeated. "We're going to spray people—like bugs." She tried to speak, but Jack held up his hand to stop her as he picked up the phone and summoned some medics and the rest of the team to the Command Center. He didn't want to have to explain his solution five different times.

The medics arrived, but Marla was arousing on her own accord and was speaking, both good signs to Jack. She had no recollection of fainting. Jack suspected it was more than a simple blackout. No more than 30 seconds later, the rest of the team arrived.

"What's goin' on, Jack?" Ted asked glumly. "Yet another damn glitch?" The four watched WNN in the commons room back in the quarters. Everyone appeared shell-shocked from the constant flow of bad news.

"I think I have the answer to the vaccination mayhem," Jack said. "We have roughly two-to-three billion people to vaccinate, and we can't even get off the ground in the U.S. But even if everything went perfectly, it would be impossible to vaccinate everyone one at a time. We were fooling ourselves. It takes time to give an injection, and we made the presumption that we'd be able to have the process working 24/7. The process was painfully broken before we even started. Hell, our own military is shooting U.S. citizens. It's close to a civil war in a country that reset the brutality meter in the 1860s and said, 'Never again.' Yet, here we are."

"Great. So we know the process we designed doesn't work. What do you suggest?" Rick asked.

"Self-mutilation and crop dusters. Or, more accurately, scratches on the forearm and using crop dusters to spray the vaccine over people," Jack said, grinning. To him, the ease of the plan was its brilliance, just like Jenner. "Marla gave me the idea."

The idea was met with deadpan stares, except Marla, who was grinning too, as her rural roots provided her with immediate understanding. The others didn't grasp what he was saying.

"Look," he said, "the poxvirus is very contagious. I mean *very*. The scab from a chickenpox infection sheds active virus for about five days. And the infected individual sheds the Pox virus through respiratory secretions for three days, even *before* the rash breaks out. In other words, you can get chickenpox by breathing in the virus or having contact with the virus on your skin. The smallpox vaccine wasn't an injection with a single needle. It was given with a circular bunch of short needles that just scratched the skin, depositing the virus just below the skin's surface in the dermis. It doesn't have to be injected into the muscle like the flu or tetanus."

"So what, Jack? We have a gazillion doses of injectable vaccine. I ain't followin' you," Ted said.

"Yes, we have lots of vials of vaccine, and currently no way to give it. That's where the crop dusters come in. Look, you guys, we need to distribute the vaccine in a way that makes it easy — and eliminates the 'Someone in this crowd will get it and I won't' mentality. We tell everyone to get in the middle of a street or a field or at the airport or Yankee Stadium... wherever. We tell them to bring a needle, a pocket knife, a damn paper clip — anything with a point sharp — sharp enough to cause a scratch on their forearm, just deep enough to cause just a little bleeding. We blast a siren one minute from the time the airplane shows up, a crop duster, its sprayer tanks loaded with the vaccine. It flies over and sprays the crowd. The crowd will be instructed to breathe deeply, expose their scratch to the mist, and rub it in. Even a relatively dilute solution of the vaccine should result in inoculation. If the scratch doesn't do it, the virus inhaled into the lungs will. It is a belts-and-suspenders approach." Jack was grinning broadly now. He hoped they were beginning to see how this lunatic plan could work. "The other benefit is that the solution is transportable and doesn't require many supplies. We don't need to ship syringes and needles, and alcohol sponges to Tanzania. Call up ACE Hardware and have them send weed sprayers! You just spray them! "

"So, lemme see if I got this straight. We're going to take crop dusters—airplanes that spray toxic chemicals to kill bug-infested fields—and put a vaccine in the tanks to spray humans?" Ted said, with no small amount of concern in his voice.

"Yeah, Jack. That worries me. How in God's name do you decontaminate organophosphate-laced chemical tanks on the crop dusters?" Rick queried.

"Calcium hypochlorite," said Jack matter-of-factly.

"Huh?" said Lucy.

"Calcium hypochlorite. Commonly known as household bleach. I looked it up on the internet while waiting for you guys to get here. You just mix one part Clorox with 10 parts of water, wash out the tanks a couple of times and test for organophosphates after the cleaning. Once there's none detected, probably after a couple of washings, just fill the tanks with a neutral salt solution with the same pH as human serum, 7.4. Dump in the vaccine, slosh it around a bit, which I imagine will happen when the duster takes off, and spray the masses. Bueno! End of story. World saved. Praise be to the team! Glory! Glory! Hallelujah!"

"Jesus, crazy as it sounds, I like it! What on God's green earth made you think up with such a darn fool plan?" Ted asked.

"Aphids, again."

"Huh?"

"Aphids. We used to be human markers for the crop duster on the farm. I just switched out the aphids for humans, and instead of spraying toxic chemicals to kill bugs, we're spraying a vaccine to save humans. Bugs were my inspiration," Jack said. He was pleased that the global solution harkened back to his down-to-earth experiences on a Kansas dirt farm.

"Surely there aren't enough crop dusters out there to handle this, are there?" Lucy asked. "I mean, I can understand there might be enough in the agricultural parts of the U.S., but what about major metropolitan areas?"

"That's where Catherine comes in again. The military should be able to equip helicopters with spray rigs pretty quickly. The forest service has planes for putting out forest fires. They can be outfitted. There are tractor-pulled portable spray tanks that can cover a twenty-yard-wide swath. I realize it isn't a delicate solution, but it should work," Jack said.

Catherine was coming back to life as she listened to Jack's solution.

"Yes! Jack, this is a great idea! We can designate by zip code where people should go—where they need to be, what time of day, what date. We could send people to Yankee Stadium and not just fill the seats, but fill the entire stadium, the field, the parking lot. From 0700 to 1000, everyone from a certain zip code would go. We'd encourage people to carpool, getting them mutually invested in saving time and achieving the same goal: to get them and their loved ones vaccinated. A couple of fly-overs by the sprayers, and in a few minutes, tens of thousands, maybe hundreds of thousands of people, would be vaccinated, all inside of three hours."

"There is a benefit of this besides just straight vaccination," Jack said.

"What else?" Lucy asked.

"The wind will no doubt carry the virus, spreading it well beyond the designated spray zones. Many people may get enough active virus to become inoculated by what's in the air."

"Any objections to Jack's concept?" Catherine asked. No one dissented.

"Great. I'm going to send the directive out and put a stop to vaccination attempts."

Jack watched as Catherine clicked the mouse, sending the memo hurtling through cyberspace to governments around the globe. He could only imagine the faces of those receiving the message, morphing from puzzled confusion to enlightened smiles. The final line of the statement read:

IMPLEMENT AT WILL, AND MAY YOUR GOD, WHATEVER YOU CONCEIVE HIM TO BE, BE WITH YOU.

The Command Center doors banged open, revealing a rather robust woman wearing a white nursing uniform, pushing a stainless steel cart. She navigated over to Marla as Jack watched.

"It's time for the team to get their shots," she said, a slight French accent making the comment sound almost gleeful.

"You first, young lady," she said, rolling up Marla's sleeve.

Jack watched as she pushed the needle through Marla's skin. Just as quickly, the needle was out and a Band-Aid on.

Jack frowned, thinking of the sensation created by injections—warm pressure as one cubic centimeter of clear vaccine pushed the deltoid muscle fibers apart. He smiled and shook his head. The desperation of finding the cause and solution since death first appeared in Mto Wa Mbu was summarized by a pinprick and a fading throb in the arm.

Jack watched as the entire team received their vaccine. He insisted on being last. As he was rolling his sleeve down, he said, "Now, let's pray it works."

CHAPTER SEVENTY-SEVEN

"Hey, Jack," Ted shouted across the room, "You gotta see this." Jack looked up from the book he was reading, other team members pausing, too. Ted reached up and turned the volume on the TV up.

The video was like a documentary on crop-dusters—clips of bi-planes, single-wings, helicopters, and the like, all spewing a misty fog. A female reporter narrated, her raspy voice sounding like she had smoked one too many cigarettes in her lifetime. "Since the novel solution to the vaccination catastrophe, an unusual air force of a non-military nature has taken to the airways, laden not with bombs or missiles or machine guns, but with liquid salvation for the masses. Huge throngs of people have collected in pre-ordained spaces to look skyward and receive biologic redemption in the form of a mist, gently enveloping them, contaminating their forearm scratches, and filling their lungs. Planes, such as those shown here, have dropped the mist over football fields, stadiums, parking lots, playgrounds, and even prison courtyards."

The TV scene flipped to a carnival-like aerial view of Las Vegas. The reporter continued. "The entire city of Las Vegas gathered earlier today between the curbs of Las Vegas Boulevard, as brightly painted crop dusters in a V-formation soaked the crowd. As one woman on the street noted, only Las Vegas could create a party-like atmosphere that belied the seriousness of this act of life." She paused for effect, then lowered her voice what sounded to Jack a whole octave. "It's as if this city viewed the Death Effector Gene as just another gamble on life's path. Odds had been placed on the likelihood of man's extinction."

"My god," Catherine said. "What a bunch of sickos."

Jack grinned. "Come on, Catherine. People will bet on anything. But, if we were wrong, who would have collected the bets?" The team chuckled.

The TV migrated from Las Vegas to San Francisco. Jack saw Catherine bristle, still angry with the mayor. The newsperson continued her story.

"The people of San Francisco gathered on the Golden Gate Bridge early yesterday morning, fog hiding the suspended roadway."

"Jeez. I wouldn't ever fly a plane in that pea soup!" exclaimed Rick. Jack nodded in agreement.

"Just after 8:30 a.m., as you'll see in this next clip, two crop dusters used in Napa Valley to spray vineyards descended from low lying clouds in the northern sky, popped over the ridge leading to Sausalito, leveled out, and began their run. The pilots skillfully navigated under and around the bridge's massive cables, completing their mission before the winds picked up, inoculating half a million souls in less than fifteen minutes. Three full bridges of people have been treated per day, and within the next several days, the entire metro area will be vaccinated."

"Absolutely amazing..." Jack mused, fascinated by the bridge sight.

"LAPD helicopters equipped with spray nozzles flew over South Los Angeles—the location of the horrific 1992 riots— the crowded streets a model of calm and cooperation. people are waving to the pilots in thanks," the reporter droned. "Truly, the harmony is as staggering as the discord just days earlier." Shots of the city faded to the face of the reporter, who tilted her head in seriousness, then said, "This has all been possible because of Dr. Jack Cann, the farm boy, and professor from Kansas, who made lethal clashes unnecessary with a simple plan to use aerial spraying."

Jack walked over and turned the set off. "Blah, blah, blah. These folks never know when to shut up."

"Whaddya suppose they do where there ain't enough people to justify a crop duster or army helicopter or any aircraft for that matter—like in small villages in remote areas like Alaska, Montana, or Mongolia, or Tibet or..." said Ted.

"They'll use something like a portable weed sprayer. You know, the kind with the bicycle-like pump handle and a hand-held spray wand?" said Jack. "Kind of a funny visual spraying individuals like so many dandelions in the yard."

08:00 APRIL 27, MUMBAI (22:30 APRIL 26 WASHINGTON, DC)

Jack was helping Marla pack their bags for the trip back to the U.S. when there was a knock at the door. "Door's open," Marla said.

Catherine opened the door and stuck her head in. "You guys gotta sec?"

"Always for you, Catherine," Jack said. "What's up?"

"I just got off the phone with the White House. They've found them."

Jack and Marla looked at each other, temporary confusion morphing into a look of hope.

"Are you sure you guys want to do this? I mean, it is amazingly great...compassionate. But a huge commitment. And with Marla's...ahhh..." Catherine stuttered.

"Paralysis, Catherine. It's OK to say it. It's not like I don't know!" Marla said.

"It's just that it's hard enough without paralysis," Catherine said.

"We've talked and talked about it. We're positive," Jack said.

"Yeah, we're good. Watch this!" Marla said. Jack laughed as she popped a wheelie with her wheelchair. "See? Entertainment value, too."

"Well then, grab your bags, and let's go. A car's waiting to take us there on the way to the airport. The rest of the team will ride along if that's OK."

Jack was thrilled to be walking outside. It seemed like months since he, or any of the team, had seen the Mumbai morning. A U.S. Army lieutenant was standing at the back of a stretch humvee. He set the bags on the ground, and the man hoisted them into the back of the vehicle.

As they were piling into the humvee, Ted came running out of the hospital. "Hey, y'all, wait a sec." The Texan's face was apple red, clipping along in cowboy boots, puffing and trying to catch his breath. He bent over as he reached the group, hands on his knees.

"Sorry, I'm a bit late for yer sendoff. I was tied up in the lab, cleaning up some details."

"Yeah, Ted. We were wondering," Jack said, reaching out to shake his hand.

Ted grabbed the hand, pulled him into a bear hug, and held him there. It felt like he was going to be crushed.

"Ted...gotta...breathe," Jack said in staccato, attempting to fill his lungs against the squeeze.

"Oh, sure," he said, letting him down gently. "I sure am gonna miss y'all." Ted's eyes looked wet.

"Ted? Are you crying?" Catherine asked.

Ted looked up at her, then at each team member in turn. "I'd love to lie to you and say no, but yeah, I'm misty-eyed. I'm gonna miss the lot of ya."

Marla, looking up, said, "Ted, we're going to miss you too!"

"Yeah, well, maybe we'll all get to work with each other again soon," Ted said.

"Jesus, Ted, I hope like hell there's never a reason for us to work together again. I mean, no offense, but it wasn't that fun," Jack said.

"You know what I mean, Jack. But hell, I'll take a barbeque in Texas, too. Now, I guess I've held ya up long enough," said Ted, motioning them to get into the humvee.

Jack lifted Marla into the vehicle and got in, the rest of the group climbing in after them.

"Good morning, Doctors," said a man in the passenger's seat. "I'm Colonel Davis, U.S. Army. First, I've been asked by President Lopez to personally thank you for all that you've done. So, thank you! Next, Dr. Montoya has informed me that we have a slight detour before the airport. Please buckle in. We have a 30-minute drive to get to Dharavi. The airport is 30 minutes beyond that."

With Marla's wheelchair loaded, the lieutenant climbed behind the wheel, pulled out of the hospital's circle drive, and headed north. There was minimal conversation as the Americans looked out the windows. Jack was slack-jawed at the chaos of Mumbai, a stark contrast to the lily-white cleanness and order of the lab he just left. There were abandoned cars with desiccated human forms in the driver's seat. The streets were lined with children, wandering as if in a trance. Dogs carried meaty bones that were surely human. And there was garbage everywhere. The closer they got to their destination, the worse it seemed to get.

They pulled up to a relatively nondescript high-rise adjacent to Asia's largest slum, Dharavi. "Dharavi used to be a small fishing village," the colonel said. "But it was subsumed by Mumbai's growth long ago, becoming a city within a city, smack-dab in the middle of the financial district. It's amazing how this prime real estate was covered by such squalor." Jack felt queasy. It was never-ending stretches of narrow, dirty alleys, open, purulent sewers, and cramped, box-like shanties. The colonel continued, saying, "It was home to over a million people before the Death Effector Gene. Now it's the world's largest orphanage."

Jack jumped out of the vehicle and fetched Marla's chair. The lieutenant led Jack, Marla, and the rest of the crew across the street into an alleyway. They walked, Marla, rolling, between piles of refuse and open pits of sewage. Rats the size of small cats watched them pass, unafraid of the humans.

"My god," Catherine said in a loud whisper to no one. Jack wondered if the others felt ill, too. The abject poverty was surpassed only by the tragedy that the slum was populated only by children abandoned by their parents in death. He could hear every footstep of his own and the continuous crunching sound made by Marla's wheels moving over loose rocks as they walked past an unbroken line of children, mere skin bags covering bones. He felt a lump in his throat, giant brown eyes watching them, silently pleading for help that they were too weak actually to ask for. Jack was beginning to question if this was a wise idea.

After half a mile, they approached what seemed like just another hovel, indistinguishable from any other. A marine sentry was standing guard. The lieutenant stopped and turned. "This is it." He turned to the marine and said, "Corporal, are the children inside?"

"Yes, sir. Shall I get them, sir?"

"Yes, please."

The combat-clad soldier disappeared into the hut. After some muffled conversation, two children appeared in the doorway and stepped into the sun. The oldest was a girl. Although covered in filth, she was a beautiful little thing. Her face was gaunt, starvation accentuating her saucer-like dark brown eyes. Black hair, a bit matted and tied in a ponytail, hung between her shoulder blades. The smaller child, a boy, equally dirty, stood beside his sister. He was confused, scared. He reached down and clasped his sister's hand for comfort. He had no shirt. He was so thin, ribs visible, that one could see the beat of his heart through his chest. Like his sister, the hardship of the past months and the nutritional deprivation depressed his spirit and hid the handsomeness that was surely there.

"Dr. Cann, Dr. Qui. May I introduce you to Edha and Kalyan Mehta, the children of Dhanesh and Falguni Mehta."

Jack knelt to eye level of the children, and Marla rolled forward. "Hi, you two," said Jack softly. "It's so nice to meet you. My name's Jack, and this is Marla" He paused and then said quietly, "We knew your daddy. He helped save all the people of the world." The marine corporal, fluent in Hindi, translated.

Edha, now nine years old, asked, "Is daddy coming home soon?"

The corporal translated the innocence of the question forcing Jack to look down from their faces and stare at the ground. Catherine and Marla were reduced to tears. Out of the corner of his eye, Jack saw Lucy put her hand over her mouth and turn away from the children, sobbing quietly.

Jack swallowed hard, eyes burning.

"No, honey, your daddy won't be coming home. He died, Edha. I'm sorry." He looked from her to Kalyan, six. They barely reacted, other than looking down at the dirt. How could they? In the past months, they had undoubtedly witnessed horror after horror.

"Our mommy died too," Kalyan said, so softly it was almost inaudible. The corporal looked down and softly relayed the information.

"Edha, honey, where's Gagan?" Jack was referring to their little brother.

"He fell asleep and didn't wake up." Now Jack and the corporal had tears in their eyes. Jack looked away momentarily. Through his water-distorted vision, he noticed Rick and the lieutenant were wiping their eyes.

"Honey… Edha, Kalyan… Marla and I are from the United States. We're sorry your mommy, daddy, and brother are gone. We're hoping you would come home with us — to stay with us."

Kalyan looked up at his big sister with questioning eyes. He turned back to the couple and said, "Do you have anything to eat?" With that, the colonel excused himself, tears running down his cheeks.

"Yes, honey, we have lots to eat—all that you need, all that you could want. And we have a house that's warm when it's cold and cool when it's hot. We'll take care of you. Will you come with us?" Jack asked, reaching out a hand, Marla mirroring his gesture.

Kalyan took Jack's hand, Edha took Marla's, and they turned and navigated the half-mile back to the humvee, flanked by their military escort. Catherine, Rick, and Lucy trailed behind in silence.

The group loaded up, and the lieutenant headed for the airport. The two children sat between Marla and Jack on the ride.

Jack was relieved that the mood in the military vehicle was more lighthearted and the chatter more lively than it had been on the ride to the slum. Rick was divulging a funny little story about Catherine that, before their relationship, had been held hostage by her self-imposed moratorium on relationships.

Jack noticed the absence of Marla's usual cute giggle. Still smiling from the story, he looked over at her. She was ashen, a bead of sweat rolling down her temple.

"Marla? You OK?" he asked.

Marla's breathing was shallow, labored, eyes wide.

"The pain. It's so…bad," Marla said, pushing out barely audible words.

Jack leaped over the children.

"Where, honey? Where's the pain?"

"All over. Especially...legs," she managed to get out between pain-infused breaths.

Jack looked down. Her feet were rocking between flexion and extension as if she were consciously exercising.

Jack touched her face. It was icy, and her color had turned from ash to an otherworldly blue hue. He looked pleadingly at Catherine.

"Lieutenant! Get us to the airport, now!" Catherine commanded.

Jack felt the lunge of the humvee accelerating, engine roaring, and as he held Marla in his arms, her eyes lolled back, her head fell to her chest, her body limp.

CHAPTER SEVENTY-NINE

"What do you hear, dammit?" Catherine demanded of the corpsmen listening to Marla's chest with his stethoscope.

"Shhhhh..." the corpsman responded. "It's hard enough to hear, with all the road noise," he said as the vehicle screeched to a halt by the lowered tail of the C-131 taking them home.

Catherine wasn't used to being shushed, but she complied.

"It's very faint, but she's alive. Her heart rate is about 160. She needs fluids. We radioed ahead, so they should be ready."

Catherine watched as the corpsmen worked, quickly transferring her to the plane. Rick walked up to her side. She felt his hand slide into hers, an odd feeling of comfort simultaneously coexisting with mourning. She could only watch.

"IV's in," the nurse said. "What should I hang?"

"D- ten normal saline," the corpsman instructed.

"Why D-ten?" the nurse asked.

"She may need the extra dextrose. Who knows what's going on, but at least she won't die of hypoglycemia," the corpsman said.

Catherine saw Rick nod his head in agreement out of the corner of her eye. She knew he hadn't taken care of patients in years, but he was more clinically connected than she had ever been. She looked over at Jack. She could tell nothing was reassuring him.

"All right," the colonel said. "Let's get this bird in the air. Dr. Cann, it has a fully equipped sickbay, so we can continue to monitor Dr. Qui, but we have to get going. She'll be better off stateside."

Catherine felt reassured by the efficiency of what was happening as she watched the colonel's order mobilize the personnel. Within five minutes, Marla's litter was strapped down, monitors were chirping her vital signs in real-time, and the tail ramp was closed. Another five minutes, and they were in the air, headed for U.S. soil.

Jack hadn't left Marla's side in the three hours they had been in the air. He talked to her, trying to get a response, but she remained silent. He would lift her arm a few inches off the bed, trying to detect the slightest bit of muscle tone, but it flopped back to the coarse, green wool standard Army issue blanket. Her breathing remained shallow and rapid.

Jack felt something touch his shoulder. Startled, he looked up to see Catherine looking down at him, her hand squeezing his shoulder. He searched her face for encouragement, for any sign of optimism. He was disappointed. She sat down beside him.

"How you are doing?" she asked.

"Shitty, Catherine. Really shitty."

"We should be able to get her to Bethesda within 30 minutes of landing. We're only eight hours away," Catherine said. Jack was hoping to hear her say something truthful and positive but knew those things were mutually exclusive at the moment.

Jack looked down. He noticed the rivets in the floor were identical to the rivets that he and the SEALs had removed from the Air India plane en route to North Korea. He looked back up and into Catherine's eyes.

"She's dying, isn't she," Jack said weakly. "Be honest."

"I don't know, Jack. It looks bad."

"Do you think it's related to the vaccine? I mean, do you think this could be a reaction?" Jack said.

"I suppose so, but I doubt it. She only received it two days ago. I doubt it would be having any effect yet," Catherine said. "It's most likely to be..." He knew what she didn't want to say.

"The mutation. I know...the goddam Death Effector Gene," Jack said, relieving Catherine of the need to complete her sentence.

"I guess we've answered the question of whether the vaccine will reverse any damage that's already occurred," Catherine said.

Jack sighed. "Yeah. Now we know it doesn't."

CHAPTER EIGHTY

Bob bumped along, gnawing on a two-inch stump of a cigar so wet with spit he couldn't keep it lit. He reached up and scratched an itch on his stubble-covered cheek with a hand as calloused as most people's feet, the tips of his fingernails black from engine grease.

He buckled a fleece-lined pilot's cap around his chin, squinting as he pulled the goggles over his eyes. He needed neither the cap nor goggles, as the Air Tractor AT-400 Turbo Crop Duster had an airtight glass canopy that he pulled shut and locked. It was all just part of his routine as a WWII ace wannabe. He pivoted the machine at the end of the dirt runway, just a mile south of Smith Center, tapped a few gauges on the instrument panel, then pushed the throttle just enough to coax the plane a few feet forward. He grinned at the sound of the engine. *This ain't no pussy Cessna 172.* No. It was a powerful sound—a droning, throaty bellow—a *manly sound, like me.*

Bob, pre-flight ceremonies complete, shoved the throttle up. He loved the sensation of the plane lurching forward and gaining speed, bumping along the rutted dirt path, which he knew few outside rural America would have comfortably described as a runway. He lifted off to the south at exactly 7:00 a.m. according to his Timex digital watch, barely readable through the dirt-filled scratches of the plastic face. He climbed to about 200 feet and then banked hard left and headed north, lining up with Highway 281, running right through the middle of town — Main Street.

Bob felt pride as he leveled off. He remembered Jack Cann from when he was just a little shit. *Smart son-of-a-bitch.* Now he was preparing to treat Jack's hometown. *I'm the doctor today.* He hoped everyone was on time, gathered like they had been told between the curbs on Main Street. He knew the town's 1,600 people could fit within a block and a half, stringing from the Center Theater to just past the intersection with East Kansas Street. It wasn't any different from the Old Settler's Day celebration when everyone crowded into the street for barbecue.

Bob radioed the volunteer fire station, instructing them to blast the emergency preparedness siren, signaling he was a minute away. "And for Christ's sakes, make sure they don't forget to scratch themselves. I only got enough for one run," he told the woman on the other end. He laughed at the thought of her slamming the radio mic into place and running a block east to Main, making sure she got her vaccine.

He dropped down to 20 feet above Main Street as he entered the town, a quarter-mile to his living target. *It'll be damn quick at 120 miles per hour!* He throttled back.

Bob focused on the road ahead. It looked like an ant colony, teaming with color. He reached over and put his finger on the silver switch that activated the sprayers. He would have to be right on today. *Three... two... one.*

Curiously, everything slowed down as he flipped the switch. Bob saw a collage of faces, ages, and colors. He was pretty sure he saw a couple of arms with blood rising in fresh, superficial wounds. He imagined that more than several of Smith Center's World War II veterans had flashbacks to their time in the South Pacific and somehow mustered the courage not to run for cover.

Bob looked back as he pulled up from the ground, his payload delivered. He could see the crowd below, enveloped in an odorless, cool, water-like mist he had just created. Wounded extremities were held skyward. Bob could see a few rubbing their forearms, presumably forcing the wetness into the scratch.

He banked left and headed back to the airport. He set the Air Tractor down, taxied to the plane ties, and shut down. He climbed into his 1963 Ford pickup, rust widely metastatic, its original aqua blue paint faded by the Kansas sun to dirty light green, and headed into town. The Lion's Club had arranged for coffee, hot chocolate, and donuts after the event, bloody arms and all. *I ain't miss it for nothin'.*

10:45 MAY 8*TH*, MTO WA MBU, TANZANIA

Riley heard them before she saw them. She held the red square of bright red curtain open just enough to watch U.S. Army humvees roll into the village like a small invasion force. They stopped in the town center, the dust their vehicles had kicked up catching up with them as they stopped, a brown cloud and creating an almost mystical appearance as it settled.

Riley watched as children slowly congregated around the Army vehicles. She was amazed at their innocent curiosity regarding these strange people who had shown up unexpectedly.

More children arrived, ranging from toddlers barely walking to older teenagers. She had watched several of the teenagers die shortly after their 18th birthdays, and it wretched the heart from her chest. She watched as the soldiers folded back a large canvas covering a bunch of cylindrical canisters.

She burst out of the shack. "Stop! What are you doing?" she said. Despite the stark limitations, she felt after Mosi's death, Riley had continued to mother about forty children. Even though it wore on her more and more each day, she took the mantle of motherhood with gusto and the ferocity of a lioness protecting her cubs.

A soldier in the back of one of the humvees immediately shouldered his M-16, lowering it just as quickly when he saw she wasn't armed.

"What are you doing?" Riley said again, more demanding, pointing a shaking finger at the soldier. She looked around and found Abasi, pulling him close.

"Well, ma'am, we're here to vaccinate the village against that gene thing," the soldier said. She figured he couldn't have been more than 20.

Riley heard on BBC that some people, including that Jack guy she had met in Jos, had been working on solving the problem, but with no electricity in the village, she had lost touch entirely with the outside world. Paradoxically, considering she was a reporter, this had resulted in the sense of great freedom for Riley. She didn't want to know what was going on elsewhere. Right here and right now was all that mattered. *Wait. A vaccine?*

"You mean a vaccine that will prevent death from whatever it is?" she said, hopefully.

"Yes, ma'am. It stops the genetic thingy from turnin' on or somethin' like that," the young man said. "Look," he said, pointing to their weapon—garden weed sprayers sloshing with the vaccine.

Riley could only grin for a few moments, hugging Abasi. "Well, do you need me to tell them to roll up their sleeves? They haven't had much experience with needles," Riley said.

"No, ma'am," said the soldier. "All they need to do is scratch their skin a little and breathe in some of the mist we spray. Rub the watery stuff into their scratch. Easy peasy."

Riley translated the instructions, noting the puzzled looks on the kid's faces. She looked around and found a pointed small rock, picked it up, and made a shallow scratch on her skin. Blood slowly appeared in the wound. She instructed the soldier to spray her. He complied, and she took deep, exaggerated breaths and rubbed it into her scratch, blood streaking up and down her arm, diluted by the vaccine. The children began to nod in understanding, and found stones of their own, wounding themselves and helping their younger — and far less willing — siblings.

The soldiers stood high on the humvees and sprayed the human hive with the vaccine. Riley moved in and out of the children, her dress—hues of blues and greens and oranges— looking like a dancing rainbow, laughing and twirling and lovingly tousling the children's hair, kissing the tops of short heads, moist with the vaccine.

In less than an hour, the soldiers pulled out of Mto Wa Mbu after every village survivor seeded with the genetic cure. It was a poetic conclusion to the global disaster, originating where they stood, in mitochondrial Eve 200,000 years earlier.

CHAPTER EIGHTY-ONE

Riley was no different from any other parent after a near 48-hour trans-Atlantic trip that began in Mto Wa Mbu. She was frazzled, and the words, *What the hell am I doing?* had entered her mind more than once. As the 747 descended, the frequency and volume of the words increased. It was one thing to chase a kid around a small village in the middle of nowhere. Not losing Abasi in Washington, DC was another issue.

Her eyes closed, despite the fact she was trying to stay awake, and she felt that beautiful sensation of the world falling away when the wheels of the jet banged down on the runway at Reagan, startling her. She was sure the jolt would awaken her new son, curled up in the window seat beside her, head in her lap. She looked down at him, his eyes closed, face relaxed, slow breaths continuing as the plane decelerated and shimmied to a stop. As the turbines whined back to life, she watched Abasi stir to life, sit up, and rub his eyes. Riley leaned forward so she could watch his face as he looked out the window. He was squinting from the brightness. She continued watching him, the plane taxiing slowly. Across the river, Riley could see the Capital dome—she wondered if he had noticed. The smile on his face told her he saw it too.

"Is this America?" Abasi asked, looking up at her, eyes wide, smile proportionally big. Riley's concerns about her new path melted at the boy's eager words, hopefully, offered. She reached over, stroked his head, and smiled at him.

"Yes, Abasi. This is America," Riley said softly, pulling him close to her.

She continued to watch his face as he looked out the window. She could only imagine what was going through his mind. She noticed every minute facial expression immediately saw twitches that would have been missed by a passing stranger as if his mind were directly connected to hers. Happiness, wonder... a little trepidation.

They waited in the aisle to get off the jet, holding hands. She noticed him alternating glances out the window and up at her face as if he was unsure it was all happening.

They exited the plane, went through customs, and found their luggage. Abasi was silent the whole way. They piled the bags on a trolley and pushed it to the curb, and Riley flailed her arms. A cab careened unscathed across an impossible number of lanes and screeched up to the curb. Riley helped the cabbie load the bags, keeping the parental eye on Abasi, who stood on the curb, taking in his surroundings.

Riley joined him on the curb and opened the back door. "Where are we going now, mamma?" Abasi asked innocently.

"Home, honey," Riley said. "We're going home," she repeated, kneeling and wrapping him in her arms.

04:45 MAY 31, ARLINGTON NATIONAL CEMETERY, ARLINGTON, VA

President Lopez opened the limo door before the car had stopped. Secret Service men scrambled to assist him and Tom Nakamoro, his Chief of Staff, tried to keep up, limbs flailing. He usually did this for two conscious reasons—one, because he had never gotten used to people opening his car door, and two, because he got a chuckle out of bucking protocol. Today, however, it was neither. It was sheer anxiousness. He wanted to be there now, needed to be there now, even though the sun was not up and the park was still closed to the public.

"Right this way, Mr. President," a giant black-suited attendant said. The president glanced at him and nodded. President Lopez had seen this agent before and always thought he must be on loan from the Washington Redskins, a defensive end in the off-season. He walked down a path, Nakamoro, one of the few inexplicably surviving Asians in his administration, trotting along behind him.

He followed a bevy of agents off the path and out into the grass of the cemetery. It impressed him how the headstones lined up perfectly as if standing at attention for him, the Commander in Chief. He saw four marines standing erect up a slight incline, two on each side of a headstone, obviously waiting for him. They snapped a salute as he walked up.

"At ease, soldiers," the president said.

Tom said, "Mr. President, this is highly unusual. People are going to say you're abusing executive power. To exhume a body and have it placed here without any family permission is…"

"Quiet, please, Thomas," the president said, taking several deep breaths. "What family exactly are you concerned about? There's no one left. I had an extensive search done, and we can't find them—they don't exist. And few deserve this honor more than him," the president said as he knelt.

He reached forward and gently ran his hand along the smooth, up-curved marbled edge of the stone. "Hello, old friend," he said quietly. He looked at the block lettering:

FRANKLIN JONES
Kentucky
PFC, 31st Infantry Regiment
Vietnam War
June 3, 1943
March 25, 2013

The president looked at the stone for a long time, one hand on the headstone, head bowed. Thomas broke the silence.

"Mr. President?"

"Yes?" the president said.

"Mr. President, I... I certainly don't want to be insensitive, but I'm puzzled about why you moved his body. And why are you here? He was quite critical of you before his death," Tom said.

President Lopez stood slowly and faced his Chief of Staff. He looked at him with brows furrowed in question, and then, over Tom's shoulder, the president noticed a flicker. He squinted. In the residual darkness of the early morning, he could see the light from the eternal flame of JFK's memorial. He stared at it for a moment and then refocused on Tom's face.

The president asked, "Who did Reverend Jones fight for, Tom?"

"For black people, Mr. President," said Tom.

The president smiled weakly. "That's only partly correct, Tom."

"What do you mean, partly, Mr. President?"

"I mean Tom, the reverend spoke for people of color."

"Uhhh... I know that. Maybe I'm not following you."

"Tom, do you recall the reverend ever talking about the whites doing 'this' or doing 'that' to 'the blacks?'" There was a pause.

"No, I guess not."

"No, you didn't. You see, the reverend intentionally used the words 'colored people' because he meant everyone. He put no parameters on the word 'colored.' Most people assumed he meant black folks, not bothering to listen deeply. But he was intentionally inclusive. He was an advocate of all people—brown, yellow, white, and yes, black. He embodied tolerance that few seem to understand and even fewer demonstrate." The president paused. "I remember some of his last words, Tom. 'May the Great Almighty God bless you, my brothers and sisters—those of all colors—'"

The President watched Tom ponder this for a moment and then reached over and put a hand on each of his shoulders and spun him around. He directed Tom's eyes to the eternal flame and said, "Tom, that's the reason I had Franklin Jones' remains moved here. Because his ideas, despite the horror of the past months, must live in our hearts as we rebuild the world. Franklin Jones was, unlike the Death Effector Gene, colorblind, and I intended to make sure this country doesn't forget that whatever happens on this planet, we're all in it together."

Marla rolled over in bed, a sliver of the Kansas morning sun beaming through a slit in the blinds, and looked at her husband, still sleeping soundly. She didn't notice the tingling in her feet that she'd had when she went to bed the night before. *It's better today.*

She lay quietly, watching his chest rise and fall. It was so quiet that she thought she could hear his heartbeat. Her left hand swept down over her breasts and belly, coming to rest just above her pubic bone, and she smiled so subtly that, had one been watching her, the change would have been almost imperceptible. She continued watching Jack, motionless except for her breathing pushing against him, as the sliver of natural light slowly ascended from his chest toward his face, settling over his eyes. He stirred, tilting his head away from the light. His eyes fluttered open to find himself nose to nose with Marla.

She looked at him with a soft authenticity that had eluded her for what seemed like an eternity. Finally home in Lawrence, she wondered if his body felt to him as hers felt at this moment—as if every cell in her body was sighing. Marla reached over and touched his face lovingly, and smiled. She kissed his lips gently and said, "Good morning, babe."

"Uhhh... yeah. Morning," he said.

She could see he was still groggy from sleep, blinking a bit more sleep from his eyes. She hesitated and then said, "Honey, I need to tell you something."

"Huh? Sure."

"Jack..." she said, sitting up to face him, "I'm pregnant."

"OK," said Jack, as he looked at her, blinking. There was a short silence, ending with him sitting straight up in bed.

"You're pregnant?" he said. Marla thought he sounded both confused and startled—not what she was hoping for. "What? How — uh." He scratched his head, clearly confused, incapable of putting a coherent sentence together.

"Yes, honey. Pregnant. Maybe just six weeks pregnant, but still pregnant. I picked up a urine pregnancy test in Washington before we got on the plane, and, well, it's blue."

"But we only had sex once in the past... Hell, I can't even remember." Marla could tell he was trying to unravel the timeline, and they were both sick of timelines.

"The past six weeks. But it only takes once, as you no doubt know."

"But I thought you were on birth control. Yes?"

"Yes, but it's funny how the importance of an international crisis seems to eliminate one's interest in some things, like trying to figure out where to get birth control pills in a foreign country amid half the world's population dying, when, frankly, the opportunity for us to jump each other's bones was rare. I blew it off when I ran out and, frankly, just forgot about it the rest of the time. It didn't even hit me that I hadn't had a period until we were on the plane headed home."

"Wow. Pregnant," Jack repeated. Marla couldn't tell if his stunned look was due to the news or caffeine deprivation. She hoped the latter.

"Why don't I get up and make the coffee this morning?" Marla suggested, thinking Jack might want a moment alone.

"Uh... OK." He remained upright, still looking substantially confused.

Marla got out of bed, slipped into her robe, grabbed her crutches, and ratcheted herself to the kitchen. She was worried that he wasn't happy about the news. She filled the pot with water, put one scoop more coffee than usual in the filter, and flipped it on. A few minutes later, the aroma of the coffee predictably resulted in Jack appearing in the kitchen. Marla took this as a good sign, his reaction seeming more related to adjusting to jet lag and the need for a good strong cup of joe. She watched him as he walked over to her, stretched his arms skyward, and wrapped her in a tight hug. His grip loosened, and he leaned back and looked at her, smiling with tenderness. "I love you, Marla."

"I love you too. So," Marla said with a pause, "You're OK with the whole baby thing? I mean, you aren't going to freak out or anything after you get some space to think about all of this? We weren't going to have kids, and we've just increased the number under this roof from two to four. Is adding a fifth in about seven months going to put you over the edge?"

She watched as Jack poured each of them a cup of coffee and sat down at the table. Marla rolled her eyes, realizing he was intentionally delaying his response for dramatic effect. "Jack?" She watched him pull a mouthful of the steaming liquid off the top of his mug, swallow, roll his eyes slowly skyward, and act as if he needed time to consider his answer. Marla picked up a potholder and flung it at him like a Frisbee. It whizzed past his left ear. She giggled at the silliness, Jack grinning.

"Come here," Jack said. Marla struggled without crutches to walk over and plunked down on his lap.

"Jesus. You're already heavier!" They both laughed. "Yes, I'm am going to freak out, but I'll be OK. I'm already better than OK. I'm excited. I mean, we didn't plan any of this. Now we have two kids sleeping upstairs and one in the oven. Kalyan and Edha are amazing, beautiful, and the surprise... the timing of you being pregnant is at once anxiety-provoking and wonderful, don't you think?"

"Yes, both," she said. Marla looked down and away unconsciously, momentarily.

"What?" Jack said. "What was that about? That was your *Something is bugging me* look."

"I don't know, honey. It's silly but, maybe not..."

"What is it?" Jack pressed.

"I probably conceived before I received the vaccination. Won't the baby have the Olduvai defect? Won't they have active copies of the Death Effector Gene?"

"Probably, Marla, but we'll just vaccinate the kid once he's older, maybe the same age as when they would get the chickenpox vaccine. I guess I don't think it's something to worry about." His smile reassured her.

Marla sat on Jack's lap at the kitchen table, drinking coffee for the next hour, shifting from leg to leg, with Jack squirming as numbness set in. She luxuriated in the time spent touching and talking about nothing important. She was relaxed in a way she hadn't felt in months and could tell Jack felt the same. The coffee ran out as they basked in the sun shining through the bay windows. Marla stopped talking and took some deep breaths, just enjoying being home. A meadowlark sat on a branch just a few feet away from them on the other side of the window. She smiled at Jack as the bird chirped his cheerful melody, a beautiful sound synonymous with the western plains of North America.

Marla, arms around Jack, felt a deep sigh and looked at him. He smiled and said, "Yep. I'm OK being a dad, honey. And I'm pretty sure our vaccine has assured our baby will have at least another 100,000 years before Homo sapiens has to confront extinction again." Marla laughed until tears flowed, Jack, laughing in unison. It wasn't clear to Marla whether her giddiness was based upon the silliness of his statement or a deep-seated, pervasive, unspoken nervousness about the accuracy of the assumption that his statement was true. *Did the vaccine really buy Homo sapiens another one hundred millennia?*

They continued chatting until Marla noticed Jack looking out the window, suddenly focused on something outside.

"What, honey?" Marla said.

"Strange," Jack said.

Marla struggled to get off his lap as he stood up and headed for the front door. She heard the door open as she grabbed her crutches to follow. By the time she got to the front porch, Jack was standing at the curb, looking north. Marla crutched down the stairs and worked her way to his side. She looked to Jack's face and, following the path of his eyes, saw what had stolen his attention. A dust devil was slowly swirling down the street, undulating between the curbs about 200 feet away. She had seen dust devils a thousand times before, but there was something strange about this one.

"Weird," Marla said.

"Yeah," Jack said. "Really weird."

Marla reached down and took Jack's hand, squeezing it tight. Mesmerized, she watched the dirt funnel snake toward them. Her curiosity suppressed the compunction to get out of its way. Fifteen yards before reaching them, it dissipated into an explosion of dirt resulting from a powerful gust of wind. Marla instantaneously slammed her eyes shut and stopped breathing, a reflex from years of dust devil encounters on the farm, in anticipation of the transient but intense sting of wind-driven dirt. It came instantaneously to the thought—a thousand red-hot needles in a coordinated attack on her face, exposed arms, and ankles. It was over in seconds.

Marla blinked some dust out of her eyes and looked up at Jack, still squinting, rubbing his eyes. She tugged his hand in a *Look at me* prompt. Her eyes met his, her feeling matching his look of puzzled, ineffable concern. She felt suddenly weak. She clumsily adjusted her crutches and turned slowly, almost stumbling, to make her way back to the house with Jack.

Halfway to the door, Jack paused. Marla turned and looked at him. He was groping in his right pant pocket, then the left, a sense of near panic on his face.

"What's wrong, honey?" Marla asked.

"Have you seen my Rubik's Cube?"

NEXT FROM MICHAEL WOODS

LATITUDES
A JACK CANN MEDICAL THRILLER

Petroleum personnel returning from Brazil develop an insidious form of dementia that rapidly evolves into an irreversible catatonic-like state. A few isolated cases evolve into a national health and security crisis, as multitudes of healthy Americans, initially in the western U.S., are immobilized by an unknown disease. Despite reports of near-ubiquitous, self-resolving, severe headaches in Brazilian citizens over a two-week period, officials deny anything unusual, and President Carlos de Santos' government is bizarrely uncooperative with the U.S. The outward appearance of an infectious cause of the disease results in Jack Cann, the world-renown Midwestern virologist, and his Asian-American wife, anthropologist Marla Qui, leading teams on two continents in a terrifying—and dangerous—hunt for the cause. Marla uncovers horrors in the Amazon not meant to be found and finds herself methodically pursued by unknown killers. At the same time, Jack narrowly escapes a brazen assassination attempt in the U.S. heartland after identifying the cause of the illness: an inexplicable cross-phyla mutation between a plant and primate virus—and a previously unknown, highly lethal, genetically-modified strain of influenza. The team finds the virus rapidly working northward from South America through plant root systems. Mass panic spreads as people are confronted by choosing between starvation and complete CNS shutdown—not dead, not alive. The seemingly unrelated findings of Jack, Marla, and their teams coalesce into a complex, chillingly opportunistic plot to take over the United States—the confirmation of which relies on a teaspoon of dirt from a mass grave.

ABOUT THE AUTHOR

Michael Woods is a general surgeon and healthcare executive living in Lawrence, KS.

He grew up in the Midwest and developed a love for the outdoors and life's rich complexity and interconnectedness while working on a western Kansas ranch.

He attended the University of Kansas, majored in Cellular Biology, did research in a virus lab, and minored in anthropology. He then completed medical school and general surgery training, becoming a board-certified general surgeon.

Tiring of the practice and politics of medicine, he became a researcher at a major pharmaceutical company, where he became the global medical leader of a worldwide drug development program. In this position, he traveled the globe, giving him rich insights and a deep appreciation of other cultures.

His background in anthropology, combined with his broad knowledge and experience in clinical and research medicine and extensive travel, is a potent combination for creating rich stories based on scientifically plausible— even factual— scenarios, as in *Olduvai Countdown*, his first fiction novel.

Michael is a well-recognized author in the medical trade press, having written and published four non-fiction books in the healthcare genre. His most successful book is *Healing Words*, a best seller for the publisher, generating combined sales of 19,000 in a niche market with very little promotion (First and Second Editions). He is the editor of a fifth publication that has sold 15,000 copies. His non-fiction works have been favorably reviewed in the industry press.